"Where do we, how do we navigate this artifice of the future world we're in? Saul Leslie lays it out, like an 18th-century progress, in all its sensate, surreal, abusive detail, the way we are forced to live our lives, seen through screens, felt through words and bodies, told back to us in visceral media, sold back to us in turn. Imagine Charles Bukowski rewritten by John Milton and James Joyce for a post-pop cultural age. This is exciting, fearsomely brilliant and witty writing — a stunning and engrossing fictional debut, a brilliant head-rush — and it never gives in."

—Philip Hoare, author of *William Blake and the Sea Monsters of Love*

"Saul Leslie has divined the deflating end point of Bataille's unproductive expenditure in the abandoned shopping trolley, stuck in the mire halfway between damp valediction and the base matter of bureaucratic Albion. A sacred conspiracy of consumer ennui, scried in his mordant sweep round its British aisles."

—Sophie Sleigh-Johnson, author of *Code: Damp, An Estoreric Guide to British Sitcoms*

""Finally: the great supermarket novel. A wickedly sharp tale of work and life under modern capitalism that will resonate with anyone who has ever worked on the tills."

—Dan Evans, author of *A Nation of Shopkeepers*

"I'm all lost in the supermarket, Joe Strummer sang half a century ago... Saul Leslie's inventive, perceptive novel is a sharply funny but also often poignant social satire centred on the precarious existence of someone who, despite his intellectual aspirations, is condemned by the contemporary capitalist economy to stack supermarket shelves and surf the sofas of those only marginally more fortunate than him. Full of revealing observations about metropolitan life in the early twenty-first century, it is written in exuberant, richly enjoyable prose."

—Matthew Beaumont, author of *Nightwalking: A Nocturnal History of London*

"Lovely, clever, both incredibly silly at points and also deadly, heartbreakingly serious. There are some really shattering and delicately drawn insights to be found about class, the nature of work, and the dream of upward mobility. I saw flashes of other texts, like Truffaut's The 400 Blows *and Hamsun's* Hunger*... there is a similar spirit of desperation mixed with ribaldry, of bleakness that gets rounded out, at points, by humor."*

—Sheila Liming, author of *Hanging Out: The Radical Power of Killing Time*

A WORKING TITLE I WANT TO CHANGE

A WORKING TITLE I WANT TO CHANGE

Saul Leslie

Published by Repeater Books

An imprint of Watkins Media Ltd

Unit 11 Shepperton House

89-93 Shepperton Road

London

N1 3DF

United Kingdom

www.repeaterbooks.com

A Repeater Books paperback original 2026

1

Distributed in the United States by Random House, Inc., New York.

ISBN: 9781917516235

Ebook ISBN: 9781917516242

The manufacturer's authorised representative in the EU for product safety is: eucomply OÜ - Pärnu mnt 139b-14, 11317 Tallinn, Estonia, hello@eucompliancepartner.com, www.eucompliancepartner.com

Printed and bound by CPI Group (UK) Ltd, Croydon, CR0 4YY

For Lloyd, beloved outlaw

CONTENTS

CHAPTER ONE

FRESH MEATS

No thundering herd in this windowless room, just new recruits lowing to our seats. We've all been designated a square desk, and mine is lopsided. If I lean on it at all, the tabletop tilts, and the pen I was given as I entered — branded with the Tesco logo — rolls noisily off the grey surface onto the grey carpet.

"Open your booklets to the Induction page," we're told.

I flick through my ring-bound wad of colourful, laminated pages — past the History of Tesco, past the sepia-grained portrait of a moustached company founder leaning against a wooden cart piled high with tins, fabrics, and fruit. We're advised to memorise all that in our own time.

'What is Induction?' the next page asks. In the margins I scribble, pressing down to pierce the page's laminate skin:

> **/ɪn'dʌkʃn/***n.* **1.** Inducting or inducing; (arch.) preamble, prologue, introduction; (esp. Med.) bringing on by artificial means (*induction of labour*). **2.** Production (*of* facts) to prove general statement; inferring of general law from particular instances (cf. *deduction*)

This definition comes courtesy of the Oxford English Dictionary, a pocket version I keep in my rucksack for just such a situation. When we're told to turn the booklet's page

I discover it has its equivalent within Tesco's windowless walls.

"Induction," explains the woman at the front, "means getting to know your store. And for all of you, that's this here — the flagship, Tesco Kensington."

Something about this woman makes me think of old lettuce — maybe it's how tightly her hair has been pulled back against her scalp, showing up the poor dye's pale veins. Or it's her crinkly, scrunched up face, as when an iceberg gets cross-sectioned. Or it's her chilly voice and the way she marches or rolls along the carpet between our desks. She passes mine; her skin has that whitish yellow of rotting leaves.

"I'm in salad," she announces. This jolts me, and my knee bangs my wobbly desk. The sudden pain of the thought criminal.

"I'm part of the region's Garden Greens team. In fact, you'll all have seen the posters around the store for the launch of our Rapunzel Range? That's all me." She says this proudly, her grin no kind of little gem. "Now, if all of you turn to page six, you will see the JBT. The Jargon Buster Tesco. This is the supermarket's lifeblood. It's our bread and butter."

We turn the page to an A–Z of words and phrases.

"All employees," she continues in a tone that mimics the ceiling fan, "are expected to use the JBT to ensure that we can more easily understand one another."

I browse the list, passing over the more self-explanatory, less interesting terminologies: 'Achievements', 'Availability', 'Branch Accounts'.

In my periphery, a hand goes up. The Rapunzel woman stops mid-step.

A lady with colourful glasses looped on a golden chain around her neck points an acrylic finger at a page. "I wanted some clarification, if I may. Just here under 'C', there seems to be some confusion between definitions."

Rapunzel, unblinking, looks down at her clipboard. "It's Francesca, isn't it?"

"Oh, Fran, Franny, whichever you prefer."

"Well Franfrannywhichever, please go on."

"Okay. I can see the term 'CAGE', but then, further down the list, I can also see the term 'CAYG'."

The room bows to examine the page in question, on which is printed a photograph of an enormous wire-meshed trolley. This is called a CAGE, which Tesco workers use to shift produce around the shop floor and warehouse. But Fran is correct, because further down the page there's also an anagram that Tesco workers must follow: Clean As You Go, which is abbreviated for convenience to CAYG.

"Just a bit confusing for me, really."

Rapunzel waves a palm, and from the back of the room there is movement as two men — one with a large brown wart under his eye, the other small and feral — step over to Fran's table, take up her belongings, and escort her out. The door hisses on its hinges as it closes behind them.

Still unblinking, Rapunzel goes on, "Some people just aren't cut out for it here, I'm afraid. It's quite clear what the difference is between CAGE and CAYG, and you should all take the time to read the JBT thoroughly, so that everyone follows our 'Customer–Colleague Interaction Policy No.3', which is to maintain hygiene standards at all times. And this involves Cleaning As You Go. It's that simple."

Rapunzel goes on with her marching and her script, but I'm still thinking of Fran's sudden exit and wondering how this most single entendre of doublespeak — CAGE/CAYG — might manifest on the shop floor. I flick through the booklet to its index of aisles and pick one at random.

Aisle No.10. World Foods.

I imagine myself stacking shelves with basmati rice and Reggae Reggae Sauce, when a senior colleague passes by.

"Cage," they murmur.

I must swiftly discern if they are saying CAGE (as in, 'There is a CAGE that needs moving to the warehouse') or CAYG (as in, 'There is a spillage on a neighbouring aisle, so please clean as you go'). There's the slimmest of fat-free slimming wafer-thin chances that this senior colleague who's just murmured the word 'cage' to a new recruit is referring to John Cage, the avant-garde composer. Perhaps this senior Tesco member despises the tinny pop tunes that swell and surge over supermarket speakers. Perhaps they're asking that the instore playlist include pioneers of musical indeterminacy and electroacoustics. '4'33', on repeat, forever. Perhaps they value silence not as a privation but as an affirmed presence. Just as Isaac Babel proclaimed that he'd invented a new genre, that of silence, to keep the regime at bay; and just as Kafka's Sirens possess a weapon more powerful than their song — namely, their silence — so here at Tesco, there might be those for whom sound is not the desired norm.

I look down at the page, with its index of aisles. In the margins I've scribbled the words 'cage', 'Babel', and '*Ungeziefer*'. I cross them out for fear of going Franward.

Her script complete, Rapunzel wraps her clipboard with solid knuckles in what could be an imitation of applause and grins another gemless grin. "Welcome to the store. Those of you who still remain are no longer new recruits but are now confirmed Team Members."

Our reward is another windowless office, this one identifiable by its door plaque: Screening Room. As I enter, hauling the huge rucksack that comes with me everywhere in London, Rapunzel puts out an arm like a parking barrier. She gestures to my rucksack. "You going hiking with that? It's not part of our uniform, so you won't be able to take it onto the shop floor with you after the Screening. Meacham?"

A meek assistant appears.

"Take this rucksack up to the Staff Canteen, to the ♂ Changing Room so that—"

"But I..." I butt in.

"—so that our new Team Member can get it when he changes into his uniform. It'll be safe there. We're one big family, remember."

Meacham takes my rucksack and disappears. I feel like a snail that's lost its shell as I settle at one end of a long beige sofa, shoulder to shoulder, hip to hip, with other new Team Members, facing a wall-length TV screen.

We are subjected to a series of CUSTOMER–COLLEAGUE CARE videos and given little paper bowls of strawberry laces and Haribo Starmix to chew cud-like as we absorb the key ethos of the company. A voiceover makes much of the supermarket's colour-scheme, tying Tesco to stiff-upper-lipped notions of national pride. When compared with its retail competitors, my new workplace is doing solid patriotic marketing. Sainsbury's has alienated a key customer base with its orange logo: it looks too much like EasyJet, and we all know where EasyJet prefers to fly. Towards Europe. ASDA and Waitrose have committed the same colour-scheme cardinal sin with their choice of green, which grinds the disgruntled gears of those customers who associate it with environ*mental*ists. Above them all, ruling triumphant, is the red, white, and blue of the Tesco brand. It is unmatched, unrivalled, and as the video continues the logo morphs into a Union Jack, and thus completes the allegiance of Great British shoppers and us supermarket staff.

An image of a face appears on the screen. There are *umms* and *ahhs* of recognition, but I'm clueless. Looking back at me is an old woman with a round, kind expression, smiling, varnished blue eyes, comically large, grandmotherly specs, curly grey hair. Endearingly grey. Royal grey. In fact, her cloche-style hat, sitting slightly back on her head, is crown-ish.

The voiceover, in accurate RP, explains: "Here is the actress Prunella Scales, a significant member of the Tesco family." This is pronounced as '*femeleh*'. "And to remind you, here's her contribution to our adverts over the years."

A murmur of joyful ascent fills the room as fuzzily coloured clips plume on the screen, with that iridescent shimmer along the monitor's edges of VHS recording. This is a montage of adverts from the 1990s, with Prunella Scales playing the main character, who fusses and dashes around a utopian Tesco. Its aisles are gleaming, its shelves perfectly stacked and ordered, and its staff diaphanous — limbs, whites of eyes and teeth all marble-coloured. The nostalgia is thermonuclear, blasting any notion of the now — of October 2013 — out of the way. Recruits around me shed tears of appreciation, pointing to the fictional aisles stocked with Tamagotchis, bottles of Sunny Delight, Lunchables, and Cheese Strings. Nostalgia and national pride knotted together with VHS tape.

And now that I look more closely, the Prunella Scales character does possess a superficial resemblance to Her Majesty the Queen. It seems that the creators of this CUSTOMER–COLLEAGUE CARE video recognise the fact too, as the screen freezes with Scales mid-regal smile, her trolley brimming with affordable produce, and the voice over announces: "In fact, our beloved Prunella even played Queen Elizabeth in a theatre play, in Alan Bennett's *A Question of Attribution*."

At this, the image of the Queen — or perhaps Scales in disguise — appears on the screen, and the 'Jerusalem' hymn plays. Without any prompting, everyone stands, including me, tugged to my feet by sovereign strings, while the anthem soars, as the screen flashes with a montage of Spitfires, rain-drenched caravans, well-kept allotments, bobbies patrolling council estates, golden ale filling a pint glass. We blink out of this and sit down again as the video concludes without any credits. I'm all twitchy and fidgety, probably from the Haribo sugar rush.

We members of the Tescommonwealth now nod along as Rapunzel recites the supermarket's policies, asking that we read along with her from our booklets:

- Customer–Colleague Interaction Policy No.1: BE PERSONABLE, which means wearing a nametag at all times.
- Customer–Colleague Interaction Policy No.2: CUSTOMER FIRST, which means the customer is always right.
- Customer–Colleague Interaction Policy No.3: MAINTAIN HYGIENE, at all times, both in body and in-store.

The brown stains on the long sofa's arm and smell of stale coffee call into question the enforceability of No.3, though maybe the policy doesn't apply to parts of the supermarket where customers are absent — in those places where we find filth and grime, where waste and fatigue are the currency of communication, where the secretions of labour are permitted.

Each new Team Member is given a plastic card printed with a barcode. This is my unique numerical identifier, like a chemical compound not yet illegalised: 6655321. We're handed our uniforms. Mine comprises three pieces in a cellophane wrapper: blue trousers, blue zip-up fleece, red long-sleeve jumper. The others are directed towards other departments or teams, while I'm instructed to go to the Food2Go Counter and introduce myself.

"Look out for the Bosnian, that's Bisera, and a Somali woman, that's Jasmeen," is Rapunzel's head-flicked instruction, before she turns away to her meek assistant. "Meacham, which store's next? I want to be done with these Inductions before midday."

"Bayswater," Meachem meekly squeaks.

Along corridors and on stairwells I experience that disorientation of a recent journey in reverse, where left is now right, right is now left, up is down, and down is up. A few times I double back along non-descript passages, finding my path blocked by a closed door that requires a code. One of these doors even requires a tap-in lanyard. UPPER MANAGEMENT, it reads in silver lettering, and on the floor is a cardboard box printed with the outline of a champagne flute. The box is taped shut.

Eventually I discover a staircase which feels familiar; I recognise four pale blemishes on the wall where once there was Blu·tack. At its base is a sign I follow to the shop floor. Everything has a different aspect now, as if charged with electricity. The shimmer, the light and shade of belonging. In my hands my packaged uniform crackles as I survey a whole store which I've been instructed to call home, colleagues now *femeleh*. Close to the supermarket's entrance is the Food2Go Counter, my assigned team, and I approach two pant-suited women each carrying a clipboard. I introduce myself.

Bisera and Jasmeen. Team Leaders.

Neither has a nametag, nor a lanyard. Their rank and authority seem to derive from their clipboards, which they wrap with long nails, explaining that a miscommunication means the Earl's Court branch was expecting an Irish man to fill the position on the Food2Go Counter. He's not shown up, and Bisera and Jasmeen turn this into a character-building lesson for me, their new recruit.

"Never end up like *that* Irish."

"Typical Irish."

"You *must* show up on time and not let down your team."

"Your family."

"You won't, will you?"

They converse and complain for a bit, using 'he' interchangeably about me and the absent Irishman, until I can't tell who is being bollocked and who is being praised, before turning back to me and giving me broad, strained smiles:

"The good news is that since there is no one else to share your responsibilities..."

"...the Food2Go Counter is assigned to you and you alone."

"CONGRATULATIONS," they harmonise, then take it in turns to thrust their clipboards in my direction, and I hurriedly sign dozens of badly photocopied purple forms. This parody of autograph hunting complete, Bisera calls over a colleague.

"This is Monojit," Jasmeen explains, "I've instructed him to show you around."

"Actually, I instructed him," Bisera adds quickly. "He's from Bangladesh."

"But don't hold that against him," adds Jasmeen.

I'm sure I detect a sneer buried in this quip. Maybe I'm just on edge because of how she described the absent Irishman. After all, being from a place does leave you open to both criticism and jocular ridicule. Monojit's shorter than me and wiry, with round glasses and a stern, hard-set mouth. Pinned to his blue fleece is a badge that explains he's a Counter Manager.

The JBT states that the Tesco hierarchy goes like this: beneath the CEO is Upper Management of a particular store. Beneath them are Duty or Department Managers, Store or General Managers, then it's Team Leaders, and beneath them are Counter Managers like Monojit. As

Counter Manager, he's Bisera and Jasmeen's inferior, and therefore my immediate superior.

"You get a group of women together to organise things round here," he says as we walk through the store, shunting CAGEs out of the way, "and it goes bloody wrong."

A set of heavy NO ENTRY double-doors slows us. Skirted along its bottom is a dented steel plate which Monojit kicks with a well-practiced boot. A staircase leads us to the Staff Canteen. Brightly lit, low ceilinged, wide but also somehow narrow. There's a pool table, which requires loose pound coins to use.

"Nothing for free," Monojit shrugs, tapping the little toaster-like slots where the coins should go.

There's a large flat-screen HD TV mounted on the white-washed brick wall furthest from the window. This morning's viewing? An episode of *The Jeremy Kyle Show*. We linger for Monojit to take in whatever bear-baiting Kyle is playing ringmaster to.

"It's a repeat," Monojit says, pointing at the bottom left corner, where the episode's topic is displayed. "The cousin turns out to be the father in this one." Perhaps it is no simple coincidence that *The Jeremy Kyle Show* is on: what better way is there to keep up the morale of a workforce than by showing them the lives of people who are worse off?

In the canteen, Monojit introduces me to what he whispers is "the Women's table." Somehow, Jasmeen has rematerialised ahead of us and is sitting with two others, and now she stands, points at me, and addresses the women, "He's from *Cam*bridge." Both raise their pencilled eyebrows. Out of approval or disapproval, I don't know.

"I thought you said he was meant to be from Ireland," says one of the women, taking me in from foot to head, from new work boots to my last clean shirt. Jasmeen throws her head back and laughs. She's got a tooth missing on one side, just behind her right canine. She winks at me as if we're in on a comedy of identity errors. "No, no, the Irish didn't show up," again pointing at me, "so he's taking that role. He's from Cambridge. He's much better. I can tell."

I don't bother explaining that I'm not actually from Cambridge, that it's simply geographical shorthand as the nearest well-known place to my hometown. Instead, I tell them that I am a friend of Alby's, that he helped me get this job.

Their pencils flatten into lines of Morse code, so Monojit clarifies, "You girls know Alby. The white guy on the Deli Counter? Scouser."

A chorus of recognition, followed by a swift invite for Alby and me to the Xmas party, with each talking over the others:

"It's still two months away, but we need a headcount and dietary requirements."

"We don't have any English whites going yet."

"Yeah most of the workers here are from Eastern Europe."

"Like Poland or, or, where's Bisera from?"

"Bosnia. Or they're from, like, Africa, like Isaiah."

"Get it right. He's from Southwark."

"Souf of the Thames. Might as well be annuva country."

"Another planet, boss."

"Watch it. I'm from Plumstead."

"And there's others here from the Middle East and South Asia."

"Remember we'll need meat alternatives and non-alcohol options for the party."

"That's a well good point. We don't want a repeat of that whole Diwali fing last autumn."

There are solemn nods and a lot of notetaking on clipboards. It appears that no one here is from Cambridge nor East Anglia. As Monojit and I move on, I wonder if I should've followed policy No.1 — become personable — by explaining that my hometown is equidistant between Mark Fisher's containerised, vanishing Felixstowe and Sebald's inherited guilt-plain of Norwich. What blank faces would've looked back at me? Next time, if anyone asks, I'll say I grew up near Ed Sheeran, where few are anything other than English or white.

We stop at another table, and I'm introduced to Dan the fishmonger, who takes up most of the space, not just physically but with an expansive character. And then Nick Dale, the store's data analyst and techxpert, flicking through a *Doctor Who* magazine, head lowered.

"You smoke, mate?" Dan says, rolling up a cigarette, his baccy paraphernalia spread around the table. "This," holding up his creation, "is the key to getting ahead here." Loose tobacco on the table, so he uses his palm to scrape the residue towards the table's edge, snatching Nick's open magazine, ignoring a feeble *I was reading that*, scooping the pubic wires into the crease, funnelling it all back into his pouch.

"I was reading that," Nick repeats.

Dan scans the page, reads the title: "Suction cups and skirts. Didn't know you was into fetish, Nick."

"They're parts of the Dalek anatomy." Each lens of Nick's glasses flashes HELP signals.

"Still buildin' your shagger machine?"

"Just a hobby," Nick murmurs quietly, eyes returning to the page.

"Just banter, fella," is Dan's reply.

Monojit continues his tour, with a few exclamations of, "See, I told you we're mad," showing me to the ♂ Changing Room. "You can change into your uniform in here," he says as we enter the dark. He waves his hand around until a sensor sparks the lights. "See that? Magic."

Two benches, lockers, tiled floor and walls. There's that swimming-pool echo and smell of bleach and Lynx. A mirror's cracked in one corner into the shape of a Glasgow grin. Leaning against an open locker is my rucksack.

"You can put your clothes and bag in there. Have you got anything valuable in your rucksack?"

I disgorge my iPod, my phone, the laptop which the university has loaned me.

Monojit points at the iPod and laptop. "Lock them up." Then he points at the phone. "Why've you got a burner? You a dealer?"

It's a Nokia 105 and I've never had anything more sophisticated. The iPod is my only concession, and even that is out-of-date with its beige click wheel. No Blackberry, no iPhone. The best minds of my generation have been destroyed by fruit-themed tech.

I shrug.

Monojit continues, "You won't have to worry about the phone. Anything else in there?"

"Some books. Magris's *Danube*, Jean Rhys, McEwan's *Sweet Tooth*, Sheila Heti, Nabokov's *Speak, Memory*, Borges's *Labyrinths*, Ballard's *High-Rise*, Solomon Northup's *Twelve Years a Slave*, Venedikt Yerofeev's *Moscow Stations*. *No Logo*."

"You got all that in there?"

He doesn't need to know that I don't have a room of my own, that I don't have a house to live in, that I'm sofa surfing, that I've been sleeping in the university library for the past few nights.

I nod.

He snorts with laughter. "Your phone is fine and no one'll touch your books, boss. Anyway, meet me back at the Food2Go Counter in three minutes." And like that, poof, he's gone.

I unwrap my cellophane package, change from civvies into uniform, and relace the work boots I bought specially for this job. My first shift hasn't even started and I'm already out of pocket from paying for the boots and for an all-zones Tube travel card.

I look at myself in the mirror, limbs and face disjointed by the crack. The fleece's collar is blue, but does that really make this blue collar? I push my rucksack into the locker, pocket the key, and return to the shop floor.

The Food2Go kitchen is a thickly furnaced cabin where industrial fridges hum, and extractor fans sigh hotly. Instead of windows, there are beige tiles, off-white with the guffs of grease from the ovens.

"Right then, your job today is CAYG." Monojit looks at me expectantly. "You know what that means, yes boss?"

"It's Clean As You Go," I reply, with the image of Fran's expulsion in mind.

"Good. CAYG all the surfaces. Haroon will help you. HAROON!"

From behind a fridge, a head appears. Very thin face, sinewy, a peppery moustache seasoning his lip. "He's a Team Member who usually stacks the CAGEs but today he's CAYGing with you," Monojit explains.

Haroon and I fall to our task. Or rather, I fall to it while he returns to his place behind the fridge and continues trimming his tash and nostrils with a pair of small scissors, and intermittently yelling his life philosophy over the fridges and fans. In the humming reflection he checks his hair and announces: "I am certain — one hundred percent, no doubt in my mind, — that *Allah al-Qadir* will punish all those who've taken what other people need."

"Do you mean, like, globally?" I ask.

"I mean, *locally*. Right here in this very store."

"So greed is an issue here?"

"Greed. And waste."

"Waste?"

He pauses, the scissors' V flashing, and proceeds to make a speech into the fridge's cleanly mirrored side about the amount of wasted food at Tesco. Then he looks at me. "You not been to the warehouse yet, have you boss?"

I shake my head.

"You'll see, it's like nothing else."

- - - - -

The remainder of the shift is dedicated to scrubbing the tiles, fridges, and industrial-sized sinks in the Food2Go kitchen. It's easy enough: spray then wipe with blue paper towels, scrunch up and aim the towels at the gaping mouth of the bin by the opposite wall. Despite the gradually building strain on the elbow joints, the chemical crinkling of my fingertips, and the growing nest of scrunched blue paper around the bin, I hope it's this sort of commitment to cleanliness which will make me a good housemate if and when I ever secure permanent accommodation somewhere in the city. I'm already falling behind on the MA course I moved to London to pursue, and I'm still sofa surfing.

"You're free to go now," Haroon yawns, pointing at the clock. "Monojit said that for your next shift, get here early if you want the warehouse tour. But personally, I don't think you're ready for it yet." A can of Red Bull in his hand hasn't yet given him wings. I march through the store, past customers beginning their rush-hour shop, take the stairs two at a time to the ♂ Changing Room, eject my rucksack from the locker, and clock out. To do this, I hold my unique ID card against the little monitor mounted on the wall, the beep signalling that the machine recognises the gurning barcode and its digits. 6655321. The monitor reads 17:04, despite my speed I've still been on-site for four minutes longer than my contract obliges. What could I have done with those precious minutes, totalling two-hundred and forty entire seconds? That's enough time for nearly the whole of John Cage's piece, missing the last nineteen seconds. Probably the most important bit.

I've hauled my rucksack onto my back, a snail with head down and eyestalks lowered to avoid getting caught by colleagues or customers, trying to exit without leaving a trail of slime, sliding, streaking all the way through the store, through the glass doors, out into the autumn dryness of late afternoon. Time is well and truly all over the place, and it's not just the season. Fallen leaves freckle the pavements, covering the blackheads of ancient chewing gum. As with the rush-hour flood of customers, the streets and the mouth of Earl's Court station are busy with crowds moving in frantic order. It's vaguely apocalyptic, recalling the shuddering pensioners in Raymond Briggs's *When the Wind Blows*, whose preparations for the four-minute warning has Jim roll up his sleeves and slosh white paint on their cottage's windows as the bombs begin to fall, while Hilda starts to panic because she's left the oven on.

I descend the escalator to the station platform in a thicket of coats and hats, and board the Tube. The unsevered string of bratwurst that makes up a London train, each carriage greasy and sweating. Maybe this is where we'd be advised to shelter in the event of a nuclear attack. I take out a notebook, an idea for an essay emerging: 'The Apocalypse in English Prose and Poetry'. Our lecturers have advised that we devise a title based on the MA syllabus reading list. I scribble some thoughts. Unlike the laminated booklet, my pen lightly presses, and ribbons of ink trail in its wake: I put down some notes about Peter Porter's poem 'Your Attention Please'. It's a parody of a public service broadcast minutes before a nuclear attack, which takes as long to read aloud as there is time left before annihilation. The poem advises religious citizens to follow the dictates of their faith, urges that all disabled and elderly are abandoned to the imminent blast, since *you can do nothing for them*.

The train fills, and I have to shuffle and tuck in my elbows, closing my notebook.

What would I do with a four-minute warning? Would I help others? Would I adhere to Tesco's policies? Would I read something? Would I scribble something? Would I send texts to loved ones? In which order? Alphabetically? With my limited phone credit?

I need to top up before I reach tonight's accommodation.

The clattering carriage is taking us (my window's scrawny reflection and me) towards Angel, to stay at the house of a family friend. The daughter of my mum's oldest schoolmate. A decent level of familiarity — I've met the daughter at family functions over the years — should make conversation easy, but also risks the possibility of a long discussion about how my family is doing. After today's tiring shift I really don't want to have to detail my sibling's incarceration.

Their questions:

Have you heard from him in jail?

Why did he steal that garden furniture?

And how's the family?

My answers:

No I've not.

How should I know?

I left my hometown to get away from all of that.

The florist outside the station points me in the direction of a side street I need to go down, the second right I need to take, the first left by the hairdressers I need to turn onto, and so on, and so on, until I arrive on a dimly lamplit row of terraced houses, the tiled roofs stitched together into a vast dark, shiny snakeskin.

I knock. There's a doorbell, but I knock. We all know someone who palms the door, and someone else who rattles the letterbox, and someone else who tinkles the glass with fingernails. Each method of announcing yourself says something slightly different, expresses a variation on formality.

The door opens, and there follows a hug with my hostess and a handshake with her boyfriend. Off come my work boots. I'm conscious of the hole in my sock's big toe — the black-rimmed nail pokes through, begging to be clipped. It's humiliating, particularly when measured against their identical pairs of grey house slippers, which sink into the snow-drift carpet as they lead me inside.

The house's communal space has that coarsened atmosphere of a couple who've been together for a long time and have discovered that the idiosyncrasies which initially drew one to the other are now the basis of daily conflict. While Lottie prepares the dinner ("You'll have to wait and see" — sourly coquettish through the open kitchen door), Vic shows me to the spare room, describing, as we ascend the stairs, the frustrations he's faced at work with a client.

"He won't, just will not play ball, here's your room—"

Vic's recently been made the head of a team of hedge fund managers who all oversee the portfolio of one famous...

"—and I mean fucking famous, and here's the bathroom—"

...client. But it seems this VFIP doesn't believe in the fiscal structure that Vic's team has worked on.

"I want to tell this wanker, 'You stick to your cycling, and let us handle the assets,' but these celebs just don't understand. They're still dining out on their London Olympics fame."

I'm not exactly sure who Vic's describing, but I reckon his face was plastered on every billboard and was endorsing every sugary sports drink in the build-up to the Games last summer. How long ago it all seems now, that open-armed spectacle.

"I can't tell you his name for legal reasons," he's demonstrating the switch on the electric shower, and the only clue he gives me is that a lot of this VFIPAnon's chagrin comes from being runner-up in 2013's Sports Personality of the Year. Apparently, Vic and this person had travelled all the way up to Leeds for the ceremony, and got the return train in total, trophy-less, silence. The tension seems to have been absorbed into this household, with Lottie choosing not to announce that dinner is ready but texting Vic's phone instead.

He and I are in the upstairs corridor, monochrome wall hangings on either side depicting London as a kind of Guernica-on-Thames. He's pointing to landmarks where his company has deployed what he terms 'activations', when his phone pings. "Ah, *she* wants us downstairs." We descend, and take our places at a hostile table.

Fuck. I forgot to top up my credit.

As the house guest, you become the porous membrane through which a couple's aggravations pass. During the dinner, Vic recounts more dramas from his office, describing serves-and-returns between himself and his team in which he comes out on top each time. He keeps using the phrase 'deployed activations'. To signify the punchline, he swigs from his bottle of Becks, his Adam's apple cutting into his neck.

Our sets of cutlery provide clattering applause.

Vic wipes his mouth and lobs a couple of questions into the table's centre. "So, how's your bruv? Heard he got nicked? How'd he manage that?"

"Vic!" Lottie stage whispers from behind her glass. "I told you already. He clearly doesn't want to talk about all that stuff."

"What. I'm just asking. Making convo."

Eyes on me with a *well-do-you-mind??* expression. I shelter momentarily behind prolonged mastication. Vic's blunt and tactless question prongs me, and Lottie is correct that I don't want to talk about it. My brother's theft of antique garden furniture from the grounds of a stately home is so uncool there's not even poacher's pride to be had.

Still, their eyes on me.

I am an anxious Caesar, picking at the egg whites of my namesake's salad, with the power to decide the conversation's course. I could say how much better this tastes than Tesco's value range on the Food2Go Counter, but this might prompt a misguided inquiry about my workplace. It's a tricky situation, and this is a tense meal with a couple who're both wearing house slippers and matching tracksuits, and whose bookcase comprises sports star biographies, Jordan Belfort's guide to finance, and two copies of *The Casual Vacancy* — there is no easy way out.

"It's all good," I answer mid-mouthful of lettuce and crouton, "though I wanted to ask you both, where *did* you get that wall hanging?" Attention swivels to the wooden mask by the bookcase, an exotic emblem brought back from a couple's visit to a Barbadian retreat, paid for through Vic's job but organised by Lottie's superior admin skills. Their joint recollections of their sunny hols brings the dinner to a neutral, even happy conclusion. Plates are cleared. Leftovers are tupperworn. I offer to wash the dishes. No, no, they both insist, and instead Vic invites me to "sit soft" in the living room and watch him play *Grand Theft Auto V*.

I can hear Lottie's sighing in the kitchen. "First, it was *House of Cards*, and then since last month, it's been this." But a bit of mindless screen-time might help me disengage from today's shift, readying me for sleep, so I softly sit.

"Have you played it?" Vic asks as he ploughs a car into some pedestrians.

"No, but I saw loads of copies of it on the Electronics aisle today."

"I should've asked you for a discount," he murmurs, throwing a Molotov cocktail at an ambulance.

"It's very violent," Lottie remarks from the doorway. "All that blood."

"I know. It's great, innit?"

"No, Vic love. That's not what I meant."

"Alright." Vic pauses the game, flicks through the menu to Settings, clicks through some options. "There. I've turned off the splatter. Happy?" He unpauses before Lottie can answer and continues to pulverise a scantily clad roller-skater with a baseball bat. Somehow, without the blood, it's more sinister.

On their grey-hatched sofa in their large living room — the lights dimmed, and the big TV screen glowing — Vic is undertaking the heist of a jewellery shop. The shift from one character to another throughout the theft (from Michael grabbing the diamonds, to Franklin doing the getaway) is a good way of imagining ourselves into the bodies and lives of others — like taking Ayahuasca in Peru, without the risk of yellow fever or bumping into Paddington. Vic reassures me it shouldn't take long to finish the mission, but Lottie keeps coming in to ask reasonable questions or comment on the game, and each time Vic makes a show of pausing, or complaining that he's getting distracted, as the screen flashes up WASTED. He then reloads the mission and begins again. This happens three or four times, and with each interruption—

"Ohh Vic babe, I'd love some bling."

—and each pause and restart, Vic crushes the controller in his palms so hard there's a creaking sound. Eventually, the jewels are stolen, and the getaway drive is completed. Lottie stands in the darkened doorway, holding her glowing laptop: "Now that's finished, why don't we look at the photos from our trip to Barbados?"

Before I can put together a plea for sleep, she's hopped onto the sofa next to me, a waft of hairspray mingled with cooked onions, explaining that she's still planning to get all the photos printed at Snappy Snaps. She places the laptop on the coffee table in front of us and clicks SLIDESHOW.

▬ ▬ ▬ ▬ ▬

My first full shift. It's a nine-to-sixer, a *Dolly Parton+1*, long enough for Monojit & co to show me the retail ropes.

He takes me aside in the kitchen, fumbles in his pocket, produces a badge. *Sans* ceremony he pins it to my chest.

"Bisera told me to tell you that they've ordered your own nametag," he explains as he pinches my long-sleeve's fabric and a bit of my skin too, "but it might take a while to arrive." I look in the fridge's reflection and decipher my back-to-front working title:

MAƎT OT WƎИ

My skin hurts from where Monojit caught it between his fingers. Not the full-on purple nurple, but nearly. Not enough for a complaint about assault in the workplace.

I'm nameless. I'm new, and he's telling me to stack shelves, and refill the Food2Go salad bar.

"What about filling CAGEs, in the warehouse?" I ask.

Monojit and Haroon exchange a look.

"He's not ready yet," Haroon diagnoses. "Give him a few more weeks."

I wheel out my trolley stacked with fresh produce and begin stacking and refilling the Meal Deals. I hear a *pssst* and turn. It's not directed towards me. It's Dan the fishmonger hissing at a security guard standing by the entrance's sliding glass doors. Dan's holding a lobster's blue claw, gesturing upwards. The security guard's eyes follow the pincer's point up to the mezzanine floor, where a young woman from the F&F clothing department has appeared on the balcony.

"Oof, I swear I can see up her skirt," Dan ogles.

She's wearing trousers but that's a minor detail.

"Oi, lov. You gonna let your hair down or wat," the security guard half-calls.

Dan's reaction: open mouthed, teeth-baring laugh, with a slight hint of phlegm in the back of the throat — less a laugh than a rattling squelch. The pincers clatter jaw-like as he chucks the lobster onto a bed of ice. He begins to descale a salmon. The young woman leaves the balcony, oblivious to or deliberately ignoring the exchange. Dan notices me, beckons:

"You started smokin' yet?" Again, that grin. His teeth are the colour of a gutter's leaves, yellow-brown along veins of enamel. I shake my head. "Well, you should start, boss. You can sneak away for a swift smoke anytime ya want." This appears to be the only legitimate reason to take a break from a shift. To smoke. If I was to just stand outside for ten minutes, that'd be a problem, but if I'm holding a cigarette, then that's okay. Maybe it's because smoking still looks like work, an effortful way of destressing — it's labour intensive; it's the piston, valve, and steam of the pin factory floor — whereas just standing there avoiding emphysema looks like idleness. Pinless. Pointless.

Later, the security guard meets Dan by the Euphorium Bakery, the former re-entering the store to return to his lectern, which is plastered with photos of banned customers; the latter heading out, cigarette already rolled. They pass a plastic lighter between them like the Olympic torch. Dan taps his watch at me, bunches thumb and index finger against his lips, and jerks his head towards the glass doors; gestures that convey *there's time for a cigarette break if you come now*. I signal back *give me one minute* and park my trolley by the Meal Deal shelves. I'd decided earlier that if the opportunity presented itself, I'd call Dan out on the way he and the security guard leched over the F&F girl. Now I gear myself up for the reprimand, with chapters and paragraphs from Steinem and *The Female Eunuch* appearing in my head as I approach Dan. With his boot's toe, he's impatiently scrubbing away the skidmarks left on the white floor tiles by customers whose soles are made of weak rubber. We step outside into the dark, lampposts turning our faces to fish roe amber; standing, shoulder to shoulder, as cold wind scatters newly fallen leaves like shards of stained glass. We watch the stringy blur of headlights cross Cromwell Road, as if we're passengers looking out through the same dim windscreen in the same traffic jam.

"How's the shift goin', boss?" he asks, his cupped palm an encased globe of flame.

"Yeah, I've got a few hours left, but it's okay."

"Hours are fucked, wages are fucked. It's like bein' a chicken on one of those farms."

"Battery."

"Battery's fucked, boss. Yeah, but you'll get used to it."

I bide my time, waiting for the right moment to spring on him the date 1792 and *The Vindication*.

"I can't tell you how much I fuckin' hate this job," he says, the 'f' and 'ck' forming their own grey plumes. I brace myself, anticipating that he'll blame the job for his previous comments about the young woman.

"Sometimes when I'm smokin' an oily out here, I face that road there and I just fink about runnin' and throwin' myself into the traffic."

It's important that we're not looking at each other, that we're side by side, when he says this, because it helps to blunt the blow to the veneer of social convention that exist between new colleagues. I don't feel I have to arrange my face in any affirming or shocked or concerned expression. Nevertheless, I am stunned by what he just said, so totally sideswiped by its candid, earnest fantasy of self-annihilation that I can't speak. Neither Wollstonecraft nor Steinem are anywhere to be seen. They've done a runner, and left me without a script.

But then the reflexes kick in, those emotional defence mechanisms we possess, which shield us from fully absorbing another person's plight. For me, it manifests in a kind of cognitive dissonance, where suddenly Dan seems very far away, as if we're talking to one another through two ends of a Bounty kitchen tube. And I'm aware I should say something:

"Well, that stretch of road is where J.G. Ballard sets the key scenes of his novel *Crash*."

He shakes his head, sipping smoke. "I don't know it, boss."

"You see the billboards? That's where the main collisions happen."

"You sayin' I should read it?"

"Absolutely. I'll get you a copy and bring it in during my next shift."

I take a deep breath, the scent of traffic mixing with the cold. "Now, I was going to say that, you know earlier, with that girl—"

"Awright there, Mrs Friel. Mind how ya go."

Dan's looking past me, and I turn to where a very old woman shuffles across the store's threshold towards us. The wind catches her and she stumbles, carrier bags creaking. Dan flicks away his cigarette and rushes to steady her, offering help.

I step over to him and tap his shoulder. He turns, still supporting Mrs Friel. "Dan, have you heard of the tyranny of man?"

"You what, mate?"

"Mary Wollstonecraft argues in her book—"

"I'm a bit busy here, boss." He turns back to Mrs Friel, and they limp away towards the bus stop.

By this point, any moment where I can pivot into an interrogation of his sexist comments has surely passed, so while he sees to Mrs Friel, I return inside, walking over the faux-marble, feeling very far from a philosopher at the Forum I'd hoped to be — dazzling and persuading with argument and evidence.

To my next shift I bring with me a paperback Ballard from the Oxfam by Angel Underground (70p without a carrier bag), and leave it on the bench in the ♂ Changing Room. I don't see Dan on the Fish Counter, but when I clock out, the book has disappeared.

A week or so later, I'm replenishing the Italian salads and notice through the glass windows the fishmonger smoking a cigarette. Taking a breather. His back is to the glass, so I can't see his expression, but his shoulders are broad and his feet far apart. He's facing the stretch of road where his fantasies deliver him. There's no traffic today.

▬ ▬ ▬ ▬ ▬

The shifts throughout the next couple of weeks are straightforward. Scrubbing walls in the kitchen, replenishing what's running low on the Food2Go Counter, CAYGing, but not CAGEing.

"Still too green for the warehouse," is Monojit's assessment.

Most of my time is spent in the kitchen, alone, now that Haroon has been returned to the warehouse. So no more philosophical or religious meditations on the horrors of wasting. All these hours CAYGing on my own makes my mind wander. I've even taken to hiding a book under the fridge, and will crouch behind it to read a few pages, until I hear the kitchen door open, at which point I pick up the spray and towels I keep nearby and continue to scrub the tiles.

"I'll let Bisera know how well you're following policy No.3," Monojit remarks when he assesses my diligent cleaning.

Over the last few days, my illicit reading behind the fridge has been Henry James, one of our required authors on the MA. I've been making notes for an essay I plan to compose: 'Retail Cages Retold'. Today, I'm tucked down on the floor, notebook open on the tiles, James's 1898 novella *In the Cage* in my bleach-wrinkled hand. It tells the story of an unnamed telegraphist as she navigates life in London.

The young woman is trapped amongst wires and wooden frames of the little telegraph-office which shares a wall with a grocery shop next door. This physical divide of wood and wire separating one business from the other is, of course, also a social gulf that spares her from making any effort with her professional neighbours.

My current circs, here on the tiled floor, head against the humming fridge, with the room's tawdry oven heat and pebble-dashed ceiling panels, are the opposite of hers. She's working in an office; I'm on the other side of that divide, a grocer-recruit beyond the heaped spaghetti of telegraph wires. She and I will never meet.

And yet in this same city, and on the laminated page of the JBT with the photograph of the CAGE, there's the same rigid frame and imprisoning mesh. Over a century later from when Henry James wrote her feelings into existence, here are those same unbridgeable social structures, professions, and feelings. The cage might be different, but the confinement is the same.

"Well, comrade, I'll have to report ye."

I'm startled. I'm caught. I've been found out. Job's done.

Alby's standing there, grinning, arms folded.

"Ah mate, you scared the shit out of me," I gasp, rising from the tiles.

"What're you calling this then, The Scatological Library?" Alby helps me up, pulling me into a fraternal embrace, then recoils, nose creasing. "Lad. Not following policy No.3 for yourself?"

I smell my armpits. The sour onion tang is there, now that I'm off the bleached floor. "I'm down to my last set of clean clothes."

Alby looks concerned. "Still sofa surfing?"

"And falling behind on the MA, as you can see."

"You do look like shite. You look, and smell, like you've been kippin' in landfill."

"Cheers."

"I thought the plan was to leave all that student livin' bollocks up on Merseyside?"

I met Alby when I moved from East Anglia to Liverpool to study English. Him being a Scouser, he led me through a city and a series of rites of undergrad passage: becoming pals in halls, playing cards and sharing spliffs, going halves on a bottle of wine or whisky; moving into a shared house on Smithdown with a half dozen others; queuing in the cold to get into Heebie Jeebies and the Raz; nights in feasting on takeaways, the Styrofoam accumulating in the kitchen of our student digs — a grim burrow with both of our rooms below ground, the two of us sharing tenancy with worms and slugs. Each night, they'd creep over the edge of loose skirting boards and leave silver ley lines across the floorboards. Alby vowed that if he ever came down south, he'd never live in such squalor again.

"Yeah, well, it's not been that easy," I exhale, rubbing my eyes with my palms, then regretting it as a chemical sting makes them teary.

"Alright, alright, lad. You hungry?"

"Very. Monojit told me there's no food allowed in here."

Alby drops his backpack onto a metal work surface. "Yeah, well, we're not allowed bags or books in here either, but I see we're of the maverick persuasion." He takes from his backpack a couple of buns and a pot of Deli Counter's finest Coronation Chicken. "Go and keep watch while I make 'em up."

I push open the kitchen door very slightly, so I can see a thin view of the concourse. Behind me, Alby sets about making our scran. It's reminiscent of those times when we'd duck down the alleyway off Colquitt Street or lock a bar's cubicle door to do a few lines.

What a difference a few months make. It used to be coke, now it's Coronation Chicken.

I look out through the narrow gap at families pushing prams, and at pensioners nudging their baskets towards the checkout. I'm suddenly struck by just how long ago all that seems up in Liverpool, but also how far away all this seems in front of me: children, growing up, responsibility. Take me back to the worms and the slugs.

"Here," Alby passes me a sarnie.

"Not bad," I compliment after a huge bite. Other than the meals I'm occasionally invited to at Lottie's, I've not properly eaten since I arrived in London, and I'm not sure if employees are permitted to take donated produce from the foodbank at the store's entrance.

"Corrie Chicken's a national institution," Alby, muffled.

"Speaking of which. I'm going to the British Museum after my shift today."

Alby swallows with difficulty. "You not finishing at five?"

I shake my head. "Sorted it with Bisera. Just a half day."

He gives me an *Et tu, bro??* look. "That's shite. Was gonna see if you wanted a bevvy. Wanted to hear about how all this has been since you started."

"Can't today, but next week?"

"Ye, ye, we'll see. I wanted to ask about your 'Spooktacular initiation'. They was talkin' 'bout it in the canteen."

Alby's referring to the adverts which have been plastered all over the store recently, ahead of Hallowe'en. Four or five times an hour, the Tannoy interrupts the playlist of the latest pop songs to play a minute-long blast of ghostly cries, lightning cracks, and witch cackles.

But Tesco doesn't stop there.

The retail imperative means that New Year's Eve, Valentine's Day, or any other annual event becomes a marketing opportunity. This month it's Hallowe'en, which has manifested in ghoulish meats, with cuts of beef advertised as 'blood red for your vampiric pleasure', and lychee on the Fruits aisle advertised as spooky eyeballs.

But Tesco doesn't stop there.

The retail imperative also requires the participation of staff, and so the other day I was subjected to a Spooktacular ritual: here in the kitchen, Monojit and I stood in the centre of a horse-shoe of already-initiated Team Members, their faces smeared into ghoul and zombie gurns with cheap paint. He held my chin gently with forefinger and thumb, and to the rhythmic drum of the fridges and whirring extractor fans, he applied lipstick and eyeshadow.

"Now you're a zombie like us!" Monojit remarked. My undead colleagues cheered.

I recount this to Alby. He laughs. "Why didn't you just say no, lad?"

"Is it that easy for a new Team Member?"

"True. Fuck me. Thinking ahead to Christmas, I hate to think of staff-bonding when there's mistletoe hanging up."

"The other thing that pissed me off about the face painting was that I had to buy a pack of wipes using my own wages to clean off the make-up. And now I've got a wad of wipes I don't have any use for. A proper waste."

"Eya, at least you've shown your loyalty. They love that here. Speaking of waste. You bin to the warehouse yet?"

"No. But I've heard."

"You've heard?"

"That it's bad in there."

"You could say that. I dunno who'll be showing yous around, but just be prepared for it."

"I'll keep my wits about me."

"Nah, I'm serious mate. When I got you this job, I was thinking that the warehouse is the worst bit. It fucks with ye head in there."

"How so?"

"I dunno. It's like, you lose your way. To be fair, that's the whole of this place."

"So how've you kept it together?"

He taps his nose. "I have my ways. You'll see. It's not just nicking Coronation Chicken."

I stop eating. "This is stolen? For fuck's sake, Alby. I don't want any of that hassle."

Alby knows about my incarcerated sibling, knows how I feel about accusations of theft.

"Don't worry, mate. This stuff was gonna be wasted anyway. It'll make sense when you've bin in the warehouse. But for now, just stay critical."

"How?"

He shrugs. "Make use of that English degree. Pen summit. Prove to me it's useful." This goes back to our undergrad days when he was studying politics. He dropped out not long after we'd moved into the shared house, claiming a Damascus realisation on the 699 bus that uni was a con, that he didn't need to roll around in the academic playpen. So he'd taken a job at the Tesco in Liverpool city centre, risen up its ranks, been recruited for a job at the flagship store in Kensington and, once our tenancy was up, moved down here. I used to sneer at his decision, but now that I've joined him both in London and in his workplace, I find my sneer reduced to a complicit murmur.

"I tried it, keeping a journal," he explains. "I mean, jotting down what I saw on the Cheese Counter. I called it my dairy diary. But then Bisera found it and got me bollocked." He brushes off crumbs from his jumper. "Right, I've got to get on the Deli Counter." He pulls from his backpack white overalls, an apron, and flips a white-mesh trilby onto his head. He hesitates, then reaches into his bag again. "You'll need this, lad, if you're going to be in the sophisticated atmos of the British Museum." He hands me a roll-on deodorant. Then he's out of the door.

I finish my shift, mulling over Alby's 'dairy diary' idea. I'll try it but with more ambition than just cheese.

Food for thought? *Store Stories*? *Word salad*?

Maybe one of these could be an essay for the MA.

I get on the Tube, and the train shudders off along the green line. I change at Embankment onto the black line, getting off at Tottenham Court Road. That's zone 1+2 I've passed through. I calculate how much Tube travel has cost me today, adding it to my running total since I started working at Tesco. And there's the work boots I'm still paying off, as well as the pack of wipes I bought. There's also the bouquet of flowers I felt obliged to get for Lottie for letting me stay. This doesn't bode well for saving up for a room of my own.

At least the British Museum is free entry. But even that concession is under threat. It wasn't long ago that the Conservatives were talking about introducing admission fees for museums and galleries. Is that really within the scope of David Cameron's 'Big Society'? I'd already moved to Liverpool in July 2010 when I watched on the TV as Cameron announced his policy down the road at Hope University, flanked by gaunt schoolboy Rory Stewart and egg-in-a-jar Eric Pickles. I remember Alby and I watching on the TV in The Dispensary as the automated subtitles tried to make sense of Cameron's plan:

What is it that we're doing that's stopping you from doing what you want to do?
How can we stop stopping you?
And how do we stop stopping others?

At TCR, I exit and escalate to the street, towards the British Museum. By this point in the afternoon, there's a long queue for the bag inspection. I join at the edge of the well-clipped lawn, watching the pigeons greyly loop in the grey sky. Ahead of me, a pair of young women wrapped in cardigans and scarves of the 'vintage' variety are also watching the birds, which ascend so high that they blur with the gridded armour of Centre Point.

One says: "...famously unused. Except by pigeons, obvs."

"Like literally hundreds of empty offices."

"They should put the homeless up in there."

"The unhoused, is what we're supposed to call them. But, oh my God, one hundred percent. I remember my dad telling me of years ago when you could, like, literally walk through London, and there'd be no one sleeping on the streets."

"Was that because there were more places to help them, or because they weren't so lazy?"

Before an answer can be given, the pair have reached the bag inspector. I imagine the thousands of metres of unworn carpet rising up into the sky, all that space for shelter and rest. Perhaps housing the homeless in Centre Point would constitute not Big, but High Society.

Usually, I'd pause to admire the museum's pillared entrance, but I've not got time, so I aim first for the BM's toilets and use Alby's roll-on for my armpits. Refreshed, my boots skip lightly into the Parthenon Room, and before me a whole afternoon dedicated to my MA unfolds. Our lecturer recommended that we get out into the city as much as possible, to see art and history whenever we can, because it'll help us compose our essays. This afternoon, I'm planning to make notes for an essay entitled 'Losing Your Marbles: Unreliable Narratives in Occupied Greece'.

The room's shape and dimensions are vaguely reminiscent of a sanatorium, with polished floors, stern, silent staff on hand, while the public saunter in every direction. I join the sauntering, beginning with an examination of a particular frieze which depicts a cow being led to sacrifice. A plaque explains that of this frieze Keats wrote, '*O mysterious priest, lend'st thou that heifer lowing at the skies/And all her silken flanks with garlands drest.*' I open my notebook, creasing down a clean white page. This is what it's all about.

I scribble a few notes: porcine, bovine, fowl, lamb. I've hit upon the idea that the observations and interactions I have at Tesco can feature in my essays for this MA, as part of its focus on city life, the everyday. I continue to scribble: '*Throughout each shift, the aisle is replenished with the pink parts of burdened beasts. Perishable goods. Sacrifice is their purpose, on the altar of human digestion. Does the cow go willingly, or does it dig in its hooves on the slippery ramp, strain against the bit, yank back its head to groan at the abattoir's bare ceiling?*'

There's such ceremony in this frieze, in Keats's lines. The priest, the silken flanks, the garlands. What ritual accoutrements are found in the abattoir? The exhausted foreman forced to work overtime, the spray can of blue paint which brands the cattle for slaughter. But maybe, for the figures in the frieze, it's the same. Just another day at work, the daily coalface of Athenian ceremonies. Maybe those rituals were as fake and cosmetic for the ancient Greeks as Tesco's Spooktacular initiative is nowadays. What the frieze doesn't show is the priest's frown, his yawn, his blistered feet, his boredom at yet another sacrifice. And then there's the hidden labour: the young man who went into the field to gather the flowers to weave into garlands. Maybe he pocketed one, in the hope of giving it to his sweetheart, but was caught and condemned for the theft of sacred goods.

Keats saw this frieze and took it for his own purposes, repackaging marble in the more portable form of a poem. Just as the abattoir cuts up and disassembles the cow to sell at the supermarket, so the poet butchers a hefty slab of frieze so that it sits neatly and lightly on a bookshelf. With his customer base in mind, Keats did us all a favour by converting the hulking ancient artefacts into something accessible, and much more cost-effective than getting the Tube into Central London. In fact, I didn't need to come to the British Museum at all today. I could've just picked up a collection of Keats from a local library, one of the few that remains open.

By this point, my notes look unhinged, all scribbles and arrows, with question marks scattered around. But maybe it'll be a way of arming myself against the many negatives of this job, using pen and paper to stave off the numbing effects of the supermarket. Writing and retail, I'd like to think, are contrary pursuits, different industries. In the JBT, the only pertinent entry under 'R' is 'Retail design group: A group of high-level Managers who meet fortnightly to agree store layout plans'. My pocket OED is more generous in its definition:

> **/ˈriːteɪl/***n., a.,* & *adv* spec. use of OFr. *retaille* piece cut off, shred **1.** The sale of commodities in small quantities **2.** To recount or tell over again; to relate in detail; to repeat to others (1594).

The Francophone root has something of the act of butchery to it, of the dramatic dismemberment or mauling of an intact body. Retail as losing parts of yourself. I picture the Deli Counter, Alby donning his white overalls, flipping on the white-mesh trilby and thumbing the switch that sets the meat cutter's blade whirring. Is this really that different from writing? Isn't writing also a severing of tissue and selling it on? And what about these other OED definitions: the sale of commodities; to recount, relate and repeat to others. This is the commodifying and packaging of raw materials, to pass on to a customer, to a reader. Perhaps writing and retail aren't that different. Retell, retail, and repeat.

Some seasoned authors say that writing is like hospitality. In the Michelin Guide of consummate literary hosts, the most renowned is Nabokov, who'd welcome you, dear reader, indoors and offer you the best wine, invite you to take the chair nearest the fire, promising you a full, rich meal. He gets a few of those coveted stars. In the language of retail, he'd maintain, if not excel, at all three of Tesco's Customer–Colleague Interaction Policies. James Joyce, by contrast, would not be a good host. His welcome, if it came at all, would be dreary and mystifying, with gruel-thin pleasantries. The wine he'd offer would be the discount stuff hastily put out when there's a rush on, its label suggesting itself as 'suitable for any occasion' (which means it's suitable for none). The chair would be a footstall, creaking and rickety, the ones on wheels we use to reach Tesco's highest shelves. And there'd be no fire, so you'd have to keep your coat on. That's Customer–Colleague Interaction Policy No.1 and No.2 flouted right there:

~~BE PERSONABLE.~~
~~CUSTOMER FIRST.~~

And if Joyce's letters to Nora Barnacle are anything to go by ('*shit your drawers, dear, and let me fuck you*') then the same goes for policy No.3:

~~MAINTAIN HYGIENE.~~

Yes, he's got *Ulysses* on his CV, but I doubt he'd pass his probation period here. Writing and hospitality, writing and retail, they're different industries.

CHAPTER TWO

SKIN CARE

AM in the Underground's rattling carriage. I've claimed a seat, avoided the eyes of anyone left standing who deserves it more than me. Staring into the immediate distance, focused on the curved windowpane above the dozing, nodding heads of commuters opposite. Beyond the glass, the muddy dark of the tunnel slides past. Out of this darkness, a gargoylean scrawn stares back. *C'est moi.* Yours falsely.

Tired pale face, tired tight mouth — those are about the only features that show up. Otherwise, the heavy brow, the rash of stubble, the shadowed cheekbones, these dissolve into the dark backing. The eyes, too, are like coals scattered on bitumen. Hair dyed by grime and grease sprouts and trails too loosely to be deliberate. A hairline slick to the touch — it could ease these screeching railway tracks to a whisper. Posture-wise the reflection is a jarring mess: gangly, dangling, a clutch of gnarled twiglets, insect-like, a mantis without a prayer. Spindly. One shoulder lower than the other, accentuated by the warped window but nonetheless a real, bodily symptom of years of slouching to one side. I'm more at ease when there are surfaces to lean against. I'd be a mess in Tiananmen Square. Years and years of leaning, and turning my head at an angle, thus turning my neck, thus leading with my left shoulder, thus sloping my back. It's not quite as blatant as Richard III's scoliotic slant, but it's definitely there, distorting my gait, supplying me with continuous back pain. Slipped disks, spasms, inflamed vertebrae — over the years I've been pulled apart, acupunctured, cracked, and crunched. These were costly pursuits that too often fell under the misleading category of 'pampering', rarely covered by NHS funding, instead taking place in the grubby front room of a crystal-reading hippy whose post-menopausal wakeup call coincided with the 2008 financial crisis.

The train shunts and shudders, clickety clacking along the Piccadilly Line. Beneath the window, the drooping head of the guy opposite sinks further, his chin on his chest. He's folding in half towards the briefcase at his feet. I can see his neck's wrinkled nape and the pale groove of his uppermost vertebra: Cervical 1, the Atlas on which the skull's globe teeters. When he lurches awake to get off at his stop, there's going to be some proper strain around Thoracic 11 and 12. He'll have to work it off.

As for *moi*, the vertebral drama isn't helped by having to drag my rucksack from labyrinthine Tube to lobotomised Tesco every day.

The fenland county where I grew up gets a lot of stick from our Norfolk neighbours for being populated by hunchbacks who live in peat bogs, prone to incest and brawling. The Underground's system of tunnels and denigrated dens should be, a Norfolkian would say, my natural habitat. Our riposte, perfected over centuries, is to accuse the Norfolkian of possessing eleven-digited hands. It's not the most sophisticated comeback, but the alternative is to just knock him out. Call it the wit of the marsh.

Few of us make it out of the Fens. My hometown orbits Cambridge, which implies a geographical familiarity with academia, but just as I'm the first in my family to work at Tesco, I'm the first to go to university. And without a nepo-connect, studying at Cambridge was not on the cards. A family scandal I'm trying to avoid facing full-on, combined with sufficient undergrad grades to study an MA at a London institution, made me bypass Cambridge, dodge Colchester and Chelmsford, haul myself out of the boggy Fens, and straighten my hunched back as best I could. Here I am following in the footsteps of Bob Hoskins, cleaning my muddy boots on the capital's metaphorical door scraper, in an attempt to remodel myself as a Londoner.

The carriage's cinema screen above the drooping guy's head plays on repeat this film of subterrain, and from time to time, in the glass, I see my dad rushing towards me on the bank of the River Orwell — newspaper in one hand, the headline announcing his elder son's incarceration, and in the other hand, the open letter announcing his younger son's acceptance onto this MA. These are the visions that tiredness brings about. This early in the AM, there are no cognitive fortifications to stave them off. I'm grateful when the carriage opens onto Earl's Court's platform. At least at work there won't be time to think of all that. I ascend the Underground's escalator, glancing back through the train window to see the guy's head sunk down even lower. That's his lumbar region fucked. Along the busy street, I shoulder-barge oblivious coffee-clutching commuters, enter Tesco, and skip up to the ♂ Changing Room. Before each shift can start, there's a daily task I must undertake. I have to go in search of an identity.

I'll explain.

I begin each day in the Staff Room, rummaging in a vegetable box. For my first few shifts, I'd worn a badge that read: 'NEW TO TEAM'. This is standard procedure until an employee's personal nametag arrives. But so far mine has not. During the weeks that have followed, I've asked several Duty Managers and a number of Team Leaders about this delivery, citing Customer–Colleague Interaction

Policy No.1 from my Induction. The response from all staff to my inquiry has been the same: a glazed look followed by the phrase, "*Delays in delivery like this can take weeks, even months*," and the directive that I should do what other colleagues have done in this situation.

"What's that?" I asked.

"In the Staff Room, there's a box filled with the nametags of ex-colleagues. Just pick out a name that suits you."

Like a schoolboy before PE, every day since, I'm sifting through Lost Property, selecting an alias. Every morning, I rummage in the box, asking myself the same question. Do I feel like Bruce? Harry? Omar? Zoe? Siobhan? Mitch? Sharon? Daryl? Jonno? The names of the forlorn. We won't remember them. In my palm, I weigh each plastic badge like a *pinakia*, the small bronze disc incised with a citizen's name when he voted in ancient Athens.

Today, none of these names quite fit with who I feel like, who I saw this morning in the carriage's reflection. What's his name? Customer–Colleague Interaction Policy No.1 states that he needs to BE PERSONABLE, and being personable means having a name, but he also looked tired, pleading to be ignored. So today I am 'Huw'. Short, neutral, almost inconspicuous.

And Huw's task this morning is in the cosmetics aisle. 'Presentation is everything' is a motto here. All staff must be firmly committed to the process of 'facing up' which, even though it doesn't actually appear in the JBT, is defined as ensuring that all products stand uniformly shoulder to shoulder along the shelves, with no gaps in between. When all the shelves are stacked in this way, the aisles resemble those from the '90s gameshow *Supermarket Sweep*. Huw remembers lying prostrate on the living room carpet on a Saturday morning, in Burglar Bill jammies, watching Dale Winton camply quiz a pair of Welsh contestants, Ian and Sian, before they helter-skeltered around the supermarket in a desperate search for a mystery vegetable which would win them the game. Ian and Sian thought the answer was potato salad, but the bellowing audience insisted it was a leek they needed. The couple gave way to the masses, becoming more and more irate as they rushed about, shouting at the audience which shouted back. In vain they ran, distracted by patriotic allegiance to their national vegetable. Their time ran out, and they were eliminated. But this was a time when gameshow contestants still went home with something. For Ian and Sian, it was an accumulated £311, a decent cash prize in 1999.

Failing to 'face up' means facing the consequences, which is a stern word from any superior, which in Huw's case is everybody. 'Every customer is a target' is another motto here. All items on an aisle must be positioned so that the particular brands' logos project towards potential buyers as they pass along the aisles. They may spend half a second lingering to consider a purchase. Huw walks to aisle No.15, begins to rearrange the mascara and moisturisers. Endless rows of bottles and tubes like chess pieces. That lacquer of dust, wax, spermaceti, lotion, which make up the mask — 'make up', the name of the tribal balm. To be 'made up' is to be pampered, with manicures and pedicures. Cutex's nail repair range has been soaring from the shelves of late. Maybe early November's chilly air brings on brittle keratin. To be 'made up' also means, from roughly Nottingham northwards, to be enthralled or exhilarated. Both cuticle varnish and the disposition of *bein' dead 'appeh* share the trait of brevity. Being made up is short-lived. The comet of delight that briefly streaks the heart's sky has its equivalent in the world of cosmetics. Almost as soon as the polish or the nail paint has set, it begins to peel. There's a temptation to pick and tear at what's been so perfectly rendered. Likewise, think of those occasions when you've felt the impulse to sabotage a happy moment, to destroy what's good. To point out flaws. This is the fate of happiness. This is the enamel's fade. The faces of the models on the packaging of this set of fake eyelashes or that pot of lip gloss might promise permanence; but in real life, the lashes always fall off, the gloss inevitably dissolves, the nails predictably crack, the comet disappears in darkness. It's temporary. It's an artifice. It's made up.

The truth is what's underneath. For instance, under Huw's nametag, under his red long-sleeve jumper, is his skin. A battleground of aggressive acne and sweat, grafted onto spasming muscles and aching bones. And yet he has to be grateful for his dermis, because, crudely put, it was his skin that got him this gig. Nearly two months ago, in mid-September, his old uni friend Alby was working on the Deli Counter, and a member of senior staff approached him:

"Do you know any white boys with a posh accent who could do Tannoy announcements?"

It was Bisera, the Bosnian woman who would become Huw's Team Leader, who had asked this. What does such a question contain? Who is the typical Tesco worker? When taxonomising the relative merits of skin pigmentation and accent, did Bisera understand that the UK is stuck like a trolley in a muddy field between its desperate need to modernise and its deeply feudal subterrain? Is this why Alby recommended Huw as the ideal worker for this particular branch? There's the white skin and almost-RP accent, a combination which evokes nostalgia for the quasi-gentry clientele who frequent this part of South Kensington. The literature degree provides a bit of poetic flourish if someone asks for a recommendation of Wiltshire ham or Rioja.

An inspired choice, madam, for which your palate will surely thank you. Yes, of course I can carry your basket. Never forget what Dryden asks us: what can power give more than food and drink, To live at ease, and not be bound to think?

The OAP clientele love that personal shopper shit, and since they're regulars it's worth inhabiting the role of a Jeevesian valet on an unsustainable wage. And there's the simple fact of Huw being a worker in a Tesco, instead of (say) a Waitrose or a Harrods. This all reinforces the skint, homeless, humanities postgrad in his early twenties as subservient to modern commerce, even if he's not exactly *dead 'appeh* about it.

So it was Huw who, in mid-September, had received a text from Alby.

> eya m8 I know you said you were looking for work here in the Big Smoke. got you an interview at Tesco Kensington. The flagship store no less! If you're down then get here for 9AM tomorrow. Clean-shaven, smart shirt.

As Huw read this message, he was standing in the smoking area of The Fitzroy Tavern in Bloomsbury, on his first night out in the city. The most interesting conversations always have a habit of taking place in the smoking areas of pubs. He was with his new coursemates from his Literature MA, inhaling tobacco and talk. This was the MA he'd moved to London to pursue. This was what he'd been told it was all about. Enthusiastic bookish types who knew the source material well enough to speak in shorthand:

"All I'm saying is there'd be no *Kubla Kahn* without Mary Robinson, like there'd be no Virginia without Leonard."

"Kingsley or Martin?"

"I prefer Mantel's earlier work. *Fludd* is just wow."

"*Beowulf*, it loses something in translation."

All of these earnest conversations swirled around Huw, borne from a shared passion for the subject. One of the cohort, a generous guy from Hungary called Dominik, a self-confessed acolyte of William Blake, had already been kind enough to offer his flat on Scala Street for Huw to crash for the night. So with his accommodation sorted and with the possibility of employment the following day, Huw was in a very 'yes and' frame of mind. Yes and I'll get the round in, yes and I'll have a rollie, yes and *The Ghost of a Flea* is a masterpiece of a painting, yes and let's stay out for another few, yes and I'll come to Abra Kebabra.

Yes, he'd texted back to Alby at the night's end, and crashed out on the carpet of Dom's third-floor flat, his jacket for a pillow. But alas, this kind of evening is not consonant with the solid night's sleep necessary for a job interview first thing. He'd been woken early the following morning by the polyphonic chirrup of his Nokia's alarm. He'd hurriedly shaken Dom awake to ask for a razor and for a suitable shirt.

"Dom? Dom, mate. Can you spare some clobber? Nothing Gatsbyesque, just smart." From the bunker of his duvet, Dom gestured vaguely at the wardrobe, murmuring in broken phrases: "Shirts in there... take any... in the bathroom... foam in cupboard." Shave, shower, shirt. Huw considered adding 'shit', but time was limited, and who dumps after a douche?

Huw had descended the building's communal staircase, the banister a lifeline, his back feeling the carpet's aftereffects, buzzing himself out through the heavy front door, tripping over a collapsed Brompton padlocked to the railings, falling, his right knee taking the brunt of the porch tiles. To his feet, he tumbled along Scala Street towards Goodge Street station, autumn air on his freshly bladed cheeks, a limp asserting itself with each stride.

There were problems even before Huw had arrived at the store. Like the crooked, split paving slabs of London, the cracks in this endeavour were showing. One such fissure was geographic. The store's closest Tube station is technically Earl's Court, and yet the supermarket is confusingly referred to as Tesco Kensington. Huw was almost late because he'd assumed that a store which calls itself Tesco Kensington would actually be closer to South Kensington, or West Kensington, or Kensington (Olympia), or High St Kensington. Having pinballed between these four stops, he'd finally found his sweaty, hobbling way out of Earl's Court station and along Warwick Road towards the store. As he sweated and hobbled, he still had no idea why this name existed. Maybe, to the Tesco powers-that-be, 'Kensington' sounded better than 'Earl's Court', though surely this was splitting regal hairs. He'd heard of another example of brand recognition overpowering common-sense geography: the confusion of building a Westfields in East London.

He arrived at the sliding doors, sweating out the residue of last night's poison, his face prickly with the salty booze that pooled in his newly bared pores, stinging him into reluctant alertness. His mouth was still a furry fermentation of booze. What he'd give for five minutes in the Toiletries aisle with some Listerine. Ditto on deodorant. The shirt he'd borrowed from Dom, crisp and fresh an hour ago, was now soaked through and itchy, onion-scented and waterlogged. The right knee of his trousers had been torn by the Brompton. He imagined its owner, cursed their bicycle clips, their hi-viz jacket, their environmental conscience, whoever they were. Maybe if he crossed his legs during the interview, left leg over right knee, he could hide the tear and the bleeding while passing himself off as vaguely contemplative and relaxed.

During the interview, the previous night's kebab was like a bailiff in his gut, and yet he still managed to reply in a measured tone to whatever was put to him by the panel: *When have you gone an extra mile for a customer... Describe yourself in three words... What's your greatest strength... What's your biggest weakness...*

His answers, he's forgotten them nearly two months on, were packaged superlatives and a basket of stock phrases. All the time, his thoughts pinged from his knee, to the churning doner, to the tufts of hair from his poor razor work. It felt like a victory for bodily restraint when they actually offered him the job, and he managed a handshake without defecating. Back through the sliding doors, he guided himself streetward, along Hogarth Road, to the nearest greasy spoon, where a toilet and celebratory fry-up welcomed him. Then back to Scala Street for another shower, another drop-off of doner+full English cargo, and a return to the carpet.

And now here he is: in early November, less smoothly cheeked and less sweaty, but on subtle self-inspection (he reaches to a high shelf and turns his nose into his armpit) no less in need of deodorant. He's directly contradicting Customer–Colleague Interaction Policy No.3: MAINTAIN HYGIENE, at risk of being reprimanded on this most fragrant and cosmetic of aisles. And now here he is: clocking out before his shift is over, exploiting the daylight savings that has pushed time back an hour. And now here he is: crouching to grab his rucksack from the carriage floor, his knee scabbed over but still itchy when he bends, the fibres of his trousers snagging on the scab's edges. And now here he is: back at Lottie and Vic's, Lottie compliantly resewing his botched attempt to mend his torn trousers, while Vic pilots a submarine through a San Andreas abyss, grits his teeth when he's WASTED. And now here he is, in the spare room, listening to Lottie and Vic arguing then fucking in the next room. And now here he is: hoping that very soon he'll amass enough money to buy a second pair of trousers and to secure a deposit for a room of his own, assuming somewhere will have him. Then he'll be made up.

▬ ▬ ▬ ▬ ▬

The Staff Canteen is cloying with warmth, even this early in the day. I unzip my fleece and fold it awkwardly over one of the radiators, hoping to sear away the morning's drizzle. Even though the tables are occupied, it's oddly quiet as I join Alby at a table. I can even hear Jeremy Kyle on the TV.

"Ey, lad. Look over there," Alby nods to the far end of the canteen, where a mass of Upper Management's black and grey suits have surrounded a shop floor worker. Everyone's attention is focused in the huddle's direction.

"It's a strip-search," Alby murmurs over Nick Dale's head bowed over his magazine. I take a seat, and watch as the shop floorer empties his pockets.

"That's Callum, works in Homeware," Alby whispers. "Surely he's not the thief."

From a neighbouring table, one of the Euphorium bakers leans over. "*Psst*, Alby. £10 says it's Callum what's stole all that stuff."

Alby grins. "Okay lad. £10 says it ain't."

But before the terms can be agreed, Callum walks away accompanied by the grey and black suits of Upper Management.

There's a baffled pause, then the baker calls over, "Well, that'll be £10 then, Alby."

"Piss off, mate. Callum walking away with them lot doesn't prove anything."

The baker grumbles and tuts. "We'll have to wait and see if the strip-searches stop then."

The strip-searches have been a recent feature of our shifts here, a result of what's being referred to as 'wasting'. This term doesn't appear in the JBT; it's part of an unofficial language which exists here, hidden in plain sight, a *lingua tesca* that I'm still learning. 'Wasting' is what occurs in the warehouse, with produce being thrown away once it's passed its sell-by date. 'Illicit wasting' is the theft of these items. And there's been a lot of it going on recently, and one big theft in particular, right here in the store, has been the talk of the canteen. A number of colleagues are under suspicion. No one for sure, but there are a lot of suspects. The scuttlebutt is that a colleague managed to steal £1,500 worth of DVDs, video games, electronics, and kitchen appliances.

"It's all pretty nuts." Alby shakes his head.

I ask: "Who's on your list of unusual suspects?"

He holds up a single digit. "There's only one hombre I reckon would attempt somethin' so fabulously fucking audacious." He affects a drumroll on the bin lid. "Heath."

"Heath?"

"Heath."

"Which one's Heath?"

"If you don't know Heath, let me get you up to speed. Heath, AKA Heath with the Teeth."

"Oh. HEATH." The image of the toothy giant strides onto my mind's stage. He puts the 'sex' in 'Essex boy': blunt, gelled hairline, reddish-brown skin that's been so copiously creamed and cured that when Heath raises his eyebrows, his forehead looks like layers of a geological survey. And when he accompanies this eyebrow-raise with a smile, you're dazzled by a blast of polished teeth like panels from a NASA space craft. "Toothy, yes, but I'd not cast him in the role of robber."

"Who would you, then, Sherlock Holmeless?" challenges Alby. He's told me before that being a Scouser down here still brings with it outdated and stale stereotypes. He half-jokes to feelings of guilt that he's betrayed his sectarian city by leaving it.

"Very good, dear Watson of Walton. I know that there was someone who was searched, and they found a packet of tofu in her coat pocket. She said she'd left the receipt somewhere else, but I dunno if anything came of it."

"You mean Cármen?" Alby, haughty, defensive even. "I doubt she'd steal."

"But you're certain about Heath?"

"Oh sure, mate. He's Heath the Thief with the Teeth. It rhymes too perfectly for there not to be some truth to it. Thought you'd see that, being literary and all." Alby draws breath before the exposition begins. "I've heard that he's addicted to fabric softener..."

"Aisle No.13?"

"No.14, but close. He used to hang around the detergents, close to hyperventilatin' with each sniff. He'd buy bottles and bottles of pink, blue, yellow fabric softener, and he'd stash 'em in his car. First it was just Tesco's own brand, then more spenny stuff, then valuable goods like DVDs and tha'. In his car parked out front, in plain sight."

"That does sound suspicious."

"And if that's not enough of a sign of guilt, I dunno what is."

This broad accusatory mood has spread across the store, with everyone living in a dual reality of accused and accuser, with all sorts of stories circulating which at any point could be used to support a claim of criminality.

Alby nudges Nick. "Hey, Nick. Have you had your strip-search?"

Nick glances up. "I'm on the phone. What?"

Alby puts his hands out in front of him, wrists touching. "Have you been strip-searched yet?"

Nick shakes his head, puts his phone back to his ear, waves a hand. "Shhh. Yes, hello, I'd like to place an order for the fender?" He sighs, presses the speaker button so we can hear the tinny sound of hold music. "They make it so bloody hard to get what you want. What were you asking, Alby?"

"I'm asking about the wasting."

Nick, more spectacles than face, shakes his head. "You mean the illicit theft of produce? I do not steal," he says, putting the phone back to his ear. "Yes, the fender, with a next-week delivery date, please."

"No, I know. Wasn't accusin' you, my mace. You're a store favourite, as far as I see it." Alby inspects the literature. "This still your robot?"

"Dalek, yes." Nick is certainly made for Tesco. He might as well carry a barcode, with his dedication to the store, with never a bad word to say about it. A typically nice guy, but also a scrupulous master of miserliness, a man expert in saving his wages, never purchasing snacks or cigarettes from the store, always prepared with Tupperware from home, the crusts snipped from the bread's edges, saving up his wages to build his own full-scale, fully functioning Dalek.

"Robot. Dalek. Same thing more or less?"

"No. Not more or less." Furiously punching in numbers. "The word 'robot' comes from the word '*robota*,' which means literally 'serf labour'."

"So, drudgery, hard work, et cetera?"

"But a Dalek is a much more complicated being, for example..."

Alby nods away the inquiry. "Sorry, Nick. We'll have to pick this up in another space-time continuum."

"That is not the correct use of the term." But this is announced into the gap left by Alby's swift scarper. I peel my damp fleece from the radiator and follow him out before the staff double doors have swung back towards me.

Alby: "I do like Nick a lot, but all that *Doctor Who* stuff I find..."

"Trying?"

"Beyond my pay grade. Y'know, the other day, I overheard Dan laughin' about Nick's 'retardis'. I know, shocking, right. But it's really stuck in my head. Why is it always the really deadly insults which last the longest?"

On I go with my own serfdom, first picking out today's nametag, wondering if the answer to Alby's question is a built-in obsolescence that makes us exalt in insult and injury, a bit of false wiring to keep us downtrodden.

Today I am 'Samuel'.

Samuel grafts sleepily, unstacking pots of couscous, wondering what was in the water of the Vltava River when Josef Capek and his brother coined *robota*. When Karel Capek visited London's East End in the early 1900s, he observed how the mass of human beings looked like piles of soot and dust. This was not a natural occurrence but a deliberate organisation of industry so that the workers became the very geological material on which the capital's capitol grew. This is the excess of work, the quarry out of which a city is built.

All this scuttlebutt about illicit wasting, supposedly committed by one individual, is an interesting distraction from the real, official wasting that occurs on a daily, hourly basis in the warehouse. Sam hasn't been given the warehouse tour yet nor witnessed the wasting himself, but from what Alby has told him, it's a travesty that so much perfectly good, edible produce is thrown away once it's passed its sell-by date. Sam has started noticing many signs and posters which warn of the consequences of 'illicit wasting', and yet no reprimands seem to exist for the official practice.

He's tried to keep a dairy diary, to note down what he's heard Upper Management saying about the wasting, but the growing threat of a strip-search like the one Callum just went through has prevented him from carrying a notebook.

But he's got an alternative strategy. One of the authors on his MA's syllabus is Thomas Pynchon, and from wider reading he's found out that apparently Pynchon was employed as a civil engineer and wrote the first draft of *Gravity's Rainbow* on the type-paper he was told to use at work. When walking the aisles, one of Sam's tasks is to aim a price-tag gun loaded with yellow REDUCED sticky labels at products that are on the cusp of their sell-by dates, at risk of being wasted. The adhesive backing to the sticky labels is a long reem of plasticky parchment, ideal for scribbling on. During a shift, Sam tucks this ribbon in his apron pocket and, from time to time, when he hopes no one's looking, scribbles what he notices. For instance, today he sees a poster on the wall in the kitchen:

CCTV
Recording in operation for the prevention of illicit wasting and for the protection of our customers, staff and stock.

On the ribbon, he copies out the poster. There is no visible sign of any CCTV in the kitchen, which makes Sam think it's much like a cardboard cut-out of a policeman in a shop window: a piece of social conditioning that's cheaper than surveillance cameras.

He'd be interested to know if there are any cameras in the warehouse, too, since that is where the official wasting occurs.

You know when you look up at the night's sky, see one star, then others suddenly emerge? Well today, Sam's been woken up to myriad other posters warning against waste. On his ribbon of REDUCED parchment, he notes down a few examples of these gleaming clouds of eternal dust. There's a green poster through the heavy NO ENTRANCE double doors:

What Can I Do?
If you see illicit wasting, report it to your manager who
will deal with your information
in full <u>confidentiality</u>.

There's a blue poster halfway up the stairwell to the Staff Room:

Why Sould [*sic*] I Care About ILLICIT Waste?
Through increased prices at the shelf
At pay reviews, due to lost profits
Shares in success reduced
Ultimately it hits OUR pockets

There's a red poster at the warehouse entrance:

SHOPLIFTING IS A CRIME
[picture of handcuffs]
[arrow pointing to handcuffs]
Free bracelet with each theft.

The spelling errors, the weird tenses, the fudged suffixes, this all confirms that big money suffers from illiteracy. It goes far beyond the original sin of '10 items or less'. Sam realises he's surrounded on all sides by hitmen of syntax and grammar. And it worries him that this might be affecting his own scribbling style. He notices that none of these posters are visible to any customers, so they're all aimed at colleagues — the main enemy who must be kept under control. Elsewhere, Sam notices a yellow poster at the top of the stairwell to the Staff Canteen:

What's UR Duty?
Minimise waste & report suspicious behaviour while remaining anonymous

This directive to snitch, to dob, to go and tell, is the modern equivalent of the medieval practice of anonymously placing a name into an iron mask in the middle of the market square. It's also a blatant evocation of Kantian deontology that argues that lying is *verboten* in every circumstance, because it flouts the Categorial Imperative. Alright, Immanuel, what about if Sam's brother, convicted of a crime, was hiding in his house, and the police came knocking. Wouldn't Sam be right to lie to the police and say he didn't know where his brother was? What say you, Manny K.?

Kant: *Nein*. The duty to be honest triumphs over all other values, including familial loyalty.
Sam: But surely this just proves the folly of your Categorial Imperative?
Kant: *Ja*, you may think so, but there's a way around this issue. Imagine, Sam, that your brother is hiding and the police come to your door. You have a binary choice: tell a lie ("*Nein*, I have not seen *mein Bruder*, officer") or tell a misleading truth ("I saw *mein Bruder* an hour ago at the supermarket"). The misleading truth is always the morally sound option.

Sam wanders the aisles, imagining what he'd say if his brother appeared, un-caged.

- - - - -

I've made an error. I've allowed myself to get too settled at Lottie and Vic's, even folding a few pairs of boxers and socks in the spare room's chest of drawers. And now they've moved me along. Not maliciously, but just via a few winks, winces, nods, and eyerolls, they've indicated that, for the time being, their hospitality has expired. I make a note in my diary to check back with them in a few months — February, say — by which time, hopefully, my guest-status can be reinstated. Anyway, with this removal comes a reduction in accommodation quality. For instance, at Lottie and Vic's in Angel, I had a room with all the trimmings (towel, freshly ironed sheets on a decent mattress, bedside table + light). But this nomadic lifestyle has now sent me south, to a house in the Borough of Lambeth, specifically Streatham Hill, where, instead of a spare room, there's a blow-up mattress in what used to be a utility cupboard. This is what's on offer when I stay at Freddy's, a friend from East Anglia who made the giant leap out of the Fens to London about a year ago. His landing on the city's fissured pavements was softened by the help of an older sibling, who sorted him with board, a job as an *au pair*, and a cultured, older, cooler, longer-haired network in the South London neighbourhood.

At the end of his road, by the train station, there's a *sklep* which, gratefully, is still open at this late hour, with an entire shelf dedicated to discount tins of Tyskie. I've had to accept that the proprietor sells each individually instead of the six-pack they arrive as, but it's not neighbourly to bring up that sort of thing. I'm a guest at a friend's house on the same street, and that friend has asked me to restock his stash of lager for his bedroom's fridge. That's the price of my accommodation.

Approaching Freddy's house, sagging carrier bag of beers in one hand, Tesco discount pizza in the other, I have to set down the bag to text Freddy to alert him that I'm outside. Looked at face-on from the cold, windy dark, I can see stars emerging above and to each side of the house. Unlike most London streets where houses are pressed as tightly together as the trays of baklava we sell on the Euphorium Bakery, this three-storey Edwardian is detached from its neighbours. For the myriad aspiring DJs living within its walls, this is an architectural benefit, as their separate jockeyings go on at all hours, at all levels, including Sunday night and Monday morning. Obscuring the off-white façade is a grand, wrinkly ash tree. Its leaves and branches tremble and creak whenever a train flattens the tracks under the railway bridge. Tall, loose hedges further wall off the house's narrow path and front yard, where late-autumn leaves bruise the ground when they fall.

First red (creeping Virginia), then brown (oak), finally black (mulch). Once the door is opened...

"Yeh, like you're, like, Freddy's mate? Solid yeh no worries he's, like, up on the top floor."

...and I feel my way past bicycles stacked in the corridor, I find myself in a Piranesi tangle of dim rooms and hallways — the walls vibrating with gabber bass, the bare wooden floorboards thudding and splintering with breakcore. Freddy's room is at the very peak of the façade's arched, red-tiled brow, his small sash window looking out onto the tree's loose-leafed branches. Picture postcard, it might've been a century ago; now, it's a living situation which I covet. This is what a senior sibling can help with, easing the path through the city for the younger. At mate's rates, with his part-time *au pair*ing gig, Freddy's remained pretty stable, at the top of the rickety house by the ash tree, teetering on the edge of the rattly railway.

"Ah, nice work, brovva. Cheers for bringing supplies." Freddy nods me to his fridge, while he stays at his desk. He's in casual steam-punk attire tonight, his leather coat bunched over his chair, his goggles on his desk, but he's still got on his fingerless studded gloves, and his digits are busy rolling a joint and tapping at his keyboard.

Freddy's a cinephile, one who'll take the Tube to East Finchley's Phoenix Cinema *because* it's far away. But his job as chief childminder for a seriously moneyed couple in Hampstead only pays so much — their stinginess is a continuous conversation between us — their ponies-in-hand only covering X amount of weed per week, X cans of Tyskie, X Tube trips to the Phoenix, and so he more often than not resorts to illegal downloads of new releases, for which the stoned digital traipse to find a decent-quality file is part of the thrill. In fact, sometimes Freddy'll deliberately seek out the grainiest, flimsiest bootleg recording, just for the howl. He'll search on websites with names like cinemimesis.co.uk or manwithamoviecamcorder.com for these bootlegs. He'll sometimes review a recording, analysing those moments when the pirate's grip on the Kodak loosens and the frame strays into a silhouetted crowd. These frame wanderings correspond, Freddy tells me, to the most expositional parts of a film, which, he's certain, proves that plot is kaput.

Anyway, as well as being a cinephile, he's also very interested in the career of Cillian Murphy, one of his few concessions to mainstream cinema. And this evening, we're settling down to watch the finale of the BBC's *Peaky Blinders*, a series that's infected even his texting style — **Bring Tyskies, by order of the PBs** — in part, I reckon, because he shares his name with one of the characters: the handsome communist with the crisp haircut, Freddie Thorne. So impressed was our Freddy with FT's short sides and long top that he's chosen to airdrop the haircut from Small Heath in the 1920s to Streatham Hill in 2013.

As he grinds some weed onto his desk — and I sit on the floorboards, schrushing open a Tyskie — Freddy's preamble begins with an analysis of Cillian Murphy in *28 Days Later*:

"This," Freddy begins, raking back loose strands of hair out of bloodshot eyes, "is Murphy at the opposite end of the scale to the character he plays in *Peaky Blinders*. Yes, it's true that *28 Days Later* is brutal, it being a grim post-apocalyptic London, but it has a light-hearted, friendly, and nice moment, which is confined to a minute and a half montage of the assembled pandemic survivors shopping in a supermarket, soundtracked by Grandaddy's 'A.M. 180'. In fact..."

Freddy drops the spliff paraphernalia, and his fingers scuttle across the keyboard, "I'll put on the song."

We sit through the unskippable YouTube adverts, and then the seaside slot machine bleeps of Grandaddy's tune begin. Freddy returns to his labours, explaining that Murphy and his co-stars cruise their trolleys along unrealistically well-stocked aisles. "It's one of the film's few errors because it's basically saying that, even after a zombie plague, supermarkets would still keep their lights on. The levity of the scene derives not just from this well-lit, civilised order, but also from the familiar way in which the four characters peruse the shelves. 'We can't just take any crap,' comments Brendan Gleeson in a convincing East End cab-driver accent, as he chastises the friendly, nice Murphy for his poor whisky selection. Gleeson chooses a superior alternative, a single malt: 'Dark, full-flavoured, warm but not aggressive. Peaty aftertaste.' Meanwhile, the post-apocalyptic product placement continues as the two female characters..."

"What're they called?" I interject between Tyskie sips.

"...erm. Can't remember. But one of them is played by Naomie Harris, later Moneypenny in *Skyfall.* Anyway, they're both giggling over Terry's chocolate oranges. It's all jovial, upbeat, the only hint of menace is the baseball bat that Murphy keeps in his shopping trolley amongst the carrier bags."

"Cricket bat."

"Huh?"

"It should've been a cricket bat. Since when would a Londoner have a baseball bat?"

"Fair point. *Shaun of the Dead* did it better. Edgar Wright gets it right. But the point of the whole supermarket montage and the bat in the trolley is to predict that Mr Niceguy will not be so nice by the end of the film. And..." — Freddy pauses here to run his tongue along the edge of the spliff — "the trajectory of Murphy's acting choices from then to now confirms this transition from friendly, nice Jim, to brutal Brummie gangster Thomas Shelby. Gleeson's lessons in whisky selection also had an effect, as Murphy's Shelby slams down, repours and knocks back drams as part of his workday."

This is how Freddy likes to begin every viewing we have of a film or TV series when I'm crashing at his. It's symptomatic of the way the stoned mind exaggerates the grandeur of an occasion, so that it's not just the two of us in his bedroom but a whole audience in a cinema listening to the auteur's preamble before the main feature.

Freddy lights up as the episode begins, and the weed and Tyskie and tiredness begin their collaborative work on my blood and brain. Fortunately, my stoned paranoia is very low-stakes, and tends to manifest in moments like this when I suspect that Freddy dumbs down his choices of films or TV when I'm here. Like, for instance, on that wall above where he's sitting is a poster of Yelizaveta Svilova. But not once has he ever suggested we whack on *Энтузиазм* or *Klyatva Molodykh*. And I'm grateful to him if that is the case, because, after a busy shift like today, I can't handle anything with even a vaguely Cyrillic title. So I'm here in the smoky and earthy world of gang violence in early 1900s Birmingham. Whisky flows like wine. Noses dribble in the cold and must be continuously wiped. Cigarettes are cupped against the blowing wind. Watching the series, you pine not necessarily for those inter-war years, but for the streets the characters walk along. Liverpool is where most of the series is filmed. There's Gwydir Street in Toxteth, there's Tobacco Warehouse at Stanley Dock, on the road out towards Crosby. And there's the pillared, grand St George's Hall, in disguise as Birmingham Art Museum, where the blonde secret agent passes her intel to the villainous Inspector Campbell.

Freddy and I pass the joint back and forth, and the heady mix of free associations becomes more centrifugal...

...The blonde secret agent has more than a passing resemblance to Serena Frome from Ian McEwan's latest novel *Sweet Tooth*.

...Campbell's not the real villain.

...I should be reading *Sweeth Tooth*.

...The real villain is official paperwork: the contracts, the dossiers passed between overworked clerks who lower their heads when the Shelbys pass by. The paraphernalia of bureaucracy.

...But I can't just whip out a book, I'm a guest afterall.

...There lurks throughout the spectre of PTSD, the 'shell shock' of veterans, Danny Whizzbang's swollen cartoon eyes when he remembers the trenches.

...I'll just skim a few pages before bedding down.

...There's the soundtrack, raw and deliberately anachronistic, like showing Sky Sports in a saw-dusted pub.

...And there's the joyous cameo from Benjamin Zephaniah, whose presence as the local preacher outside the grimy Garrison is the kind of literary intervention that elevates any TV show. B.Z. is the biz, a dyslexic second-gen Jamaican poet of 'Inna Liverpool', 'Propa Propaganda', and 'London Breed', who triumphantly rejected an OBE.

...There's something Shakespearean about the pubs frequented by the Shelbys, with stained glass and wooden partitions, through which the baritone timbre of the Brummie voices, coarsened by cigarettes and whisky, vibrate the exposition for the benefit of an eavesdropping barmaid.

...At Tesco, by contrast, the Upper Management's offices are sealed far away from the ears and eyes of us on the shop floor. No chance of dropping eaves.

...Another way in which the Shelbys and Tesco differ is how they motivate their respective workforces. In an earlier episode, the older brother Arthur rallies his platoon of gangsters ahead of the Cheltenham races, distributing bottles of spirits as fighters' fuel. Boozing on the job is forbidden at Tesco, or at least it is for us on the shop floor. I've seen disposable plastic flutes and bottles of CAVA stacked by Upper Management's private doors. So, in a century, it's gone from whisky socialists to the fizzy wine of the nouveau riche.

- - - - -

The day's not nigh; it's now. As I pass through the sliding glass doors for my shift, the Tannoy calls for me — by name — as sinister as a passenger announcement issued in an airport. I'm instructed by the vaulted ceiling's echo to meet Monojit by the warehouse entrance for my warehouse orientation. I catch Alby's eye as I pass the Deli Counter.

"So it's time for yous to witness the wastehouse," he says, turning off the cheese cutter and rummaging through a cupboard by his knees.

"You call it the wastehouse?"

"Yes lad. Like an oasthouse but instead of kilning hops it's killing hope. Yeah see? You're not the only one round ere who can do portentous wordplay."

"You mean pretentious, Alby."

"No no. Portentous. You'll know what I mean once you've been in. Here." He stands, his hand out. "You'll need these for the warehouse. Really, we should all be issued with hard hats and torches — you never know what'll fall on you — but this will help with the sight and the smell."

I inspect what he's given me. Two small vials containing dark, viscus liquid.

"That's oil from euphrasy," he explains. "A few drops in the eyes, and you'll adjust to the darkness and the dust much quicker. And that one is oil from rue. You'll definitely need that for the smell."

I give him a look which is supposed to connote suspicion.

"Come on, lad. You've put much worse up your nose behind Colquitt Street."

"But that was good old-fashioned cocaine–washing powder hybrid."

"Ey. Just yous make sure to dab a bit on the inside of your nostrils."

"Isn't this excessive?"

"Trust me. I always keep a couple of bottles here just in case I'm asked to go into the warehouse. Get on now, and find me afterwards when you're out. We'll debrief in Felon Place."

As I head to meet Monojit, I run a rued fingertip around the honker, then drop a few beads of euphrasy into each eye, blinking away the momentary blur to see Monojit ahead of me, already pushing aside the plasticky tendrils that hang down at the warehouse's entrance. I'm reminded of Gulliver's return from his travels, and the smell of the Yahoo Englanders he couldn't stand. To combat it he took to stuffing his nose with herbs.

We enter the unlit wastehouse. Not even the shop floor's shimmer in here. Having regularly complained, I now pine for it. My eyes blur. I miss my footing, skid in something, almost fall.

"What's that?" I ask, mid-skid. There's a large white smear on the dark concrete. I step away from the patch and feel scrunching under my boots.

Monojit crouches, looks closely: "There's been a breakage. Hellmann's mayo, probably."

I begin to sideswipe my boot to gather up the shards of glass into a dim, glittering pile.

"No, no. CAYG doesn't apply here." Monojit leads us into the darkness, across this sulphur-smelling threshold, as we move deeper into the ominous cavern in which lurks grief, disease, the stench of mould and damp. Despite the rue thoroughly balmed, the stench of putrefaction, unashamed mulch, the smell of rotting eggs is unavoidable. We come across a pile of reeking bin bags, on which has been thrown the bent and buckled skeleton of a CAGE. A procession of warehouse workers passes us, each hunched figure under a huge sack, each bag leaking, dripping, with juices that in the half-light glisten darkly like petrol, gathering in the fissures of the concrete floor, seeping into grim brooks and pools. You could go puddle hopping in here.

"You could go puddle hopping in here," I say, but Monojit doesn't turn. He doesn't even hear. Yes, I have a barrier against the sight and smell, but Alby failed to prepare me for the sound. Ruinous noises swirl around. Workers in shrieking paroxysms of hideous destruction, and their wheezing combustion, their hands and forearms, constricted by black rubber gloves, are manacled in endless perdition to the huge rattling CAGEs.

Monojit leads us still deeper into the midst of this place, into full-fat darkness, where the pale light from the warehouse entrance barely reaches, to the mucky, boggy katabasis. Lots of slopes and ramps that lead confusingly back to where we started. I feel that impulse to ascend, which guarantees I'll plummet. More figures pass us, and their creaking CAGEs teeter on these steep slopes, in desperate need of repair, with squeaking wheels threatening at any moment to free themselves from the worker's grip, to speed down the concrete ramp and smash into the dustbins where all this food is destined to be thrown. There's a sound like rheumatoid joint-cracking, and everyone cackles, a monstrous crew in deep, mean laughter, as CAGEs collide somewhere in the dark.

Faces peep out from dark alleyways of CAGEs, wordlessly shunting trolleys and palettes, bin liners sagging with produce, towards the ugly backend of waste disposal lorries that hiss and gasp with pneumatic greed. Although the faces of these workers are gaunt, their bodies are well-built, muscled, broad — as if, to prolong their suffering, they've been made endlessly strong. These CAGE workers and cart rattlers are the wasters who run their errands down into the deepest gloom.

I take my phone from my pocket, tap on its torch, the beam a singly thin curtain of light against the dark, which nonetheless highlights thick dust floating in the air, drying my eyes. I dab more euphrasy and survey the dismal situation — sad, noisy. The light illuminates a multitude, all in dark overalls, none in Tesco outfits, none with nametags. I think I recognise one as Haroon, his face grizzled and unwashed. Just as CAYG no longer applies, neither does any other policy. Nameless, in dark oblivion they dwell and work.

In the midst of this visible darkness, with ragged wraithlike figures flittering about and pulling their skeletal CAGEs, their jeers mixing with the metallic shunt and squeal, there congeals in my mind's whirlpool of oil-slick associations a question — I'll seek out Alby and ask him: who is to blame for all this?

I re-emerge back through the plasticky tendrils, into the harsh, relieving light. The shop floor is a land of bright unpleasantness and distortion, and only now do I turn off my phone's torch and notice on the screen that the little bars are returning, one by one, like self-righting dominoes. While in the warehouse, I've had no signal. In there, no one can hear you call.

I'm relieved to be out but still feel coated with grime, so I get up to the ♂ Changing Room pronto, lean over the basin to wash, scrub, and breathe deeply. I look at my reflection, notice where my nametag should go. There wasn't time to select one before I went into the wastehouse. On the blank piece of red fabric is a pair of small but distinct holes, maybe an inch apart, like the precise wounds left in flesh after a snake has removed its fangs.

Alby materialises, puts my fleece around my shoulders, and leads the way. I follow him without really registering anything. To witness such wastefulness is to discover woeful sights, where there's neither peace nor rest, only dolorous disorder, where shelter from conscience is nowhere to be found, where dreadful shadows dwell.

The cold air brings me to my senses as we step through the FIRE EXIT at the back of the store, but Alby still has to repeat himself many times before I tune into what he's saying.

"Sohaveyoureadit?"

Have I read it? Have I read what? I scan my internal Rolodex of required reading for the MA. Pynchon's *Bleeding Edge*, Silitoe's *Saturday Night and Sunday Morning*, Karen Green's *Bough Down*, *Savage Messiah*, Nadeem Aslam's *Maps for Lost Lovers*, Henry Green, Achebe, Tao Lin's *Taipei*.

"Hello, mate. Welcome back. I'm tryin' to take your mind off all that in the warehouse. So I'm askin' ye, haveyoureadit yet?"

As I try to understand what he means, Alby takes from his apron pocket a selection of snacks: packets, tins, jars, laying them on the flat top of a dustbin lid.

What's Alby referring to, his eyes so expectant? Then the brain fog clears. He wants to borrow *No Logo* by Naomi Klein, one of the books I want to use on my course. I was supposed to bring it in for him today.

I shake my head, taking a sheet of Emmental. "This weekend. Promise."

"Is that a Tesco colleague guarantee?" Alby spits out an olive stone into the brambles nearby. Our location is Felon Place, a crooked alleyway behind the store, dead-ended, weeded, walled by a mesh fence, where we've been holding our lunchbreaks over the last few weeks. Despite the fact that the last of autumn's agile heat is yielding to

November's incomprehensible cold, this is a good spot for a debrief.

We've taken to eating the produce that's destined to be wasted, rescuing it from its landfill fate by bringing it here and dutifully despatching it ourselves. At first, I was reluctant to engage in anything remotely similar to the ILLICIT WASTING warned against on those posters all around the store. Since my brother's incarceration, I've been desperate to avoid all associations with theft, or borrowing (my stomach drops whenever I have to take something out of the library, for fear I'll be fined). But now that I've seen the fate of all this perfectly edible produce when it is CAGEd and wheeled to the warehouse, I tuck in to the scran heartily.

It's a broad church of cheese and olives, elbows of baguette, with the odd stuffed pepper or pickled onion and a fuck tonne of canapés. By a country — no, a continental — mile, it's the best food I've eaten since arriving in London. Weird, then, to be enjoying this delectation with a dustbin lid for a table. There's a twanging sound as another of Alby's olive stones ricochets off the flank of a crumpled Stella can that's embedded in amongst the torcs of thorn and thistle. "What do you reckon I can do that again?"

"I reckon a pint."

He scoops up another olive from the pot, swills it loose of flesh in his mouth, and aims the stone can-ward. The twang is dulled by a car horn along Warwick Road.

"I'll applaud when we're at the pub." I reply, aware that part of this little picnic operation relies as much as possible on tactical gourmet espionage. We've agreed that if we get caught, we'll pretend we're cottaging, and in the meantime, we've made a pact of Tescomertà.

"So what say you to pubbing it?"

Alby's speculative nod: "Maybe tomorrow. Got a lot on tonight." For a moment, I wonder if this is a rebuke after I chose the British Museum over a beer the other week, but then I remember that his twin brother is having a rough time (divorce, one of the first of our age-group to embark on that peculiar galleon), and quite rightly it's the sibling who gets first dibs on Alby's sofa. It's not even Alby's sofa, since he and his brother are beneficiaries of a generous, London-based cousin who is always away for work in Dublin.

Alby's previously described this cousin, nearly a decade Alby's senior, as not quite a brother but not quite an uncle either. Shakespeare had it right in *Romeo and Juliet* — to focus so much on the fractures in family life — but more attention should've been given to the role of cousin, who is at a relieving remove from the tangle of immediate kin, and whose distance permits a clearer view of family problems. Like watching a foreign film with subtitles, the *gentle coz* may miss the nuances of speech or syntax, but they see the bigger picture and place more attention on physical cues, facial expressions, and gestures. This means that instead of offering to sit Alby or his twin brother down and talk, talk, talk about what's on their minds, this cousin apparently just sent a simple text when Alby first came to London:

> **eyup heard you need a spare room. Ours is free and all that.**

That's a gesture, that's a figurative handing over of keys. Nevertheless, staying at Alby's place in Canonbury has been out of the question since I arrived from East Anglia nearly two months ago. If I asked, Alby would oblige, probably even giving up his own bed for the sake of a guest. It's an enviable generosity I've never had, and would rather not call him to account for. He's an exact, precise bloke — was always quicker, sharper than the rest of us living together at university. During our undergrad, in our shared house, he was always quoting Diogenes, telling people to get out of his light; he had a poster of Hugh Gaitskell on his bedroom wall, claimed the Labour leader was "THE Labour leader, in favour of social welfare and hard on crime. Attempted to remove Clause 4, wasn't up for nuclear disarmament, was healthily Eurosceptic." Depending on Alby's mood or booze-intake, these attributes of Gaitskell's were merits or deficiencies, and Alby could always argue the case either way. But ever since I've known him, he's also been anxious for intellectual approval, for the knowledge that his arguments hold up. He's the only person I know who got a grant to study from sheer, well-deserved talent and hard work, and so when he dropped out, I regarded his decision as a waste. His personality is fiercely fortified, defended with bastions and earthworks rarely breached. He loathes not knowing a film or a book — wants to be part of a complex conversation or a scheme if there's one going.

Inevitably, then, I can see him dying to get stuck into my warehouse experience. So we get into it, going back and forth about the avarice with which Tesco seems to commit to wastage, its immoralities, what it tells us about consumerism and greed.

"There are the words of Orwell, that it's unfortunate how England is exceptionally wasteful of food. He points out in *Wigan Pier* that you'd never see such wastage in France."

To this Alby shrugs, passing me a chunk of bread: "Lad, if I lived somewhere that ate snails as a matter of course, I'd want to waste." He's in one of his lightly Eurosceptical moods.

I go on: "Orwell's got a point, but even he couldn't have predicted that this English wastefulness would have gone beyond the domestic."

"And been supersized by this demonic house."

"It's not just the store. It's the city itself. It's been the site of so many pestilences, and this is the latest infection."

"Lad, it's a country of waste, and it's the warehouse workers — all those inside its dark, damp, cold walls — who are implicated as cogs in a national wasting machine."

"So, at whose shoes should the blame be placed?" I ask.

Alby considers this. "Do we blame the managers or the workers? Polished shoes or work boots?"

"Exactly. There's a line by John Betjeman, '*It is enjoyable to taste/These items ere they go to waste*.'"

"Eya, slow down lad" — Alby rolls his eyes — "this isn't a poetry slam."

Although I've tried to engage him in poetry, Alby's interest lies in the real world, rarely in fiction, never in lyric.

"Anyway," he goes on, mouth gummed with brie, "what I wanna know is what should be done about it?"

"About what?"

"About all this wastin'. Not the theft by individuals, but the system. It's not right."

"I dunno. What did you have in mind?"

Alby looks off down the alley to the cars flitting past, as if a solution to systemic hypocrisy and injustice might be sloganised on the side of a passing red bus. "For starters, someone should stop all those CAGEs getting churned out into the dustbins in the warehouse."

I shiver at the memory of what I've just witnessed, of rows and rows of CAGEs all waiting to have their contents wasted. "Can something be done?" I ask.

"Always."

"Aisle No.13. Baby/Sanitary."

"Very good. You're getting it, lad. I just reckon there's loadsa people bein' shifty and sketchy in those Upper Management offices in this buildin', and they need to be held to account. And all that wasted food — it's not right. It's not right at all."

I've seen this expression on Alby's face before, eyebrows knitted, jaw clenched. It's the origins of a scheme. At uni, it was the face he had when he was planning to pick up some gear via some creative means, and it was the expression he'd have once he'd done that coke. 'Getting on the Gradgrind,' we'd call it, more or less ironically.

"Well, if you mean the 'illicit wasting', like that incident with Callum and the strip-search, maybe there's no actual theft. Maybe it's like a warning."

"Could be, lad. There's a lot of guilty faces in there, though, I'd say. It's class to watch everyone look so sheepish. It's like you're at a gig and someone nearby farts. You look around to try and suss out who did it, but suddenly you know that by lookin' around, you might look like you're looking around because you're the guilty one, so you quickly flick your head back round and try to look innocent, but this just increases the likelihood to those looking at you that you're the one who dealt it."

"Whoever smelt it dealt it."

"Whoever did the song did the pong."

"Whoever did the rhyme did the crime."

"Whoever did the riff did the whiff."

"Whoever denied it supplied it."

"The point is," Alby strokes his chin, "who looks more guilty than the innocent?"

It's certainly the case that since the announcement of the strip-searches, all the staff have had that look of guilt-posing-as-innocence-posing-as-guilt-posing-as-innocence, an impossibly layered onion of potential wrongdoing, where you don't know who to trust, where everyone is watching everyone else.

Alby and I collect our rubbish and tip it into the dustbin, then return along the alleyway. As we walk, I try to sneak an explanation of this problem of guilt and innocence from literature.

"I know you don't rate it, but there's a bit from Dave Eggers's *The Circle* like this."

"Another book on your MA syllabus?" Alby mimics a massive yawn and looks at his wrist as if he's got a watch.

"What else would it be? The protagonist, Mae, and her digital followers try tracking down a fugitive from justice, in a socially networked manhunt. Their prey is Fiona Highbridge, forty-four, from Manchester, convicted of murdering her children. With the help of a prison guard she'd seduced, Highbridge escapes. A decade on, and police had given up the search, but Mae rallies the Circle's followers, and within minutes, there are hundreds of photos posted with likenesses of Highbridge. Votes tally up which of the photos are most likely her, whittling it down to five prime candidates. One Fiona in Oregon. Another Fiona in Canada. Another in Glasgow. She is eventually tracked down to a town in Wales, where she'd been using the alias Fatima Hilensky. Mae instructs the keyboard warriors of Carmarthen to record on their phones Fiona-Fatima's attempts to get away from her pursuers. But she's trapped. Surrounded by an encircling mob with their phones aimed towards her, capturing her every gesture, finally she collapses to the ground, covering her face."

"And this is considered a victory, is it?" Alby asks.

"For Mae and her followers."

Alby stops still, his palm flat against the FIRE EXIT door. "You know. That does actually remind me of a real scandal, also involving an online army and a Manc woman. Back in July 2011, that Rebecca Leighton was arrested for murdering five people at a hospital in Stockport. Police leaked her name to the media and made her social media public, then journalists and civilians with a self-righteous digital mission plundered her Facebook page, using photos of her out on the town as evidence of guilt. But the mobilised, mobile mob had assembled and pursued its prey in error. Leighton was totally innocent. When eventually she was cleared of the accusations, her troubles didn't end. The digital damage was done and she chose to enlist the services of Max Clifford to help salvage her name and reputation."

"Did her rebrand succeed?"

Alby shakes his head. "It all came to an end last year when Clifford was arrested for sex offences as part of Operation Yewtree."

"And what happened to Rebecca?"

"Dunno. Probably had to get an alias and change her identity. Hopefully she just got back to work."

"Like we should."

CHAPTER THREE

CANNED GOODS

Nobody should be this familiar with sofas. You might not know it, and fair play if you don't, but this standard piece of household furniture has its own distinct qualities and attributes, depending on the household to which it belongs, and on the room in which it's positioned. Its weft, its weave, its particular sag and sigh from the strained imprint of a hundred arses, or countless pairs of cheesy feet tucked up under its cushions. The pouf, the futon, the couch — each poses a unique threat against a good night's sleep for the weary Tesco worker, who can never quite just fling himself down. No, in situations like this where you are a guest for two, or three, sometimes four nights, you must begin your acquaintance with the furniture in the same sitting position as your host. You're keeping up appearances, after all. You're trying to prevent the slip of your pleasant mask, working hard to disguise the exhausted mug beneath, whenever your host asks you how you are, how the job's going, how your family is.

And that's not to mention the zeppelin of yawns that's been steadily ballooning inside you, for which you must use your final cells of strength to suppress whenever your host turns the page of a family photo album slung across your aching knees, or suggests another episode of whatever, or another level of whichever video game. Then finally, the gauntlet of amicability run, the politeness toll paid, you are permitted to lie down. The futon unfolds into a bed; blankets are brought, to keep out December's advance; a duvet to hold you firm if you're startled awake in the night by the immersion heater switching on or the family pet clattering through its flap. A stilton-scented cushion transforms into a pillow. Crumbs that sequin the couch are brushed away. They ping upwards like performing fleas. And you're almost on your way, your host clicking off the living room light, for there are no bedside lamps in here, and you're drifting, vaguely aware of the last atoms falling from your waking day, wondering whether you should pocket the £2 coin you've just found in the folds of your makeshift mattress.

Sleeping quarters of this variety are nothing like the artful statement of Tracey Emin's 'Bed'. It's the object removed from the grandeur and safety of the gallery and reinserted into an obscure dwelling. Nor does my sofa surfing have anything in common with West Coast couch tripping. There's none of that loose, sun-bleached slouching — dandruff, yes, but no far-out flowers in my hair. Nor does it resemble Britain's couch potato culture, with its enviable anchoring to a place, and its glorious cruise through TV channels. In fact, the only TV I've watched since arriving in London is the wall-mounted HD monstrosity that frames Jeremy Kyle's face. Perhaps Proust could render all this romantic; perhaps Xavier de Maistre could chart the voyage, but I can't, I'm on the road to sofa serfdom, so I try to get my head down. This body won't revive itself.

There's one crucial thing that you take with you from house to house: impostor syndrome. You may've demonstrated your adequacy as a guest in the past, but every conversation in the corridor, or dinner time chat, or request to use the washing machine, brings up the thing you most suspect: here I am not wanted. Like a smelling salt, you're suddenly woken up to it if you receive a text or an email from your previous host...

> **did you take out the bins?**
>
> **did you leave the key in the drawer?**
>
> **do you know where the laptop charger is that you borrowed?**

...you read these messages and feel your mind's tinfoil cuirass buckling. Yes, you took out the bins; yes, the key's back in its drawer; but no — no, you don't know where the charger is. Even if you're not responsible for its whereabouts, even if your laptop uses a different port, it still makes staying there in the future that bit harder, puts off the point when you might be able to ask again.

You wake with a *what-what-where-am-I* gasp. Get up and immediately rearrange the cushions and blankets to return your temp. bed to its sofa-state, then get in the shower ASAP, where you'll stand naked and tall above that model citadel of miniature shampoos, tonics, and lotions, all arranged in a financial district of green, pink, and cream bottles. This is a city planned by cosmeticians, thought up in the shower: the colourful buildings seen through the hot rain from the showerhead, a drizzly vision, a perfectly clean idyll of London. Today's Big Smoke was created in mist and fog: in steam rooms, at steam fairs, over steamed veg. If steam is the vapour of affluence, then damp is the green laddered growth on the side of new-builds, and mould is the base-matter of the marsh, which threatens to pull you back in.

Always be wary during the AM shower. Your judgement might be skewed in your lathered lethargy, but never ever use a host's shampoo, not even a cheeky squirt, unless you've been explicitly invited to. And even then, the permission could've been uttered in a grudging and *I'd-rather-you-didn't-but...* tone of voice, so make sure to judge your choices carefully. Never finish a bottle. Opt instead for the inconspicuous bar of soap tucked somewhere at the back, the one with the marshmallowy underside that's been softened by collected water droplets, and always avoid using products that look like they've come from a salon or direct from a barber. Keep out of Neal's Yard. Always remove the crescent moons of nail-clippings. And pubic hair. It's your job to wash away any of those wiry nautilus fossils stuck to the tiles, any groinal twine that's draped itself on the tap. Even if none of it was clipped or plucked from your person, always CAYG. And of course, remember to pull up the kelp that's coagulated in the plughole.

Leaving a wet towel on a floor is terrible guest etiquette, so the doorframe is fair game. If you're in a spare room or study, then the back of the chair is available, too, though not if it's a leather or cushioned chair which will absorb the moisture. If the towel is sodden, take note of the flooring. It's a bad move to let your towel drip dry onto a carpet. You'll return to the room to find a puddle spreading out. At this sight, your impulse might be to get tissue or toilet roll to soak it all up. Never do this. The sheet of paper will disintegrate under your palm as you scrub, and the little white flakes will embed themselves in the carpet fibres, and as they dry, they'll become permanently fixed like crusty white barnacles. If this happens, then your best bet is to use the wet towel as a mop, thereby rescuing you from the puddle faux pas, but exposing you to the original terrible etiquette.

Only after all that can your day begin.

- - - - -

Flats, boots, heels, all shuffling towards the exit, all stopping, all scuffing the scuffed floor. The rush-hour two-step through Earl's Court station. All of us on our way to work. At the barrier, there's the wildebeest blockage of commuters. Every beep of an Oyster Card is a Pavlovian prompt to step forward. While I wait for my turn to tap out, I glance at the whiteboard propped against the grimy tiled wall, which each morning has a different 'thought for the day' scribbled on it by a bleary-eyed Underground worker. Today's offering: '*Every child is a different kind of flower and all together makes this world a beautiful garden.*' My blue Oyster on the peeling mustard disc, red light flashes green. The barrier's beep releases me, and I step forward, my swollen rucksack almost catching in the reptile jaws closing behind me. Winter layers and the thick chthonic heat of a city in transit froths sweat down my back. This morning's shower was a waste. Fortunately the store's doing 30% off on anti-perspirants at the moment; I can knock off another 15% if I aim my price-tag gun at our Nivea range. Ten steps further on, at the yawning exit to the station, I pick up a copy of *City A.M.* from its leaning grey stack. The front-page reads 'KEEP WORKING UNTIL YOU'RE 70, GEORGE OSBORNE SAYS'.

It's drizzly. It's London. A cold clot of wet dust scoops up loose cardboard into brown wings, which flap for a moment and splat to the pavement. I step over these, avoiding the cracks. Childhood habits are hard to break. My eyes on the paper. Chancellor Osbourne has just given his Autumn Statement, and this has been swiftly printed and duly distributed to all the rush-hour news-stands in the rented clefts of London's Underground stations. I read column after column laying out the implications of the policy for people born after 1990 — millennials, we're being called; mundanials, we feel like — who will have to work five years longer than any previous generation before our state pension kicks in. I was born at the tail end of 1990, my twenty-third birthday was only a matter of days ago. Birthday cards are crumpling in my rucksack as I walk, sent to the most recent address where I'm staying, so this headline is aimed at me and many other millions in my position. An obedient dog's condition: the world of retail whistled, and I came running to where there was work.

I wait at the traffic lights of West Cromwell Road and watch as a homeless fella pushes a trolley towards the dropped curb. Its wheels lodge in the flat grey gaps of the blemished pavement, and he leans heavily over it. It looks sturdier than he does. He's got a second overcoat folded over the handlebar, like a hotel's trouser press, so I can't tell which supermarket the trolley belongs to. The colour code from my Induction lives on:

Orange = Sainsbury's.
Green = Waitrose/ASDA.
Blue or red = Tesco.

The sleeve of Trolley Fella's overcoat trails along the damp pavement, leaving a bubbling track in the morning drizzle, raking fallen, sodden leaves as the trolley trundles.

"'Av yer got a one paaand coin, matey?" he asks me. His accent is familiar, of the Wash. No doubt he was sluiced into the capital along the estuaries. He elongates the *aaa* of 'pound' just as the market square fruit sellers do around East Anglia.

I give him the international gesture for no-cash-on-me-sorry (shrug, with hands miming empty pockets), and am grateful that Trolley Fella turns away to face the slowing traffic.

I busy myself with *City A.M.*, the raindrops fuzz and dapple my newspaper, ink sliding before I have time to finish a sentence: '...today's announcement will see that increase to 68 by the mid 2030s and 69 by the late 2040s, with the age increasing... someone aged 40 today would retire at 68... a person aged 30 would be working until they reached 69...' The mushy paper becomes a makeshift umbrella as I dodge Trolley Fella, the traffic lights' heart monitor beeping me over the Warwick Road–Cromwell intersection and through Tesco's sliding glass doors.

It's bright, all tremble and ricochet, a cathedral of clattering sounds and strip lights that I bow to avoid, only to find the light rebounded off faux-marble flooring. Somehow brighter than the lights above. An end-of-days white.

I heave off my rucksack and stuff it into a locker, aiming shoulder barges and elbow pummels against the wet, cold canvas to get it in. No Queensberry rules at Tesco. There's nothing breakable inside: it's books and clothes and birthday cards — probably all damp from sweat and rain. While my sofa surfing continues, my most recent host (a friend of a friend of a friend who lives above a chicken shop with his ancient golden retriever in Bethnal Green) has let me leave the university's loaned laptop and my toothbrush at his flat, and even put up a few balloons on my birthday. These've already begun to deflate to a sad scrotal limpness. It's been nearly three months since I arrived in London to start this Literature MA and still no luck with a room whose rent I can afford. Maybe the problem is that people don't want a new tenant in winter. Maybe no one wants to be shut in with a stranger in the darker months.

When I can't get a sofa or my temporary accommodation falls through at the last minute, I've been sleeping in the university's library. If coursemates ask, I tell them I'm pulling all-nighters, and as such I've already developed the reputation for a committed, studious work ethic. The library staff may well have worked out what's going on. The ponytailed guy on the desk was suspiciously willing to loan me a laptop from their stash. It's supposed to be for students from low-income households, but perhaps the scheme extends also to students with no household incoming.

All around the store, tinsel has spread like weeds. It's been a steady, relentlessly triffidian encroachment throughout the weeks. Even in early November, Tesco got ahead of its supermarket rivals in the Christmas advertising race, launching its TV adverts with Usain Bolt-like speed, taking totally by surprise John Lewis, Sainsbury's, and ASDA. The Lowe Howard-Spink agency with whom Tesco has been partnered for decades recommended that Tesco begin its festive campaign on ITV, during the advert breaks of *Coronation Street* and *Downton Abbey*. It continues to be a hugely successful manoeuvre, managing to appeal to two demographics that Tesco has had its baubled eyes on: the Corrie-watching provincial who thinks of Ant & Dec as on-screen nephews, and the Maggie Smith-wannabe for whom *Downton Abbey* is a guilty pleasure. These are the upstairs and downstairs of England's class structure, both of whom Tesco markets itself to and employs. Every little Englander helps.

Between colleagues, there's much talk of the upcoming Christmas party, which I've decided not to attend, on the grounds that the day I have to rely on Tesco to supply me with an evening's entertainment is the day I offer my neck to the cheese cutter on the Deli Counter. Discussing the party inevitably leads to compulsory chit-chat about Xmas plans and traditions. In the Staff Canteen, one of the women from HR explains that December 25th for her means visiting her family's graves. Mother, father, brother, all killed in the same car accident:

"And then it's back home to heat up my dinner. And I always get an extra can of carrots and peas to boil, 'cause those ready meals never come with enough veg, do they."

Almost everyone else is going home to see family and friends above ground. Trains from London into the Fens are pricey and the service often cancelled because Black Shuck's been spotted padding the tracks, so it's probable that I'm going to stay in London over Xmas Eve, Boxing Day and beyond. Bisera's already mentioned that there'll be shifts that need doing, alongside my non-Christian colleagues. It's not the most festive way of celebrating the birth of Our Lord J.C. I mean, I know my solemn hymns from school and like most people I know Ezekiel 25:17, but that's about the extent of my religious upbringing.

Today I am 'Kevin', and Kevin is on aisle No.16 (Pets), wheeling a squeaky CAGE weighted down with produce destined to be wasted: wet dog food, Meaty Chunks, Butcher's Tripe, Whiskas Poultry Feast. Being the committed employee that he is, Kevin goes along the shelves 'facing up' boxes of moggie dental treats and worming tablets. At the far end of the aisle, a group of Upper Management has gathered, inspecting the latest range of breathable muzzles, a lacky at their elbows with a clipboard making notes, her eyes darting like a muntjac caught in a forest clearing. Kevin imagines this aisle on a slant, he at the upper end, Upper Management at the lower. He imagines his grip loosening on the CAGE, its wheels steadily picking up speed as it hurtles down past fur brushes and chew toys, with gathering momentum, a CAGE off its lead that crashes into the crowd of pantsuits and ties. The lacky would be alright, Kevin reckons, her doe-alertness springing her away before impact, her lanyard flailing. Suppose, however, that a customer came into view just before impact, and the squeaky wheel made the CAGE shift direction. It'd save Upper Management but injure the customer. If there was a way Kevin could readjust the CAGE to avoid the innocent civilian but hit Upper Management, would he intervene? Is one customer's life worth more than four or five senior staff? Policy No.2 tells us that the customer is always right, so maybe Kevin would be contractually obliged to do something.

- - - - -

Break out the fizzy wine, douse the logs in lighter fluid, set up an awning. We're celebrating. My quarterly probation period is complete. In a windowless meeting room on the first floor, Monojit stands by as Bisera spreads out documents across the desk and taps on a keyboard. It smells of coffee and farts, the latter fresh. Her swivel chair cries like a banshee as she leans forward.

"Now this is your long-term contract, and here," she's pointing at the screen's Excel spreadsheet, "are your shifts for the next few weeks." I scrawl an approximation of my signature on the first page as I'm looking down the neon column of shifts.

"This one I can't do," I point to December 16th's column.

There's an event on at the university that I can't, that I won't, categorically no, won't, will not miss. A.S. Byatt is visiting our department, to talk about her novels. This coincides with the b'days of Arthur Clark, Philip K. Dick, and Jane Austen, which means the event will get triple the amount of funding; that's triple the amount of booze and nibbles. It'll be a chance to watch my coursemates smoothly and more successfully rub shoulders with a proper, real-life author, and ask her in loud, bright voices for advice about how to get published, while in the corner, my oversized Adam's apple rots in its groove and makes my throat mushy.

It's been the talk of the pub for weeks: who's read Byatt's stuff, what everyone makes of it, what might anyone ask her if they get the chance. I've already made a special effort to read a selection of her back catalogue, *Possession*, obviously, *Still Life*, and a particularly expensive, pain in the arse debut to get hold of, *The Shadow of the Sun*, in which Byatt recalls in a Foreword that her first novel was 'written in libraries and lectures, between essays and love affairs.'

So far, my experience of all of these has been minimal to non-existent. Byatt is a master of the baggy monster, and the accumulated weight of her oeuvre has done my back in. If I get a chance in the Q&A, I might take her to task about it.

The banshee cries out again as Bisera leans back. "Listen, I hate disloyalty. You really need to do this for me. The big boss is coming in for a tour on December 16th, so we need the Food2Go Counter to be manned."

I plant both boots on the carpet, a posture ready for combat.

"There's no other way," Monojit adds, tapping his clipboard, shaking his head, "Loyalty here today..."

"...is loyalty from now on. You need to prove it."

Feet planted, my sweaty hands on my work trousers, I summon all of my negotiating skills, gather all of my eloquence, recalling those hours spent reading the sharp replies and honed arguments of the literary greats. I must out-manoeuvre these Tescomotrons. My rhetorical genius will flash, will floor them, sparks will fly. I am Demosthenes. Watch how I defeat through my wit and watertight reason...

I emerge from the meeting room, and it looks like I'm missing A.S. Byatt. And somehow I've agreed to work Xmas Eve, Boxing Day, the ensuing days, and New Year's Eve. I hadn't bargained on Bisera simply raising her hand from her mouse, palm towards me, and saying, "Let me stop you there," while I was beginning to set up my counter-offensive. I folded, and before I knew it, I was agreeing to her directive: *prove your loyalty*. The compromise is that I'll be on double pay for those shifts, so that's Byatt's back catalogue retrospectively paid for.

What threw me, I think, as I wander back to the Food2Go Counter, is how Monojit and Bisera kept telling me to prove my loyalty. Literature overrun by an appeal to Tesco fealty. Bisera had turned her computer screen towards me and pointed out a graph whose axes evilly charted an upward diagonal trajectory, of loyalty vs £££.

M.: “That’s loyalty.”
B.: “We know you need this work.”

I considered protesting that there’s such a thing as excess of exhaustion brought about by endless shifts without a decent break. I considered citing Plato’s *Protagoras*, in which he refers to the maxim ‘Nothing too much’ that was carved in Apollo’s temple in Delphi, alongside the inscription ‘Know Thyself’. But this was too esoteric a bit of argumentation, so I began to explain that the phrase ‘Know thyself’ is used by the oracle in the Matrix, when Neo breaks the vase, just as she predicted he would. Knowledge. Intelligence. Data. How did Monojit and Bisera so expertly harness and wield it? How did they grasp and contain it?

“What’s wrong with you?” Alby asks, entering the kitchen where I’ve retreated behind a half-empty CAGE.

“I’ve just been done over by technocrats.”

“Huh?”

“Upstairs. Bisera and Monojit have got me working over Xmas and New Year. They’re winning, the technocrats.”

Alby nods sadly. “It was ever thus. Look at Lord MacLaurin.”

“Who?”

“In your JBT, there’s a whole section about the Tesco Clubcard scheme, in the early ’90s. It was basically the moment when Tesco embraced tech over knowledge. Yeah, lad. People complained about the Nanny State. It’s the Nano State that’s the problem.”

“And Lord… MacCulkin is it?” I’m still dazed.

“MacLaurin. He told the number-crunchers in charge that what terrified him was that they’d learned more about his customer base and worker habits in three months than he’d learned in three decades.”

I picture again Monojit's shaking head — "You need this work," repeating, "Prove your loyalty" — and the computer screen's columns: an impenetrable fortress of data.

It's only later on in the shift, facing up the Naked Smoothies, that I glimpse the bare facts of my current situation: I moved to London to do the MA, and to support that venture, I've been working at Tesco, and now I've forgone the literature to get more money so that I can live in London and do the MA which I've just agreed to skip. This startling realisation — the kind with the **!** above your head — comes to me as a pair of Upper Management approach. I'm too stuck in my meditation to notice that they're sneaking in my direction. When they reach me, it's too late to move off with my trolley without looking suspicious.

The second clipboard of the day presents itself. "Hi there. We're from upstairs. We're just doing the routine spot checks."

"This is the strip-search?" I ask.

"We call them routine spot checks," says the one with a large brown wart under his eye. I feel like I've seen him before. "If you look on page eight of your JBT, you'll see..."

Flanking Wart is a small feral man. Ditto, I recognise them both. As I sign away my consent for the search, he's telling me that it's just routine, but that under Section Such-and-Such in Paragraph Etc.-Etc. of my contract's COLLEAGUE EFFICIENCY AGREEMENT...

" — that purple document you would've signed on your first day here — "

...I'm dutybound to agree to spot checks. I pause, waiting for them to guide me to the privacy of the kitchen or the Staff Canteen as Callum was, or at least out of the sight of passing customers. No invitation is forthcoming, with Wart and Feral just looking at me expectantly, and so begins my shop-floor Full Monty.

I suddenly remember these men — Wart and Feral — as the pair who escorted Franny from the Induction a couple of months ago. It seems, then, I am at risk from being wiped out, being wasted away, if this strip-search goes south.

I untie the string of my apron, as a mother passes us pushing her toddler in a pram ("Mummy, is that man in twubble?"), unhooking it from my neck, and before I can place it on my trolley, Wart has an arm out and has taken hold of it. "Your pockets first," he says, "on the trolley top, if you don't mind." Keys for my current accommodation (a flat-share in a scaffolded cul-de-sac off Whitechapel, occupied by a coursemate who smokes jazz cigarettes indoors). A lidless biro. Nokia 105. Ribbons of REDUCED paper — fortunately blank.

Each item prompts Feral to note something down on his clipboard. I pull up my red jumper to display the trousers' waistband below my pasty navel. A tumbleweed of bellybutton fluff, dislodged by the search, floats down to the floor as a dandelion head might descend. More customers pass, tutting expressions. Bisera's phrase *prove your loyalty* is having a few free spins on the mind carousel. I follow where the fluff leads, crouching to unlace my boots, rising again to remove them, my thin socks no match for the cold faux-marble that makes my toes and ankles tingle.

"Anything else?" I mutter to the fluff.

There's nothing incriminating, but my capitulation feels like it carries guilt. The optics surely aren't helping anyone, as shoppers continue to pass us. Surely the general paying customer doesn't count as a witness.

My out-turned pockets flop at my sides like elephant ears. Attention turns to my apron. Wart is still holding it up, and now he raises it higher, seems to weigh it.

"Bit heavy, this," he runs his hands over the edges of a rectangular object contoured by the fabric. "What's inside?"

From the pouch he brings out a thick hardback. Frayed stitching, the corners peeling. He looks at me, then at the book, opens it, the pages are stained and annotated with decades of desperate marginalia.

"It's from my university's library. Hard to get hold of," I explain for not much of a reason.

He flicks through the pages, the spine crackling like a chiropractor's dream. Stops at a page highlighted in an array of pink, green, yellow, where indecipherable cursive adorns the thin borders.

"These your doodles?"

"Some are, yes."

"I'll level with you," Wart holds the book up to the side of his mouth in a gesture of confidentiality. "When I felt the shape in the apron, I thought DVD boxset, one hundred percent."

"Same here," Feral adds. "*Mrs Brown's Boys,* series 1 and 2, I reckoned."

"So if this is what you think is valuable, I think you'll be alright." He puts the book back on the trolley, runs a finger along the spine. "Blindness. Green. What's that about, then?"

"Henry Green. British novelist. *Blindness* was his first novel. 1926. Stopped penning stuff when he went deaf."

"Wouldn't find this on one of our shelves, I'd wager," winks Wart.

"No. Green's an author with merit."

"You saying Dan Brown's *Inferno* doesn't have merit?"

"It's at number 1 on our shelves," Feral chips in.

"Not literary merit," I can feel the floor's chill creeping up my shins. "A lot of value but not any literary merit."

"So who do we sell that you're saying is worth reading?"

"Chimamanda Ngozie Adichie."

Wart frowns. "Chim-iminie who?"

Feral laughs, bends over slightly with his feet out,

Wide Boy style: "*Chim chim-in-ey, chim chim-in-ey, Chim chim cher-oo.*"

Wart laughs widely, also bending over slightly. "*Me cap would be glad of a copper or two.*"

"Her name's Chimamanda Ngozie Adichie," I repeat.

Wart and Feral link arms, grinning broadly.

"She's Nigerian. Wrote *Americanah*. It's about the complexities of race and gender in the US and the UK."

The pair of Upper Management aren't paying any attention to this, too busy with their arms linked, each doing his best Dick Van Dyke.

Into the Poppins void, I add that it's a good book, with both commercial value and literary merit. "It's number 2 on the Tesco shelf."

They both abruptly pause. Feral, suddenly interested. "Hold on. If it's at number 2, I know the one."

"You do?" asks Wart.

"Yes she's the one who does that speech on the Beyoncé song."

"Ah yes. *Flawless*. It's on our new instore playlist. *I woke up like this* and all that. Cracking stuff."

"I'd recommend the novel." My knees are freezing over.

"I won't be reading that."

"Maybe you'd prefer Danielle Steele," I suggest.

"We're getting her new book in," Feral, excitedly, "in the summer. *A Perfect Life*."

"That'll be more your speed."

Feral picks up *Blindness* and presses it into my chest, not so firmly that I step backwards but firm enough that I register the object. Instinctively, my hands take hold of the book, and he taps a pen against the cover. "Anyway," the sound is hollow, "that's all fine. But so you know, reading on the job, not alright, alright?" He writes something on his clipboard, and he and Wart move on.

I return Green to the apron's pouch, loop the apron around my neck, put on my boots, then, as casually and innocently as possible, smiling blankly at passing customers, wheel my trolley into the empty kitchen. First I retie my laces, doublecheck behind the fridge for Haroon, then open the book to page 205, on which the author asks, 'Why did one always talk baby-talk to someone who was crying?' where, tucked between the yellow pages, there's a small, feint-ruled piece of paper. If Wart had found this, that would've taken some explaining. I smooth out the creases.

'Draft No.3', it reads ambitiously at the top, and I scan the page of what is an attempted communication to send to my brother. My Letter to an Incarcerated Sibling. Not an easy genre to get right first time, which is why I've taken a few run ups. I've already penned one in my own voice, but it was all over the place. So for Draft No.2 I tried a Joycean stream of consciousness, with Finnegan-inflections ('*the pax in embrace or poghue puxy as practiced between brothers*'), but it was even more unhinged than my own scribbles, so for Draft No.3, I've kept it realist. I read it through. The letter needs work, the tone is not right, too naïve, the themes and questions I'm asking lack that fraternal supplication that a younger sibling should express to the elder. Too many adolescent parentheses as well. Too high modernist. Too Green.

Bisera enters as I'm folding the draft and pouching it. She looks at me with bland confusion, asks me to fetch a few boxes of Coca-Cola from the warehouse and take them up for colleagues in one of the staff meeting rooms. When I ask why, her blandness morphs into stern bewilderment.

"It's for a motivational speech. For some reason Upper Management asked specifically for you to do this. Be careful in the warehouse," she adds, and for a moment my heart lifts at this show of colleague concern, "there's mess all over the cola boxes which you'll need to wash off before you take them upstairs."

And the next moment, I'm in the warehouse holding a bucket, sloshing down some weird grey streaks on the boxes' sides. They've been left under the corrugated beams by the warehouse's back entrance, where pigeons roost and let rip. Now the boxes have become crusted in guano. Each bucket I slosh dissolves the droppings, then I run back to the kitchen to refill the bucket in the big sink, and again I slosh, thus fulfilling both my loyalty to the store, and also proving the store's internal Gaia Hypothesis: if someone, somewhere is getting motivated, then someone, somewhere else, is scrubbing pigeon shit.

- - - - -

The whiteboard outside Earl's Court station reads: '*Growth is painful, change is painful. But nothings as painful as being stuck somewhere you dont belong.*' Cold grips the pavements and the windscreens of passing cars. I'm early, so I detour from Warwick Road to Niven Square, a secluded garden, the faded trees of which hang over the street. There are straggly leaves scattered all around in an unsettling wind. Others that have already found their way to earth are too waterlogged from this morning's harsh rain for that cornflake crunch underfoot. Nevertheless, it's a comfort that little nooks of tranquillity like this can be found — that, from time to time, the inextricable knot of Misery City can be momentarily loosened and a quiet spot located. Here is where happiness can be glimpsed through the iron bars, if only briefly, and at a distance. This and other nearby squares have been privatised. Each is surrounded by grand terraces with tall, startled windows, all gated and walled, only available to those who can afford a residents' iron key. The last of the year's leaves cling like insecure tenants to the damp branches. Through the gaps in the railings, I can see blackening heaps, like giant molehills, raked by someone who almost certainly doesn't live here.

As I turn to continue towards Tesco, there's a dark blur in my periphery, and the sound of heaving, the rattle of thin metal. Clambering over the wall and now dangling from its granite lip is Trolley Fella, who asked me for money the other morning in the drizzly street. My first instinct is to dash off before he asks me for another *one paaand coin*, but I can see he's in a precarious position. The toes of his crumbling boots are teetering on the wobbly edge of a trolley wedged up against the high wall; his thick overcoat has caught on iron spears that threaten to make Emmental cheese of the garment. For a moment, he hangs there, his feet skirting the trolley's mesh edge. I rush over to hold the trolley still. Gradually, he unloops the holes from the spear tops, steps down from the trolley, and returns to street level.

He smells like he's just burrowed out of that molehill of raked leaves. He grins and thanks me, "I bin sleepin' 'side the gaard'n, fo' long time now. Bin usin' these trolleys to get in and owt." He grins at me. "Genyus innit?"

His accent takes me back to the estuaries of East Anglia, to the eel-basket weavers of Kings Lynn, to the grumpy woman with pink earmuffs at Hunstanton's Joke Shop. I wonder how he came to be here. Maybe he'd arrived here on a tide of goodwill but soon found himself out of work and wandering London's streets and canal sides looking for trolleys to dredge up and return to their respective stores.

Pointing at the trolley: "But y'see 'ere. It's got a big old hole and the wheels don't turn no more. I needa gettit back to Tesco to get the coin owt."

And he's right. Poking out from the handlebar's lock is the rising sun of a pound coin, which will only be released when the trolley is connected up to the line of other trolleys outside the store. Between the two of us, we carry it back onto Warwick Road, towards Tesco. He tells me of the neighbourhood's Domestic Revival architecture, pointing out the bay windows and balconies of the tall terraces, terracotta and rubbed red brick, decorated pediments, elaborate chimneys funnelling richly warm smoke.

"You could be a tour guide," I gasp at the traffic lights.

As I catch my breath, inhaling the machine-breeze coming off the abyssal plain of the busy road, Trolley Fella continues with his folklore: "You see these 'ere steps outside Tesco. These was made famous by ahh Mayor of London, Boris Johnson. Ow yeh. 'E dun a vox pop here befaw 'e was an MP, when 'e was a journalist workin' for *The Spectator*."

It's the sort of overload of data which adds weight to the trolley's deadlift.

"That's as far as I can take it," I tell him as we reach the other side of the road.

I'm late and pace it up these historically significant steps before Trolley Fella has a chance to ask for spare shrapnel. During my shift, I scribble down the details he told me, and later, when I'm stretched out on the most recent sofa at the Whitechapel cul-de-sac, I open up my laptop and look up a YouTube clip of a younger Boris Johnson, featured on *Newsnight* in October 1998. Johnson goes 'undercover' at our flagship Tesco to find out... well... whatever sorts of things he thinks are important to find out on *Newsnight*. Having watched the clip, I fall down a YouTube hole and discover that earlier in that year, in April 1998, Johnson appeared on *Have I Got News for You*. At the time, the Mayorship of London didn't even exist, and so Johnson was introduced by Angus Deaton as a *Daily Telegraph* journalist and failed Conservative candidate for Clyde South. This got a sympathetic laugh from the audience. The episode would become a launch pad for Johnson's public persona, due to Ian Hislop asking Johnson to explain his friendship with a convicted fraudster named Darius Guppy, with whom Johnson had conspired to assault a journalist. Johnson had guffawed and mumbled his way through the accusation, which again received forgiving laughter from the audience.

"Richly comic," was how Johnson summed up the whole snafu with his Old Etonian Guppy buddy. Evidently, *Newsnight* weighed the risk of using a thug-accomplice as a presenter and decided that he was just too 'richly comic' a character to pass up for their vox pops.

There are definitely advantages to moving in the circles of Mayor Johnson, and Guppy. It grants you certain protections against criticism aimed at you from the plebs below. Like when the entire Paralympic stadium booed George Osbourne as he presented the medals for the Men's 400m T38. A life spent breathing the rarefied atmosphere of privilege must've helped him through that moment, and it's probably why he responded to the booing with a cold, thin smile. A lesser man might've been affected, might've taken stock, might've changed economic course, when met with fury, contempt, and hatred. But Georgey just grinned then got to work.

And there's their education. I was glad to be spared the mental torture of Latin, not that it was an option at state school, but looking up the definition of 'vox pop' now as I readjust the cushions on this sofa I learn that it means 'the people's voice'. Moreover, 'pop' is a term from the deliberately impenetrable discourse of Eton College. Officially called the Eton Society, 'Pop' is a closed circle comprising the most well-regarded and able boys of the English ruling class, and the future of that unflappable upper crust. Its members wear white and black houndstooth-checked trousers, a starched stick-up collar, a white bow-tie, and flamboyant waistcoats. Previous members have included the current Prince of Wales but not his younger brother (who failed to be elected); *Les Misérables* actor Eddie Redmayne; and Liverpool-born Prime Minister William Gladstone.

My grubby forefinger skids across the laptop's touchpad, and a further Google search shows that Johnson has returned as a panellist to *Have I Got News for You* many more times over the following years, despite saying and writing the sorts of things that should've ended his career. A Wikipedia scroll explains that in 2004 he published an article in *The Spectator* in which he referred to Merseyside inhabitants as wallowing in victimhood and described Liverpool's 'excessive predilection for welfarism' and the 'peculiar, and deeply unattractive, psyche among many Liverpudlians.' A brief scan of the Goodreads page tells me later that year he also published a novel called *Seventy-Two Virgins*, about a tousle-haired bicycle obsessive who must use his position as an MP to save a respite centre for disabled children from closure. Either of these publications should've been disqualifying, but nonetheless, by November 2005, Johnson was fully rehabilitated and promoted to the position of guest host on *HIGNFY*.

Richly comic.

- - - - -

Alby and I assemble for our covert Christmas Meal, under the discreet cover of greyness in Felon Place. That bluish winter light makes our skin corpse-like. Brambles. Dustbin. Festive cheer. We're foregoing party hats and we're keeping it brief because of the cold.

"How was your strip-search?" Alby asks, glugging from a miniature of Merlot. It's Xmas, after all.

"It was as you said. Weird. On the shop floor, too."

His brow creases, eyes like searchlights in the gloom.

"Right there in front of customers. I swear I could see them shaking their heads. I must've looked like I'd been properly caught out."

"Caught red right handed."

"*Rubente dextera.*"

"Repeat, please."

"You been watching *Peaky Blinders*?"

"Best intro music of a series in a long time, I reckon."

"'Red right hand' is a phrase from Milton."

Alby shakes his head. "Alright, it's Xmas. Come on, then, impart the wisdom of the poet."

"'*What if the breath that kindled those grim fires,*
Awaked, should blow them into sevenfold rage,
And plunge us in the flames; or from above
Should intermitted vengeance arm again
His red right hand to plague us?'"

"That degree's paying itself forward in spades. You know, at some point, I reckon I should borrow that Milton book."

But before I can express surprise at his concession in favour of poetry, a dark shadow flits across us and we turn to see a figure silhouetted by the marmalade smear of lamplight. It lopes towards us.

"If you've summoned Milton's ghost..." Alby begins, then scrambles at the bin, "Quick, hide the fuckin' booze," but it's too dark, and his hands knock an open bottle, which tips and rolls off the dustbin's lid. It doesn't break when it hits the ground but continues its roll towards the approaching figure. A man, tall, skinny. He stops it with his foot, like a holding midfielder preparing the counter-press.

"S'alright, lads. Good choice, that." He picks up the bottle, sniffs the rim. "New Zealand. Oyster Bay, I reckon." He steps towards us and takes in our obscure little party, replacing the bottle on the bin lid. "This is a sad scene, isn't it." His smile ignites the gloom. "Don't worry, though, I won't tell. I've got myself roundly fucked with the whole snitching thing."

"Heath!" Alby shouts, "What're you doing back here?"

"They've found me out. In there. They've done me in. I'm sacked." The smell of fabric softener comes off him in heady, sickly waves. "And I would've got away with it if it wasn't for that meddling Upper Management. The problem was when the sensor of the sliding doors stopped me. Someone had already changed the setting so that no one could get out. And as I turned, I could see Upper Management rolling towards me. Steaming, they were, 'cause they'd had to run down all those stairs from their tower at the top."

Alby: "You know we all placed bets on whodunnit."

Heath's grin as wide and bright as a reg. plate: "Ha ha. And now you can all collect your winnings!"

"Why'd you steal all the stuff?" I ask.

"I was gonna sell it on at my local market down in Deptford. There's a geezer there who buys these things and sells them on. I lost my flat recently because the landlord wanted to put up the rent. Wanker. I asked Tesco for more shifts — they said no. I couldn't find any other work so I was gonna make a swift £1,500. But that's that. I'm out."

"So what now?"

"They've said something about a court date, but I don't know when. I'm almost looking forward to it. It'd give me a chance to wear my new suit. I nicked it from F&F. Hope it's soon. Might not fit me if I lose any more weight. I dunno. Anyway, if you don't mind." He steps past our dustbin, crouches by the brambles and begins to pull and yank at the thorns and weeds. "Aha," he rises again, a small box in his hands, turns towards us, million-watt grin again. "My getaway dosh. What, you think you're the only ones who use Felon Place? Here."

He opens the box and chucks something towards us. Alby catches it.

"For your silence. You didn't see me." Then he's walking away back along Felon Place towards the main road, not even checking left or right as he crosses, dissolving into the traffic.

"Fuckin' hell. Well at least the strip-searches will stop."

"And you've won that bet with the baker."

Alby holds up the object. "Won't need that now. Look at all this. That's five £20 notes right there. Pub after work?"

"Agreed."

"And I reckon these picnics should stop. No more savin' the stock from waste. Too risky with all these poets and thieves about. Never know who's watchin'."

"Agreed again."

We walk back inside, where we're met with a wall of noise from the store's speakers.

"Christ, they know how to fuck up Xmas songs here," complains Alby, wiggling his fingers into his ears.

"What even is this?"

"It's either 'Silent Night' or Mariah Carey. Can't tell, the acoustics are so shite."

"Maybe we should do some karaoke," Alby suggests, "with it being Christmas. Get on the Tannoy and blast out a festive ditty."

"I'd go for 'War is Over' by John Lennon."

"Or George Michael's behemoth?"

"That's a good tune. Already totally ruined."

I know what Alby's referring to. These songs have passed their sell-by date. They're clearly classics, but we've been subject to Tesco's over-use, over-exposure, and it's only mid-December. These and other tunes pump out from the speakers hour after hour, so much so that you're totally sick of them.

I return to the Food2Go Counter and re-pin today's nametag.

I am 'Samuel' again, and Sam gets on with shelving tins of soup. If this graft was good enough for Alex DeLarge's mother at the Statemart, then it's good enough for Sam. He hums along to 'A Wonderful Christmas Time' by Paul McCartney and scorns himself for it. His mind still returns regularly to the horrors of waste he witnessed. Since his visit to the wastehouse, he can't shake the memory of the smell, the fatigue, the sound. It lingers. He's found himself much more aware of just how many CAGEs there are everywhere — not just in the store, but noticing those CAGEs out there around the city. Abandoned CAGEs near derelict buildings, or CAGEs wedged in piss-tanged alleyways, or CAGEs keeled over and dented next to multistorey carparks. It's as if these runaway CAGEs have seeped like damp through the walls of the warehouse and tried their luck on the streets of London.

Of all the difficulties faced by someone possessing even a fairly average moral compass on this flagship, 'wastage' is by far the most difficult to negotiate. Armed with a smear of rue around his nostrils, and his eyes dabbed with euphrasy and a clipboard, Sam ventures back into the warehouse. Why the clipboard? When he was small, Sam's grandfather once told him that while stationed in British Ceylon during WWII, he would get out of doing jobs around the camp by carrying a clipboard. He'd march around, occasionally stopping to inspect some equipment, scribble something down, and then move on. If he was spotted by a senior, the clipboard was enough of an object to signify BUSYNESS.

Clipboarded and balmed, Sam enters the warehouse. Uninhibited by Monojit's presence, he moves about with stealth, though this isn't really necessary since none of the workers in here are paid enough to pay him any attention. Nevertheless, he ducks, hides, flattens himself against CAGEs to avoid detection, solidly snaking his way to where the CAGEs ready for wasting are kept. From behind a box, Sam watches as a few workers slot these huge mesh-wired rectangles on wheels next to each other. He approaches one CAGE at random and by Nokia-light makes a list of its contents on the clipboard. A figure limps by under the weight of a bin bag, staring at but not really seeing. Sam nods, which is not reciprocated, and returns to his notes.

Kalamata olive selection (3 boxes, 3 kilos), Borettane onions (3 boxes, 3 kilos), cherry peppers (2 boxes, 2 kilos), pitted Kalamata olives in piri piri marinade (3 boxes, 3 kilos), green Kalamata olives and jalapeno peppers (2 boxes, 2 kilos), mixed Kalamata olives with chilli and basil (5 boxes, 5 kilos)...

Sam turns over the page and continues writing,

> colossal Kalamata olives with lemon and garlic (2 boxes, 2 kilos)...mammoth Kalamata olives stuffed with chili (2 boxes, 2 kilos), mixed pitted Kalamata and Spanish olives with basil and garlic (2 boxes, 2 kilos), garlic stuffed Kalamata olives (2 boxes, 2 kilos), Kalamata green mammoth olives (2 boxes, 2 kilos), pitted green Kalamata olives with roasted vegetables (2 boxes, 2 kilos), Kalamata olives stuffed with lemon (3 boxes, 3 kilos), Kalamata olives stuffed with garlic and pepper (1 box, 1 kilo).

This is by no means all of the produce Sam witnesses being wasted; these don't even make up half of the things that Tesco orders in for the Food2Go salad bar. Nor does this particular list make up a full CAGE's worth of waste. He does some swift maths and works out how many boxes it would take to completely fill a CAGE: 16 boxes stacked high, 4 boxes side-by-side, 4 boxes back-to-back. 16 × 4 × 4 = 256 boxes. If each box weighs 1 kilo, that's 256 kilos.

When these sorts of figures are considered, then the present and future threat posed by wasting to the ecology of the mind and the planet is obvious. Perhaps the way for Sam to continue functioning in a place like this is to become numb to the reality of the practice, following the example of the warehouse workers, and their gaunt, blank faces. Thus numbed, wasting becomes a game, with a time-limit, levels, missions, and a points system. This might remove him from the awful reality of what he's witnessing. No, he's not just a witness, he's complicit — in the most shameful and unethical game of Tetris: shifting these huge blocks of perfectly edible food around the warehouse and then tipping them into dustbins.

> It's Game Over.
> WASTED.

The alternative is for Sam to think long and hard about who it is that is suffering from the bureaucratic and bucolic nightmare of wasting. There are, of course, victims in the immediate proximity, the people who starve on the streets around Kensington, and a few stops down the Tube is Embankment, where there are often torn cardboard 'Homeless and hungry' signs leaning against a cross-legged figure on the damp pavement, whose eyes Sam avoids. But there are also the people in the green hills of the Peloponnese who suffer. From October onwards, when the tourist season has finished, the Greek inhabitants in and around cities like Kalamata stop their summer jobs of running tavernas and driving taxis in order to get on hands and knees and pick millions and millions of olives from green and purple hillsides. If Sam could stand in a silvery olive grove in autumn's clean Hellenic light, he'd see the farmland all carpeted in green and purple and see the factories where the region's most precious export are picked, boxed up, then driven to Kalamata's seaport, then shipped across to England, to Felixstowe, where gigantic dangling cranes transfer crates of olives from Greece, sauces from Spain, and pastas from Italy, onto trucks headed inland, to London, to W14, to Tesco Kensington. Here, the boxes are opened, and the produce sits in the fridges until it is displayed on the Food2Go Counter for a single day. And at the end of that day, people like Sam put the out-of-date but perfectly edible, untouched food in the CAGEs, and these are wheeled into the warehouse, where gaunt, funereal processions of workers empty them all into the dustbins, which are then loaded into lorries and taken to a landfill site somewhere in the Midlands.

There's a bleak moment later in his shift, when Sam is in the World Foods aisle. He steps in to help a colleague struggling with a weighty CAGE, and together they push the CAGE into the warehouse. As they pass through the plasticky tendrils, headed towards the dustbins, Sam realises that he and his colleague are murmuring along to Band Aid's Xmas song, singing the words 'Feed the world' to no one in particular, as the wasting begins.

CHAPTER FOUR

DAIRY

"As our presence here in this pub literally attests, the world didn't end in 2012."

"The Mayans, like, lied to us."

"That's, like, a mischaracterisation of the Mayan calendar."

"The *baktun*, I think it's called."

"*B'ak'tun*, I think it's pronounced."

"So we've been living for two years in the aftermath of non-apocalypse."

"What kind of person, like, emerges from that kind of non-event?"

"Look at us here, this cohort. Here's your evidence."

Everyone looks around the old wooden table, sticky with beer spills. Rings of wet from collected empties have formed the Olympic logo. The Fitzroy Tavern is populated by bored, enraged, suspiciously naïve, innocently jaded twenty-somethings. Above our heads, there's patterned Lincrusta, off-white décor, and hazy chandeliers. It's not a sawdust establishment, barely anywhere is anymore, but there are still clues of the good ol' days. Between the bar bit and the back room is a square wooden arch where once a door would've been set, a relic from the decades when watering holes were segregated by class or gender. There's no jar of pickled eggs on the bar, none of that nettley smell of vinegar. This has been replaced by a donation pot for a charity to build a well in some Third-World country, and there's this punishing reek of undiluted bleach recently swabbed. Old iron radiators blaze, grilling your back when you lean against them. Wooden furnishings that feel vaguely maritime. It's the sort of pub where UKIP might stage a pint-swilling photo-op.

Our discussion isn't really about Mesoamerican calendars, so much as a ping-ponging debate about broken promises. There's been some trouble with that over the last few years. The Mayans' bullshit, if it's mischaracterised correctly, pales in comparison to a lie much closer to home, more corrosive, and much more eschatological: the rise in tuition fees.

We all remember Nick Clegg clogging up TV and computer screens back in 2012, saying, "we made a pledge...we didn't stick to it...and for that, I'm sorry." This apology was turned into a dance mix on YouTube: "*Sorry, sorry, I'm so so sorry.*" The clip became so popular that its creator could've used the money it made to pay for his tuition fees, and probably taken out a mortgage, too, had he not decided instead to donate it all to a charity in Clegg's constituency. A digital entrepreneur and philanthropist for Sheffield Hallam in an epoch of fibs. For the rest of the student body on campuses across the country who lacked the ingenuity to make YouTube vids and instead attended their lectures, they'd taken to the streets to protest — not about the YouTube clip, but about Clegg's broken promise. The state's reaction was end-of-days: baton-wielding police, penning in the protestors. Pepper spray, truncheons, water cannons, imprisonment. The full English. When their demand to be listened to wasn't being supressed or ignored, the newspapers mocked the sight of so many adolescents playing up. Ungrateful, wilfully ignorant, entitled, avo-eating, sourdough-baking youths, who should neither be seen nor heard, was the broadsheet view. But for those others who kept seeing, kept hearing, a different kind of infantilisation emerged.

With this kettled cohort, it was their parents who'd footed the bill for the raised tuition fees. After all, the mums and dads, most of whom had themselves gone to university when it was their turn to leave home, had been through the process, remembered the rite of passage, and thought their children should do the same. On top of that, these parents who'd made money in careers off the back of worthwhile degrees had more influence as the customers paying for a service. This is how the structural infantilisation got going.

So, two years on from the broken promise, in early January 2014, in this pub, is the first generation of graduates whose purpose for pursuing higher education is not to accrue learning, nor is it even to participate in the collective pooling of knowledge. Rather, we are here to validate an economic investment made by a parental patron. And, as a customer base, we have certain customer rights, or rather, our parental funding body has certain rights. They have a right to know that their investment hasn't failed, that their money is being used to prepare their precious little tot for the labour market. Move over critical ideas, bring on CV fodder. Never forget — the customer is always right. Parents and campus admin across the land benignly and banally conspired to coddle, to check in, to demand feedback. So a student might look down at her phone and read the text, **when can we Skype? Love mum & dad x**, or a student might open up his emails and read the automated university message, **please spend 5 mins filling in this form. Win £10 Starbucks vouchers.**

Continuous intervention, to protect the student from dangerous ideas, from challenges, jolts, disappointments, anxieties, and failures. And yet, through this effort, the student develops just a higher order of those feelings, and remains socially and emotionally incompetent. Look around this pub, and you'll see a paddock of pampered cattle, a group of terrified, brittle, recent adults whose role in the customer base economy makes them yearn for an apocalypse that was guaranteed but never occurred. This group of young people, with cartoon character keychains swinging from their backpacks, lied to by the state, who protested against the lie, were then sent to their rooms as punishment for the protest, while their patron was asked to pay for the room. In a post-2012 world, neither the Mayans nor the government can deliver a future.

Here we all sit around, sipping Sam Smith, watching the evening snow gather its greatness beyond the cross-hatched windows. We're all aware of a vague disappointment, to which our MA syllabus hasn't provided a solution, for which our reading lists haven't given us a vocabulary. So we internalise the problem, absorbing it as grey matter, and instead spend our conversational efforts trying to perform phrases which fifty-fifty between sincerity and politeness. If one of us could diagnose it, we might say, *words at once not untrue and not unkind*.

"Ahh you do realise that's, like, based on a Philip Larkin poem?" someone might respond.

"He's a fascist, isn't he?"

"But what about his poem for Sidney?"

"Sidney Larkin? His dad? He *definitely* was a fascist. Attended rallies in, like, the '30s."

"No, another Sidney. The jazz saxophone player, from New Orleans."

"Bechet. Sidney Bechet. He gets a name check in Nadeem Aslam's *Maps for Lost Lovers*."

"'A practitioner of music should be a musicianer.'"

"That's the one."

"Well what about him?"

"Larkin, the son, not the father, wrote a poem called 'For

Sidney' about the musician: '*On me your voice falls as they say love should, like an enormous yes.*'"

"Not half bad."

"Exactly. I'd be buzzing if the son of a fascist wrote something like that about me."

"So you're saying that just 'cause he wrote a poem about a jazz player, he's not a fascist? That's your evidence is it? Sounds like a 'some of my best mates are jazz players' excuse to me."

We all sip our pints and look to the snow for salvation. Shit shit shit.

Someone else might want to say, "I need a room of my own to avoid this awkwardness."

And someone else might add, "But hang on, a room of one's own is a phrase from Virginia Woolf."

"Yes, 'intellectual freedom depends upon material things.'"

"Like a room of one's own."

"Defo."

"Obvs."

"But wasn't Woolf a eugenicist?"

Shit shit shit. Can't get away from problematics. First the Mayans, then Clegg, and now it's our own literary intuition. No one can be trusted.

We're rescued from the sullen double-bind by the appearance of a PhDer who enters the pub, scrubbing crusts of snow from his hair. Contrary to the popular notion, universities are not these great information highways leading to spaghetti junctions where bachelor's, master's, PhDers congregate. In actual fact, we seldom mix.

The PhDer, pasty-skinned, round spectacles, tweeded, dressed for the role he wants, circulates the room handing out the latest edition of the campus magazine, π. On the front cover is Nigel Farage's face, and we all flick through the nearest copy, past the open letter to President

Obama, past an article about a student's holiday in Kyiv, to read π's interview with the UKIP leader. We read lines aloud.

"What about when he says, 'You can prove what you like with facts and figures'?" This leads us to mull the nature of truth.

"What about when he says, 'Just because Uncle Sam says 'jump,' we don't need to say 'how high?''" This makes us nod, not quite in agreement, but not quite with disapproval.

"Or what about this bit, when he claims that every person 'who lives in the centre of London' is under threat from a Romanian?" This leads to sideways glances at our East-European cours mates.

Dom interjects: "You should all read Lucian Blaga, translated *Faust* into Rumanian, doesn't get angered or get angsty over the loss of peasant ancestry, and doesn't exult in the misery of being from a lower class. He calls his model of life the Mioritic space, which means the landscape is the Rumanian soul."

"The whole UKIP and Farage thing is just a flash in the pan. They'll be defeated or fizzle out."

"Like Nick Griffin."

"He was ruined when he appeared on *Question Time*."

"And now he does his own cooking show."

"What?"

"Yeah, I saw that. Making beef stew, on YouTube, in his kitchen."

"Strictly British beef stew, of course."

"Of course."

"Goebbels Ramsay."

"Marco Pierre White Nationalist."

"His wife's German isn't she?"

"Pierre White's?"

"No. Farage's."

"Think so."

I watch the PhDer explaining to the barman about π, holding up the magazine, pointing to Farage's face, putting a stack on the bar next to the charity donation pot. The barman waits until the PhDer has turned back towards us, then removes the stack of π from sight.

I'm reminded of a comment made in the ♂ Changing Room recently. One of the marketing bods was complaining about a LIDL that'd opened up near another Tesco. He called it an invasion, saying that he has friends who work at Sainsbury's and ASDA who say the same. An 'invasion' from Europe. It seems that the rivalry between British supermarkets has been put aside with LIDL's recent arrival. When it comes to tribal allegiances and the demarcations of class, education, and culture across supermarkets, the divides collapse when the isles look towards the continent and see foreigners approaching, with their yellow logos and suspiciously competitive prices. To shop at LIDL is tantamount to treason, it is to besmirch the Queen.

To the assembled students I ask: "Did anyone see that interview he gave last year about supermarkets?"

There's a collective headshake.

"Farage and the journo discussed the future of UKIP, and the need for the party to talk about more than just immigration or Europe if they're to succeed at the next General Election. Schools, hospitals, the economy. To this the journo asked: will these policies be your ideas or will you just buy them off the shelf, as suggested by the Institute of Economic Affairs? 'Why not?' Farage replied with gusto. 'If someone else has produced brilliant research, I haven't got a problem with that.' And the journo described this as supermarket shelf policymaking, where you don't have to believe in what you're buying."

Dom, elbowing me in the ribs. "All that supermarket stuff is getting into your bones."

"Right everybody," the PhDer announces, "I'm not sticking around, my literature review isn't going to write itself, but just to say...the English Dept has managed to procure a ticket to the stage adaptation of *Wolf Hall* and *Bring Up the Bodies* in Stratford."

"It's already sold out," someone objects.

The PhDer shakes his head. "A member of senior staff has got hold of just one single ticket for a performance in mid-April. So I'm here to notify all of you that the ticket will be awarded to the MA student who writes the best 140 words about the role of monarchy in 2014."

"Why 140 words?"

"So that it's like Twitter, I presume," shrugs the PhDer.

"Why? That's such a limitation."

"And I swear down," someone else interjects, "Twitter uses, like, 140 characters, not 140 words."

"It's about keeping literature relevant," replies the PhDer, fiddling with a cuff's loose thread.

"So why choose the monarchy, then? Might as well make copper farthings the theme."

"Take it up with the senior staff," the PhDer sighs. "Anyway, the only other stipulation is that this is a competition for what the Department is calling 'Home Students'."

"Students with a home?" I blurt, panicked.

"No. It refers to students from the UK." There's a murmur of unrest. "As I said, take it up with the senior staff. I'll leave the rest of these here," he says, dropping the remaining stack of π mags onto our table. A dozen or more Farage faces stare up to the ceiling with flared nostrils and the thin, straight mouth of a tortoise.

The PhDer takes himself away, presumably headed to The Bricklayers Arms on Gresse Street, the hangout for PhD candidates and early-career staff. No one really knows where the seniors congregate. As he leaves, there's hissing and grumbling, particularly from Dom, who complains into his empty glass about discrimination. The mood sinks further each time he uses the phrase 'cash cow' to describe international students like him who end up subsidising the research, admin, and teaching of so-called home students.

No one pushes back. He's probably right, but we can't really do anything about the injustice, can we? After all, us UK natives will benefit from a smaller pool of competitors for this desired ticket. There's no fraternity here. There aren't enough resources to go around. Man is wolf to man.

I lean back and shift my weight to give my phone a quick pocket check. No text from a coddling parent asking for Skype, but the numbers lined up on the screen jolt me into a gosh-look-at-the-time scenario. I'm going to be late for my scheduled arrival at the next accommodation. I gulp the last of my pint, say my goodbyes, haul on my rucksack, and exit the pub, leaving the wall of noise and heat to join the cold and curious quiet of a busy street muffled by snow. I set off in the direction of the river, enjoying that pestle and mortar crunch and squeak of my footfalls — I'm grateful to be wearing work boots on my day off. They were an expensive purchase and my daily outgoings (Tube travel, gifts for my hosts, pints of Sam Smith) mean that I'm still paying them off these months later.

It's like that Terry Pratchett thing, about cheap boots. The rich are so rich because they've worked out how to spend less money. They buy a pair of boots for £300, which last years and years. The poor, by contrast, can only afford a pair for £19.99 which after a few miles in a few different seasons start to tear and leak and break. The poor then have to buy another pair, and another, and another, and another, and another, and another, spending £19.99 a pop — and all the while, the rich have the same pair of well-made, dry boots.

It's the same with a house purchase, instead of renting. It's the same with bulk buying, instead of single item shopping.

Pimlico is where I'm aimed, to the high-rise apartment of Lance Waddle, sometime musicianer and majority town planner. His is a friendship I greatly value because it was a chance encounter, following a gig Lance was playing at The Woodman pub a couple of months ago in Highgate. He was the double-bassist in an ensemble doing Alice Coltrane covers as a backing band for poetry readings. The gig was held in The Woodman's back room, named the Rod Stewart Room for some reason. After the gig I'd been at the bar, and Lance'd passed me, tripped on my rucksack, and knocked into a man standing next to me. This man, it transpired, was the BF of one of the poets, a pretty girl in swishing suffragette hues, like Ada Shelby when she introduces baby Karl to the Blinders in the finale. The BF had turned on Lance, pushed him, tried to headbutt him. The poet rushed over, a blur of lavender, nettle, cream, and got herself between her BF and Lance, reached up to grip her beloved's skull between her palms, stared placatingly into his bulging eyes, moaned, "Babe, babe. Remember the words of the Dylan Thomas poem, '*Oh as I was young and easy in the mercy of his means, Time held me green and dying, though I sang in my...my*err.'" But she fumbled her words, seemed to forget, and the BF clenched his fists, ready to go again.

Over his shoulder I'd mouthed to her, "'*my chains like the sea,*'" which she'd repeated, and somehow this subdued her man. She led him away, leaving me to buy Lance a consolatory pint. We ended up shooting the shit about jazz and poetry until closing and drunkenly agreed to jam together, Lance doing the instruments, me reciting famous poems. Not often that you meet someone organically, without the ropes and pulleys of digital interaction or mutual friends, and crucially, he lives in his rich uncle's apartment at the top of Astrocity Tower in Pimlico, and a lot of the time can put me up.

All the way there, with the poems in my rucksack ready to recite, the falling snow appals those stuck in traffic along gridded roads. They look imprisoned in their little cabins, black wipers battling the white like insect antennae. But it delights me because of the way it settles on the streets. I want to grab the arm of a passer-by and say, *Look! if you catch the headlamps' beams at the right moment, you can trace a shadow in the textured drift and make out the name of the local authority which funded the drain covers.* WESTMINSTER CITY COUNCIL, in this case.

A week or so ago I stayed at Freddy's, and as he was grinding the weed (that same sound as walking through this snow), he did his cinephilia thing, the auteur's turn towards his bedroom's imagined audience, and he introduced that evening's film: David Cronenberg's *Crash*. As part of his preamble, he commented on the scandal that the film caused in the UK:

"About *Crash*, Cronenberg said there was a 'strange island response, a siege mentality in England and a fear of being contaminated from the outside, enclosed on the island with no way to get off.'"

"Meaning?" I asked, stifling a spliffed cough.

"Meaning," Freddy replied, already preparing the next joint, "that it's an expression of isolationist cinema. The controversy with *Crash* was so out of control that *The Daily Mail* printed the headline 'Ban This Car Crash Sex Film', and then doorstepped the BBFC's examiners — as in the guys who dish out film certificates — and published articles about their private lives." He packed this joint into the end of a Bakelite cigarette holder, the latest addition to his steampunk get-up. "Apparently, the campaign succeeded in banning *Crash* in the Borough of Westminster. To this day, the DVD is like a samizdat, covertly circulated around Trafalgar Square. They have to use carrier pigeons to disseminate it."

It wasn't until the next day that I'd concluded it was probably bollocks. Weed can make me gullible.

I pass the low fence cordoning off St James's Park, each perimeter post frosted and glittering. The fence is made of that thin, lattice-like wire that reminds me horribly of Tesco's CAGEs, and immediately I'm transported back to those endless rows of metal and mesh. To the wastehouse. I shiver, but not from the cold.

Beyond the fence, a curiously discernible darkness glows, all shadowy whiteness and blearily bright. Apparently, a family of pelicans lives here, gifted to the British by a Russian Ambassador. This Siberian weather must really baffle those poor animals, so much more at home in warmer climes. I imagine them bristling their frozen feathers and wondering, *what the fuck did we do to deserve this gulag?*

This whole perimetered park is their CAGE.

I'm entering gloomed Pimlico, following the Thames's wintry current. Snow, nighttime, streetlamps. White, black, amber. As I progress along the river's most protruding bend, I trace descending snowflakes from upper darkness, down past street level, into the silvery green of great flow. The cycle of each snowflake is fixed: dissolved in the churn, carried out to sea, absorbed up into the sky, orbiting the globe as cloud a few times, then tugged back down here in time for next January's snowfall. The free movement of particles unconstrained by economics or policy or people. I'm not sure of the science, but I like to imagine each crystal fragment diluting the filthy smoothie ingredients of this river.

A frosted blue plaque announces that Millbank Prison once stood on this site. Apocryphal as it might well be, the appealing fact floats down that the slang term 'pom' used in Oceania (not Orwell's) derives from the acronym for Prisoners of Millbank, who were transferred from the clink onto ships and sent down south to one of H. Royal M.'s most successful colonies: the land of Oz. The British Isles certainly promotes a unique brand of migration: POMs out; pelicans in. If I ever reach its mouth, the Thames has got some explaining to do.

My thumbs are cold as MiniMilks (aisle No.12), but I retrieve my phone and send a message:

Hey man approaching your building. You about?

A delay, long enough for the automated text to come from O2: **15p per text. Remaining credit is £06.70**, and long enough for me to look up at the criss-crossed glass of Astrocity Tower, its square and rectangle windows all wholly whited out by snow, like a Mondrian paint-by-numbers.

Still on the bass bud. Give it 20 mins?

To keep warm, to stop my legs from seizing up, to stave off the familiar humiliation I feel when I'm waiting around for someone to let me in, I stroll along Grosvenor Road until my host can start hosting. Never key another man's car; never cockblock another bloke; never interrupt another guy's musicianship. Three maxims that seem to make sense. But maybe it's the cold; maybe it's some iridescent fragrance coming up off the river and mixing in my lungs. Whatever it is, there's some base bravado in my midst, and I choose to stride rather than stroll, only slowing as I approach a pub's lamplit entrance. I fumble in my pocket for the cellophaned pack of cigarettes and the new lighter that I've taken to carrying around with me. This is Dan's influence, I hate to admit. I still don't smoke regularly, but I hope it might be a way to meet someone. I'm hoping that someone — anyone, preferably a woman — is standing outside: a woman whose cigarette I can light, a woman with whom I can pass a few minutes, a woman with whom I can quickly fall in love, then move in with, and be done with this sofa surfing.

No one appears outside the pub, and I've used up my beer allowance already earlier, so I walk on to the edge of St George's Square, where the fallen snow is so thick it's rendered the rigid demarcations of curb and road, double yellow and red lines, totally boundless. My eyes splinter with cold, but my heart is burning, swelling, as the skin of snow grafts itself freshly and fiercely onto the city's coarsened bones. If there's no person to attach my feelings to, the city itself will have to do. I feel dilated with the snow's constant renewal. I am dissolved in each layer's hazy swirl, the black sky above scattering with such a generous hand, the spread of iced jewels, and I can't tell if these are shivers of cold or the trembles of lively joy. I'm dizzy from the exertion, snowy data cascading all around me like code.

I cross the road to get closer to the river, sidestepping static cars wedged in snow-stopped traffic, the white falling on them like an enormous yes. I pause at a statue, leaning heavily against its stone plinth. Looking up, it's easily recognisable as one of those Industrial Revolutionaries. Probably a slave merchant moonlighting as a philanthropist. In posterity he's had his era's coattails and cravat removed and instead been draped in a Roman toga like he's on his way to a Freshers' initiation. Rather than the iron or steel from the age which brought his wealth, he's been built from marble, so ivory white that it's impossible to see where the stone stops and the snow begins. His bare shoulder is heaped up and his head thickly crowned with what looks like whipped cream (aisle No.4). With an elbow, I brush away the crust of frost on the plinth to read his name: William Huskisson MP. Here, then, is the overlapping of snowy, drifting history. He was Secretary for the Colonies, which included Australia. He also holds the unlikely title of the first fatality from a locomotive train accident. In 1830, on the inaugural journey of the Liverpool–Manchester railway service, this here Billy Husks tried to climb aboard the Duke of Wellington's carriage, but slipped and fell back onto the newly laid track, where the oncoming Rocket locomotive crushed his right leg. He died from the injury later that day. I note that the mason of this marble recreation has given back to Husks both of his legs. The railway line was built to make it easier to transport cotton from the port of Liverpool to Manchester's textile factories, so maybe Huskisson's right leg was a minor amputation taken by history's unrelenting sense of irony as a price for his part in the trade.

All done. Let me know when ur here.

I return the way I came. Word on the street is that when WWII ended, Elizabeth Windsor disguised herself as a loyal subject and went out to celebrate amongst her people. I wonder if she ever does that now. I might bump into her. Is that glossy pool of frozen sick her doing? What about that stubbed cigarette? Is that figure on the other side of the road, arm being swallowed by a bin, the sovereign looking for something to eat?

On Astrocity Tower's porch, the doorman shelters from the gathered snow. He eyes me noncommittally as I bang my boots and pass through the revolving doors. They spin automatically. I'm sure that part of the doorman's stern vibe is that automation of this kind threatens his profession, just as self-service checkouts threaten Tesco staff. They should unionise: Doormen And Checkout Allied Union. DACHAU. Maybe not. Inside, it's glass and marble, but a totally different tint and grain to Tesco. This here is black, grey flooring, which this evening is scattered with yellow CAUTION signs where the foaming snow from tenants' shoes has melted.

I'm in the foyer. Ping me up?

While I wait for Lance's reply, I settle on the couch by a huge cheese plant.

He's had the good sense to get himself born to a man whose brother is a shareholder in myriad companies around the globe, the dividends from which make this Pimlico accommodation one of many, alongside Frankfurt, Milan, New Zealand. Basically, Lance's uncle is loaded. Minted. Wadded. Loadsa dividendz. Lance's done well to make use of family links to get hooked up with this pad. With the uncle being abroad so much of the year, it's more or less unoccupied.

On a low coffee table, there's a selection of mags, including a lot of copies of *GQ*. I flick through the September edition and scan the list of award winners for 2013's Men of the Year.

Russell Brand — Oracle.

Piers Morgan — TV Personality.

Boris Johnson — Politician.

I can't remember who it was, maybe Trolley Fella, maybe a coursemate at The Fitzroy Tavern, but someone was saying recently that, during his acceptance speech, Johnson expressed mock-scepticism about his worthiness for the award and likened it to Ed Miliband's demand for more evidence and a second vote before intervening militarily in Syria.

Richly comic.

A delivery man enters, then leaves, and then a well-dressed man and an elegant woman in thick, cosy coats leave together. When all is quiet, the concierge moves from behind his desk, carrying a mop and a bucket. He catches my eye, shrugs at what must be a question arranged on my face, answers with, "I'm not even *paid* to wipe." He begins to swab the marble floor and realign the yellow CAUTION signs, murmuring as he goes, "Wipe, wipe," which, in his accent, sounds like "Weep, weep."

When Lance had first invited me to Astrocity Tower, this concierge had been very hostile. Since I was neither a worker in the building nor a resident in one of its apartments he didn't want me waiting in the foyer. He'd even insisted that I use the 'Poor Door' around the back, by the bins, so that the executive guests and tenants didn't have to endure the sight of me waiting for Lance. But through perseverance, by gradually wearing him down by repeatedly turning up over the weeks, the concierge has permitted me to sit here in the foyer waiting for Lance. It's the sort of mutual arrangement between people who don't belong in a marble place of this prestige.

Another delivery man enters, doesn't bang his boots and instead walks muddy snow across where the concierge has cleaned. The concierge complains, the delivery man replies. Both voices are raised in argument, swiftly accumulating into unintelligible and unresolved echo. The delivery man leaves in anger, kicking over a few CAUTION signs. The concierge stares after him before continuing to wipe. WAYG might be in the concierge handbook, along with a policy to tolerate but not intervene with delivery men. I walk over and help to realign the signs.

"That's it, bro. I know that guy. I seen him around here all the time. Always in a bad mood."

The concierge begins a diatribe against that delivery man in particular, and then delivery men in general. "They all be like they can just walk in when they fuckin' like, and nevva showin' respect." The revolving doors spin, as tenants enter and leave, but the concierge continues his invective. Thoughts and doors revolve, his manner of speaking reflects the rotation, always circling back to the same topics: entitled delivery men, how long he's got left of his shift, his divorce, his girlfriend who works on the door of a hotel in

Marylebone, his favourite album (*The College Dropout*), his gal at the Holmes Hotel in W1U, his divorce ("a slag, bro"), how long he's got left of his shift, and "these fuckin' guys." I align the CAUTION signs and nod, waiting for Lance.

The phone blurbles on the desk. The concierge answers it, looks over to me. He used to say, "Mr. Waddle will see you now," but these days it's a nod towards the lift. I'm pinged up.

This is a monochrome mod-con building, with its external ladders of dark glass and its internal sequences of grey columned concrete and black carpet. In the apartment, we're talking electric hobs, electric underfloor heating, electric power shower, speakers in each room, all to a backdrop of exposed concrete walls. The uncle (and presumably the auntie) subscribes to the kind of décor that thinks these walls need amending, hence NO COFFEE NO WORKEE. This is printed above the state-of-the-art barista machine. LOVE LIFE LISTEN above the sofa. BE OPEN in the bathroom, opposite the toilet. If you stand in the right position the mirror reflects everything backwards, so it reads ИƎꟼO. And then mounted on the wall of the mezzanine, positioned in front of the treadmill: CREATE YOUR OWN WAY OUT OF NEGATIVITY. I picture Millbank's convicts scratching their names or impassioned last words into the walls of their cells before being shipped off to Australia. They too would've needed that talent for an economy of language. In a different era, maybe they would've found work for the companies which come up with these wall-phrases.

I sit at the marble-topped island on a high swivel chair. Lance is in loose trackies and joggers, heating up some leftovers from a colourful stir-fry. As he serves, he clears aside boxes of Pampers, heaps of babygrows in rainbow hues. His sister is on the cusp of giving birth, and she's using the uncle's flat as a storage unit.

I gulp down the stir-fry in minutes.

From a fridge the size of one of ours at work, he takes an array of vials in a sealed bag and explains that these are colostrum, ready for the baby. "Sweet, sweet nectar. My sister said it's good for body builders."

"You're going to drink your own sister's breast milk?" I ask, my stir-fry stirring.

He shrugs. "We drink milk from cows and goats. Why's this any different?"

This is a sibling bond gone too far. Since the altercation at the jazz gig, Lance has been thinking about working out, getting hench, bulking up. This colostrum archive must be part of it.

Lance reopens the fridge door, takes out a number of bottles filled with milk formula, rearranging what's inside to make room for the leftovers of the leftovers I haven't got round to eating yet. If he'd given me a few more minutes, I'd've managed it. The bottles are opaque with whitish liquid. Maybe it's milk+, maybe it contains Vellocet or Drencrom. Maybe it's got knives in it, o my brothers.

"You know what I overheard today?" I offer between digestive belches, nodding at the line of bottles.

"What's that?" Lance is already setting up for our jazz-poetry jam: tuning his double-bass, plugging the microphone into an amp, opening up the recording software on his laptop. He likes to use this room because of its shimmery acoustics.

"I overheard a conversation in the nappy and talc section between two women. One was telling the other that when a woman is pregnant, her nipples go dark — properly purple — because newborns can't see colour, just basically black and white, and so the nipple skin darkens to contrast with the skin of the breast. And I was thinking how odd that is — that infants live in the world of black and white."

Lance looks around the room, wistfully, at the black and white furnishings. He's feeling out his imminent role of uncle: "This place would be perfect for a newborn, then, wouldn't it?"

I kick myself as I realise I might've just done myself out of accommodation once the baby arrives. If the sister wants to raise her baby here, I'll be out in the cold. I move the conversation along, retrieving from my rucksack a thin anthology of poems from which I'll read while Lance plays. He hands me the microphone, gripping the elephant head of his double bass, looks out at the night, at the snow falling beyond the wide, wall-length window. "It's like, Anneliese's little baby was an accident, right, not planned or anything, but she's really looking forward to being a mum, and it'd be hard to say that it's been a loss. Everyone's going to gain from it."

Not quite everyone, I almost mutter into the mic.

▬ ▬ ▬ ▬ ▬

'You're a good girl... I know you want it... I know you want it... You're a good girl.' No, this isn't Henry Reed. No, this isn't Walter de la Mare. No, this isn't Elizabeth Barrett Browning. It's 'Blurred Lines' by Robin Thicke. People no longer hum Tennyson beneath their breath at luncheon parties. Instead they tap their toes, like this young mother, as the song thunders from the store's speakers. *'You're a good girl... I know you want it...'* I get these lyrics mixed up with those from another song on the store playlist: *'You're a good girl and you know it... You act so different around me... 'Cause you're a good girl and you know it.'* That comes courtesy of Drake. The Thicke and Drake albums sit next to one another on the shelf on aisle No.18, and so far, I've never been asked to restock them. Ever. That doesn't necessarily imply that their albums are filled with vacuous, empty lyrics churned out in mindless repetition to satisfy the lowest common-denominator audience. Not at all. It might just be that fewer customers are buying CDs. The mother is

absent-mindedly mouthing along to the words of T.I.'s rap. '*Had a bitch, but she ain't bad as you/So, hit me up when you pass through/I'll give you something big enough to tear your ass in two.*' While she reads the label on a pot of yoghurt, her toddler reaches out from his pram's restraints to brush his pudgy fingers against the colourful wrapper of a *Frozen* lunchbox. A few shifts ago, I was tasked with positioning these on the lowest shelves.

"*I'll give you something big enough to tear your ass in two*," I hear Dan the fishmonger murmuring as he continues mechanically to wrench a bony spine from its fleshy wallet. He slices, descaling a seabream which flecks silver jewels all around the blue slab of chopping board. "*I'll give you something big enough to tear your ass in two*." His thick thumb and forefinger lodged in each of the bream's eye sockets. "*I'll give you something big enough to tear your ass in two*." He discards what's not needed. There are all sorts of complaints about what will happen if automated checkouts are brought in, and surely soon after, it will be automated butchers and mongers. Dan's robotic conditioning has already begun. Can Dan be blamed for his attitudes towards the women on the F&F mezzanine ("smashin' those backdoors in on the regs, if I could") if this is what he and everyone else is listening to? And what about my conditioning? Am I also susceptible? Maybe there's an essay in it, but I can't quite think of a title. All I see is blurred lines.

There's a tap on my shoulder. Monojit: "It's your turn."

"For what?"

He holds up a clenched fist. "You've got a posh voice." Thumb sticks out. "You've passed your probation." Index finger points upwards. "It's time for you to do the Tannoy." Middle finger joins it. I begin to protest, but he reminds me, "This is what Bisera hired you for." Trailed by Monojit, who blocks my way when I try to retreat, I reach the Customer Service Desk, next to which the lanes of checkout terminals beep like monitors in a coma ward. These will soon be replaced with self-service, apparently, and even now I picture bagmen with earpieces and tinted sunglasses first tasering and then carrying off elderly workers, putting them out to pasture, and installing in their place compliant machines which never complain of backache or realign their dentures on the shop floor.

"You have to hold down the red button there," Monojit instructs, passing me a piece of a paper. "Speak into the microphone and say what's written here."

There's a metallic swooning sound, like a guitar caught off-guard, and the bit of 'Blurred Lines' when they sing, '*Do it like it hurt... What, you don't like work?*' automatically fades down. There must be some software that Nick Dale's devised for that. I clear my throat. "Welcome to Tesco Kensington, this is a customer service announcement. On the Fish Counter today, we have whole seabream better than half price, £4 per kilo."

"And the last bit," Monojit mutters sternly.

I hold down the red button again. "That's a Tesco promise. Please let us know how we can enhance your supermarket experience. Thank you."

As I leave the desk, a regular is waiting. Montgomery. He's always wearing a brown flat cap, a green puffer jacket, and, beneath it, a shirt patterned like a noughts and crosses board. His trousers are the colour of Colman's (aisle No.17). It's the attire of a grouse-shooter during the off-season. He doffs his broad hat in mock deference to my announcement, bows slightly, his scalp red, flaked, and bleeding beneath an ambitious combover. He's maybe seventy, very posh and well-off, returning to the store daily — "Just popping in for some pop," by which he means a bottle of champagne. He sometimes asks me to accompany him as a personal shopper around the aisles and has a habit of rubbing his jewelled hands on his mustard thighs. He talks in a very flowery way, not really to you but near you, no sentence nor sentiment ever quite ending, just buttressed by "*yupyupuhuhyup.*" He told me the other week, on one of our store sojourns, that he used to work undercover for the government and went to North Korea to do deals with them on the Crown's behalf.

But today he wants to talk about stuff closer to home.

"And from which fair land do you hail?" he asks.

"Suffolk," I answer.

"*Yupyup*ah, the Fens of Anglia East. A wonderful place to stalk deer. I used to know a fellow there. Hervey. Do you know his people?"

I'm startled at this pointed and accurate question. I tell him that I once went on a school trip to the grounds of a large manor house outside a nearby town. Where the Hervey family lived.

"*Uhuh*Oh *yupyupyup* I know the place: Ickworth House. I knew the fellow there. Mark Hervey. Terrible end for the boy. Opiates wasn't it? You know, Mark and I were meant to go into business together building hovercraft for the British government. Oh yas, but then Mark went off the rails and, well, one rather loses touch in such circumstances."

I don't share it with Montgomery but I do remember very clearly the reports of Hervey's demise in the local paper, the same publication which years later announced my brother's arrest.

Montgomery signals an end to his story by stumping his cane woodily against the faux-marble floor, moving off, doffing his cap to staff as he passes them. They nod back politely, he being a tolerated regular who openly displays his bafflement at the tracksuited variety of customer who has, in his words, "corrupted these fine aisles." For Montgomery, this Tesco is his own extended pantry, and as far as he's concerned, the riffraff should bloody well clear off elsewhere. I imagine the schema like this:

Fortnum & Masons	Upper
Waitrose	Middle-upper
M&S	Lower-upper
Sainsbury's	Upper-middle
Tesco	Middle-middle
Morrisons	Lower-middle
ASDA	Upper-lower
LIDL	Middle-lower
Iceland	Lower-lower
Foodbank	Lowest

I continue my aisle rounds. By now, 'Blurred Lines' has segued first into Macklemore's 'Thrift Shop', then into Pharrell's 'Happy', and is now blasting out Miley Cyrus's 'We Can't Stop'. *'To my homegirls here with the big butt/ Shaking it like we at a strip club/Remember only God can judge ya/Forget the haters 'cause somebody loves ya.'*

"Can you believe this fucking music?" Alby asks as I pass the Deli Counter. "I'm one song away from puttin' my neck across this blade. Well done on the Tannoy, by the way. You sounded suitably unenthusiastic. I doubt they'll ask you again."

"Mate, I'm dying of hunger right now. I'm surprised my stomach didn't drown out the announcement." Since Alby and I ceased our espionage picnics in Felon Place, each shift is an orchestra for the gut, with no food to digest. It's made worse by the fact that the Euphorium Bakery by the store's entrance has some sort of ventilation system that pumps the smells of freshly leavened bread into the store. A similar technique is used by high-street coffee houses, which release the fragrance of ground beans into the street in front of the doors, to entice, to condition. The warm yeasty fragrance of the nuclear family's oven swills around the store. I've heard one of the Upper Management describe this as 'experience', as in: the first thing that customers should 'experience' when they enter the store is the smell of baking.

"You do look a bit gaunt," Alby observes. "If you're that hungry, go over to the Bakery. That guy still owes me from the bet he lost about Callum's strip search."

"You sure?"

Alby shrugs as he tugs cellophane over a cold cut, and pats a sticker onto it: PILGRIM'S PROCESS. He weighs the kg, and hands it to a customer.

"Yes, lad, but on the condition that we get a few scoops after work."

"Alright. What time do you finish?"

"Five thirty."

"I'm clocking off at five, so I'll go on ahead to the pub and get us a table."

"Boss."

I turn and, with as much self-control as possible, try to walk casually, not desperately, towards the Euphorium Bakery. Looking in the dictionary (my pocket OED, not the JBT), the term 'euphoria' means an intense or exaggerated feeling of elation. Its origin is Greek: 'euphoros' meaning a false sensation of well-being in a sick person. The term 'euphoriant' refers to a drug which produces euphoria. 'Euphorium' is not an actual word which exists in current usage. It's pure corporate coinage. As with so many commercial strategies which seek to harness and control a target market, a group of pie-chart wielders will have sat around a large shiny table while a lacky takes the minutes, with way too much money sloshing around for way too little thought. Their task? To come up with a new name to capture the imaginations of customers buying bread. After numerous spreadsheets and sentences that begin,

"Focus groups indicate that..." they will have settled on 'Euphorium'. To me, however, the term conjures up Robert Nozick-esque visions of bubbling tanks in which brains float. This imagery clashes with the connotations of 'home' induced by the choice of décor and smells at the supermarket's entrance.

The baker, in his white cap, white trousers and white shirt resembles a Bedlam inmate. I remind him of the bet, tell him Alby says I'm owed a sarnie. He rolls his eyes but concedes. "I was sure it was Callum, but yeah, should've suspected that Heath tosser. So come on, boss" — he points at the cabinet of sandwiches — "pick one and move along."

I mull the names of what's on offer: Euphorium's Ham&Cheese, Euphorium's All Egg Brunch, Euphorium's WhoCan?Vegan. How hard is it, really, to come up with a name and marketing strategy for these products? If I do away with my apron, select a tie and shirt, trim back my greasy locks, grab a whiteboard and march into the meeting room upstairs, I could make my pitch:

"Hi there. I'm here to ask you one very simple question. What is the Tesco experience? Answer: sensation. And what do we want? Satisfaction. Well, ladies and gentlemen, I give you 'SENSATIATE', the latest evolution in supermarket baking."

I'd present the audience with the names of the products, each based on thirteenth-century baking techniques invented in Stratford: "That's right, ladies and gentlemen. We're putting London Town back on the map of global bread production."

I'd hand out samples: "We have **Le Pouffe**, after the French term for bread. And these two here are the '**Simnel**' and the '**Wastel**', which are white, fine, and common. Great for low-income customers. We're also introducing the '**Bis**', which is brown bread. And the '**Tourte**', a tasty treat, because even the Londoners of the thirteenth century had a naughty side."

I'd turn back to the whiteboard to conclude my pitch. "Our slogan? 'SENSATIATE', because history is our story."

I blink back to the now, to the baker's expectant face. "I'll have a Euphorium's Ploughwoman's, please. Could I have a cup of water with it too?"

The baker sighs as he chucks the sandwich on the counter. "We don't do water. I know Alby won the bet, but if you want a refreshment, you'll have to buy something."

"Can't I just have some from the tap?"

"'Fraid not, boss. We're not authorised to use the tap."

One technique I've developed over the months here to try and dissuade the stomach from kicking up a fuss is to fill it with water. It's hot in the airless kitchen, and six to seven hours doing circuits on the shop floor, no matter how slow, makes you thirsty. Food is not allowed to be consumed in the kitchen, that's been well-established, but neither is water. There are no cups in the kitchen, and the tap leaning over the industrial-sized silver sink drips scolding drips. But it seems the same applies over here at the Euphorium Bakery.

'Water, Water, Everywhere, Nor Any Drop to Drink.'

"Come on, just a sip." I protest.

The baker loses his patience, slamming down a rolling pin that makes a pile of flour plume. "Look, do you remember Roberto? He used to work here on Euphorium? No? Well he doesn't work here anymore, and I'll tell you why. He was spotted by Upper Management drinking from that tap over there. No tribunal, no inquiry, they just showed him the CCTV footage, of him breaking all sorts of hygiene and health and safety standards, and he was sacked. I was standing just here proofing the brioche when those two fellas, the big one with the wart and the little weedy one, came and escorted Roberto off site. So the short answer is, no mate, I'm not gonna risk it. Now fuck off with your sarnie, I've got baking to do."

I decide not to point out to him the hygiene infringement implied by the sign in the sandwich cabinet: PLEASE USE TONGUES TO RETRIEVE BAKERY GOODS. Instead I return to the Food2Go kitchen, to hide behind the fridge and scoff my sandwich. I begin to unwrap it, but notice growing along the crust and spreading across the bread the green and syphilitic black spots of mould. I return to the Bakery and show him, asking first for another Ploughwoman's, then for a cup. This is water. It's seldom tasted so sweet.

- - - - -

After my shift, I go on ahead to The Troubadour on Old Brompton Road. It's a spenny establishment, for sure, but tonight Alby and I will be drinking on Heath's dime left over from our encounter in Felon Place. I set up a tab on the bar and get a decent table. With half an hour until Alby arrives, I use the time to finish off this week's required reading for my MA: *The Diary of a Nobody* by George and Weedon Grossmith, a comic novel from 1892 which most of my coursemates have already finished. When they've been discussing it I've stayed quiet, listening to one half despondently describe it as a waste of time to read a novel that negates itself even in its own title. They think we should be reading more useful texts, the kind that could get us a job. And the other half have been arguing that this self-negation is exactly the point, a blankness which should galvanise and delight. I always keep schtum in this kind of discussion, only ever sharing my views once I've finished the novel in question. It's a real malady of my generation to talk about a text without having done the graft. An unfinished novel is like a fly-tipped mattress, once abandoned it's wise not to talk about it. All I can say, as I approach the final few paragraphs, is that the collaboration between these Bros. Grossmith is the stuff of lacerating envy that brings tears close to the ducts.

I take out the latest draft of my Letter to an Incarcerated Sibling, the version that most accurately reflects what I want to say. In as simple terms as I can put together, I ask him for an explanation for why he committed the theft, for assurances that he is trying to change, and express hope that we'll have a better relationship in the future. It still needs work (the draft and the brotherly bond), but just before I can scribble some edits, Alby arrives, so I rub my eyes and tuck the paper into the book.

"Good?" He asks.

"Yeah, I'm fine."

He nods at the cover. "I meant the book."

"Hard to say," I murmur, dabbing the corner of my eye, pretending it's an itch.

"*Diary of a Nobody*," he reads. "Would you recommend?"

"To you? Mr I-don't-read-fiction. Actually I would. Authored by two brothers."

He nods in approval, sets his coat down and goes to the bar for us to commence our boozing. This doesn't happen all that often. His duties of fraternal heavy lifting for his twin take precedent over one-to-one time chatting breeze in the pub.

This particular pub's appeal to me is its impressive alumni of performers: Charlie Watts, Bob Dylan, Joni Mitchell, Robert Plant. For Alby, he likes the significance of knowing that, within these walls, Ban The Bomb morphed into the Campaign for Nuclear Disarmament. Pub folklore goes that Gerald Holtom designed the famous peace symbol over a pint of Guinness, scribbling it on a beermat, so when we order, the bartender dutifully scrawls the ☮ in the foam.

"Here's to Heath." We clink glasses.

"Still can't believe he stole all that stuff." The Guinness

tastes richly of iron, like licking away the blood when you cut your finger.

"Lad, he would've got away with it if it wasn't for the door sensor. He told us so."

"Yeah, what do you reckon he meant by that?"

"It was something about how the settings on the sensor can be changed so that the doors don't open to let people out."

"What about CCTV?"

"Yeah, that too. He'd've needed to disable it. Nick would know."

"And there was Upper Management."

"Yeah, you'd need to find a way to keep 'em upstairs."

"Just get them one of those crates of champagne. That'd keep them busy."

"I still can't believe you suspected Cármen." Alby scoffs and fidgets with his glass.

"Did I?"

Alby nods. "You said she'd stolen some tofu."

"Yeah I mean I'd heard she was up on the F&F mezzanine doing her samples pitch and someone accused her."

"She'd never steal." Alby's looking out of the snowy window.

"She seems to've stolen something of yours."

He looks at me, alert. He hates being caught out, loathes not being a couple of steps ahead.

"You're into her. Nothing wrong with that. She looks good."

Dark orangey hair, a bob almost the colour of red brick, with endearing freckles that she tries to cover up with foundation. A big Steinway smile of ivories, and hazel eyes. A ponderous manner, her dark red eyebrows often frowning at a question she poses, and immediately clearing when the answer is provided. From Argentina. The Customer–Company Liaison Assistant. Her job is to invite the public to

Taste Sessions to try a variety of the most delicious produce. She goes from store to store, dropping in every few months, or whenever there's an important event (Christmas, Valentine's Day, Easter), each of which is a fertile opportunity for marketing. From time to time, she'll come into the Food2Go kitchen and, along its surfaces, prepare a spread of cakes, plates of chocolate, and platters of expensive nibbles. She has a blueprint of the layout of the whole store, which she annotates to show where her Taste Sessions will be most effectively deployed. Sometimes she even offers Alby and me a few pieces of something (out of Monojit's sight, of course). She always gives Alby bigger portions.

Alby sinks the rest of his pint. "I tell you, it's been a drought for me, and she does give me the eyes." He stands. "Do you want another?"

I get out my wallet instinctively.

"We're still on Heath's money, lad."

I return my wallet to my pocket, notice I've dropped something. Bend down to retrieve it.

"Wait. What the fuck is tha'?"

"It's my hairnet."

"It looks like somethin' for your shower, for putting soap bars in or whatever. Who gave you it?"

"Monojit. Apparently my hair has reached a certain length."

"It is pretty long. More power to you." Alby, slapping his head. "I'm not long for the land of the receding hairline."

"You know the solution for that? Lay off the self-abuse and give Cármen a ring."

"Bit too soon for marriage, lad."

"Get on the dog and bone."

He looks back at me, animated.

"Don't, Alby. Don't lower yourself. What I mean is, as you very well know, you should call her up."

He turns noncommittally back towards the bar.

I know what he means about the drought. It's been one year, five months, twenty-nine days of unchosen chastity for me. No amount of jerking the gherkin (aisle No.5) can replace sex with another, actual person, and besides, an earnest wank is tricky when you haven't got your own place to pull it off. While Alby fetches the next round, I open my diary and check my accommodation schedule for the next few weeks. I'm due to return to Lottie and Vic's soon, after what feels like a decent absence. Then it's a few overnight hauls at friends of friends, the odd camp out in the university library, and whatever else I can blag. This is the cynical cycle of the unhoused, whose forward-planning must always be ready to double-back on itself when circs change. One day, someday, somehow, somewhere I'll have enough money for a deposit for a room of my own, where I can masturbate to my cardio's content.

I thumb backwards through the diary's pages...28th... 22nd...17th...12th...5th...4th...to the beginning of the year. When the countdown had commenced on New Year's Eve, I was stacking shelves of bran flakes. I made a list of resolutions. As fireworks burst beyond the store's windows, strobing the glass in colourful spiderwebs of red, white, and blue, I committed myself to getting laid and to getting a room of my own. With ten seconds to spare, I'd dashed from Dairy to the store's entrance, stopping just short of the grey carpet which demarcates the sliding doors' movement sensor. On this threshold, I watched 2013 burst and spill into 2014, feeling like a lowing heifer, my eyes ceilingward, almost hoping for the steel buttresses to collapse, for the whole thing to fall. Maybe the Mayans got it wrong by just one year. Maybe there was an error on their paperwork — an exhausted low-level Yucatán clerk on some Friday 9–5, 5–9 including overtime triple shift, who'd just simply made a typo. He'd written 2012 by mistake, when actually he meant 2013 as the end of the world. Let's count down and hope for this ancient bureaucratic cock-up... 3... 2... 1...

Welcome to 2014. In those first few seconds, I'd felt duped, betrayed by a Mesoamerican people who'd promised an end to all this. Someone else had put in the grump work to orchestrate the prediction, and I was primed for it. When it didn't happen, I was very deflated, and didn't feel proactive enough to do the annihilating all on my own. *La petite mort.*

CHAPTER FIVE

FROZEN

I press the red button. The store explodes.

Naughty Boy's 'La La La' cuts out — '*When your words mean nothing, I go, "La, la, la,"*' — as I clear my throat. "Good afternoon, welcome to Tesco Kensington. This is a customer announcement. We are so pleased to tell you that, ahead of the DVD release of *Frozen*, we are giving away a free digital download when you purchase any of our amazing range of *Frozen* products: that's a lunchbox; or one of Elsa's dresses; or our instore kids' mag, which comes with a free Olaf toy. Thank you, and please let us know how we can enhance your supermarket experience. And happy Valentine's Day."

I release my finger, the Tannoy clicks off, the song fades back in — '*When your words mean nothing, I go, "La, la, la,"*' — and I cower behind the Customer Service Desk as a collective scream gathers in volume from all around the store, a cacophony of tantrums as toddlers yelp at their parents for one of the items I've mentioned. Sam Smith is wholly drowned out. This is a la-la-less land, more like a scraggy rock off the Galapagos where a million gannets shriek and squabble in their own guano. Almost inevitably, a furious-looking father marches towards me, dragging with one hand a tear-stained blob in a woolly jumper, and in the other a bouquet of drooping roses.

"I tell you what would enhance *my* supermarket experience, for you to stop doing those fucking announcements when I've got my little boy with me. How am I supposed to get him home now without one of them toys or whatever? Cheers pal, really done me over there."

"I'm sorry, sir. Can I interest you in one of the *Frozen* Collectable Card packs? Ten percent off?"

"Piss off, mate. I can barely afford the DVD, let alone all this other stuff."

The sobbing blob heaves snottily at the man's side, "Buh-buh-buh-buht pweese, daddy."

"Shane. Stop wantin' for everyfink. I'm not made of bladdy maney." The man has turned the colour of the rose petals, the veins in his forehead about to burst. It'd only take a thorn...

To me, he replies, "Yeah, since you've fucked up my evenin', I guess I'll 'ave one n all. Give us one of them, then."

I slide a kids' mag across the desk as he taps his card as aggressively as he can against the payment monitor. He grabs the mag and shoves it into his toddler's hands.

Little Shane pulls at the magazine's packaging to get at the toy as the doors slide open, and the white-knuckled father with his hiccupping son dissolve into the icy afternoon.

Monojit erupts with carrot-grating glee, "Hceh, hceh. I thought he was going to bloody well hit you."

I scrunch up the piece of paper Monojit handed me for the announcement, throw it towards the bin below the desk, brimming with unsuccessful scratch cards. Yes, the most addicted Lotto gamblers in Tesco are the staff.

"That was my last act for the day. I'm off," I call over my shoulder to Monojit, hauling my rucksack and weaving through the store's gannety wall of sound, towards the sliding doors. As I reach the entrance, but just out of range so that the sensor doesn't detect me, I notice on the faux-marble floor an ID card. I scoop it up and inspect it.

NAME: MRS Mollie Friel

DOB: June 15th, *1941.*

Concessionary travel funded by HM Government with your local authority.

It's a Freedom Pass, a card that gets its owner free travel on buses and trains around London. I look around for Mrs Mollie Friel, but no one fits her photo — staring up at me: an ancient woman with wrinkles and startled blue eyes.

Free travel.

I look around again. The security guard is busy at his lectern. I should hand it in but...

Free travel.

A troupe of angry mums pushing prams and towing toddlers advances past the guard, as one, in Monojit's direction. They all have to swerve around Wart and Feral, who are in the midst of escorting a colleague called Isaiah across the foyer.

"I'm telling you I've got the receipt," he's remonstrating with them, "and it was only a tin of sweetcorn!" as the double doors to the staff area swing open. Poor Isaiah. I liked him. A softly spoken man in his early thirties from Southwark, he once explained to me when we were stacking shelves on World Foods that where his parents are from, in the Lower Niger, sweet corn is called *eze-agadi-nwayi*. "It means, 'the teeth of an old woman'." He'd also pointed out to me that the World Foods aisle is full of cheaper and better-tasting produce, but that it's just that most people want the 'British' label on their foods, and so prefer to shop on other aisles, even if it's more expensive and less well made.

No one's looking my way. This gives me a moment's cover. Not theft; borrowing what's lost. I swiftly pocket the Freedom Pass, and feel the chilly satisfaction of being spat out through the doors into the cold. I crane my neck to survey the frosted concourse of Warwick Road, but can't see any furious fathers with sobbing toddlers. A month ago,

I would've been able to trace their footprints in the snow, tracking them like deer, but now the ice has come, there's no trace. Snow is dreamy, wistful, a benign apparition which floats down from all the way up there. It soothes the mind like whisky and makes tenuous connections believable. Snow is the weather of aggregation. Ice isn't. It's disparate, coarsely separating out what wants to be together. So who decided that mid-February was the best time for the most romantic day of the year? Valentine's Day, February 14th. Whoever did Cupid's PR really didn't think it through. It's totally at odds with the season.

The road is clear of paternal debris, dropped petals, and footprints, so I walk towards the nearest bus stop on Holland Road. Not towards the Tube as normal, nope. Thing are different today. Things are worse. The icy wind keeps squaring up to me as I try to navigate slippery paving slabs. I take out my phone and reread the text which Freddy sent me as I'd arrived for my shift this morning:

> **No probs if you need somewhere 2nyt last minute but just so you know my house mates already got a mate staying in the cupboard and I'm gonna have a girl over this eve (the one from that steampunk convention!) so you'll have to take the upstairs bathroom. We've got rugs and cushions though. Let me know if you're happy with this**

With bluish fingers I thumb a message:

Hey manthanks for this. Erm I'll have an ask around and see what's what, but thanks any way then open a new text message and type to another contact **Heya mi old mucka sorry it's so last minute but is there any chance I could crash at yours tonight. My accomm's fallen through last min and I'm a bit desperate.**

I look up as a bus passes me before I've got time to wave

it to a stop. It cruises on, bare branches from road-lining trees rake its side and etch the frosted glass like it's been flogged. I'll wait. Other than the cold and the wind that's picking up, I'm not in a rush. The plan was to stay at Lottie and Vic's for another week or so. That's what we'd agreed. But for reasons I can't get to grips with yet, those plans fell through yesterday evening.

Behind me there's a rattling sound of metal meeting metal, of steel clashing with steel, of a sinewy wire entanglement. I turn to see the shuttered front of a shop, ASH'S FROZEN MEATS & FABRICS, outside which a huddle of CAGEs has been left, each overflowing with whatever's been discarded from the day's business. The icy wind keeps shoving the CAGEs against the metal shutters, and the sound takes me straight back into the warehouse, to the squeaking, screeching, shrieking wastehouse. I look upwards for respite, but the leafless trees overhead just flail and spread their bare knobbly fingers into obscene gestures.

A queue gathers at the bus stop, a procession like Aleksey Sundukov would paint if he had hours to kill while he tried to secure some accommodation: some in ragged scarves, some with cheeks bruised blue by frost, one with shoes broken at the heel. The soles flap as their owner shuffles forward. A lot of carrier bags filled not with fresh groceries but belongings. Never a good sign, suggests a metro no*mad*.

If the father reappeared now, when I'm beyond the store's jurisdiction, I wonder what I'd say. His anger was understandable, even excusable. We should all probably let it go when a parent has to appease their little monster by purchasing this or that toy. Parents and children are all the victims of myriad signals that encourage a child's reaction and condition a parent's response.

We shuffle forward.

But surely the same should go for (say) Dan, who spends day after day humming along to 'Blurred Lines', not by choice but by its endless loop over the speakers. He's been just as conditioned as Little Shane or Shane Senior. Or the newest edition to the store's playlist: Dapper Laughs's 'Proper Moist', which Dan — and, for that matter, many other colleagues and customers — sings along to.

The other day Dan was humming while he went about his mongering — "*I'll track her down and fuck her mum*," and then, "*if she's lookin' at me but playin' with her hair, by the end of the night she'll need a wheelchair*." From the diamond carpet on which the fillets and shells rested, he selected a whole plaice. He weighed it in the silver dish. Not those of Justice, but Prunella's scales. "*She wants a little kiss, and I ain't gonna stop her, it's only taken one glass of knicker dropper*." On the blue chopping board was a juvenile conger eel, its flesh segmented like a toast rack. With one gloved hand, Dan placed a thick cleaver into each groove, and with the other, brought down a mallet onto the blade's top edge, splitting through the eel's thick vertebrae. These eel steaks went into the silver dish, and the scales seesawed to one side with mesopelagic weight.

"*There's no choice, you'll be feeling proper moist*." No one can really judge Dan for this. But it makes me wonder if there is a time and place for Dapper Laughs's particular brand of fierce, laser-guided humour?

The actor who plays the character of D.L. is an Addlestone native — where H.G. Wells has his Martians spaceships arrive in *The War of the Worlds*. If D.L. had been around in Wells's day then maybe his bants about rape or sexual harassment could've been enough to dissuade the aliens from landing. Put D.L. there as the spaceship approached, and he'd be shouting, "Oof phwaoh check out the tripod legs on that Martian *beyooutay*. Phwoah, go on luv. Give those tentacles a twirl, will ya?"

So there is a time and place for Dapper Laughs, but it just seems to be in a post-apocalyptic hellscape during an alien invasion. We must cherish the D.L.s of our nation, for they are the best deterrent against attack. Banter is cheaper than Trident.

I check my phone. No reply yet. I tap a few keys to check my Outbox and reread the text, to make sure it did actually send, and that it doesn't sound too desperate. My plan is simply that I'll keep texting different people to see if they can offer me a place to sleep tonight. I'll keep riding the buses until I hear back. Can't do this on the Tube because down there, like the warehouse, there's no signal.

Another bus appears, and this time a middle-aged woman who is still a little way off along the street turns to wave for it, and tries to dash to reach our queue. There's a sudden gust of icy wind and, out of nowhere, one of the CAGEs by the shuttered shop detaches from its moorings and slides across the pavement towards her. At the last moment, she sees it coming and dodges, but in the midst of her dodge, she steps on a slippery paving slab and falls, only just managing to grip onto a metal bench's slat to prevent a full-on collapse. Mid-February ice — splintered, skidding, treacherous — it's a poltergeist which makes the earth a magnet for bruised or broken wrists, elbows, and hips.

I watch from my neutral place in the queue as she gets back to her feet. Customer–Colleague Interaction Policy No.1 BE PERSONABLE only applies within the confines of working hours. Then I watch as the CAGE continues its slide around in the icy wind, only slowing to a standstill when one of its wheels rolls over what looks like the remains of a pigeon, the grey frosted wing acting as a wedge.

Up onto the top deck, empty. Bliss. Through the glass, I can see the woman has sat on the bench. It's one of those austere iron benches shaped like a wave: aesthetically pleasing, ergonomically devastating, and for the homeless it's a hostile piss-take. She's grimacing, holding her side. This city has been taken over by a class of indiscriminate frost that punishes both the pavements of Tower Hamlets and the ponds in the Royal Parks, the darkened frost which scowls at the prospect of its own thaw, stubbornly frosting the surface further. I've looked in many an icy window of many a shop front, searched the frosted glass for myself, and I don't know what I see. There should be an affinity between our physical resemblance and our reflection. But I don't recognise what's there.

From here on the top deck, I'm level with the icicles hanging from the lips of roofs like walrus tusks. Thus elevated, I survey this frozen island, dark and wild, where storms and wind and dire hail perpetually beat, where the firm soil never thaws, where ice banks heap ruinously and massive buildings dash the hopes of those passing beneath their icy glass.

I check my phone.

Sorry pal I'm out of town for work and don't have a spare key. Good luck tho

I thumb another message to another name in my contact list. The automated text from O2 appears: **15p per text. Remaining credit is £14.02.**

I've got thinking to do. The last twenty-four hours have been... well, I need to get down to some serious scribbling to make sense of whatever the fuck happened with Lottie and Vic yesterday. I've looked up this bus route, and it'll take about an hour, which should be enough time for me to get some last minute accommodation, and if I get to the other end and need to take another bus, then I will.

This is the No.9 to TEMPLE. The next stop is WARWICK GARDENS

It's not the bus tyres over potholes that makes me shudder. It's whenever I think back to what happened. I take out my notebook and scribble a few words to help me: 'drought', 'flesh', 'onanism', 'caught', 'shame'. Also from my rucksack I take a folded newspaper, unwrap it, revealing a dripping pork pie, saved by Alby from its fate in a CAGE and covertly passed to me.

"Someone needs to benefit from all this wasting," he'd shrugged, with that scheming expression he sometimes has. "It's not theft; it's salvage."

In the past, I might've had the energy to push back on this, but I was and still am so fucking hungry and tired. I'd added to this a tin of cabbage leaves, sprats in tomato sauce, and finally, a small bottle of vodka, all plastered in REDUCED stickers. This is how I'm fortifying my Valentine's bus journey.

And of course there's the Freedom Pass. I do intend to return it soon, but if it lets me do circuits of the city for free, in the warmth of a bus, until I find somewhere to sleep, then I'll use it today. When I boarded the bus and tapped the card against the yellow disc, I made a point of covering the photo from the bus driver, but now that I'm sitting safely alone, I inspect it more closely. Yes, I do recognise her — Mrs Mollie Friel. She's a right regular wrong 'un, who stalks the aisles with her trolley, snarling at everyone.

The next stop is HARRODS

Friel comes in every day. Like clockwork. She's an ancient Irish woman with bloodshot, milky eyes, crusted porridge coloured skin, and one of those headscarves that made old women even back in 1950s photos look out of date. She is always leaning on her trolley round the store, which might be the disability that grants her this Freedom Pass, always snapping at anyone who is on the margins of being in her way. Tesco conditions us to say "*I'm here to help*," so I have in the past stepped out and asked her if there's anything I can do to enhance her supermarket experience. About a week ago, I saw her hobbling along an aisle, her burden of a headscarf tied tightly around her gaunt face, giving her the proportions and shades of cellophane-wrapped gammon — faded rouge and dull bone. I asked if she needed help.

Maybe it was her lack of teeth or the wall of music blaring from the speakers that made me mishear, but she answered back in a slur: "O Christ, those fucking darkies down that aisle. With their Caribbean muck in tins. Dose bloody migraines." She may've seen the horror on my face, so she followed this with, "I'm not racist, but I'm saying just send 'em back to where they came from."

I wanted to ask her if she remembered a time when billboards and signs outside pubs across the country read 'No Dogs, No Blacks, No Irish.'

I wanted to point out the similarity between those billboards then and what she's saying now in February 2014.

I wanted to say that it's a 'hatred breeds hatred' sort of thing — that once a group becomes absorbed into the culture, it gives that group a license to oppress whoever else remains outside it.

I wanted to point out to her that the parish records from St Giles in the Fields — not far from where this bus now is headed — note that, as far back as 1640, pernicious views persisted that Irish immigrants were idle beggars, who'd perfected the disposition of workshyness that set a bad example for Londoners.

But Customer–Colleague Interaction Policy No.2 kicked in, and the customer is always right, so I felt it was my Tesco duty to say, "*Yeah, yeah, one hundred percent, madame. You're so, so right. Right on. They should all go back to where they came from*" — namely, the port of Tilbury, where they'd been welcomed in 1948 and invited to settle through the

British Nationality Act that gave citizenship in the UK for anyone born in a British colony.

With anti-Romanian and anti-Bulgarian sentiment very much in vogue right now, it's confusing that the list of those no longer welcome has been expanded beyond your classic 'Paddy beggar' and 'Windrush darkie'. The signs outside the proverbial pubs will have to be massive to fit all the words in.

But her eyes were so startled, so milky and bloodshot, so wildly unfocused that I thought I'd leave it. Instead I simply repeated,

"How can I enhance your supermarket experience?"

She didn't bite, nor did she seem to feel the hook. She just repeated that 'they' needed to be sent back, and she limped off wheeling her trolley.

The next stop is ALDWYCH/DRURY LANE. This is the final stop of this service.
All change please.

I disembark onto the Strand's gentle crescent, and linger by the retired bus's exhaust pipe to heat my hands. This works until the fumes make me dizzy, and I have to cross the road and lean against another bus stop to clear my head. I scan the routes. Yes, the No.1 will take me deep into South East while I continue to try to fix up some accommodation. A bit of good fortune: the bus pulls up and I board. Again, I hide the Freedom Pass photo from the driver as I tap in. Upstairs I slot it back into my wallet, between my Oyster Card and Draft No.5 of my Letter to an Incarcerated Sibling. Annoyingly, I seem to have lost the last one, the one which I felt had the wording almost correct. This new draft I wrote in the style of the Soviet absurdist Daniil Kharms, in an attempt to inject a bit of levity to the bleak earnestness of my inquiry. But reading it back now, I see just whimsy and caprice. It'll need another attempt.

I mull over the name 'Mollie', not feeling quite the connection to it that I usually feel when an alias comes over me.

This is the No.1 to CANADA WATER

My pocket vibrates with the latest response. **Ah bruv no good I'm afraid. You tried the YMCA?**

I thumb another message to another contact. The automated text from O2 appears: **15p per text. Remaining credit is £12.97.**

The bus gives a horse snort as it moves off, with its new assortment of passengers shuffling around, filling up the top deck. More commuters come aboard, many with towering bouquets and bags of chocolate boxes. That furious father will probably be home by now. Maybe Little Shane has calmed down too, probably squatting in front of the TV watching the *Frozen* digital download, while upstairs, mummy and daddy grab a precious moment.

These are the fruits of all the weeks of preparation for Valentine's Day, a carefully orchestrated campaign of toys and films to keep babies distracted while parents make babies. Already by mid-Jan, there were F&F mannequins beginning to crowd the mezzanine in their drapings of lace and sexy string. Lingerie, négligées, suspenders, stockings. The feathery silks, thin as smoke, the colours and contours somehow edible. And around the rest of the store, on every billboard and hording, there appeared in early February images of bras, rouge lips, and coal-smudged eyes. Caress, pout, gaze. All of this contributed to the unwelcome reminder that my drought's been elongating itself across the months. Phone companies should devise some sort of automated text, like a warning about impending nuclear annihilation:

ALERT: It's been 1 year, 6 months, and 18 days since your last fuck. Reply for more info on how to end it. This is not a drill.

I'm not any good at maths, but this totalling of days is one I've never forgotten. My last lay was during the London Olympics opening ceremony, which was streaming on a laptop screen while I and a member of the university's netball society undressed in her room. Just as I was rolling on the condom, I glanced up to see Daniel Craig in a tux escorting the Queen along a palace corridor, corgis around their feet. How long ago that all seems, with the pair's Union Jack parachutes descending into the oval of the stadium.

One day ago — T-minus 1 to V-Day — I was in the Staff Room, rummaging in the veg box for a nametag. I'd begun hoping to find a 'Lothario' or a 'Casanova', aliases that might manifest a relief to the frustration. No such luck. Instead it was 'Michael' that I pinned to my chest, a name which now, on this shuddering bus, makes me shudder even more.

I've been holding off from thinking too much about this, but I need to make sense of what happened with Lottie and Vic yesterday. The bus is now rattling along Waterloo Road, just passing Morley Street. I could do with some fried chicken. Ah yes, my picnic. I retrieve some snacks and snap open my bottle of vodka, with my notebook open on my lap. I'll graze and gulp while I try to make it make sense.

Yesterday I was 'Michael', and throughout his shift, Michael found himself staring at the Deli Counter's circular blade and thinking of flesh. He'd blink away and realise he'd been watching how the brie and other soft cheese was being wrapped up. Hard to know if this frigidity was self-imposed or the result of some deficit in his personality and constitution. During his lunchbreak, he did a quick stat check, like in *GTA V*, to try and understand why he'd been failing to bring about the circs of any kind of sexual congress. *GTA V*, the coloniser of the Electronics shelves, a video game which Vic had recently been so vehemently driven to each night. You might think that playing video games doesn't get you girls, but Vic is evidence to the contrary, with Lottie curling up beside him each night as he takes a hatchet to a passerby on Del Perro Ferris wheel.

From a drawer in the Staff Room's kitchenette, Michael took a greasy spoon and inspected his warped reflection in its convex silver, while the communal fridge hummed merrily in the corner. Michael's stats were:

Stamina: 17%
Strength: 28%
Stealth: 64%
Flying: n/a
Driving: n/a
Lung capacity: 52%

This self-evaluation revealed nothing about why the approach of V-Day was affecting Michael so badly, why his sexual frustration was so fierce. All morning he'd noticed a solid, leaden feeling, an accumulation of days' worth of weight. It felt like between his legs was a pair of those easy-peel Jaffa oranges you get in the netted bags. And he planned to do something about it when he got back to the Angel accommodation that evening.

After his shift, he treated himself to a few mini-bottles of Merlot from aisle No.20. There was a discount on these minis, so he bought five. That was already a win. He unpinned the nametag but still felt the need for an alias, given what he had in mind for the evening. Fuck it — he'd pretend he was Casanova. So he got on the Tube as he imagined Casanova would. He unscrewed the cap of the first of his mini Merlots as he imagined Casanova would. He read from Sheila Heti's *How Should a Person Be?* as he imagined Casanova would, nodded along in wine-fuelled agreement to the line '*there's so much fucking to do*' as he imaged Casanova would. When the train stopped, the momentum jogged his hand mid-sip, and he'd dropped his copy of *How Should a Person Be?* and spilled his wine, wiping a streak from his cheek as he imagined Casanova would. He arrived back in Angel with one mini remaining.

Michael-cum-Casanova had always prided himself on a healthy approach to carnality. By their early twenties, most young men count themselves as connoisseurs of hand relief. But to maintain this expertise you need to practice. Regularly. And regular practice necessitates privacy. And privacy necessitates a room of one's own. But Casanova faced a predicament. He had the status of pauper, not king. Without his own space, he put the 'wan' in 'wank'.

He was four mini Merlots in, and he'd arrived at the Angel accommodation. No *GTA* on the living room TV, Vic was out — working late, apparently. Lottie was at the kitchen table, making a surprise gift for Vic: a 'his and hers' pair of T-shirts printed with a photo of the happy couple embracing on a beach. She'd been working on them for weeks whenever Vic was out, asking me (no, not me, asking Michael, or rather, asking Casanova) for advice on which photo to use, what size T-shirt, what colour to go for.

"Blue," Michael'd slurred as he dashed upstairs.

So Lottie was busy downstairs working on her gift. Good. This covert operation needed some time alone. Well, a couple of minutes. Two Mins Love. First, he closed the spare room's door.

Stealth: 83%

Then unbuttoned his work trousers. Then it was all about efficiency, working at it, with all the desperate, grim vigour of someone who recognised its necessity. In the immediate aftermath, he'd probably feel rotten inside. *La petite mort* never has a sell-by date because it was never fresh to start with.

But he was doing this as a dirty duty to himself. He didn't want to be one of the grocers, flower sellers, or pastry makers in Sheila Heti's list, all of whom have no joy, have no fucking, who have nothing but dreariness. No. This is how a person should be, he'd said to himself.

This is how a person should be.

Strength: 32%... 66%

This is how a person should be. Getting a grip of himself to lose himself just for a couple of minutes. Going AWOL. Disappearing.

Flying: 30%... 60%... 90%

"Oh, I'm..."

But that wasn't him saying that. It wasn't one of those outer body experiences out of which poems spring.

No.

A head swivel and Lottie was in the doorway.

Stealth: 0%

Strength: 24%... 15%... 8%... 0%

"Oh, I'm," she repeated. "Oh, oh, sorry, I..." A T-shirt was draped over her trembling forearm, like she was waiting on a table "...wanted your opinion but..." — she withdrew, her arm lowering as she recoiled, the T-shirt heaping on the floor — "...it can wait..."

The door closed with a squeaking click.

This bus is being DIVERTED. The next stop is INNER LONDON CROWN COURT

Casanova was nowhere to be seen. In his place, Michael, the naked ape, was hunched alone in his silence. He unhunched, re-buttoned his trousers, his belt buckle jangling like a tawdry sleigh bell. He hobbled over to the closed door, pressed his ear to the wood to catch the steady thump of footsteps descending. He picked up the T-shirt that Lottie had let fall. She'd not taken his advice and opted instead for the crimson fabric, the rouge of Cupid, the colour of a crime scene. He held it up. It was entirely red except for the clear white and blue image in the centre — of Lottie and Vic in beach-bod attire, clutching one another, Lottie's huge smile as curved and bright as the white sandy cove behind them. The words printed across the bottom of the image, in lovey-dovey squiggling cursive read BE MY LEVANTINE.

Either this was a reference to Vic's East Mediterranean heritage of which Michael was not aware (*Vicangelopoulos*?) or it was an epic typo. Either way, this T-shirt was a gift intended to be kept secret and so he'd tucked it into his rucksack in case Vic should follow Lottie's lead and enter the room without knocking.

Shit, the T-shirt. Twenty-four hours later and it's still in my rucksack, somewhere buried beneath all the snacks I've brought with me. I take a deep swig of vodka as the bus rattles on.

This is GREAT DOVER STREET. The next stop is BARTHOLOMEW STREET

Michael'd stayed in the spare bedroom for a bit, feeling less and less like anything. The Merlots' rich taste had swiftly soured the flesh of his tongue and gums. After a while, he'd heard Vic arrive home, and then the three of them had assembled in their respective places at the dinner table: Vic and Michael opposite one another, Lottie to Michael's left. Out of sight but so acutely not out of mind.

To a passive audience poking their plates of lentils and greens like it was playdough, Vic was full-throttling the anti-immigration engine: "...all I'm saying is that there are too many cars on the roads, too many people in supermarket queues, too many in GP waiting rooms. It's a population explosion that's all a consequence of what's happening in Syria. It's all true, I heard it on a podcast. That region, where all these people are coming from for a better life, we just can't take any more of them. If they want a better life, they should stay where they are and fight for it."

Michael had occasionally responded with a non-committal murmur, and all the time was aware that Lottie was there, just there, her head bowed over her plate. He could only assume her eyes were lowered too, but whether out of embarrassment for what Vic was saying or out of disgust at what she'd witnessed upstairs, Michael didn't know. Judging from the way Vic was going on about skull sizes, about master and worker bees, about native extinction, about how he'd found a cheat code to get a flame-thrower to torch cars, Michael reckoned she'd not told him.

TOWER BRIDGE ROAD

After the long evening meal, Michael had scooped up the plates and reached out for the salad spoons just as Lottie did the same. Michael's little finger, the naked ape's last digit, grazed the back of hers and they'd glanced at one another, her eyes widening in a way that Michael couldn't quite discern, somewhere between pleading and fear.

So, this morning, I'd woken up. There was no sign of Casanova, nor was there any residue of Michael. The shame about the previous night still lingered, as did the heady effects of the Merlots. But any aliases had fizzled out sometime in the early hours. No stat check was required. It was simply:

Personality: 0%

It was *moi*. Yours falsely, back to the old self, left to face the day and my hosts alone. In the bluish light of 6AM, I dressed but stayed in the spare room, listening to the sounds of Lottie and Vic's slippered feet padding along the corridor and down the stairs. Theirs is an early rising sort of household and I'd learned to adjust.

I waited for my moment to dash for the front door, to avoid any small talk. Something about this time in the AM makes it impossible to put on a front of any kind, let alone construct the sort of Norman fortress required to protect the self from the aftermath of last night if I bumped into Lottie. I heard the muffled sound of coffee beans grinding, and shortly afterwards nosed the brew's heartening waft. I bided my time for them both to depart for work, sitting on the floor by the spare room's door. While I waited, I opened my laptop and checked the morning news.

A news report from this time last year had resurfaced. In February 2013, a dead sperm whale was found washed up on Spain's south coast. It had swallowed 17 kg of plastic waste dumped into the sea by farmers growing vegetables for British supermarkets. Apparently, Almeria had transformed itself into Europe's winter market garden thanks to the plastic greenhouses where the veg grows. Local farmers reported that Tesco, Waitrose, and Sainsbury's are all valued customers.

GRIGGS PLACE

I'd heard the front door slamming. This was my chance. I grabbed my rucksack and heelied down the stairs, but found my path blocked. Vic, dressing-gowned, steaming brew in hand, leaning in the lounge's doorframe, blocking my lunge for the front door.

"Y'alrighty, mate?" he asked.

"Yeah, just thought you'd left for work."

Vic folded himself onto the sofa, scooping up a controller. "Got the day off, 'cause of my working late," grinning. "How about a bit of *GTA*, then?"

"Sorry, I've got to get to work myself."

"It's not even 7AM. I swear last night you said you weren't due in until later this morning."

Did I? Fuck, that Merlot must've messed with my mind.

"C'mon, mate. Just half an hour. I might have to force you, this being my house and all."

I paused.

"Ah just joshing with ya, mate."

"Why not," as I turned from the front door and dropped my bag.

"I can show you the flame-thrower cheat code I found. It's proper funny."

He unpaused the menu and continued playing.

And then out of nowhere, *ex nihilo*, Vic said, "So, Lotts said about you wanking last night."

"What no I mean but..."

"Ahhh maaate. Don't worry about it. She told me this morning and I was like, what's a man to do? He can't help it. Men are apes, it's biologically impossible for us not to want to cum."

"I um it's ah..."

"You seen *Wolf of Wall Street* yet?"

"No I..."

"Well there's this bit where Matthew McConaughey orders DiCaprio to wank like two, three times a day, to make sure his mind is focused on all those screens and digits. He's not wrong. I've started doing it at work too. Keeps me focused long into the night."

It was too early for this.

"Eh, mate, there's no shame in it. Lotts catches me all the time. And I'm always saying to her, 'Look, I'm a man. I can't help it. I'm biologically programmed to produce semen. What do you want me to do about it? Cut my balls off?' Ah, here's the flame-thrower. Watch this."

He incinerated a bus, with little avatars falling out in flames on the road.

"It's good, isn't it?"

"Very. Look I've got to get on."

"Yeah, alright."

"Cheers for understanding, Vic. Particularly with Valentine's Day and all that."

He pressed the pause button. "You what? Fuuck. That's today innit? I'd forgot all about Valentine's. Cheers for the reminder there, got me out of a bollocking with the missus."

"Yeah, in fact I'll make other plans and stay elsewhere tonight. Give you and Lottie some time alone together."

Vic snorted. "It'll just be *GTA* and a suckjob, hopefully, but yeah, nice one. That's probably a good idea."

I was then out into the punishing, bracing frost, contorted by the cold morning but relieved at having dodged the conversational draft. I put on the burners through the streets, avoiding the iciest slabs, to the Tube station and clattered westwards, thinking it'd be tricky to arrange alternative accommodation at such last minute but knowing I had nothing else. Outside Tesco, I'd texted Freddy:

> Hey Freddy sorry it's last minute but my current accom has fallen through and I'm pretty desperate. Is one of the rooms free at yours or anywhere? I'll really take anything cheers.

It was to this message that Freddy had responded that the utility cupboard was already taken, that he had a girl staying over, but that the upstairs bathroom was on offer. At 9AM that had seemed a preposterous offer but now, after a day replaying the *onan interruptus* in my head, with no other accommodation secured... it's looking more tempting.

ANCHOR STREET

A man and a woman settle in the seats in front of mine, both in black coats and black ushankas. Her head is resting on his shoulder. A big bouquet across her lap, dropping pollen and floral lint onto the wet floor. They snuggle and nuzzle one another in that private way that is so compelling in public.

To block out the kissy-wissy sounds before the couple begins their V-Day PDA, I retrieve my iPod, plug in my headphones, and thumb the wheel to a new track that Lance and I recorded — of our poetry-jazz jams. The Waddle Cantos, we're calling them. His double bass thumps pleasantly, and cymbals borrowed from some music software sprinkle rhythm all around. It's an Oscar Peterson-ish jaunt, with me reading from 'Love's Philosophy' by Shelley. '*What are all these kissings worth, If thou kiss not me?*' Lance suggested we do a whole album of classic poems set to jazz. I like the idea, but since his niece burst onto the scene only like a month ago or whatever I haven't heard from him. No chance of crashing at his for a long time I reckon.

Love is everywhere, ubiquitous, so mainstream, so fucking marketed it should be stamped with a ©. '*The threat of the arrow is everywhere at once, not just in the heart,*' as Karen Green puts it. We can only suspect that, like the man who invented karaoke, or the internet, that Cupid seethes with outright fury for the other 364 days as he calculates what his earnings would've been had he gone in for a full patent.

During my lunchbreak earlier today, I'd reached the end of World Foods and seen Cármen, up on the mezzanine, with Alby. He was making her laugh, and she was even stroking the metal banister that's supposed to stop anyone jumping to the shop floor.

Shortly afterwards Alby had entered the Staff Canteen and dashed over to me. I already guessed what he was after: "I need a gift for Cármen. Any ideas?"

"You can have these."

On the table was a box of Ferrero Rocher.

He looked sideways at me. "You're not giving them to anyone?"

I'd bought them with the intention of sending them to Lottie as an apology. But somehow a 5 × 5 box of small wafery hazelnut confection balls didn't seem like it'd be enough to make up for what she'd walked in on.

"A barren wasteland of a V-Day for me. Go on, take the chocolates. Maybe you'll have more luck."

I slid them towards Alby. "Cheers, lad." And he'd sped off, peeling the REDUCED sticker from the box. I returned to work, spending my afternoon trying to secure some accommodation other than Freddy's.

SPA ROAD

The woman in front shifts slightly, more pollen falling on the floor of the bus. The man puts his arm around her and holds her shoulders tightly. I'm still listening to the jazz-poems, so I can't hear the sweet-nothings he's surely murmuring into her ear. Why can't I have a bit of this? I've got all the lines of poetry ready to go. She turns towards him, and I expect to see a clear, smiling face gazing up at him. Instead it's tear-drenched. He passes her a tissue and she sniffs away a sob.

I unplug my headphones and listen in.

"We should really write the card before we get there," he sighs.

Through her sobs, she nods.

I notice that the bouquet is not of the romantic kind but made up of lilies. And their clothes are not the amorous armour against winter but the jackdaw feathering of grief.

He's got a card open on his lap. "Shall I start with 'We're sorry for your loss?'" he suggests.

The gloom of London, a melancholy that asserts itself even in the midst of the designated day of romance.

I'm surprised he's managed to get a funeral card. We removed all our Sympathy and New Baby range to free up space for V-Day.

Throughout Tesco, where all the cards are stacked like red and gold telegrams, you can tug any one of them from the shelf and open it to find some trite phrase. Love creates its own lexicon, and those trying to learn the lingo may be shocked to discover how many of the diminutive nicknames that one lover might bestow on another are borrowed from other aisles: 'pickle', 'chickpea', 'dumpling', 'cupcake' — love absorbs each of those food groups into its all-consuming lexicon, while annual inflation makes the cards on which these nicknames appear increasingly expensive. Cupid swoops down and lets fly, administering an annual wound on the bank balances of the romantically unimaginative and gullible.

But even love's language has its limits. Yes it's big on jarred, vinegared veg and tinned pulses, but it's never 'gammon', 'spam', or even the cutest of culinary abbreviations: 'spag bol'. Perhaps it's the 'i' and 'u' sounds vs the 'a' and 'o'. Or maybe everyone just needs to start looking beyond the Tesco aisles for their romantic inspiration.

This bus is being DIVERTED due to ROADWORKS. Please await driver's instructions.

The driver explains our redirection, though I'm not listening. I'm texting Freddy to ask if the rugs and cushions are still available for the bathroom suite. I ping the bell.

"I'm sorry," I mutter over the shoulders of the couple in front, as the bus coughs and splutters itself to a pneumatic standstill, and alongside pensioners and prams I exit with my rucksack snail shelled across my back, leaving streaks of melting slime across the frosted pavement.

An hour later, having walked to the nearest Tube stop and used Mollie's Freedom Pass to get to Streatham, I'm at Freddy's house fortifying the porcelain sides of the upstairs bath with cushions. I settle down in the mossy garden of the bath, cocooned under a rug, and though my limbs are constricted by the narrow crib my eyes follow the route of black mould growing up the grooves between the shower tiles. It isn't that the tiles are covered in mould so much as the black fur has fenced off the white porcelain. Other than the mould, my belongings, and a fly at the window, the bathroom is empty. Fortunately, there're another two toilets in this enormous house, so I shouldn't be disturbed during the night.

My phone vibrates on the lino floor. I lean over the bath's side to retrieve it.

> hey there! just wanted to say thanks for staying at your friend's house 2night. Vic and I really need some time today for Valentines. And also So sorry to ask this but is there any chance you could find another place to stay for a while? I think me and Vic really need some time. BTW you can chuck out that T-shirt, you must've picked it up by accident and put it with ur stuff. it had a spelling mistake anway. L.

On top of the cistern is a scented candle, usually on hand to cover the smell of defecation or rising damp. Tonight I turn off the bathroom light and hold a match to the wick, watching amber glow and flit across the shower curtain's folds, against the tiles. By the flickering hues and shadow, like the cross-section of a Jaffa Cake, I take out my diary and ceremonially draw a line through the upcoming dates when I was scheduled to stay at Lottie and Vic's. I'll have to find alternatives on a long-term basis, but for now I'll lie here, head against the bath's hard, cold rim, watching the house fly dart around and settle on a white tile. I didn't know flies could survive the winter. Its head is pointing downwards towards me, its wings pointing up towards the shower curtain's rail.

The white tile makes a silhouette of this *musca domestica*, its little black body tapered and its curved wings protruded to create the shape of the quintessential Valentine's Day heart. The candle soon dies out, its wick too stubby for lingering light.

I wriggle slightly, skin squeaking against the sides of my porcelain coffin. Perhaps this is why we all like a deep soak at the end of a long working day, because it readies us for the grave.

CHAPTER SIX

ELECTRONICS

London in March 2014, the swagger of capitol in all directions. North, south, west, but particularly east: past Greenwich, Dagenham, Tilbury Docks, and Grays, along the Thames Estuary by Gravesend's ASDA, where pre-urbia is demarcated by skidmarked brown belt to which developers will give names. Every so often, overhead, is an electricity pylon, like a centipedic clothes airer. All will be washed away by the daily slurp of the tide into the Narrow Sea.

It's hard to imagine but, once upon a time, the Thames was a tributary of the Rhine. Some thirty million years ago, give or take. That probably explains some of the resentment that the British feel towards the Continent: our most famous, identifiable body of water is an off-shoot of something European.

Next to me on the Tube is a tourist family. How do I know? What are the clues? The anoraks, the sensible GORE-TEX shoes, the bumbags. The strained concentration on the faces of the adults and the bored leg-swinging of their tired offspring. *Mutter* has a *Deutsch zu Englisch* phrase book in her coat pocket, and *Vater* has an Ordnance Survey map spread out across his lap. It looks like uncooperative bed linen. In Germanic voices, they're talking about London, studying the map.

"*Sehr groß*," she murmurs.

"*Etwas groß*," he replies.

The little girl runs her finger along the blue Thames, following its loops and bends, like she's playing the buzzing wire game.

"*Schätzchen, bitte*," the father says sternly.

The girl takes her hand away, kneels on the seat, then stands and reaches up to begin tracing instead the more angular Thames as it appears on the wall's Underground map. By the time her finger has reached the Cutty Sark bit, the train doors open, and her family beckon her away. I follow them off the train and can just make out her protestations which, although German, I imagine go something like, "Bwut I didn't get to finish twacing my finger along the wiver."

Up the escalators and burped out of Earl's Court. Today's whiteboard: '*May your choices reflect your hopes, not your fears — Nelson Mandela.*'

Inside the store, along the newspaper shelves, there's a theme: *The Daily Mail* is using an enlarged image of the 'Oscar Selfie', under which is a headline about a Downing Street arrest for child pornography. *The Guardian* is also using the enlarged image of the 'Oscar Selfie', under which is a headline about Putin's tightening grip on Crimea. And *The Times* includes the 'Oscar Selfie' story but only in red letters at the top, accompanied by the phrase THE BEAUTIFUL AND THE BLAND, under which it dedicates the rest of the page to an image of houses on fire and the headline: UKRAINE CRISIS SPREADS AS RUSSIANS ADVANCE. It's hard to know which of these papers Mandela would have me choose if I wanted to communicate my hopes. The publications which most regularly fly off our shelves are *Take A Break* and *That's Life!*, both of which are owned by Bauer, a German Media Group, another channelling of Europe to these aisles. Today there's a mag running a headline about Chris Martin and Gwyneth

Paltrow's divorce. It's being described as 'The Conscious Uncoupling of Heaven and Hell.'

There's the sudden sound of smashing and shouting from another part of the store, and a Tannoy announcement asking for security on Wine & Spirits. A few minutes later, I'm called for, along with Nick Dale. We've been given the directive of CAYG, each of us starting at separate ends of the aisle to mop spillages and sweep the glass. There are great gaps in the shelves where there are usually bottles of French and Spanish claret, that now slosh bloodily on the floor. The 'Kent' selection, as we call it, of cider and hoppy ales remains untouched. As we approach one another using squeegee-tipped brooms to wipe, we drop to our knees and crawl, scooping up the more slender fragments. We get close enough for me to ask him about the ranting customer who's caused all this damage. He fills me in on the details while our thin rubber gloves barely remain intact against the shards, trying to mop up these rivers.

"I think he was a very troubled individual," Nick surmises. "The blue tattoos above his eyes indicate this."

"That's how tattoos run and fade, into blue, over many years," I explain over the tinkling of gathered glass.

"Ooow!" Nick suddenly yelps, recoiling his hand, folding it into the crease of his armpit. He whistles through his teeth, eyes scrunched. "Ow ow ow." Then he's silent, frozen, he opens his eyes, looks at me, smiles in the manner of Ledger's Joker, and snorts, holds up his stigmata'd palm. And then after a pause that's slightly too long follows up with, "Ha. Got you. It's just the red wine."

"Very good, Nick, but April Fools' is next month."

Nick continues his CAYG. "There isn't any glass on this planet that can puncture my skin." He holds up his hands towards me. "All these years of building in my garage have given me an extra hard layer. It's really a superpower."

"How is the Dalek coming along?"

Nick closes his eyes as if recalling a wonderful memory. "Yesterday, I drove to Basingstoke after my shift to buy a new flame-thrower. Today is my last shift for three days. It will just be me and my new Dalek in my garage. Bliss."

Cyborgs and robots no longer belong to the realm of outer space. Judging from Nick's tranquil smile, these machines serve a desire to inhabit inner space. We want tech to fill our intimate, most internal nooks and crannies.

"Look here." He takes out his phone and begins to swipe through the photos. "When it's ready, it'll be centre-stage at next year's Comic Con." He shows me a step-by-step of how he's built it.

"The silver dome for its head is actually a fibreglass casting from an original Imperial prop. A rather nice bit of lineage."

He swipes the screen.

"That's the manipulator arm, and that's where the fender will go when it arrives from Texas." He double-taps the screen, and the robot's midriff enlarges. "That's the suction cup" — he runs a finger vertically up the screen — "and there's its skirt." He swipes his finger left across the screen, and the photo changes, from metal and rivets to flesh. Soft, rosy, curved flesh. Woman's flesh.

"Ah, that's my fiancée. Sorry, that was not meant to happen. Sorry. Error error error," he snorts nervously and affects a Dalek voice, "EXTERMINATE. THIS. IS. A. MALFUNCTION." He quickly swipes again, and the Dalek returns, but the atmos down here amongst the sticky wine and broken glass has changed. His fiancée's body lingers, imprinted in the conversational space between us, standing in profile in black lace underwear — from our F&F V-Day range it looks like. Her face towards the camera, her grin huge, and her arms and palms out in a show of celebration as she presents her swollen belly.

"Sorry," he says again as he pockets the phone. "I should have put those on my desktop by now. Stupid, stupid, stupid Nick."

There's a crunchy quiet as we swab the floor. For once I'm grateful for the store's playlist, with Beyoncé's 'XO' soaring loudly over the speakers. I've heard this so many times now that I can quote not only all the lyrics but also the sample featured at the beginning, which is a recording of Jay Greene, the Flight Director for the 1986 Challenger Spaceship disaster, uttering the famous words: "*obviously a major malfunction*." Apparently Greene wasn't supposed to oversee the spaceship's launch on that fateful day, but due to staffing shortages, he was assigned the working title of Flight Director.

How far along is she, I want to ask Nick, but this kind of intimate curiosity might precipitate the building of a relationship that neither of us is looking for.

'Your heart is glowin',

And I'm crashin' into you.'

"The skirt looks good," I venture, and his startled expression makes me clarify with, "on the robot, I mean. What about the claw and the sensor, when're you attaching them?"

He breathes more easily. "Already got them. The claw's straightforward, just a stainless steel thing that a welder I know made for me. Only £600, mate's rate. And the sensor, actually it's one of the same sensors we have here on the main entrance's doors. Same company that Tesco uses. Just a binary sensor that activates when there's motion. Very simple to operate, if you know how."

I'm reminded of Heath's foiled getaway, thwarted by the doors that refused to open for him. As if by telepathy, perhaps one of his other superpowers, Nick adds: "Yeah, a few months ago there was a colleague — ex-colleague now, I'm pleased to say — who tried to escape with a lot of expensive items, but I'd caught him on the CCTV and knew what he was doing, so I changed the settings on the sensor so that no one could leave the store. He was waving his arms like a madman, but the doors wouldn't open."

So Nick was the tech hero who discovered Heath's crime.

Nick's phone is safely away in his pocket, but as we continue to CAYG he keeps taking it out to check its blank, dark screen — as if it's listening in, or as if his fleshy, pregnant fiancée might choose to climb through the screen, expand to her full, fleshy proportions right here on the aisle, and accuse him of showing off photos of her to his colleagues.

'We don't have forever,
Oh baby, daylight's wasting.'

While Beyoncé continues to sing, we carry on cleaning, but our attention abruptly turns to the aisle's end, where one of the elderly checkout workers, Drew, is being escorted by a pair of men — Wart and Feral — out of the store. Drew tries to resist, pulling his thin arms against their grip, but they hold him firm.

"That is a sad sight," says Nick.

"Was Drew involved in this smash up?"

"No, no. Incorrect. It's just that he's not been able to keep up with his role on the checkout till, so he has to go. See?"

I turn back and watch as a hi-vizzed delivery man wheels a self-service machine into view. He begins to wire it up to cables across the floor.

"A beautiful unit, isn't it?" admires Nick. "It'll take Drew's professional responsibilities and be much, much more efficient."

This is the latest scuttlebutt aboard the HMteSco. Self-service machines are soon to be introduced, and many members of staff will lose their jobs. Drew is one of the first replacements.

"So everyone's job is under threat?" I ask.

"I'll be alright," he follows up. "I'll keep my job. Upper Management have already primed me with the responsibilities to run the stats and data on who will get the chop."

"So your job will be to work out who loses their job? That's a lot to put on your shoulders."

"Not really. I don't have to do much. It's the software which is the real hero. I just input the staff member's credentials, and the info comes back about what time they clocked in and out each day."

"I mean, moral responsibility."

He frowns. "Again, that doesn't really factor into the calculations. We have the CCTV footage that does some face recognition to identify where each shop floor worker is in the store at any given time. From that, we can ascertain who is most efficient and who is not."

"Sounds terrifying."

"Be careful who you say that to. We're having a regional meeting later this month, with staff from all over the country coming here, and this new technology will be rolled out. It's the way of the future, and it's exciting. Total automation. No need for time-wasting chit-chat."

"What we're doing now?"

"That's not what this space is for," he gestures around us. "This place is for profit. I could show you a pie-chart with profits lost through time spent in non-essential communication. I'm sure there are other places for that kind of thing, but not here."

By this point, Nick has cleaned up the final shards of glass on his side of the aisle and has risen from his knees to stand over me. "It's inevitable that this tech is coming. But for now the store will want to transition towards more efficient workers. The time will come when everyone needs to ask themselves if they want to remain." Off he walks along the aisle, the bin liners in each of his hands creaking with broken glass. I plead with the universe that a shard will burst the bag's side, but Nick turns at the aisle's end and is away.

I continue to clean. Somehow, I'm less efficient, even though he was doing most of the talking. This will probably get flagged in my data and CCTV evidence. It's unpleasant to consider, but it's hard to find fault in Nick's reasoning. This is a business, not a community centre.

By the end of my shift, what Nick explained to me has congealed into something that really makes sense, and it lingers like the scent of the rubber gloves, the musk of fermenting wine, and the sting of cleaning product on my fingers.

Alby and I clock off together. I test out Nick's logic under another's scrutiny. Alby listens as we leave the store, then replies, "You do realise that all this tech can only push us to one side? Or out of the door entirely?"

"Yes, maybe. But Nick was saying that the efficiency of the store would improve. More customers, more revenue, a better service."

"And fewer of us workin' here."

"If total, effective profit is the goal, which it surely must be, then that's just the way it is."

Alby blows his nose on a folded tissue, spreads it out and examines the laddered trails of off-white snoz jam. "Look, I'm allergic to all this weirdness you're spoutin'."

"I'm just repeating what Nick was saying."

"Well you're doin' a boss job of mimicking him, for sure. Speakin' like a true autistic."

We walk on in silence, letting the dark afternoon's traffic wash through the crossroads. It's not like Alby to talk like that. It's more like Dan's style.

"Alright. Sorry, lad, that was a bit rough," Alby concedes. "I'm just so fuckin' sick of how much fuckin' waste there is, not just of the store's produce, but the staff, too. We're all for the landfill, it looks like. Pub, if you're free?"

"I am."

"Good, I've got something to show you."

"Okay but leave your Danisms outside would you?"

"Will do. It's just quite an addictive way to talk, the whole un-PC thing. Like when Dan called Nick's *Doctor Who* thing a 'retardis'."

"It's not just that. Maybe it's something broader in the culture, where autism is concerned."

"How so?"

"In Dave Eggers's *The Circle*."

"You've already told me about that book, lad. I'm not interested in reading it. I want some of that John Milton you bang on about."

In the past month or so, I've noticed that Alby has become much more warmed up to the idea of reading. This is progress.

"I'm not making a recommendation, it's a citation. But just hold off judging for a second. You might learn something. In the novel, the protagonist Mae argues with her ex-boyfriend about privacy on social media. And her ex describes Mae's adherence to tech as 'socially autistic'. And in Sheila Heti's *How Should A Person Be?*"

"Another book on your syllabus, I'm guessin'?"

"Yes. The narrator crashes at a wealthy man's apartment. He's in the tech industry, and has Asperger's syndrome. The narrator recounts that, apparently, he's good in bed because Silicon Valley boys read the 'how to' manuals on sex."

"So what're yous sayin', that we need to be more like tech bros?"

"No. Just that the culture is engaging with autism."

"Does this hypothesis extend beyond your MA syllabus, because you must be aware that 'culture' doesn't equal your university campus?"

I think for a moment. And then Vic's dressing-gowned figure sluices into my mind's irrigation system, bashing the XO buttons on his controller, flame-throwing an ambulance. "Actually, yes. You know what our most popular electronic product is at the moment?"

"*Grand Theft Auto V*, obviously."

"Exactly. In that game, there's a mission where a wheelchair-user called Lester tells Michael — he's the character you play as... well, you play as three different aliases, but anyway — Lester tells Michael that he has to behave like he's got low-level Asperger's in order to disguise himself as a web-designer so he can infiltrate a tech company called LifeInvader."

"This sounds like the beginnin' of one of your essays. 'Autism and Technological Aptitude in Pop Culture'. Somethin' like that?"

"Mate, honestly, it's been so long since I've had the time to sit down and properly think about that MA. Sometimes I forget I'm still doing it. But yeah, the point is surely that there's a broad misunderstanding of autism if it's only about being tech-savvy, and these books and videogames are part of that broadening. Just like the assumption that the majority of disabled people use wheelchairs."

"They don't?"

I give Alby a lingering look, trying to work out if he's doing a Danism again. He shrugs.

"London's Tube Map might have something to do with that assumption, since its logo for 'accessible' and 'disability-friendly' stations is a wheelchair."

The London Paralympic Games two summers ago ran all these adverts about improving attitudes towards disabled people, purporting to overturn assumptions and stereotypes about this vast, ignored demographic. As Alby's question maybe proves, this hasn't quite worked. Maybe the problem was that one of the Games' sponsors was ATOS, the tech company which provided the information system relied on by officials, athletes, and the media throughout the whole spectacle. This is the same ATOS which has been the recipient of lucrative contracts from the government to carry out Work Capabilities Assessments that judge, using stringent evaluation procedures and tribunals, whether disabled claimants are fit for work. I wonder if this is the limit of Nick's way of thinking, where relying solely on software makes life harder, if not impossible, for those who the technology puts on trial.

We continue on our route to the outer Earl's Court area, where the traffic is thick, and the pavement is rammed with crowds buffeted by the cold. All of a sudden, Alby drops back from my side, and I turn to see him skid across the street, taking something from his pocket and dropping it into the palm of a figure hunched over a trolley. Of course, it's Trolley Fella, and he looks grateful.

"The Troubadour?" Alby asks, as he returns to our side of the street. He doesn't seem to register his act of generosity, and I'm not going to congratulate him, or mention that I haven't any coins on me. It'd feel like pandering, or self-justification.

"I dunno," I answer, money on my mind. "It's a proper onslaught on the wallet, and we've used the last of Heath's hush money."

"Well, my impoverished pal, you're in luck. Our Elis has insisted that while his divorce is goin' on, he wants to contribute for his lodgings. Even though it's our cousin's pad, Elis wants to pay his way. So at a sibling's reduction, I'm still making it rain in the Mills household."

"Drinks on you?"

"Why not." And we trot to The Troub and find an empty room. "I've got something to show you," says Alby, opening his coat and drawing out a long tube. "Get a cloth from the bar, and I'll explain."

While I wipe down a table, Alby unrolls an enormous piece of thick paper, the size of a sheet from an office flip chart. The sheet curls back on itself like a swelling wave breaking on the shore, so we use empties to secure each of the four corners. Standing back, we take in the whole sheet. It's a blueprint of Tesco Kensington's shop floor, with a central walkway and the two sets of ten aisles, each drawn as an elongated rectangle.

"Looks like a ribcage, doesn't it?" Alby asks proudly.

Indeed it does. The central walkway a vertebral corridor, a stem from which the different aisles are offshoots. Looked at it from this perspective, from Leviathan's towering height, it's a cartography that conveys territory, each aisle a region, a constituency of the retail body.

"What do you think? A thing of beauty, isn't it?"

"How did you get this?"

Alby sighs, running a fingertip along the map, from aisle No.3 (Ready Meals), via No.10 (World Foods), all the way up to No.19 (Confectionary). "It's a tale of seduction, betrayal, and redemption, involving me, Borges, and Cármen."

It takes me a second to process this, and then a new tab opens up on my mind's flickering screen. I remember that look on Alby's face, of relief and gratitude, when I slid the Ferrero Rocher to him.

"The Valentine's Day chocolates. You gave them to her in exchange for this map?"

"It wasn't just the chocs, lad. I had to put in some proper groundwork myself, too."

"So come on then, Ferreromeo, share your tips."

"I shall. But first the booze," Alby pulls out banknotes and goes to the bar. There's a pause of a few minutes while he orders us a pair of pints, during which I examine the blueprint. Some time ago, I mulled over the convergence of writing and retail, but looking down at this map, I see where the comparison breaks down. Writing is unruly. It goes anywhere, beyond topography, beyond aisles, but here the shop floor's pathways are set demarcations. I can sort of see the appeal about its order. Without this arrangement, without the borders, a customer's or a colleague's route around the store would be all over the place.

I'm about to put this to Alby, as I'm perturbed by whatever change it signals in me, but he's already setting the drinks down and continuing, "So, on Valentine's Day, Cármen was up on the mezzanine doing her Liaison Assistant thing. Cheers, by the way. And I made my approach towards her."

"Cheers. I could see you from the shop floor, making her laugh."

"Yeah, I just went up to her and started sayin' stuff about Borges, how much I love his penmanship and stuff."

"You'd never even heard of him until I leant you *Labyrinths*. How did you pull that off?"

"I have to admit, I didn't actually read it — well, not properly. I just went on SparkNotes. Then I read his story, 'On Exactitude in Science', and recited it to her — in English, then in Spanish. She fuckin' loved it."

"Why didn't you ask me? I could've told you much better stuff than SparkNotes."

"It wasn't so much quality I was after, lad."

"And you don't even speak Spanish."

"Google Translate, *laddito*. Anyway, that's when I got the chocs from yous. Nice one. Then, after my shift, we went for a couple of scoops 'round the corner, and then back to hers in Camden. Proper mission getting there and back home."

"How was it?"

Alby snaps his fingers, then puffs his chest out with exaggerated bravado, rocking his shoulders up and down with a simian strut, and takes on Dan's accent…

"I tell ya, matey, that Argentinian bird went daaan faster than the bloomin' Belgrano."

"Alright, alright, move it along."

He returns to his own posture and voice. "Nah, seriously. It was boss, lad. She gave me the map in the morning."

"And why d'ya need the map?"

Alby taps his nose and grins. "A map for lost lovers. Anything to get a bit of lunchbreak nookie."

This sounds like only a partial truth. "You're an animal, mate," I sigh, "taking Nadeem Aslam's name in vain like that. And Borges' too."

"From glancin' at *Labyrinths*, I reckon Borges would've been buzzin' that his work assisted in seduction. And besides, do you know how long it takes to memorise an entire story in Spanish and then recite it word for word?"

"I swear 'On Exactitude' is only about three lines long."

"Come on, lad. Don't you tell me you've never recited lines in the hope of a fuck."

He has me there — though it's never worked.

"Still, it's a feat of perseverance, no? And now my drought's over."

"That it is. You going to see her again?"

"Not sure. You know how she's always between stores. Hard to get hold of."

"And are you going to want another book recommendation for someone else in the supermarket? Maybe you want something about electric sheep to seduce Nick?"

"Ey?"

"Some of that Philip K. Dick?"

"I mean, I'm up for another book if that's what you're sayin'. What've I borrowed so far? Naomi Klein, the Grossmith brothers, and now Borges. What next?"

"Milton?"

He gulps his pint and flicks up a thumb.

"And why did you want this map?"

He restrains a belch and says stiflingly, "Monojit's orders. He wants our Knowledge improved."

"Knowledge?"

"Yeah, our Knowledge of all the aisles, all the produce on all of the shelves. He wants it memorised, and all the shelves on all the aisles in all the parts of the store. It's all part of improvin' efficiency and customer care."

"Like cabbies do with London's streets. The Knowledge?"

"Exactly."

"So he told you to seduce Cármen to give you the map?"

He grins. "No, that part was me, but he told me the other day he wants us to have better Knowledge. And so I thought this would be a foolproof way of us keepin' our jobs. If we're not goin' to fall victim to Nick's Grand Theft Automation."

The polygraph needle in my brain jitters slightly. I don't fully buy this. Maybe Alby's got some other scheme going on. But I might be wrong, and I've got things I want to tell him: "You know, earlier today when I was with Nick cleaning up a breakage, he told me about how the homemade Dalek he's building uses the same kind of sensor that Tesco uses for opening and closing the store's sliding doors."

"Interesting. That was Heath's Achilles heel."

"Yeah. Nick was actually the one who stopped Heath escaping, because he locked the glass doors by changing the sensor settings."

Alby looks into the middle distance, almost impressed. "Might have to ask Nick about that."

"How come?" I ask, flipping a beermat, failing to catch it.

Alby shrugs. "In case I want to make the store into a prison by lockin' the doors and hold the staff to ransom. I dunno."

"Well, if you do that, just choose a day when I'm not at work. Got too much catching up to do for my MA to be taken hostage."

"Noted."

"Anyway, how's this map going to improve our Knowledge?"

"I thought this would be the quickest way to help us avoid the sack. So, let's do it. A drinkin' game, right now. The shop floor Sambuca challenge. We're goin' to beat the machines. I'll get 'em in, and each time one of us answers with the wrong aisle, he does a shot."

And so the evening proceeds, with each of us leaning over the blueprint, testing the other's memory for different items on different shelves on different aisles.

"Linda McCartney sausages?"

"Piece of piss, lad. Aisle No.12, in the freezers."

"Baby's giraffe teething toy?"

"Easy. Aisle No.13."

"Masala sauce?"

I glance at the table, I'm already three shots in and my knees are turning to sponge. "Aisle No.7, surely. Sauces."

"Wrong, I'm afraid, lad. Aisle No.10, World Foods. Drink up."

I inhale the piercing herbal flavour and gulp it down. My throat's ignited.

By 10PM, all these aisles merge into one. Somehow, Alby's still standing.

- - - - -

"What are you having?"

"Lime and soda."

Dom looks at me, confused. "You're not drinking anymore?"

The memory of forgetting my journey back to my accommodation after the drinking game with Alby has left me reluctant to booze it for a while. The next morning at work, Alby and I were both dashing back and forth to Felon Place to throw up in the brambles. A week later, and I can still feel the Sambuca ooze on my skin, an aniseed sheen that makes me feel like I've been rolling around on a hospital floor.

The MA students are all assembled in The Fitzroy Tavern, as per tradition after our seminar. But we've been joined this evening by senior staff. This is a throwback to some previous epoch when there wasn't such a separation between staff and students, and yet still the chasm has established itself across the room. Staff leaning against the bar, at a slight remove from us students, who all huddle on the other side of the tables, occasionally glancing at the staff to see if there's a natural way of instigating conversation. It's like a Year 6 disco, where the girls would stay on one side and boys on the other — the boys desperately trying to think of any legit reason to totter over and address the forward guard.

In our paddock of students, the chat is all about the Stratford ticket, and who has likely won it. All the different postures have been adopted, from outright curiosity to barely stifled competitiveness, to (possibly faux) self-deprecation. So...

"What did you write about?"

"How about you?"

"That's a great idea."

"What, mine? Ah it was nothing, really."

"I just wrote something last minute."

"Really? I spent literally days slaving away at those 140 words."

"Monarchy in the modern era. A hard topic, I thought."

Notably, Dom and the other international students are very quiet, removed. Some haven't even shown up.

The most senior of senior staff — Head of Dept. — tinkles his small glass of wine. I'd watched him order it earlier and wondered if, at his age, that eggcup-sized glass constituted the outermost limit of hedonism. His is a respectable restraint unusual in this profession. It's widely known that unfettered boozing has destroyed many a promising career. This isn't *Wolf of Wall Street*. As hush falls, he launches into a brief speech about the role of monarchy in contemporary life, "...as Hilary Mantel's novels show us, there is still a real appetite for the Royals..."

Appetite. An interesting word to use, given its associations with cravings for food, the satiating of hunger. Us paupers look at the Windsors as a meal. Sovereign flesh to consume. Mantel wrote something like that about Middleton last year, that hers is a body devoured by the public's gaze. Let them eat Kate.

Maybe I should've submitted something like that for the competition. I didn't have the time. I was too busy stacking shelves. Recently, I've been directed to spend more time in the warehouse, and all of that time in the wastehouse, around all those CAGEs, dealing in all that waste, really doesn't make me feel at all creative. It doesn't make me feel at all, actually.

The HoD continues, "...the importance of Mantel at a time of increasing political uncertainty... we need big books like hers... the vital role that you students here play, as the next generation of serious readers, and who knows, maybe even writers!"

Then he unfolds an envelope from his tweed breast pocket.

"The lucky student who has won the coveted ticket for the Stratford trip next month to see the *Wolf Hall* and *Bring Up the Bodies* performance is..."

There's a hush so complete I can even hear the buzz of a faulty lightbulb dangling from a loose fitting overhead.

"Florence Grand."

A figure glides out from our paddock towards the bar. She is tall, blonde, skinny, skinny, skinny, draped in all sorts of rich and colourful garb: a Bedouin thobe restitched and augmented with Mali bogolan fabric, and about her wrists and bare ankles are shackled sparkling bands. There's a collective hiccup as she leaves the students' side of the room. Maybe, beneath their masks of approval, the other coursemates are seething like me. But maybe they genuinely think she's a worthy winner, with her LinkedIn page and list of achievements: model, philosopher, business owner, freethinker, eco-worrier. Yes, that's eco-*worrier*. She's self-published a book of poems, *Going with the Flo*. And often she reads, unprompted, from her longest ditty, 'Himalayan'.

In any case, the momentum is suddenly with her, and everyone applauds in her wake. She waves a henna'd arm, like a wintry tree trunk entwined with thorny weeds. She shakes her messy blonde hair, all lopped to one side, straightens her padded, gilded gilet over the thobe. As she reaches the HoD, I gaze at her over the lip of my lime and soda. She has the hue and posture of a totem pole, with angular cheek bones and a haughtily Grazia'd nose, like a carved eagle enjoying its wingspan. Her eyes are glassy lightbulbs: persistent, fragile, glowing. With these, she surveys the room of losers.

"Florence, is it? Flo, I'm sorry, will now read her winning entry," the HoD announces, bowing slightly as he steps aside, rejoining the staff at the bar.

She takes the envelope from his hands and announces that, before she starts reading, she'd like to preface it all with a brief CV and a timeline of her achievements. As she speaks, her enormous, clear-skinned, domed forehead never creases; her cheekbones and pointy chin act, from the way she speaks, as lightning rods for superlatives about the universe and our place both inside and contrarily outside it. Her voice is of the Keira Knightly 'gap yah' variety, smoky, with a practiced authority. She'd be ideal for Tannoy announcements.

"What I'm really enthralled by," Flo goes on, her voice duck-like in its throaty nasalness, "what truly activates my anima is the depth of spiritual understanding which has visited me in this moment, in conjunction with centrifugal knowledge of the universe and both everything within and beyond that which can be impassioned and conceived of."

From time to time, her 't's change into 'd's, as in '*I godda lodda time for cosmology.*'

"I godda lodda time for cosmology," she continues. "We need to, collectively and individually, positively ally and interblend our discourses, because without such an interstellar integration, we will not promote ourselves beyond the current frequency of consciousness. With this fundamental notion now planted in the cortex of your minds, I will now read from my winning entry, which is entitled 'Freeing the Mind-Forg'd Himalayan Monarch'."

She begins reading, elongating the vowels, with thrusts and waves of her arms, with Kate Bush theatrics. In this crowded, small room, she risks spilling drinks. As Flo reaches the crescendo of her reading, she falls to her knees, eyes up to the chandelier. She concludes with the words, "*Himalayan, your Majesty!*" returning to her full height and curtsying. There's the sounds of many hands slapping, which in unembittered company is known as applause, but here seems to convey the collective feeling of having missed out.

The senior staff mill around, finish their drinks, and leave. When it's just us MA students, Flo pings her glass for attention and calls across everyone's heads. "I have a cosmic confession that I felt was inappropriate to vocalise in the presence of our senior colleagues. But to you all assembled here, and in order to fashion a truthful path towards interconnection, I have to admit that I already have a ticket for the play. Yahs, my mother managed to get it — she knows the Stratford people. But what I shall now do is launch my own competition, so that one of you may accompany me."

Suddenly the room's atmos of collective, shared loss, metastasises into a wary sense that everyone is, once again, everyone else's competitor.

"So here is your chance. Write another 140 words, but this time the topic is the cosmic dichotomy of fragrance and scent. In other words, how planets and perfumes are part of the same inextricable unity. I think you'll all agree that this is a much more relevant topic. Whoever wins will join me in Stratford." There's a murmur of excitement and confusion. "And, and..." — Flo waits for quiet — "I should add that everyone here is eligible. Unlike the department's competition, this is open to both UK and international students. Do you know why?"

There is silence.

"Isn't it obvious? Because the cosmos knows no borders."

- - - - -

The meeting room is empty, for now. It's low-ceilinged, windowless, and thick with the heat of over-excited radiators in winter weather's deepest trench. Too many bodies will shortly be crowded into this space, as part of an important regional Tesco event that our flagship is hosting. The room's grey panelled ceiling and walls carry the conversation while I, along with other disgruntled workers recruited against our will, unstack, unfold, and assemble the room.

"So Nick's running this?" a baker remarks, pushing a table against a wall.

"That's what it looks like. No one else would need all these wires and cables and screens," another yawns.

"Whatever this is, I'd wager that Nick's put in the graft, but it'll be Upper Management that's getting the credit."

"True that, boss. I heard Connor McConcavity's coming down for it."

There's a murmur of surprise. McConcavity. First name Connor. The Great CMcC. Not since Kafka has someone taken such ownership of letters of the alphabet. The rarely seen but often sensed most senior of seniorist supermarket staff. His name appears on all of the official literature that's sent around the store, but seldom is he seen in person.

"Yep. I suspect, whatever this is today, it'll be of importance. He doesn't come out into the open for just anything."

"I hope he mentions these redundancies. Need to know if I've got a job or not."

"Look, it's an uncertain time. All over. In all sectors."

"We should organise. Run our own workplace."

"Shit, boss. Careful who hears you say that."

"I bin watching that *Trews*, with Russell Brand. Bloke's got some ideas about collective bargaining and self-governing."

"Doesn't he also say we shouldn't vote?"

"Yeah, I heard that."

"When was that?"

"Like, last year. He was on *Newsnight* with Paxman. Brand was like, 'I ain't never voted,' and Paxman was like, 'You're a facetious man,' and Brand was like, 'being facetious is just the same as being serious, but at least facetiousness is funny.'"

"Yeah. I dunno about all that faecesousness. Sounds like he's got it the wrong way round."

"How?"

"Well, he's saying, organise collectively, unionise and all that, but saying don't vote. Like, I dunno how that would work."

"Wouldn't work here."

"Not without a lot of data and information."

"Well, that'd be Nick's job. Them upstairs have told him to start running data scans on lazy workers."

"You better pick up your pace then, fat bastard."

"I didn't realise Nick was so high up."

"When it comes to tech, Nick's who you want. He's like a false nine."

"You sound like McConcavity. He loves a football reference."

"He's got some serious data storage capacity, that Nick geeza has." The baker stands up perfectly straight, stares off into the distance. "Exterminate, exterminate." His voice is mock-nasal, doing his best Dalek. "Power. Point. Presentations. Slides. Stats."

The other bakers laugh. "Exterminate. Classic."

As we unstack the last of the chairs, the room begins to fill up.

"Fackin' hell" — one of the bakers nods at a group that's just entered — "I know them. They're from the big Tesco in Bishop's Stortford. Fack me. Today must be important."

More workers begin filing in and taking seats.

"Yeah, and there's the Dunstable crew."

"I fink I can see the Thanet clan as well. They only come up here when it's serious."

I leave these Euphorium bakers to it and retreat to the back row before I'm forced to sit at the front. If any of this is in any way interactive, I want to be as far away from being called on to take part.

Alby enters the room, takes the seat next to mine.

"Good of you to join us. Where've you been?"

"Nick was showin' me the door sensor."

"Why?"

"Just interestin', innit, lad?"

There's another gentle jitter on the mind's polygraph, as I sense that Alby's up to something, but I roll my eyes. "Oh, no. You're not planning to hold the store to ransom, are you?"

Alby stage whispers, "Keep it down, lad," and looks this way and that with mock-paranoia.

Behind Alby's swaying head, I can see Nick enter. He marches along the rows to the front, where a large projector illuminates a smeared and scuffed wall. He passes across the projector's beam, his silhouette briefly huge and commanding. But he shrinks back to size, bowing in subjugation as another figure appears.

"Fockhinell lad. Today must be a big deal," Alby notes. "There's staff here from all over the region. Not just London." He suddenly sits up very straight. "Eyup. That's Connor McConcavity over there."

"Yeah, the Euphorium Team was just saying he'd come for this meeting."

At the front, Connor McConcavity appears in the projector's relentlessly bursting brightness. He's wintry and pale, and in the light, seems to merge with or float on the squiggles of dust that pass through its beam. His hair is black and silver, like a wire pan scourer. Nick passes him a mic, and he taps its top lightly. He speaks softly into it, its cord writhes slickly to the carpet, as if McConcavity is the derrick and the mic cord oil newly struck.

"Thank you, everyone. Is this on? Nick? Okay, we've not got long this morning, so I'll be quick. First, I'd like to welcome you all to this very important regional meeting of the Tesco family. We have here staff from as far south as Crawley and as far north as Northampton. What a diverse bunch I see before me. Now I know it's been a difficult couple of months. The Christmas to New Year to Valentine's period is always tough. But you've all been working like beavers and got through it, so everyone, give yourselves a cheer."

There's a dull clatter of palms on thighs, like cheap furniture collapsing.

"Working like beavers?" I repeat to Alby.

"Lad. He's got more where that came from. Just listen."

"Also," McConcavity goes on, "I'd like to thank our tech expert Nick for pulling together the slides I'll be presenting, and also for overseeing the initiative we're proposing. Nick, if you would..."

An image appears on the screen, of a footballer in profile, gripping a camera lens at the side of a pitch, celebrating a goal.

"Who's that?" asks McConcavity.

There are jocular boos in the audience. "Ah we have some United Fans here."

"It's Stevie G.," shouts Alby.

"Yes it is," continues McConcavity. "It's Steven Gerrard. Liverpool FC's captain. Now, for those who don't know, last weekend The Reds routed their neighbours the Red Devils, and when Gerrard scored, he celebrated by puckering his lips up to the lens of a pitch-side camera. He scored two goals during the match. Had he netted the third he would've been the first player to score a hat-trick at Old Trafford since... anyone here know the answer?"

There's a lull in the room. The rusted ventilation shafts over our heads umm and ahh.

"Fred Howe, 1936." Alby, again.

"Exactly right. Sounds like a Scouse accent. What's your name?"

"Alby."

"Alby. Alby." McConcavity looks down at his notes. "Alby Mills, is it? Yes, well done. Notice how he is breathing life into the lens, performing CPR on the mechanical. This is an inspiring image for what we're proposing. Nick, if you would..."

At this, Nick walks along the aisle, distributing a stack of dark rectangular objects, muttering, "Pass them along, pass them along. Take one and pass them along." He comes over to where Alby and I are sitting, hands us the final pair.

"Here's some evil tech, Alby." Nick smiles with strained affection, then slings us a subtle 👍 and returns to the front.

"What does he mean by that?" I ask.

Alby just grins, shakes his head. In our hands are thin, heavy rectangles, sized somewhere between A4 and A5, plasticky aluminium on one side, glass on the other.

McConcavity holds up his own: "Thanks, Nick. Everybody, your attention please. These are tablets. More pacifically, they're computers but with interactive screens. All staff in the region will now be using these each day. These will keep track of all of the members of each department. The idea is to bring about a tech revolution and streamline the running of the store. These tablets are the first step. I know for some of you it'll be a steep learning curb but these will help Counter Managers keep track of the efficiency of each shift. Every one of you will need to carry a tablet when you're working on your particular counters. That includes you in the Euphorium, on the Deli, or on Fish. Everyone up in F&F, you will too. And that's it."

Nick whispers into McConcavity's ear.

"And Food2Go. Yes. Thank you, Nick."

Alby looks at me, eyebrows raised.

"It's a very forgettable counter," I shrug.

Alby continues to look at me. "Or it means you're inconspicuous. No one would suspect you."

McConcavity: "Each of you'll now be in possession of your own individual tablet. We're phasing out clipboards for good and embracing the new. Why? Well I think you'll all agree that paper is just so wasteful. And this tech offers us an opportunity. Now I could go on until I'm blue in the teeth about how exciting this is, but I want us all to try it out. So, everyone, we, together, let's all try it out now. We're going to practice as we go."

"*PAWG*?" Alby nudges me. "That's an unfortunate acronym."

"Ergh."

"Hey, lad. Have you noticed how many times he's sayin' 'we'?"

"McConcavity?"

"Yeah, it's like every other word is we we we."

McConcavity: "To log in to your tablet, just type in your unique numerical identifier, which you would all have received in your Inductions."

There's a groan in the room as people shift their weight to retrieve wallets from back pockets. In my wallet is my plastic card, sandwiched between Mollie Friel's Freedom Pass and Draft No.6 of my Letter to an Incarcerated Sibling.

Further along our row, a hand goes up. An old man who I've seen working the checkouts. "I don't think I have mine."

McConcavity looks stony, blank. "All those of you who do not have your unique numerical identifiers, please stand up."

A large minority stand, most with difficulty, because these are elderly staff, who have worked here for a long time.

"That's a real shame. But all of you need to leave. Go straight to Jasmeen in the Staff Canteen."

There's a quiet hum of confusion and doubt as the troupe of pensioners-to-be depart.

"That really is a loss, but if you're not loyal enough to carry your ID, you're not responsible enough to work here."

"Fuck," Alby whispers. "It's beginning."

"What is?" I whisper back.

"The exodus, the redundancy, the purge."

McConcavity goes on. "For the rest of you, well done on your loyalty. I'll stand toe to toe with you any day of the week. Use your number to unlock your tablet."

I lean over my tablet and enter the digits: 6655321. The screen ignites with the supermarket's logo.

"Have we all managed it? Are we all okay?"

Now that Alby's mentioned it, I can really hear the verbal life raft onto which Connor clings. The dangers of 'we' are well known, and maybe more ubiquitous in the store than just McConcavity. Monojit often makes a point of reminding me how much "WE like to have a laugh around here" and how "crazy, just plain crazy WE are round here," but maybe it's the *We* of Yevgeny Zamyatin's novel, with its false consolation of the collective and its excitement about a machine-dominated dystopia, a fictional vision that the author gleaned from his eighteen months supervising the manufacture of polar ships in the docks of Wallsend, North Tyneside.

From somewhere near the front of the room, a pasty, veined hand creeps up. "Mr McConcavity, we're all wondering about these rumours about automation. Will us on the checkouts lose our jobs to self-service machines?"

"And what's your name?"

"Maggy. Davis. Maggy Davis."

"And your ID number?"

"9781917."

McConcavity nods at Nick, who types the numbers in. The projector flashes. An image appears, all kinds of differently coloured charts and graphs.

"Maggy. This shows the specific times of day you've clocked in and out during the last two weeks." The graph undulates like the rollercoaster at Yarmouth Pleasure Beach. "As we can see, very inconsistent."

There's a charged quiet, and in the dimness, two men materialise out of the walls. It's the same pair — Wart and Feral — who'd strip-searched me and did Callum too, who I'd watched escort Franny, Isaiah, and Drew, and all those others from the store. Wart and Feral move amongst the crowd, in but not of the multitude, and escort Maggy from the room. I'm back in my Induction. How long ago that all feels.

The silence lingers, until McConcavity sighs and rearranges a cufflink. The projector's image changes. "This chart shows how efficient, or rather inefficient, Maggy has been on the till. As you can see, not very good, so it's for her own good that she'll be moved along."

He nods to Nick. The projection flashes up another image, this time a black and white pixelated box, like a chessboard gone AWOL.

McConcavity continues. "Now, I'm sure the question you all have is, how did we do that? How did we get Maggy's data up? Well, look at this. This is a QR code. Some of you might know what these are for, or maybe seen them around London. But to explain to the rest of you, if you hold up your tablets now towards this image, as if you were taking a photo on your smart phone, you'll be able to access some very important information."

In unison, we hold up our tablets. My screen asks me for my digits. I type them: 6655321, and follow the code.

McConcavity shouts over the noise. "All of your screens should now display the data about your own personal performances here at Tesco."

I look down at my screen again, confused. No data, no info about my personal performance. Just these words in capital letters, glowing against the blank background of the tablet, as if etched in stone, commanding me, directing me. I look across to Alby's screen, and on his are displayed numerous pie charts and graphs. "I think there's an error with mine," I mutter, looking up towards the front. Maybe it's just the projector's distorting light, but I swear I can see Nick winking at me.

"And let's try again," McConcavity repeats. "Let's look at the stats of our resident scouser. Alby... Mills, wasn't it?"

"What's your ID number, Alby?"

I can feel Alby next to me squirm. "Erm, 516235."

"Nick, would you?"

On the projector appear stats and charts. The whole audience leans forward to see what it tells us.

"So, as we can see, for Alby there's room for improvement. You'll notice how this part of the screen is Amber-coloured. Yes? Some of you will have Green, others like Alby will be Amber, and some of you, though not many I'm sure, will be Red."

Alby's groaning as he looks from the projector to his tablet's screen. "That's Amber, that is."

"These correspond to how efficient you are at clocking in and out, and how the CCTV facial recognition technology we've recently rolled out has noticed where you are in the store in relation to your designated work station."

There are some mutters of excitement, concern, confusion.

"Our intention is that, with these tablets, which all of you will now wear on your person at all times, using these belts, we will be able to track your movements and create a personalised heat map."

The projector changes again, to a blueprint of the store, the same kind that Alby procured during his Anglo-Argentinian summit.

I glance at him. "Did you ever ring Cármen up after your Valentine's Night?"

He shakes his head, groans again. Now's not the time to remind him of Romance 101 – Phone Her Back – because McConcavity is driving home his message: "For those of you in Green, well done. Keep it up. For those in Amber, we're watching you. For those in Red, you'll hear from your Team Leader. Anyway" — McConcavity seems to be wrapping up — “to conclude, I want to talk about family, and about loyalty. As you’ll all know, we have worked alongside the Lowe Howard-Spink agency for many years. In 1993, they worked with us to create initiatives like baby-changing facilities and a ‘no-quibble’ returns policy, which completely redefined the type of service customers came to expect from us. That’s why we have such a positive attitude towards childcare in our stores, and a generous view towards customers.”

Alby elbows me, whispers: “Does that include when Dan called that old woman with the toddler a cunt the other day, when she dropped that bag of mackerel on the floor?”

McConcavity: “We are all one big family. And I know you’ll agree with me that we really take it personally when anyone in our Tesco family is attacked. And so I want you all to join me in rallying now against a figure, an enemy, that many of you will know...”

The projector flashes to black and white. Another QR code. This one resembles a country estate’s maze if seen from the sky. A monochrome labyrinth.

Alby sits up straight. “Here we go,” he sounds bitter. I look at him questioningly. He grins grimly. “Just watch this.”

Our tablets are raised up, and suddenly there is baying and booing and hissing as a face appears on the screens. I can see Nick put on a pair of ear defenders. On my screen, there is a face: wide head, broad smile, like an ex-rugby lad, curly light hair, enormous jewellery, chunky watch, rings, bling.

Alby’s voice is in my ear. “It’s Peter Marsh. Basically, Tesco’s greatest enemy. Connor does this every time Tesco launches a new initiative or there’s a cull of staff. It rallies the troops.”

“Who is Peter Marsh?” I whisper.

“Haven’t you read about him in your booklet?”

I think back, to my Induction, skimming a page with an image of this face, with a huge X printed across it. It must've been this Marsh bloke.

Alby is whispering to me, "...he was this rebel advertiser, proper enemy of Tesco."

McConcavity points towards the audience: "As many of you will know, Frank Lowe, the legendary founder of the agency who devised our family slogan EVERY LITTLE HELPS has been mercilessly attacked."

There's a loud cheer, or jeer, of ascent.

"Mercilessly!" someone shouts.

"Exactly. Many of you will know what was said."

Another jeer, some hisses.

"Frank Lowe was described as 'a jumbo-sized piece of skin stretched over an ego.'"

Alby stifles a laugh with his palm. The rest of the crowd bellows, "Shame! NEVER! Lowe is loved."

"Thank you, everyone. That's all good. And many of you will know who was responsible for such an attack."

A huge roar, as if the crowd, the herd, recognises a threat is imminent.

"The figure who is the enemy of our family is... Nick, do the honours."

The wall screen flashes and there appears a photo of Marsh in a suit and tie, leaning against a cream Bentley. At once, the crowd erupts in angry shouts. I turn to Alby, who is sitting very still, lips pursed.

"This is Peter Marsh," McConcavity shouts over the mob. "Chairman of Allen, Brady, and Marsh, and the enemy of our beloved Lowe."

The crowd is roiling, many people jumping up from their chairs, and I have to stand to see the screen.

McConcavity shouts over the crowd, "This is your time to HATE. Shout as loud as you can." The crowd bellows at the image.

Everyone is shouting. McConcavity is shouting, and everyone rises, unable to sit, shouting and jeering along with everyone else. From somewhere, someone flings a Tesco booklet at the screen, which flaps like a paper bird and splats its laminated wings against Marsh's face before sliding down the wall.

"For the next few months," McConcavity shouts, "we will channel our hatred for Marsh. Who do you hate? Repeat it with me, Marsh, Marsh, Marsh, Marsh."

The crowd chants as one, stands as one, troops out of the room, everyone's tablets raised, everyone repeating, "Marsh, Marsh, Marsh."

The lights that greet us in the corridor as we emerge from the meeting room make me squint and blink. Alby is giving me a weird look. "I'm surprised you got so carried away."

"What do you mean?"

"You were shouting along with everyone else."

"Was I? Hard not to," is all I can say as I catch my breath. I feel charged with the tingling sensation of... maybe... belonging.

Remembering Alby's flashing tablet screen I ask him, "What will you do to get out of Amber?"

"Who says I want to?" Alby replies, looking straight ahead.

I return to the Food2Go Counter, my new tablet jangling at my waist, and re-pin my nametag. There's no 'Winston', no 'George', so today I am 'Eric'.

CHAPTER SEVEN

WINE & SPIRITS

"So, is this like an April Fools' thing? Is it pretend?" Flo exhales her cigarette, the smoke forming two prongs of a compass.

"Unfortunately, it's real." Secretly, I love that it's real.

"And you get into fights all the time?"

"All the time." Never. Ever. Except with Norfolkians, with cudgels, at dawn. "Sometimes fights come to me. When they do, I try to finish them." I chew on the butt of my unlit cigarette.

"That's Himalayan."

"It is what it is."

"Turn your face this way, so I can have a better look."

I angle my bruises and my cuts towards the angry, glowing heat lamp in the Fitzroy Tavern's smoking area. It's red-tinted, to my advantage, accentuating the purple-brown and the coagulated blood. My black eye, dashed nose, and cracked lower lip have become deliciously discoloured in their healing. The skin has that iridescent grey-green palette of a pigeon's neck.

Flo is looking very closely, her eyes darting woozily from my nose to my brow to my chin and back again. I can smell her breath, rich and dark from all the port she's been downing.

"That's positively Himalayan," she slurs again.

Over the past few days, my face has swollen on one side, has purpled and browned, like someone's poured Calpol on a manila envelope. The cheek has scabbily rewoven itself to a satisfyingly unpleasant degree. It looks worse than it is, and I'm not going to reveal how it really went down: Alby and I trying to heave a stubborn CAGE up a ramp in the warehouse, only for its mesh door to swing open and catch me with a right hook in the face. The contents of the CAGE spilled out. Monojit had come running, blamed us both for the crime of wasted produce. Our punishment? We've been put on the taskforce for a forthcoming initiative, grimly named 'The Great Insertion' in preparation for the summer release of Danielle Steel's new book, *A Perfect Life*, which is being touted as the store's next bestseller. That's all we've been told. But I'm not going to explain any of this to Flo. There's too much cachet in the black eye, too much mileage in wounds whose origins remain mysterious.

"Right," Flo declares to the evening's chilly air (spring's early nods and winks), stubbing her fag in a plant pot on the windowsill, "let's get in here. Time for the results." She checks herself in the pub's window, etched with flowery plumes. Then she enters, and I follow. This is the second time in a matter of months that there's been a feeling of anticipation here in The Fitzroy. But this time it's Flo in charge of the competition.

The pub is even more crowded than last time. Not with senior staff but with all those international students who've come too, their faces expectant, excited; they've been included. Flo stands by the bar, takes from her gilet pocket a piece of paper. "As you'll all know, this is for the *Wolf Hall* and *Bring Up the Bodies* performance later this month. I read through all of your incredible entries, many of which were almost worthy. And it's great to see so many of you here tonight for the big announcement, including international students. I really feel that amplification of interconnectedness right now. It's really Himalayan. Anyway, gosh this really is *so* Himalayan isn't it. The winner is... Dominik Ady... hope I've pronounced that right, Dom... up you come... there you are. A few words? No? Okay, let's give Dom a round of cosmic applause."

Dom retreats modestly back into the crowd, and he receives hearty backslaps and earnest congrats in myriad accents from all sorts of nations. It's a Rosetta Stone Language Course of goodwill:

"恭喜你."
"*Godt gjort.*"
"Vell deserwed, Dom."
"*Félicitations.*"
"*O_di nma.*"

There are no senior staff members to add their compliments, nor with whom to network, so we all sort of stand around, sipping our drinks, no one with the inclination to launch into a proper debate or discourse on any subject. It's as if, in the last month or so, the piss and vinegar has been drained from the cohort, like we're just going through the motions. The course concludes in June, only two months away, and still no one has any sense of what they're doing next. Where are all those eager publishers who were meant to accost us after a seminar and say, "Are you a graduate from a prestigious MA degree? Here's a ludicrous advance to write a novel," or "We're looking for a writerly writer graduate to do a weekly column for a broadsheet. Here's a six-figure salary and the phone number of a reliable coke dealer to get you started."

Flo approaches. "How about that, then?" Another glass of brimming port.

"A worthy winner, for sure. What was his entry about?"

"Huh? Oh something good," vaguely.

"You didn't read it."

She leans in conspiratorially, fermented Cockburn on her breath. "There were so many entries that I had to, let's say, outsource the process to a few dedicated readers I know."

"On this course?"

"Oh my gawwsh, no. No, my friend Tara has her own literature tutoring business, and so I asked a few of her students to read the stories and mark them out of ten. Tara said it took up an entire week of tutorials, saved her the effort of coming up with a lesson plan." She wrinkles her nose at the cuteness of the strategy. I don't ask if the students were paid for their labours.

"Did you enter?" she asks.

"You'd have to check with Tara's students if they enjoyed reading about the cosmic layout of a supermarket."

Flo throws her head back. "Ohh. Him. A. Lay. An! That *does* sound good. You know, I was going to say, Dom's won the competition, so he's got the ticket to Stratford, but he's also coming away for a party at mine, a collective, an event, a launch, a debauch, a bacchanalia, a soul search, an inter-reconnection. I'm hosting at my family estate in Berkshire. You know, my people would be enthralled to hear you speak. To hear more of your supermarket tales, and about your fighting."

She gives me details of dates and times, reiterates it'll be "generously Himalayan."

I extract my diary from my rucksack's gullet. A ream of plasticky parchment cascades to the floorboards, including another redraft of my Letter to an Incarcerated Sibling. I swiftly retrieve them before Flo notices. "My working hours are..." — I'm scanning the days in late April — "I'm working on the Friday until the afternoon and then I'm working from midday on Saturday, and all of Sunday."

"That's alright. You can come just for the Friday night, then. Dom already said he'll be renting a car and driving, so he can bring you with him and then drop you at Newbury train station on the Saturday morning."

I umm and umm.

"You really should come," she says, cajoling. "Tara's coming. She's always looking for new tutors for her business. Regal Tuition. You should speak to her about it."

I mull this prospect, a transition away from the service industry of Tesco to the service industry of education. A private individual with huge funds using the skills of others, taking substantial commission for their labours, all the while shifting produce. I'd be swapping groceries for learning, food for thought.

Conversation in the pub has warmed up. Maybe now that the suspense of Flo's competition is over, everyone's a bit looser. They're talking about the recent A.S. Byatt event. The one which I couldn't attend because of my loyalty to Tesco.

"You missed out," Dom tells me. "In the Q&A, someone asked her for tips."

"Oh yeah, I remember that," Flo interjects. "Was that when she said the thing about the villa?"

"The football team?" I ask.

"No. She was asked for advice on how to start writing. And she said that for her first novel she went to stay at a friend's villa in the South of France."

"Arles, was where she said it was."

"It's in Provence."

"It's pronounced Pro*vence*."

I make a mental note: step one to becoming a successful author — get a pal with a big fuck off property. Suddenly, Flo seems bathed by the golden chandelier, the cosmos with stars and planets.

Later in the evening, when I'm settling down on Dom's floor, I get a text from Flo: **bring your Tesco outfit**. So, it's going to be fancy-dress-themed. I could've predicted that. Dom's already snoring, so I can't ask what he'll go as.

- - - - -

Upper Management are looking even more morose than usual. They're walking in grey and dark suits, funereal skirts and tights, along the white aisles, heads bowed. Bisera gathers together Food2Go staff (yours falsely) and the Deli Counter crew (Alby + a handful of butchers-in-training) to explain. She holds up a copy of the industry inside paper: *Our Tannoy*. It's a publication with the power to bedevil and haunt many a senior manager's sleepless night, with its articles pitting one supermarket against another. The papery wraith of retail.

"It's a problem," Bisera mutters, a painted nail pressing down onto the article which has caused all this stress. "One of their journalists... his name is... Angus Caarht... has reprinted excerpts from a speech by the Prime Minister where he said that he prefers Waitrose customers because they are, and I quote, more engaged and talkative. And just like that" — she clicks her fingers — "our relationship with our posh clientele has been damaged. There's a serious worry that they will now want to go over to Waitrose instead. And we'll be left with a poor customer base. Upper Management want us to do something about it."

"They look like they're in mourning," Alby remarks as the procession passes by, a pair of lackies following close behind with a box of own-brand gin.

"Are you surprised?" Bisera goes on, "We need to be extra efficient today. Shift as much of the high-quality stuff as possible, get on good terms with the posh customers, call them clients, offer a personal shopper experience, do whatever you have to do. Really push the delicacies. I'm talking salami, stuffed peppers, olives."

"Even the Kalamata olives?"

"*Especially* the Kalamata olives."

My stomach twinges at the image of heaps of food ready to be wasted, if Bisera's plan doesn't work.

"And whatever you do, make sure you all observe Customer–Colleague Interaction Policy No.1. Which is?"

As one we all chorus, "BE PERSONABLE."

"Exactly. Be personable. You need to smile and fucking relax. I don't want any tension today. This is serious."

Inevitably, the workday is tense and difficult and inefficient. Call it trickle-down anxiety, with Upper Management in mourning, and therefore Bisera and the other Team Leaders stressing, and the Counter Managers like Monojit feeling on edge, and shop floorers like me getting a repeated bollocking whenever something doesn't adhere to company policies. At one point, I'm replenishing cocktail onions when Wart and Feral accost another shop floorer who accidentally tips over a palette of Ocean Spray Cranberry cartons. The red juice spills out and spreads like chum for a great white shark. Wart and Feral are circling and immediately take the shop floorer away. I catch Dan the fishmonger's eye, and even he looks unsettled. It's all a bit like a school during an OFSTED inspection, where the pressure exponentially increases the further down the pecking order you go, from Governor and Head Teacher down to Support Staff, students, and lollipop man.

And judging from this article in *Our Tannoy*, David Cameron's to blame.

When I have a free moment to myself, I retrieve a copy of the paper and read Angus Caarht's article. Beneath a small photograph of a man in his forties, with jowls beginning to bloat into middle-age, and thinning brownish hair on the slopes of an emerging scalp, Caarht's bio explains that he's a local journalist, concerned with political issues which impact on businesses in the SW5–7 area. His article emphasises that the significance of Cameron's remarks goes all the way back to the aristocratic infrastructure of this neighbourhood. And it's true, from my own experience here. The likes of Montgomery, Lady Harding's elderly daughter, and the other ex-gentry regulars we see on a daily basis all belong to the lower- and middle-upper classes who still linger on in Kensington and Earl's Court. But much to their chagrin, they must now rub shoulders with the lower-middle, and middle-lower classes, the types who don't get their trackies from the F&F mezzanine but from Frank Johnson's in SW9. And with the introduction of foodbanks, a whole new demographic has arrived. The Montgomerys, the Archibalds, the Cecilys — all of them guffaw bemusedly when they overhear another customer talk of "running errands." For the poshoids, they only ever just 'nip' or 'pop' into Tesco. For the trackie-wearers, their weekly shop is paramilitary, organised and conducted with all the gear and furrowed brow of Tommies sent over the top. Surveilled by cameras, calling on mobiles to check back with HQ (the missus), asking if dried coriander will do, hauling baskets or a leaden trolley, the inventoried shopping list crumpled in palm.

This curious coalition of demographics collide. Their trolleys clash, each inspects the other's baskets, frowns at their choices, incapable of imagining the lives they lead beyond the sliding glass doors.

It's my smoking break. I've taken to standing out front with an unlit cigarette in my mouth, which I hope is enough of a signifier that I'm taking a breather but not risking emphysema. No one approaches me. Maybe it's the cigarette; maybe it's the last residue of the bruise and flaky scabs on my face. I look up at the towers of London above. Surely the clouds must regularly complain about the cranes. They want a clean, clear bit of sky to cruise through, unobstructed by all this man-made clutter: the spires, the pylons, helicopters, chimneys, tower blocks. Cumulonimbyism.

Suddenly, onto the store's forecourt pull up a couple of heavy-duty, tank-like Land Rovers. Grey suits spill out, at the same time there appears an overweight journo with a big camera swinging from his neck. Angus Caarht, obviously. He starts snapping away as the grey throng passes by. I recognise the tall man in the centre of the crowd as a Lib Dem MP, a front bencher, and I watch as he and his entourage enter the foyer, and through the glass I can see them greeted by Upper Management with big, slow handshakes. The two separate groups — Westminsterians and retailonauts — congeal into one great mass of grey-suited matter. All the time, Angus Caarht snaps. A giant cheque appears, held at one end by a young F&F woman and at the other by the MP. Grins and poses as the camera flashes. Then he skids away to the Fish Counter, flips on one of Dan's white trilbies, holds up a large glittering salmon. It sags down between his outstretched arms like a long cartoon smile. More poses, more flashing. Then the grey throng turns as one, retreats back through the foyer, out of the store, climbs back into their Land Rovers, and they speed off into the thick traffic headed west.

Angus Caarht snaps their departure, then turns towards me. "Oi oi, mate. You got a spare fag?"

I take out the pack, still nearly full, and pass him my emergency lighter. Finally, a chance to use it. He lights up, the fag dangling from a parched lower lip, and rubs his eyes with his palms.

"What was all that about with the grey frenzy?" I ask.

"You might've read *Our Tannoy* and the hatchet job I did, in last week's edition?", he asks, scratching stubble scattered like dark lichen across his jowls. "It was about the government losing its Tesco vote, and this afternoon, Downing Street quickly scrambled a minister to come here for a photo-op."

Oddly I have the impulse to get his autograph.

"How long've you been a journalist?"

He rubs his eyes again. "Always been a local journo. Sometimes I get the odd piece into the *Evening Standard*, film or TV reviews, that sorta thing, and in the past I've had the choice of going national, but there's more power in the parochial."

The scent of exhaust fumes from the Land Rovers wafts towards us, mingles with Caarht's tobacco smoke.

"That MP must've been gutted he had to come and do Cameron's damage control."

Caarht laughs. Nods. "It's fun to watch 'em squirm like that, don't you think? But credit where it's due. Very clever of him to hold up that salmon. It'll win them back the posh vote, one hundred percent."

"How come?"

He struggles to relight his half-butt in the breeze. "Because trout and salmon — the French-sounding fish — are aristocratic, caught by fly-fishing, whereas carp, pike, tench — the coarse, muddy fish — are associated with the people who work the land owned by the gentry. Same goes for salt water fish. Unless it's like a marlin or a tuna, you're basically announcing yourself as a pleb. Would've been a completely different story if he'd held up a herring in there. I could've used the headline, 'Stitched up like a kipper'. But he's a pro; he knew what he was doing."

I realise I'm slightly envious of this guy, uncovering local stories, holding power to account, in his badly fitted jacket, his dwindling hedgerow short back and sides, the bags under his eyes. His smoky exhales give off the impression of a job well done. Maybe I can out-fact him. "That was George Orwell's favourite meal, Yarmouth kippers."

He nods. "One of *the* iconic journalists, he was. You know, there was going to be a statue of Orwell outside BBC HQ, but then Mark Thompson, the Director General, opposed it. Said it would be too left-wing. But one of my mates who is a local journo up in N15 is working on that."

I stamp out my unlit cigarette, see him off, then return inside, pausing at the end of aisle No.11, scanning the daily newspapers. The display covers the broad bandwidth of public opinion: *The Telegraph*, *The Daily Mail*, *The Sun*, *The Independent*, *The Guardian*. At eye level, it's the right-wing publications (the rationale, as Monojit explains it, is that the pensioners and sixty years+ customers who make up the majority of the readership shouldn't be bending over to retrieve their papers), and at shin level, the papers become more left-wing (perhaps the younger demographics should have to stoop this low). At waist-height *The Independent* is running a story about the commencement of Prince George's first royal tour, around New Zealand and Australia. The article explains that, for the past couple of weeks, the breakfast TV shows of Oceania have been referring to the miniature prince as 'the Republican slayer', because of a poll showing that, along with his mum and dad — the Duke and Duchess of Cambridge — little George's presence out there in the Commonwealth has helped shift attitudes 51% in favour of the monarchy. It is perhaps unfair to give a nine-month-old such responsibility, or to bestow on him the title of 'slayer', but it does bring to mind the image of an axe-wielding butcher of republicanism, his dummy a gum shield, his cot's mobile a mace swung at howling barbarians. A good bit of PR from the House of Windsor to breed a baby who is so camera-ready. I wonder if Bisera would approve or scorn these kinds of articles.

I beckon to Alby at the Deli Counter. "Ready for our punishment?"

He nods, hanging up his mesh trilby and white coat. "Your wounds are healin'."

"It hurts to smile."

"I wouldn't worry about that. This task force thing sounds proper grim. 'The Great Insertion'."

"I've never heard anything so unnerving."

"Do you know what it's for?"

"Danielle Steel's book is coming out in the summer. They want us to help devise the advertising campaign."

"I'm not sure that's part of my job description."

I give him a look that's meant to convey that he needs to take this more seriously.

"Yes, yes. Provin' our loyalty, to save our jobs, and all tha'."

Up to the meeting we go, to find a roundtable of other colleagues in a windowless office, including staff from Euphorium in their Bedlam inmate whites, Nick Dale, a few of Jasmeen's giggling underlings, and even some pale, excavated creatures from the warehouse.

"Okay," says Jasmeen, looking up from her tablet, "I'm the most senior member here, so I'll get us started. The Great Insertion is the latest of our initiatives. You've all been carefully chosen to help roll it out. In July, we will be publishing *A Perfect Life* by the greatest, unputdownable writer, Danielle Steel, and for this we're getting wordy. The campaign will basically mean putting up slogans all around the store to promote produce. But what's so great about this initiative is that it uses words which are inside other words." She turns her tablet around to show us the screen. It's an image of a series of matryoshkas, each a brightly painted and smaller carving of its neighbour.

"We'll be following this principle, which the Lowe Howard-Spink agency has created for us. They call it Russian Dollism, where something valuable is embedded inside something else. We'll be using the same principle but with words. Our job is to sit here, brainstorm, and think up as many words as we can that contain other words."

A lot of heads are bowed over their tablet screens. I look around at this array of frowners and temple-scratchers. Jasmeen is staring at me, an encouraging smile across her face. She nods. "Well?"

There's silence, so she goes on. "Right. The idea is that the less words the better. If you look at any item on any aisle, it's all about finding the word to describe it. Febreze. Cillit Bang. Head 'n' Shoulders. The briefer, the better. And also the '&' symbol is infinitely better than 'and'."

"I don't quite understand," Alby sighs.

"I think I get it," I murmur. I can see Alby in my periphery snap his head up. I go on, directing my explanation partially towards him. "Each word must earn its place. No squatters. So for example, how about, putting the 'fun' in 'fungi'?"

"Yes, bang on!" Jasmeen confirms excitedly.

Alby looks at me, blankly. "Thanks. That's really helpful."

"Exactly right," says Jasmeen, encouragingly. "Any more?"

I go on: "Putting the 'pro' in 'protein'. Putting the 'ok' in 'cookies'. Putting the 'aw' in 'prawns'. Putting the 'real' in 'cereal'."

"These are great! Just what we need." Jasmeen is nodding and typing away on her tablet's keyboard.

Alby puts up his hand: "Putting the 'IKEA' in 'likeable'?"

There's a silence. Jasmeen folds her lips inwards. Taps something on her tablet. "I don't think we should be evoking the names of competitors. Particularly with all that stress about the article in *Our Tannoy* and the threat of the loss of customers to Waitrose. Anyone else?"

"Putting the 'ingle' in 'Pringles'?" I offer.

Jasmeen looks blank. So does the rest of the table, except Alby, whose head is lowered. I explain: "Ingle is the name for a fireplace. So we could put it on aisle No.17. Homeware."

Jasmeen nods speculatively, looking at me as if for the first time. "I'll short-list it."

"Putting the 'ESC' in 'Tesco'," suggests Nick, tentatively.

"I don't get it, Nick," said Jasmeen, gently.

"The ESC key on a keyboard is the 'escape' key. So Tesco is like an escape from everyday life."

"Again, I'll short-list it."

This goes on for a while. It's easy, even enjoyable. As we're tucking in chairs to leave, Jasmeen leans over and puts her hand on my arm. "Great work there. The Danielle Steel launch will really benefit from your input. I've made a note of it."

As we're leaving the room, I glance at my tablet. My traffic light is bright Green.

"I see you've found a use for that English degree, then," Alby mutters as he passes by. His traffic light seems to've turned a darker scarlet.

- - - - -

At the end of my shift, I stand by the traffic lights, waiting for Dom. At 16.02, he appears in his rental: a VW Polo.

"Do you know there's a big scratch along the passenger side?" I ask as I get in.

"Yes. The man tried to give me a brand new car, but I insisted on this one."

"Why?"

"If it gets scratched again, it'll be less obvious. And we're driving into the countryside, and I foresee brambles."

He complains about how weird it is to drive with the steering wheel on the other side from Hungary: "Does the UK think it's special or something?" he asks the windscreen.

"Yes," I reply.

"Crap cars, crap food."

"Guilty on both fronts," I concede.

"Although, actually... you know, last night I made that Nick Griffin beef stew."

"The BNP leader? Why?"

"Yes. Using his YouTube cooking video. I hate to say it, but living over here, I wanted to get the most authentic British food. And, well, I remember someone recommending his recipe while we were in The Fitzroy Tavern — so I cooked it up, and you know, it's not bad. Very hearty."

Dom describes to me in great detail the method for making the BNP beef stew, the order of prepping ingredients, the constant attention you have to pay at the hob, never getting complacent as it heats up, and the little twist to the recipe of adding a mixture of Hungarian spices. Against my will, I find myself salivating.

The grey flyover sends us west, the car edging closer and closer to the road's white lines, with that jaw-trembling noise that makes the cabin rattle as the tyres run over the blemishes.

Tender is the day. Not as in 'soft' or something delicate that's easily broken. No, I'm talking legal tender. Cold, hard £££. The sky has that hue and palette of a fiver: a bit of blue but mostly grainy grey and white. On the outer curves of London's orbital, trees that line the squat suburbs all look like tenners: rusty brown with spots of light yellow. And, from time to time, we pass streets dotted with estate agent signs, the colour of a £20, nailed to a terrace wall. It's rare to see banknotes these days. Barely any customers use them. It's all cards, plastic, contactless. Like the city itself, without intimacy, everything at a distance, everyone minding the gap.

"Did you bring your invitation?" Dom asks as we pass a sign for Royal Ascot.

"I didn't know there were any."

"Flo sent them in the post."

"I haven't got an address to send it to."

"Mine's in the glovebox. Have a look."

I thumb open the gawping mouth of the glovebox, take out the piece of paper:

FLORENCE INVITES YOU for COSMIC WEEKEND
House rules:
Be respectful of the place and don't bring any of your bullshit.
Good vibes only.
No arseholes
Fancy dress theme: worker chic.
Things I need help with:
life in general
someone to make me a cake
someone to bring moonstones
someone to make drinks
someone to FEED ME DRUGS UNTIL I PASS OUT

"It's not her birthday, is it?" I ask.

"No, why?"

"It reads like a birthday. And it's very formal. She's using her full name, too."

"Yeah, she told me about that. Said she only goes by 'Flo' at university. Out here in the countryside, she's always been 'Florence'."

"We'll have to honour that, I suppose. As guests. And this worker chic. What're you coming as?"

Dom smirks. "I've got some traditional Hungarian clothing with me."

"Is that worker chic?"

"If anyone asks, I'll tell them it's what peasant farmers wear."

"What do you reckon her friends will be like?"

"Free love and free spirit types," Dom replies, "judging by Flo's, sorry *Flaw*rence's, theatrical manner."

"That reminds me. How was the Stratford trip and the Hilary Mantel performance?"

"Mostly, it was good. Hard to concentrate with Flo..."

"Florence."

"Florence just repeating how 'Himalayan' it was. But yeah, Ben Miles does a great job as Cromwell, and Lydia Leonard is perfect as Anne Boleyn."

"What was your entry for the competition?"

"Oh," Dom shrugs, "something about the reputation of Valentine Greatrakes, a healer who lived in Lincoln Fields in the early 1660s. How important his ideas about the cosmos are for understanding current genetic and cultural trajectory." He glances sideways as he indicates. "Yeah, I know. A lot of bullshit. I just copied it word for word from a manuscript I found when I was looking through Blake's stuff in the British Library. Took me five minutes."

By now the Polo is cowering beneath bare branches threaded together overhead. In summer, these will be the great green tunnels of English country lanes.

Dom flicks on the SatNav and punches in an address. A deep, slightly robotic voice speaks from the dashboard: "*Maradj ebben a sávban. A következő kanyarodásnál tarts balra.*"

"What's that?"

"It's the SatNav directions to Florence's estate."

"Voice sounds weird."

"It's Viktor Orbán," Dom chuckles. "I downloaded it to use on long journeys. His tone is very forthright and stern. Bad for politics but great for SatNav."

"*Forduljon balra.*"

Then we're along an undulating lane.

"*Forduljon jobbra.*"

Then we're along another undulating lane.

"*Forduljon balra.*"

Then we're along another undulating lane.

"*Forduljon balra.*"

Then we're along another undulating lane.

"*Megérkeztél.*"

Then we're up a steep, endless gravel path, like a trail of gunpowder until we reach a moat and a bridge. Then an inner courtyard, a huge turning circle busy with row after row of posh vehicles parking up, with a gatehouse and fortress ahead.

The Polo's tyres' delicious ligament cracking as it teeters over to a small space between a white BMW and a white Mercedes, which resemble giant elephants resting on the edge of a gladiatorial ring. Crowds are milling around all over, they barely glance towards us. We take our bags from the boot and enter through an open door into a large hallway, greeted with the acoustics and décor of a Roman vomitorium (marble, drapes, incense burning). There's also a huge white piano. Dom nods at it.

"Florence said that it's the one from the John Lennon video."

"She told me it was the Marylin Monroe piano?"

"No, I think that's in the conservatory."

The whole place is busy with identical people all crowding around in padded gilets. The men all wear boat shoes, rugger gear, cream jumpers tied like albatrosses around their necks. The women all have big curtains of hair lopped over one shoulder. When Florence spots us, she rushes over. "Oh, wonderful to see you both, and you've already got your outfit on. You've brought the hairnet? That is so Himalayan. What a hit you'll be."

On the piano, she plays a few chords and keys at the leftmost end of the Steinway. 'Ode to Joy', deep, doomy, echoing out while the gilets gather and the curtained heads turn. When there's quiet, she stands on a piano stool, one leg bent forward like a caryatid, and calls out over everyone's heads, her voice redoubling off the vomitorium walls.

"Ls and Gs, you can all dump your stuff in the sleeping quarters in a little bit, but first I am cosmologically obliged to give you a tour." She bunches her skirt in a jewelled fist and puts out a hand. Immediately a couple of gilets rush forward and offer shoulders for her to lean on as she hops down. On top of the piano is a cloth covering a large object, which she pulls away to reveal a scale 3D model of the property we're standing in, with grounds, trees, lakes, huts, cottages, the moat and fortress up on a hill, and a bungalow at its bottom. With an extendable pointer, she hovers above a bluish pool the size of a hubcap.

"Lake Agatha. It's seventy yards by seventy, which equates to four hundred and forty-seven square metres, and at its deepest part it's twelve feet. We've got all sorts in there, some catfish, belugas, but my personal fave is the Koi carp, and you can see here and here" — the tip of the pointer hovers on little dashes of white and gold in the pool, shapes sifting the surface for fallen flies — "each fish is named after a property the Fam owns in England, France, and Singapore."

Everyone applauds.

"And if you look closely here, you'll see a crowd of small figurines fishing on the bank. They've even got a little tent. I know, *so* cute, isn't it? We have a pikey family who live there all year round. They've been there night and day, fishing out the eels which slipped into the lake during the floods of 2012. It's really terrible, how those eels affect our Koi collection."

Florence moves the pointer over the grounds. The scale model is not only delicately proportioned but also accommodates for the topography, with a wide, expansive, forest that lines the hill.

"Our house is called Koh-i-Noor," she announces. Everyone applauds. Its fortress is white, turreted, flintily rooved, on the top of the large, flat-topped peak.

She points at the slope on which the house sits. "We call it Champers Hill," she laughs nasally, "as in, short for 'champaign', with an 'i', not like 'champagne', with an 'e'."

"Aha, very good," compliments one of the boat-shoed gilets with chiselled hair. They all have chiselled hair. And boat shoes. And gilets.

Florence is explaining that, from its uppermost viewing platform in the south tower, you can see three counties. "And that's where the girls'll be sleeping, with a view of Oxford, Wilts, and Hamps. And this" — her spangled, tattooed finger trails down the slope of Champers Hill along a winding path towards the lake, at the end of which is a squat bungalow — "is the boys' quarters. The stallions' stable." She laughs widely and openly, as do many of her guests. "We usually use it as storage, but Debra has cleaned it out for you all. She did warn me, though, that we have a mouse infestation, so be careful in bare feet. There are traps. Meet back here in an hour at most."

It's hard to say how many of us there are destined for the stable. I've seen a dozen or more guys wandering around, but since they all look the same, there could be only six of us, or ten times as many. The same chiselled side-parting, broadly blond, thin pouting mouth, eyebrows poised in readiness to cast out an unchallenged opinion. Shirt and jumper combos. Cream trousers or a daring pair of shorts. Boat shoes. And always gilets, gilets, gilets. I glance down at my work boots, the colour of dung beetles.

Dom and I head for our accommodation, a dusty, cool cabin that's a relief after the hot, sweaty walk down the path. From the low wooden beams hang abandoned cobwebs, with moths or flies suspended at the end of each thread like coat toggles. A lingering smell of lawnmower fuel and rotten grass. On the floor, there's a scattering of peppercorn-like particles: mice droppings.

"I'm amazed."

"This is a maze."

While I wipe my armpits with the corner of the duvet, Dom changes into his costume. Leathery boots, leathery jacket, leathery hat, and leathery belt buckle. More Berlin basement raver than what I'd assume is Hungarian folkware. I look out of the small window at the lake. I can see a thin chalky smear of smoke rising from a few tents on the water's far side. A few people are sitting on the grass bank, watching the water, but it's hard to tell if they're at ease or getting on with graft. We return towards Koh-i-Noor, passing a group of lads on their way to the stable.

"Very rich costume," one compliments Dom, who nods and tips his leathery hat. They look at my work clothes but make no comment.

Re-entering the hall, there are already guests in all sorts of attire: mechanics, waitresses, miners, oil riggers, carpenters, electricians, farm hands, pest controllers, truckers, street cleaners, parking attendants. A lot of slutty builders pass round a large inflatable hammer, to pout and pose for photos.

Over the course of the next few hours, the rooms fill up with achingly attractive people fulfilling the invitation's brief of worker chic outfits. Instead of dressing up, they dress down. Their voices all possess a timbre as solid and steady as the elegant antique furnishings and walls they bounce off.

"I don't recognise the sovereignty of Salford."

"Let's put a bet on, but I'm convinced that the quickest way to get from Inverness to Land's End is by my dad's sea plane."

"Where's Tara with the gak?"

From time to time, I retreat to a nook. Clearly it was once a hearth that's been bricked up. An ice machine and a table of gins, brandies, and cognac has been slotted into the space. I pretend to busy myself fixing a drink, each chunk of ice in my tumbler a deep inhale and exhale, an attempt to keep an even keel on the mind's ship, while I wonder what these kinds of events do, what they are for. And there it is, melting in my glass: these occasions dissolve the incasements of the human heart. Whether with rage or envy or lousy attempts at passion, the drunken party has always been a way to enliven the spirits and thaw our flesh.

I scowl at this prospect and turn to face the costumed hippydom — all dream catchers, bangles, incense, coal miners make up, and Wimpy baseball caps. I down my drink, raisiny, sweet, rich. The bottle says it's 'XO' cognac. I pour again, and again, gradually tuning into the room, picking up snippets of what's said. No notebook to scribble it in, I shut my eyes in the hope of plastering the phrases to the inside of my skull, like Post-it Notes on a study wall:

"...what I do is basically a sensual, playful alchemy, like literally witchcraft but also not literally witchcraft..."

"...I like to share my knowledge, wisdom, and passion as a craft that brings me all this pleasure, which itself informs my knowledge, which turns into craft that brings me more pleasure. It's like a cycle or something..."

"...the question is like a Jaffa Cake. If the US ever abandons Israel, the country will either harden or soften as it grows stale..."

"...I work with all of my senses and faculties fully engaged, shutting off the noise of my left brain, and turning up the volume and energy and vibrational frequencies on my right brain..."

I pass Dom — his Hungarian attire a huge hit — in mid-conversation with a woman dressed as a Viennese waitress. "The election has just been held in Hungary. It kept Orbán as Prime Minister. He described the victory as transforming my country from, and I quote, a battered, sluggish old banger with a flat tyre into a reliable, fast, and bold racing car."

She flirtatiously flaps the white cloth over her arm: "So tell me about the Rumanian-Romanian thing?"

I'm on my way out of the room before I can hear Dom's reply.

"You need to top that up, yah," a plumber suggests to me, monkey wrench pointed at my glass. I've finished the drink without realising. Need to pace myself. He then proceeds to refill it with some potent spirit. I mumble thanks, clink glasses, and move off, retreating through a wide doorframe occupied by a pair dressed in sewage treatment dungarees, chatting with anticipation about the potential of something called Bitcoin. I slip sideways through the gap between them into the hallway, retreating further, seeking out the sink in a quiet kitchen, glugging a few glasses of water. Of course, the brass tap isn't just a normal tap but is shaped like a fan of Tarot cards.

"You can drink it if you want to. But that water's not for drinking." A man in a hard hat directs me towards a fridge. "There's filtered in there." I decant as instructed, then retreat along a corridor. I duck into a bathroom. A moment's quiet. On the wall is a series of framed articles from *Vogue* magazine, where Florence did an internship a couple of years ago through a hookup of a relative. I double- then triple-take one of these articles. 'A Rose in the Desert' is a profile about the First Lady of Syria, Asma al-Assad.

I retreat from my retreat, back into the busy corridor, where voices mingle and follow me through walls.

"...it helps me tap into the chemistry and communion between mind, body, marrow, and spirit with each bouquet I arrange..."

"...I just think you literally embody what you believe, and everything you see, touch, taste, feel, hear, and especially what you smell — this can change your destiny..."

"...Bashir was the 'spare'. It was supposed to be his brother who would rule, but he died in a car crash..."

Automatically, I pat my pocket, where I can feel the contours of my wallet, in which is folded Draft No.7 of my Letter to an Incarcerated Sibling. This one I'd composed like an academic essay, with citations and references to support each claim of the harm he'd caused, but the footnotes feel too cold, too empty of feeling, and some are missing page numbers.

I walk on, past one group arguing that pollen should be its own currency, and then past another where a young man announces: "OMG, HMOs are literally my fave kind of income stream."

The corridor ends with a conservatory, the glass doors of which lead me outside onto a shadowy lawn crowded with people smoking and shouting and watching two men wrestle. They're in Tudor-ish dress. I didn't realise the theme applied across epochs. Everyone's laughing and whooping and cheering, when one of them lands a punch with his padded green sleeves.

"Get him, Crantz."

"My money's on Guilden."

It's hard to tell if those are really the names of the fighters. I retreat further, past a foursome looking up at the sky.

"...sometimes my ceramics come through total inspiration, like almost angelic influence, and sometimes my CCs — I call them my CCs, my Ceramic Creations — come through an attitude I cultivate with my frame of mind and energy..."

"...memories are like fairy tales, to get lost in, but they're also like how to rediscover yourself..."

"...each stock I've sold has its own story to tell, and I'm just so grateful for everyone supporting me on my journey into the world of finance in all its beauty and wonder..."

And by now I'm on the edge of the forest, the bluish gloom welcoming me into the fresh night's budding folds. Pausing by a mossy tree trunk, I look back at the busy lights illuminating the house through the haze of early spring foliage. I feel the bark under my palm. Damp, cold, restful. Between the branches, and through the barcode of tree trunks, I can see the lake's inkblot surface, across which there are dim torchlights rippling the water. A timelessly feudal image of fishermen whose housing is paid for by the work they do on other people's land and water.

Months ago, when Ian McEwan's *Sweet Tooth* was the set text for one of our seminars, our lecturer highlighted a passage where the narrator notes that wealthy people stock their moats with carp, while the downtrodden keep their belongings in supermarket trolleys. That novel was set during the Edward Heath administration of 1970, when both the institution of the supermarkets and the technology of trolleys were recent additions to life in Britain. I have the sudden urge to get away from Tesco, aware of its powers to drag me under. Florence did mention her friend, Tara, with the tutoring business.

I hear again that sound of Florence hitting the piano keys in her doomy rendition of 'Ode to Joy'. Snapping and stepping back over the damp grass, I return to future prospects, the hope of meeting Tara and the possibility of Regal Tuition. I re-enter the lit house, passing through corridors, joining with others as we assemble around our hostess.

"My utmost joy," Florence begins once all are summoned, once she's up on the stool, "is guiding people to their fate and fortune. My greatest *telos* is helping those around me to realise their creative destiny, allowing them access to cosmological oneness" — her bare arms are spread wide, as if scattering the words out towards us — "and I simply looove the flow state." At this, the crowd murmurs a laugh, and Florence grins, making it rain with her palms, then bringing her palms together before entangling them in a complicated mudra. "All of us in this room, in this house, in this county, on this island, on this planet, in this cosmos, we are not just content creators, we're not just continent creators, we're creators from and of the firmament, we devise and produce our own reality. So, it is my honour, it is my potent privilege, to launch my range of perfumes: under the company title 'Flo-re-scent'."

Once again she pulls away the cloth from the piano's lid, this time revealing an arrangement of jars and pots and tubes and vials.

There is quiet.

"Through these perfumes, there is a way for you to galvanise and kickstart a purpose and aspiration beyond that which you have until this very moment conceived. These scents represent a paradigm shift, and I'm so thrilled, so imbued with cosmological delight, that I have the opportunity to guide you on your journey. If you sequence these scents, it forms a Fibonaccian pattern by which you can navigate your self-realisation. So, with this perfume" — she holds up a small vial — "which I've called 'Exist-scent, you can start your day with the knowledge that, yes, I am here; I awoke like this, and I am part of the beauty of universal connection. Then there is this one, which is called 'Fermented Firmament'. It's great for when you need to access your innermost Zeus or Apollo energy. And then, at the end of the day, 'Ignight' will help you develop your sleep component. So here are just three, but as you can see, there's a plethora of smells, and I invite, nay, I welcome you, to partake and begin your cosmic conversion.

So, thank you, not YOU but U, as in, thank the universe for ushering in this moment."

Big applause, raised flutes, the early twitching gurns of Class As. Somewhere out of sight, a sitar begins to strum and pluck, as the crowd rushes for the table.

"Isn't it spectacular?" asks a street cleaner at my side, a litter picker over her shoulder, snapping the air when she squeezes the trigger. "These events are always great."

"You've been before?"

"Oh yaahs. Last month, Henrietta over there, the one dressed as a train conductor, launched her hedge-cutting business, and like two months ago, it was Sebastien's turn, and he launched his dog-walking company, 'Hiking with Hounds'. It is like sooo rogue. Then there was 'Placenta Sausages' by Septimus; and the other month it was 'Dentistree', which was basically a kind of floss for cleaning bark off ancient oaks in our gardens."

"And how're these businesses doing?"

"Oh, they don't last. None of them last. Apart from Tara's tutoring business. Regal Tuition. But that's an exception. It's all about being seen to be here when they launch. Now you'll always be able to say you were here for the launch of Florence's perfumes."

And yes, I suddenly notice just how many people have their iPhones out, posing with the perfume bottles, giving the camera a thumbs up.

Around my arm appears a long, slender, henna'd hand. Florence: "I'm so sorry Ulrica, I need to borrow this one."

The litter picker shrugs. "Yeah, no worries. Take him with you."

Off Florence trots me. We canter around the room, Florence receiving compliments and well-wishings as we pass, posing for selfies. "It's wonderful that you're meeting so many people, but I really want you to speak to Tara." She steers me towards a small horseshoe of people sitting on low sofas, with a glittery tall woman at its centre portioning out onto a low table two heaps of bright white powder.

"Tara the Terrible, we call her," Florence explains, wrinkling her nose at me.

Everyone's listening to Tara, all the farriers and welders and dockers leaning forward, watching her scoop, sieve, and chop the heaps with a pair of bank cards, listening to her as she recounts a day she spent in Cambridge:

"I was sitting in the shade of an awning at The Anchor, the waiter had just asked about my sea bass. I told him it was cooked to perfection, but really it was quite awful. Hey what was I to do? You know what those dives can be like. Anyway, I was sitting there enjoying a flute of Bolly and a line of gak..."

No one interrupts. She opens her purse, takes out a marker pen and two small St George's Cross-shaped labels, the kind with a toothpick tip that Alby sticks in cured meat on the Deli Counter.

"...and watching those punts slide by from the arch of Silver Street Bridge, and as I just sat and sipped and sniffed, I realised I wasn't paying one iota of attention to the people sitting in the boats but instead to those pushing the punts, you know, the hunks working the poles. In their navy waistcoats and straw hats, I was literally taken in by them..."

She writes on a label, and plunges the stick into one heap: CALVIN.

"...No, no. Not because of their hunkiness, but because I realised that there is such an exquisite delight derived from watching the labours of others, from a position of leisure."

She writes on the other label. Plunges: KLEIN.

Everyone laughs, "*Fwah fwah fwah.*"

"Right," she announces, gesturing at her piles, "coke on the left, ket on the right. Don't mix your drinks!"

Fwah fwah fwah again.

I shiver, maybe the breeze coming off Lake Agatha's got into my bones. Maybe it's the spirit of the River Cam, summoned by Tara's tale. A memory ebbs to me, of a story my dad told me once, of him when he was aged sixteen finishing a shift at the strawberry packing factory in what must've been 1962 or '63, the factory out in Fenstanton, and he cycled all the way over to Silver Street Bridge, taking from a jar a freshly unearthed worm, spooling it onto a hook, casting into the deepest part of the river by the weir, in the days long before flat-bottomed punts clogged the Cam, casting again and again — then, suddenly aware of an elderly man at his side, who'd just stepped out of The Anchor, betting him two shillings that he couldn't catch a trout. Well, well, well. On the next cast, he struck and reeled in a troutlet, small but nonetheless a bet-winning trout. And with his two shillings, he'd purchased a top-of-the-range face mask to prevent inhaling the asbestos which constantly drifted down from the ceiling at the strawberry factory. Never missing the chance to impart a paternal lesson, when my dad told me this story, he concluded: "Always try to make your talents and pastimes improve your professional work."

Tara goes on, divvying herself a line of Calvin, taking a £50 note from her purse, rolling it tightly between her fingertips. "And I'm sitting there, and the waiter brings over their selection of cakes. All rather average, I must say. But you know what I thought of? Do you remember Morrissey describing his first sexual encounter when he was fourteen? He called it 'grappling cupcakes.'"

She passes the £50 note along the sofa.

"*Fwah fwah fwah*, that is rich," sniffs a farrier.

"Oh my, I luuuv Morrissey." A docker rubs her nose.

"Me too."

"And me."

"'*England for the English*' and all that."

"What's it called, 'National Trust Disco'?"

"Oh, I adore that one."

"And me."

"And me."

"And me."

Florence interrupts to make the introduction.

"Pudding caress," is all I can think to say, as Tara looks up, dusts off her hand and offers it for a tender shake.

"Sorry, what?" Tara's brown, feathered hair frames her face like brackets of a bookshelf.

"Morrissey. We sell his book at the shop I work at, and I think he should've called his sexual encounter something like a 'pudding caress.'"

"Yes."

"Or red velvet clutch."

"Oh my, yes."

"Or trifle grip, or souffle squeeze."

Tara leans over the table and hoovers another line Henrietta-style. She stands, totters slightly, puts an arm on my shoulder. "How about fondue fondle?" she asks brightly, sniffing then wiping her sugared nose.

Fair play to her. That's pretty good.

"Who are you, then?" She inspects my outfit, thumbs my hairnet, pings it against my forehead. "Ahh, the Tesco worker. Florence did say."

"And you've come as?" I ask.

"I don't come as anything. Just come as me."

"No worker chic for you."

"I literally *am* a theme. But yaahhs, Florence said you're the one who wants to get into literature tutoring."

I nod like one of those toy dogs in a car's rear window.

"Well, my business, Regal Tuition, it really only uses the highest quality stock of tutors." There's a pause as she looks me up and down again. "Before I make a decision, tell me about your background." She puts her knuckles against my cheek, turns my head at an angle. "Florence told me you get yourself into fights."

"Where I grew up, there was plenty to brawl about."

She claps her hands together. "Oh that *is* good."

She hands me her rolled up £50. "Help yourself." She nods at the table. Taking the note, it feels wafery in my hand, like a Caprice chocolate stick (aisle No.19). I settle myself on the sofa, lean over the diminished heap of Calvin. The St George's Cross has started to fall sideways.

I snort and pass the note along.

Tara snorts.

The others snort.

We go again.

We go again.

"Tell me about your background," Tara encourages.

Between each line, I'm spinning some yarn of half-remembered anecdotes of lowly family origins: "It's all I know. Hard graft, earnin' me keep. I ain't learned how to act proper like everyone here." I seem to've adopted a new accent.

As the numbing nose attaches itself to the front of my face, as the whiskers of synthetic ice spread out under my cheeks, and as my gums and teeth tingle, I'm haunted by the sepia faces of ancestors, staring out from family photograph albums. They'd be so proud of where I've got to.

Tara's face is brightening like a lightbulb sparked on. "Here's what you need to know. I can't make any promises, but what Regal Tuition could do with is someone who will really work, really put the hours in."

"Pfft," laughs one of the men sitting down, dressed in wellies like he's a trawler. "Oh now, come come, Tara. You've got plenty of those. Like when you made them all write out lesson plans for you in exchange for coupons?"

"Oh, fuck awf, Archie," Tara hisses. "It's MY business that's paid for the Calvin and Klein you're snorting. Keep your nose out."

Archie returns to the table.

"I've never heard it called Calvin," I say speedily, chewily. "Properly sent me west, that has."

"Oh wow," Archie's knees are knocking mine, he's got the coke trembles, or maybe the ket shakes. "'Sent me west'. What a phrase. Where did you study?"

"Merseyside."

There's a pause, then another belting *fwah fwah fwah*. "Oh yaahhs, one of the Red Bricks. Yahh, one of the Russells. Really top to go there. Tell me, what do they call cocaine?"

I fumble through the Rolodex of terms that Alby and I used when we were in Liverpool's alleyways. For some reason, we'd made an adolescent pact never to share these terms with anyone else. Until now, it seems...

"Gradgrind," I reply.

"Why 'gradgrind'?"

"'Cause of the coking factories in Preston."

This is greeted with a hefty *fwah fwah fwah* from the sofas. Archie leans over, grabs my wrist, and slaps the £50 note into my palm. "Oh yaahs. That's rich. I'm sooo going to start using 'gradgrind'. Here's your tip."

Tara's circling a taloned finger in a cocktail she's scooped up from the table, making the green olive bob like a buoy out at sea. "So you like literally grew up round there, in Preston?"

"Here and there," I reply vaguely, trying to drop my H's. "S'where Dickens set *Hard Times*."

She gasps again. "That's literally one of the set texts at Regal Tuition."

I internalise a victorious, upward fist and subtly pocket the £50 note.

"Ha," Archie interjects. "Tara, I must protest. I bet you've not ever read *Hard Times*."

Tara shrugs. "No. It's not my job to read it. I only employ people who have" — and with a hand on my shoulder again — "and I think I've just found a new recruit." She stands, leading me from the sofa, puts her mouth close to my ear. "Come with me. I think we should make you a contract."

As we leave, there's a swirl of bawdy laughter. We pass through many rooms, along many corridors, and my firmer footing in the conversation, and a growing confidence about my prospects of working for Regal Tuition, prompts me to ask her a few things. The Calvin has loosened her tongue, and she tells me of her family's house in Ladbroke Grove: not only wealthy enough to open a couple of boutiques selling personalised, hand-woven carpets to other aromapaths, but also wealthy enough to own shares in a company which makes the steamers that clean those carpets.

I tell her I've never actually seen a £50 note before tonight, which is true, except for the replica pinned to the wall of the pub I worked in as a pot washer — above the till, so that the bartenders could examine a potential forgery. She seems enamoured, but maybe it's the coke.

We pause at the threshold of the conservatory, where the open doors bring in the faint fresh breeze. There's likely the scent of trimmed grass, maybe spring's budding flora, but smell is not a sense immediately available to me.

I launch into a distorted version of my upbringing. Each fact refracted by the silvery, numb feeling that's spread all through me, each truth obscured in the light from sulphurous yellow and green lamps on mahogany tables, each honest description fogged by dry ice sauntering under the door from another room's thumping rave. I tell her that I was brought up in the flat mulch of East Anglian Fens, sprouted between the molar-like cobbles of a non-descript market town where the dramas played out between the state school and the proud remains of the abbey.

"So you were a stable hand or something like that at Newmarket?"

"Only on weekends. During the week I worked the fruit stall," I fabricate.

She looks relieved at this. "That's good, because I only ever fuck downwards. As a rule, men are below me, and men who moved from fruit picking to work at Tesco are *definitely* below me." This is what Tara says, matter-of-fact, without the slightest hint of intended insult. She might've been describing the chemical compound of carbon monoxide. "Come on then, let's go to the stable." She seems to have made up her mind about the work she wants me to do, and leads the way down the garden path.

The thump of music and shouting fades, replaced by crackles of twigs and the rasp of gravel underfoot. Through the trees, I can no longer see the lamps by the lake. Maybe my sense of smell isn't the only one to go. In the stable she creaks the door shut, kicking off her heels, narrowly avoiding a mouse trap on the floor.

She wriggles as she approaches, her dress slipping from her shoulders and hips onto the floor, leaving a silvery puddle like rainwater. "I love the smell of a working man." And she inhales my red shirt's collar. If her senses have been dulled like mine, my oniony musk is well-hidden.

"Tell me your name," she gasps.

I rummage in my imaginary box of nametags... Darren, Mitch, Keith, and pick one out that I wager will be of service.

"Hmmnn," she breathes. "Keep your hairnet on... Des. You're a working man. Are you going to work for me?"

She's tonguing Des's stubbled cheek and neck.

"I'm so sick of toffs. Their hair product and good postures. I want someone who's dishevelled, back-broken, dirty, blistered hands."

Des holds up his palms, grubby from the mossy tree's smear. She kisses his fingertips, runs them along her collarbone, where there's a tattoo of an avocado entwined in barbed wire.

"Are you going to work for me?" She repeats.

Des acquiesces and proceeds with proletariat fervour, pistons going, chimneys steaming, conveyor belts rolling. All nuts and bolts. Screws at the fuck factory. One hand, still dirty from his day down the coal mine, is caressing the shark fins of her bare shoulder blades, while the other hand, still blistered from the smithy, bunches her loose brown hair into a sheaf of wheat.

They kiss greedily, filthily, feudally.

Classless — that is to say, without class.

Down onto the bed they go, like a pair of logs felled by a lumberjack. Des's gurning mouth greases the pinkish folds of Tara's vulva, like a tanner with his brine.

"Do an accent," she murmurs.

"What?" Des asks between mouthfuls.

"Do a worker's accent," she groans, "a labourer's accent."

Des goes into his best cockney.

"No, a *proper* worker's accent. Go northern." He switches to his closest approximation of the North East, dropping in the word 'canny'.

"Ohh, cunny," she mishears.

He comes up for air, and his digits, baccy-stained from countless fag-breaks at the steel mill, exploratorily stroke her navel… hands at her breasts like the threshing machine his forefathers sweated in. She rolls over, tumbling like a totalled car at a scrapyard.

He retreats into the familiar Fen accent.

"No," she demands, "I said a *worker's* voice." She's on the cusp of climax; there's no time to explain the variations of East Anglian dialects. Her voice is raised. "Tell me more! Give me... give me... give me your class credentials."

"My ancestors worked in a textile mill in Bolton."

"Yes."

"My great grandfather heaved crates on Stanley Dock."

"Yes, yes."

"I've signed on three or four times."

"Yes, you're going to work for me, work, work. Do another northern voice."

Des summons his best impression of Alby.

"Do you have a foreman?"

"Well a Team Leader, technically. I mean, eeerm wul ahv go a teeem leadeh my mace."

"Do it like a Geordie again. And you clock in and out?"

"Yes. Sorry. Aye man."

"More, more, more."

It could be the coke, but Des is experiencing a distinct sense of *Entfremdung*.

By the time they're in the final throes, he's murmuring the details of the tax bracket he occupies. With each percentage and decimal point, she moans.

She tugs off Des's red shirt, throws it floorward. There's a castanet clatter as the heavy fabric sets off the mouse traps.

"Pee... Pee," she gasps.

"Pee?"

"Yahh... Pee..."

"As in, piss?" He asks reluctantly, wary.

"Pee... forty... five."

"Oh, I see. Yeah I've got one of those."

At this she screams out, and he reaches the end of his trial shift, while the mousetraps continue snapping their empty jaws.

- - - - -

Eyes wide open. I wake of my own volition, without my phone's alarm clock. This already bodes well, like I've infiltrated the day unnoticed. The other side of the bed has emptied of the night's occupant. Bedsheets with oyster-shell crinkles, grooves of the duvet, a concave impression on the pillow — all suggest that a body was here and is no more. In the split second before the hangover assembles itself, what I feel is relief. I exhale, issuing a noxious draught from the landfill of my mouth. It's always best to avoid airy morning pillow-talk after a night of boozing without a toothbrush. If both of you have the breath, it's the sort of chemical-weapon exchange that could make Assad shudder.

I check my phone, see the time, and hastily jostle my limbs, pulling on my last clean T-shirt (Lottie's typo'd LEVANTINE), going into the next room, and shaking Dom. He's flat on his back, still half-dressed, still with Hungarian tights on around his Hungarian booted ankles.

"Mate, it's already 10.15. Can you drive me to the station? I've got to get to work." His lids unclench: bloodshot, glazed, failing to focus in unison. One eye looking at me, the other looking for me. There's no way he's standing, let alone driving.

Then I remember: my stealthily pocketed £50 note. I run up Champers Hill, which has somehow steepened in the night, up the gravel drive. It crackles with each step. Crunch time.

The house is still, silent, like a school after hours, where there should be noise and movement. If it wasn't for the haze and twitch of substances in my bloodstream, this would be how a character arrives for the beginning of a Jane Austen adaptation.

The large front door's handle is the ornate shape of Saturn; the brass hoop is the planet's rings. In the hallway, there's a landline Bakelite on a small side table, and yes, in the drawer, an assortment of takeaway leaflets and cab cards. I pick up the receiver, which chimes out like it's a mourning bell, and begin dialling. Dialling. Dialling. Each rattle of the phone's circular face is one step closer to something coronary. I thought I'd outrun the hangover on the jog up here, but it's caught me by the collar. I can taste my sicky burps.

"You alright, lov?" I turn, and there's a gorgeous woman standing in the wide-open front doorway, yellow gloves in hand, a roll of bin bags under her arm, earphones plugged in.

"Hi. Yeah, I'm trying to get a taxi to the station."

She tuts, dropping the bags, unplugging her ears. "Not from here at this time on a Saturday. This is the country." Her accent is north-western. Not Alby-ish but certainly nearby. My heart calms a little. She pauses, taking in my workboots, the blue Tesco trousers, the BE MY LEVANTINE T-shirt.

"Which station? Newbury?"

I nod, my brain sloshing in the tin pail of my skull.

"If you're ready right now, I can drop you." I rush past her, holding my breath so as not to comatose my saviour, then pelt it down into the stable, stuff my bag with my scattered things: Tesco long-sleeve, hairnet, boxers, and run back, pausing to be sick behind an ancient tree. This is good timing, as it'll make the drive to the station more manageable, before the next bout of nausea.

"I'm Debra, by the way" — as she takes a leafy bend with ease — "Debra out here, but Debs at home." She's originally from Warrington, been working for the Grand family for a few years now. When I mention I used to study in Liverpool, she nods matter-of-factly, but there's no geo-camaraderie forthcoming.

"And you studied?"

"Literature."

"You're studying now as well, I'd say."

"With Florence, aye. I mean, yeah."

"Miss Grand and her Grandees."

"Pah," I sneer, in remonstration.

"Ey, don't knock 'em too hard. That family's done decent stuff round here. You'll be too young to remember, but there was a big old protest just on the other side of those fields back in the '80s, the Greenham Women's Peace Camp, to rally against nuclear weapons at the RAF base. It was Florence's mother who helped a lot, by cooking and cleaning for the protestors, cared for their children, printed out hymn sheets when they all wanted to sing together. Mrs Grand even went door-to-door round Newbury to convince the neighbourhood to support the protest. It didn't really work, and the whole Grand family was ostracised by the other locals. Yoko Ono bought some land nearby and parked a caravan there so that the protestors could find shelter when the police got brutal or the locals threw faeces over their tents. It was Florence's family who supplied the caravan."

With this weighty hangover, it's inconvenient to have to reassemble my image of Florence and her surroundings. It's a pain in the arse to edit that view and give it conscience.

The country lanes are Escher-like, with corners and bends coming back round on themselves, with identical fences and the same bemused herd of sheep with their fresh lambs watching me waste more and more time. I keep clock-watching with each stomach lurch.

"Were you staying in the cottage?" Debra asks as we slow towards a T-junction.

"In the stable, yes, I was."

"Ah. The stable's what they call it. It used to house Mr Oliver, best groundskeeper going. Any trouble with the mice?"

"Not that I saw."

She presses the button that opens her window. Shit, she's trying to fumigate the car. "What're you rushing back for?" she asks.

"I work at Tesco in West London," I answer through the smallest aperture of a mouth possible.

"Not usually Florence's type."

"Actually, one of her pals offered me a job."

"And you're working at Tesco?"

"Yeah."

I explain about the job offer from Tara, "...but I'm not sure if I'll take it."

There's a long pause at the T-junction, a lone sheep beyond the fence gurning with cud in its cheek. The thick bushes on both sides of the car lean out into the road, obscuring the view of oncoming traffic. Debra has to look left, right, left, right, edging it, left, right, left, right, edging, then swerves out and onwards. She nods her head back to the country lane we've just come along. "That might not be you" — then nods at my rucksack down by my knees — "but this isn't you either. Take the job if there's one offered."

The £50 covers my train ticket, and with what's left over, I buy a sausage roll, a tuna sarnie, and a bottle of EVIAN from the WH Smith on the platform. When you're this hungover, any combination of food is fair game to line the stomach, even the most antisocial of foods for public transport. I'm in desperate need of sobering up pronto before reaching Earl's Court. As I climb aboard, duck to a window seat, and start scranning, I can practically see the stink of cheap, hot meat rising from the pastry, and the recoiling expressions of other passengers as the smell of fish spreads out around the carriage.

The rest of the journey from Newbury to Paddington is a headbanging quest for sleep. Each time I'm close to dropping off, my neck tugs me upright. From Paddington to Earl's Court, I mull over the sequence of the last twelve hours, the drive with Dom, Florence's — or I can safely say, Flo's — perfume launch, the applause, Calvin and Klein, Tara the Terrible, Debra's advice. With Tara, it wasn't so much the ecstasy of a romance novel, but rather a job application with many a messy signature scrawled across dotted lines.

We'll contact you with the results of your application, and will take your performance into consideration.

So engrossed am I in this that I almost miss my stop. I run off the Tube. It's not just the carriages which have become cloying; it's the underground walkways too, caverns of viscous heat. Then I'm up into sunlight, hauling myself along Warwick Road. Just in time. Into the ♂ Changing Room.

I rinse my face, or try to. There's a circle in hell decked out to receive people who design taps which stop running as soon as you lift your hand away. With six minutes until my shift is due to start, I peel off Lottie's T-shirt and pull from my hastily stuffed rucksack my red Tesco top. It was the first thing I grabbed up off the floor of the stable; now, it's the last thing I can reach.

Over my head it goes. Yes, it has the thick sour smell of spilled beer, stale baccy, and smears of Tara's perfume, but it will do. A quick glance in the changing room's mirror. I'm just about presentable for the shop floor, even with oily skin that makes me look like I've been lacquered.

Then my eyes drop to my red long-sleeve; to the area of fabric above my chest, where a nametag would be pinned. There is a large, frayed, gaping hole. I inspect the edges closely, and there's what look like teeth marks.

Mice.

In that conscripted proletariat passion, Tara'd thrown my shirt to the floor. In the night, the tim'rous beasties must've found it and gorged themselves. My pasty skin, wispily chest-haired, shows through. What to do? A sad solution suggests itself as the clock continues to narrow my options.

BY MY LEVANTINE.

I strip, then it's back into my rucksack, retrieving Lottie's sweat-chilled, homemade T-shirt. It's the rouge of Cupid, just similar enough to be an undershirt, to disguise the hole that's been gnawed into the Tesco top. I pull it on, recoiling at the sensation of damp cloth on my skin, then over this goes the Tesco long-sleeve. Only a very discerning observer, a Big Brother, would identify the different hues. However, now the problem is still Lottie's smiling face peeping through the frayed portcullis. I rush through to the Staff Room, select a nametag. I pinch the fabric, Lottie's smile creasing into a grimace, and I push the pin right through her face. Somewhere in Angel, I picture her flinching as my hex is reluctantly placed. Maybe it's the poisons coursing round my body, or maybe the stress of limited time, but my trembling hands make me pierce the skin above my own heart. Fortunately, blood stains Tesco red.

CHAPTER EIGHT

TOILETRIES

So begins the shift.
The work shift.
The keyboard shift.
The paradigm shift.
The silken shift.

On this occasion, it's the shift in the seasons. It reveals many buried things. New parts of a city, new outfits on the Tube (tentative skirts, cardigan+shirt combos; no overcoats). New areas of a house. Freddy's in Streatham is the only accommodation that's got a garden. Until May arrived, I wouldn't have ventured out into it, but now the season's here with her rejuvenating smells, songs, and heat, the garden appeals. On the ground floor, at the back of the house, is one of the housemate's rooms, with French windows opening out onto five mossy steps that lead to an overgrown plot. The room was obvs. once a reading room for the affluent family who lived here, but the bookcases have been removed to reveal high, wide nooks, and the fireplace has been bricked up. Sublet after sublet over the years has led to more and more conversions of this labyrinth of a house into smaller and more expensive plots of tenancy. Presumably the idea is that the more occupants, the less each resident pays towards the overall rent, but this is reliant on the whims and impulses of a landlord whose portfolio is wholly without a price cap and whose nest egg loves a feathering.

So, one of Freddy's housemates has been away for about a week, and I've been granted access to her room (free of charge… a shift in the season reveals new avenues of fortune, too). Apparently, she's trying to improve her DJ praxis by attending a month-long silent disco retreat. Having a place to lay my head has done wonders for the old hemispheres. Each morning, I unlatch then fling open the French windows like I'm about to begin a sermon. During winter, the garden is left to rainy, muddy, icy ruin, but now that spring's worked her magic, everything is renewed, and the result is a storied thicket of bushes, brambles, waist-high weeds, bursting flowers, creeping tendrils, all with a rich stock of birds, worms, bees, and leaves. Up in an apple tree is a nest, a thatched vessel that softens me to the chirruping potential of life, a nest made of watered shoots, resting on a bough which will in a few months bend with thick-set fruit. Along the base of a mouldy wooden fence which this house shares with next door, there's a cluster of molehills, each leading to a Tom, Dick, or Harry.

This overgrown undergrowth has the atmos of a post-apocalyptic cityscape once nature has retaken the turf. Out here in AM's first freshness, if I stand with my wisping mug of tea and look hard amongst the shady grove, I can see objects left over from before plague flushed out the inhabitants. Over there is the wreck of a BBQ, abandoned to thorny weeds, its rusted hull brimming with last season's rainfall. Now it's a bird bath. This wreck is evidence of the tenants' collective attempt to forge strong, sustainable relations with one another — an attempt that inevitably failed and left behind this relic, this Marie Celeste of communal cooking. As well as the BBQ, a few old bicycles lean against a lichened wall, their leather saddles like slugs after salt treatment. Over there is a coil of hose pipe from some other futile effort to keep a veg patch. And there's some mottled, peeling garden furniture, which no one would ever consider stealing.

This AM, as has become routine, a pair of squirrels appear, their tails asking me the daily question: *Heyup, pal. Where ur nuts at??* I used to be all about questions myself, but my time at Tesco has transferred me to the supply and answers business. On the window's wooden frame, there's a protruding nail on which I've hung a sock. Inside it I keep a few handfuls of quinoa seeds, borrowed from a cobwebbed jar in the kitchen. Guided by an impulse to ensure there's enough food to go around, I scatter the seed and the squirrels come hopping. Their forward-planning is impressive. Not content with indulgent grazing, they archive most of the grain in their cheeks. Industrious, these grey bastards are. I wonder where they store it all. Under the soil, I reckon, anticipating a great harvest in autumn. In the past, I probably would've tugged a reference book from a shelf and looked in the index under *Squirrel, habits of,* but it's part of a shift I've noticed. Nowadays, it's a Google search if anything — but more often, I just leave it. There's no time for these flights of fancy. And certainly not this AM. I've got a 9–5 of being full of flu to be getting on with.

I thumb open another packet of paracetamol and throttle a tube of Strepsils. Flinging open the French windows, feeding the squirrels, was a brief idyllic interlude that's left me knackered. Heavily dosed up, I lie down again on the bed and tuck myself into the sleeping bag — not my own: an item leant to me by Freddy and not used since he went to a music festival last summer. It's still crusted with muddy smears and smells of yeasty cider. Unfortunately, this flu hasn't blocked my sense of smell. I'm not using any bedclothes, bedsheets, or pillows belonging to the housemate whose room I'm staying in. I don't want to leave any slimy trace. Her fluffy towels remain in her unopened drawers. Her pink ribbon-patterned robe hangs like a candyfloss wraith on the back of the door. Her silken shift stays on its coat hanger. Instead, I've encased myself in the sleeping bag, wriggling maggoty wriggles into the bed where I'm least conspicuous. The only concession I make to expanding into this borrowed space is a Tesco Bag for Life beside the bed, which over the last few days has been gradually filling with tissues and toilet roll centres, swelling and bulging like a snotty blimp. It'll need replacing in the next day or so, but for now it's being put to use. I peel off a few squares of tissue from a toilet roll, fold them double, triple, and blow long and hard, dislodging what feels like setting concrete from my sinuses. When I look in the tissue, it looks like something growing in a petri dish. The meds take effect, and I begin to drift off — until there's a buzzing, and I squint at my phone's screen.

lad, Food2Go Counter looking pretty empty from where I'm standing.

I collapse back into my sleeping bag, the collar of which is very damp. I'm woozily falling asleep again, almost off the hook, and there's a knock on the door. Freddy's signature tap-tap-tatap-tap, tap-tap.

Through the woodgrain, he muffles: "It's me. I've got some provisions for you — dark chocolate, salad leaves, and some oranges. I'll leave them out here. I'm also sliding another DVD under the door. Freshly burned this morning. I reckon you'll like this one. It's got Scarlett Johansson in it."

I hatch from the sleeping bag and heel-drag my aching, sweaty, clammy frame towards the door. "Thanks," I say, or try to say. The Strepsils haven't even touched the sides of this sore throat.

There's a pause. "I'll take that silence as confirmation that you've received the info. Anyway, here's the DVD."

I look down at the doorframe's edge where, poking out like the moon's silvery crescent, is a disc. In Freddy's loopy, pointy handwriting, it reads *Under the Skin*.

"That's today's prescription. You just stay in there, watch that film, and email me with any comments or ideas you have. I enjoyed your last one about *Her*."

A few days ago, between regurgitating my lungs, keeping down medication, and scattering quinoa, I'd emailed Freddy with a few thoughts on Spike Jonze's latest. In the past, I might've scribbled this out on paper, with a pen, but the laptop loaned from uni is better. The ink never runs out, as long as the charger's plugged in.

By the time I get back across the room to the sleeping bag, I'm dragging my knuckles with tiredness and fever. Down onto my side, I pull the laptop towards me and insert the disc.

While it loads, I click onto my emails and re-read the review of *Her* I sent Freddy. I tried to do it in the style of one of Freddy's cinephile speeches, channelling my inner Kermode.

> After his mockumental, staged breakdown in *I'm Still Here*, Joaquin Phoenix completes his degrizzling, first via PTA's 2012 *The Master* and now as the moustached Theodore, a scribe for other people's letters. As an epistolarian-for-hire, Theodore forms an earnest relationship with his computer operating system...

With a room of my own, with its own key and lock for the time being, so have I.

...based on a series of questions which the computer asks Theodore. Freddy, I don't know how you'd answer but here are mine:

Are you social or anti-social? I want to be the former.

Would you like your OS to have a male or female voice? Female.

How would you describe your relationship with your mother? Intensely honest, with lightning strikes of haughtiness and emotional distance.

I could do with some maternal comfort about now. Hot water bottle+cold flannel. A Cup a Soup, or Marmite on toast, aisle No. No. No. ergh, this flu's ruined my Knowledge.

I think more attention should've been paid to the storyline of the unpaid surrogacy volunteer, who covets the emotional connection between Theodore and Samantha, and reveals how damaged she is, and how sensitive she is to rejection.

After *Under the Skin*'s opening credits roll, I drift in and out of seeing what's on the screen, glimpsing through the flu a vision of a worker ant twitching on Scarlett Johansson's fingertip. The camera focuses in on its mandibles, antennae, legs, propodeum. Then it's SJ herself, an interstellar labourer, a white van woman, grafting at the coalface to perform the feckless task of seducing mankind.

I sleep a bit, wake again, sleep a bit.

At the film's end credits, I rouse myself by hurling up phlegm, then gulp down more meds. I unlock the door just enough to stick out an infected arm to retrieve the provisions, before shutting myself back in the quarantine.

A thought reassures me. This is what it feels like to *be* a housemate. Freddy's brought me nourishing salad leaves, kale and spinach. They match the colour of my phlegm. As I chew, I type:

> She's addressed as 'lass', 'pet', 'love' by the Scottish Lowlanders, but otherwise SJ's character is unnamed. She passes undetected through the epidermal layers, moves amongst them (us). Stalks them (us). Hunts men (us). In that scene when she cruises in her white van deep into the council estate interiors, she's properly like a black-haired widow spider at the roadside, indicators flashing, waiting to entice, ensnare, entangle, extract, discard. Men are wasted.

I type out, and then delete the following:

> SJ's is a writer's project, predatory, taking what she can from what she sees, operating the skeletal levers of what it is to be a person, wasting what can't be used. She also exhibits a supermarket worker's behaviour. When she drives off from a man who she's unsuccessfully propositioned, her enticing expression drops, returns to mannequin neutrality. This is how my face feels each time I turn away from a customer.

I send the email, gulp down some more meds, and fall asleep.

At some point, I wake to bright light. The clouds have parted, the sun is bucketing out its rays, which splash up the room's walls. I sneeze and cough into delirium. I can't escape the light; it's flashing in my dry eyes. Some might call it hay fever, but it's much more invasive and stubborn than that. It's scorching my retinas. This is an organised assault on the eyes, nose, throat. This is flu. It films the eyes during the daytime and at night crusts the lids with granules. It takes a Bunsen burner to each nostril. It does roadworks on my throat. And the ears — oh, the ears. I jam a little finger into the whorl of my right ear, expecting to pluck some enormous knobbly spire of wax. Alchemy. Golden nuggets (Cereal, aisle No.11, with Baking), *honey crunchin' good*. There's enough wax here to make a Tussauds effigy of me. I squint again, unable to escape the light that seems everywhere around the room. I sit up, and the flashes hit me full in the face. I blink away to discover the source. Under the doorframe is another of Freddy's discs, and the sunlight has caught it and sent its rays centrifugally all about the room.

- - - - -

Two weeks on, thirty DVDs later, and everything is vibrantly HD when I finally leave the room. Now the flu's passed, it's a case of CAYG before I depart, scrubbing door and wardrobe handles, throwing the Bags for Life into dustbins, unhooking the sock, and scattering the last of the quinoa to the squirrels. And there's me to clean. I stretch my spindles, scrub my proboscis, inflate my wings, and practically fly to Streatham station and onwards to Earl's Court, so keen am I to get out, to get back to work.

I'm early. In fact, I'm so early I can afford to linger at the station's threshold. Today's whiteboard reads: '*Life is like toilet paper. The closer it gets to the end, the faster it goes.*' And I can afford to slowly stroll along Warwick Road, dodging the cyclists on Barclays Boris bikes who, at this time in the morning, hunt in packs along the pavement. I pass the Trolley Fella, who nods at me — maybe he's noticed my absence. On the corner of Philbeach Gardens, I watch toddlers with lunchboxes queueing up against the white wall of a posh old building.

"That's the LEFY, the Landun Early Years Faandation," the Trolley Fella explains, having caught me up. "Basickly a nursery. Bin 'ere for years." The children lining up look like dots of Morse code.

"I've walked past that place so many times but never stopped."

"Yaw too eager to get in ther'," — he nods at Tesco's glass façade. "'Ave it right. Work's good, but ye've gotta look around ye. You see her?" Trolley Fella points a twiglet of a finger towards one of the plump women ushering the toddlers up the stairs.

"I see her."

"Well I remembah wen she was small 'nuff to line up against that wall 'erself. Now she's rannin' the plice."

We walk together onto the crossroads, his trolley catching between the paving slabs. The warbling of bicycle bells and larking toddlers is lost to the churn and klaxon of the road. On the central traffic island, we wait, between the vehicular rivers flowing behind and in front. It's a small world of its own here. While the red man mimes my stationary stance, I do a 360° — of the tree lined busyness, of vehicles carting down Cromwell Road towards South Kensington and Belgravia, a realist's idyll, longed for by Elizabeth Gaskell's Edith, that spoiled heiress in *North and South*. And when I spin on my heel, I face the other way, with vehicles flowing up onto the warped and fabulated flyover, out of sight, past indecipherable, time-bending billboards and beneath insectoid cranes. It's been a long, long time since I looked at any of the materials for the MA, but I know that one of our required books is David Lodge's *The Novelist at the Crossroads*, which positions the artistically minded person at a junction just like this one. In one direction is realism, in another is modernism. This is a very appealing notion because it makes the author's choice straightforward and binary: WALK or DON'T WALK, left or right, love or hate, to buy or not to buy. But really there is another way. It's been revealed to me from my time at Tesco.

The green man beeps, the flow stills briefly, and I tread water before the rush of engines and chassis resumes. Through the windscreens of the foremost row of cars, the drivers are biting their thumb cuticles anxiously. I recognise the white knuckles and the trapped panic on their faces, almost as if a crash, a collision, a total wipe-out would be a relief.

What I've realised is that Lodge's image of the novelist at the junction pales in comparison to the space I'm about to enter: the 'aesthetic supermarket', with its overabundance of styles, the hintertextual, the overtly self-referenced voices, technē, simulated situations, off-the-shelf farces. The novelist, like a customer, walks the aisles, picks up an item, inspects the label, fills the basket with a combination of ingredients. This is jazz cooking; this is improv living; this is hybridity; this is pluralism; this is progress.

"I s'pose I'll leave ye 'ere then," mutters Trolley Fella, "and 'av ye got a spare two paaand coin?" he asks as I reach the store's threshold, where a group of workmen have opened up the pavement by the crossroads. In a deep trench, they're laying cable.

"Sorry, haven't got anything on me," I call over my shoulder. A few months ago it was only £1 he was asking for. Now it's £2. Inflation bites everyone.

I enter through the sliding doors as if refreshed and revitalised, as if returning from some odyssey in the land of the sick, ready to tell everyone about the cyclōptic sinus, the siren Rennies.

"You're back. Finally," is Jasmeen's comment as I enter the Staff Canteen.

"You look like shit," is Dan's contribution as I pass the Fish Counter.

"You've shaved," is Bisera's observation. During my quarantine, I'd hacked away at the face forest but left my hair to the elements.

"You've been reassigned to the F&F mezzanine," is Monojit's directive.

"What?" I ask.

He blocks my next step towards the Food2Go Counter. "At least until your sickness is totally gone, you're prohibited from being around fresh produce."

"Who'll take charge of the Food2Go Counter?"

Monojit points to a guy in an oversized suit with my trolley, wearing my apron, leaning over the cocktail onions of my section. Not a hairnet in sight, instead he's got gelled spikes like hostile architecture that stops homeless people sleeping.

"Who is he?"

"New guy. He's called Akin. Actually he goes by his full-name: Akin Walter Tidem. A decent worker. Lots of potential. Uses his tablet well. You should hear his Tannoy announcements." Monojit kisses his bunched fingertips. "Anyway. They need you on F&F."

As I make my way upstairs to the mezzanine, I eye Akin suspiciously, watching him approach the Customer Service Desk and get on the microphone. His broadcast is perfect in pitch and diction, his RP-accent the clean and sober quality that would've narrated Queen Elizabeth's Coronation. He makes Flo and all her country pals sound like estuary chavs. Having delivered the final line about enhancing customers' supermarket experience Akin steps away and nearby staff and shoppers applaud. Suddenly I feel territorial. I want my salad bar back.

Upwards to F&F, I consider Monojit's hygiene-conscious rationale: totally rich, given how many people I've seen sneezing over the open-top salad bar. The olives and other produce that people grab with bare, grotty hands. It's one thing to covet from afar, but another to reach out and touch, but yet another to transgress entirely and taste. There's very little I can do. I can't demand they regurgitate what's been greedily consumed. The customer remains firmly, solidly right.

From the balcony I watch Akin as he scoots around the salad bar, spraying the sides with the eager dedication of someone who has just landed a new job. I can't remember if I was this eager and dedicated when I first started working here. It's hard to remember what my attitude used to be. All I remember was feeling grateful to Alby for getting me the job in the first place. I was already signed on and found those interviews at the Job Centre bleak and unnerving.

I remember when I first entered that Job Centre, thinking the waiting room was like a GP's but with less joy and more ill health. When my turn had come, the invigilator sat me down and scanned my CV.

"It says here you used to be a pot washer?" She twiddled a finger around a springy perm.

"Yes. One of my first jobs. When I was thirteen. From there I became an assistant chef in the same pub and..."

"Okay, okay. If I need any more info I'll ask for it. But it says here 'Pot washer'."

"Yes. I washed pots."

She pouted and chewed the pout. "Not the best words, izzit, 'Pot washer'?"

"That's what my job was."

"And what were your professional responsibilities."

"Mostly washing pots. Almost exclusively."

"Right. Right. Okay. Well can you think of a way of sprucing up your CV a tad? Employers don't like phrases like 'Pot washer'. They like more spruced-up words. They'll want something... something..."

"Spruced?"

"Exactly."

"What would you suggest?"

She'd smirked. "I'm sorry, I can't do all the work for you. And it says here you studied English at university, so let's utilise those word skills and let's upscale and architect your CV."

"Okay then. Let's spruce this thing." I tapped a drum beat on my thighs. "How about '*Plongeur*'?"

"What's that?"

"From one of George Orwell's books. When he was living in Paris he..."

"No, no. Choose an English phrase. You want employment in England. Use English."

Riled up, I'd leaned forward, mouth dry. "How about instead of 'Pot washer', I put 'Underwater Ceramics Technician'?"

Her eyes widened. "Perfect."

"Really?"

"Yes. Just pop that in and you're good as gold. Consider your CV upscaled. Now, your appointment time is up so... just move along please. Thanks. Next."

And moved along I was, and spruced was my CV. Shortly afterwards, I'd received that text from Alby. If it wasn't for him, none of this in the last eight months would've happened.

As I reach the F&F's staff desk, I make a mental note to thank him. Or blame him.

It's an overtly metallic space up here: steel girders, steel platforms, steel walkways. You feel like a foreman surveying a factory floor. And everywhere, bookending every rack and aisle of clothing, is a tall mirror, which catches and exaggerates my every movement. In fact, there's nowhere I can stand without being forced to look back at a reflected and refracted, even more self-conscious reproduction of myself. Yours falsely. The F&F team is made up of attractive men and women, all fabulous, all wrist-snapping, all "Yes, babez," and "No, darlin'," all wearing enviably colourful outfits, and I don't feel like I resemble any of them — physically or spiritually.

I must work harder.

My tasks, I'm told, are to fold, to hang, and to drape the new spring collection.

"And wear this," says the F&F director, her headset clasped around her gorgeously shiny fringe. She's holding out a scrunchy the colour of jaundice. I suddenly wish I'd cut my hair as well as my beard.

"You're not wearing one?" I ask.

She smiles and shakes her head. "You can let your hair down too when you've worked your way up to my position."

Over the next few days, I come into work each day, ascend the metal stairs, and set to folding, hanging, and draping. Throughout my shift, I tune in to the scribbly conversations of my new F&F colleagues who only pause their dialogue when the Tannoy announces a discount on cured hams and Cillit Bang, before continuing. I've noticed this habit, with staff and shoppers alike. It's like when two people meet in the streets and get talking but will pause while a police siren wails past, with the pair just looking at each other, waiting to continue. It's the same momentary prohibition on speech that I see in the aisles, with socially sanctioned public staring.

My role as a human iron goes on all day, and it's not bad. It's not the work that's better or any less menial but the more rarefied atmos that the F&F team have cultivated. They put in the emotional labour to form meaningful relationships with one another. As they call it, the 'vibe'. Then, during my lunchbreaks, I and the colourful F&F butterflies flutter to the Staff Canteen. There we sit, in our F&F huddle, getting gassed, being fun, fabulous.

We all agree that 'panties' is a horrid word.

"What are we saying about 'knickers' and 'pants'?"

We all clap and continue nibbling on our salads.

During one lunchtime, I can see Alby squinting — or

maybe even scowling — over from the crowd of deli workers and the new guy, Akin Walter Tidem. Bisera is frantic for our flagship to shine like St Elmo's fire because, as she puts it, 'the Big Boss' Philip Clarke is coming to show a millionaire around. Clarke, alumnus of the University of Liverpool, is CEO of Tesco — the omniscient power-that-is. I'm relieved to be free from all that frenzy on the shop floor, and pleased to be up on the F&F mezzanine amongst people who seem to actually enjoy their work.

Jasmeen shakes her head. "Sorry to cut across you, Bisera. Your big clean-up is going to have to wait, because I need everyone, as many as possible, for an urgent delivery, for our next intervention."

"Erm, Jasmeen, excuse me..." replies Bisera.

There appears to be a powershift unfolding in the relationship between the two tablet-wielding Team Leaders.

Jasmeen: "Let me stop you there. It's ten years since *Finding Nemo* was released, and the rest of May is going to involve a number of Nemo interventions."

"But..." Bisera protests.

But Jasmeen goes again, holding up her tablet's screen flashing with data: "We're looking at 500+ copies of *Finding Nemo*, ten-year limited edition, for the DVD aisle. I asked Akin to compile some stats for me. Thanks Akin, and it says here that DVDs are amongst our most valuable and popular products, up 26.66% since the previous quarter. We need to push for maximum sales. And up on the F&F mezzanine, we're about to put out hundreds of different costumes and outfits from the film. This *Finding Nemo* launch is gonna be huge."

"But..." Bisera repeats.

"I'm talking facts, here, Bisera. I'm not doing 'ifs', 'buts', and 'maybes'. I'm doing 'absolutes'."

Jasmeen speaks the truth. Over the last few days, all overtime staff have been on aisle No.1 working into the early hours of the morning on hands and knees putting out shelves of colourful kids' mags, laminated and glittery, each with a toy inside of a turtle or a fish or a shark. I've been watching from the mezzanine as all of this lays the ground for the final part of the marketing strategy.

"So, all of you in F&F—" Jasmeen goes on.

I sit up straight, as do the rest of my team.

"—we need you up on the mezzanine, draping mini mannequins with outfits from the film: all fish and marine animals. Orange and white striped outfits with tails, those are the clown fish. The electric blue and yellow-streaked outfits are Dory. And the grey wiry contraptions with big toothy helmets are the shark characters." She flashes her tablet's screen towards us, on which is a GIF of three sharks in an AA meeting, fins raised as they take the abstinence pledge. I remember that scene from when I first saw the film when I was a boy, but it's only now I realise they're in a Shark Recovery Group, trying to stop their addiction to eating other fish.

These outfits have been flying off the racks already, with parents giving in to the yelps and tantrums of their offspring.

I follow the rest of the team out of the room, only to be tugged on the arm. Monojit, frowning. "Just 'cause you're up on the mezzanine doesn't mean that Customer–Colleague Interaction Policies don't apply to you."

"Thanks for the reminder."

He sighs. "You need to BE PERSONABLE."

"Again, thanks."

"Which means maintaining a nametag at all times." He pokes my chest, along the poorly mended seam where I've stitched a bit of red fabric over the hole made by the mice.

"Yes, about that. When is my own nametag supposed to arrive?"

"Can't say."

Can't say. The perfect self-negating statement which even elides the "I" that can't say whatever it is that can't be said.

So, before I return to the mezzanine, I go to the Staff Room, and my proboscis probes the box for a nametag.

Today I am 'Judith', and Judith continues to fold, hang, and drape. She avoids backache by sitting on a stool while she works, hunched like Rodin's *Le Penseur*, as she sets out little pairs of colourful boots and slippers in the 12 months+ section. A little boy passes, gripping his father's hand. One of the T-shirts unhooks from the hanger above Judith and falls silently to the floor. In the mirror, the logo on the T-shirt is reflected: OMƎИ

The boy loosens himself from his father's hand, crouches to pick up the T-shirt, and gives it back to Judith.

"Thank you very much," Judith smiles.

He retreats to the safety of the paternal chino. The father nods at Judith as they move on. "Daddy, I want a *Finding Nemo* costume. Can we get one?"

Judith stands to crack her back, stretch her legs, shake out her hair. She should take up yoga or Pilates. This time up here in the more rarefied atmos of the mezzanine has made her start thinking that a lifestyle change could be beneficial. Maybe a hot stone massage. Or getting a tattoo of her name across the small of her back. Judith. *Nomen est omen*. Your name is your destiny.

Another of Akin's Tannoy broadcasts echoes around the store, his delivery even better than before. Judith is relieved that she's not competing with him right now.

As she passes the 4 years+ aisle, she notices a blur of orange, like a traffic cone, and looks again. It's not a traffic cone. It's the same little boy who picked up the T-shirt, but now he's dressed in one of the clown fish costumes. And he's cowering and crying. There's no big father fish in sight. This is a little boy lost in the retail forest. Inconsolable.

"Where's my daddy?"

Crying.

"Daddy."

Crying.

Judith crouches.

Inconsolable.

Inconsolable.

She pulls from a stack of plastic *Finding Nemo* masks the blue tang face. "Have you seen *Finding Nemo*?"

The boy nods, his face a little *Blaukraut* cabbage of fear.

"I'm Dory," Judith announces, putting on the mask and peering down at the clown fish through the eye holes.

The boy relaxes slightly, sniffs snottily.

"I'm Dory," Judith repeats.

He giggles through his tears.

"Shall we go and find your daddy?"

He nods again, and a small flipper pokes upwards. Judith clutches it. Soft, tiny, cold.

"Do you remember what you've got to do when life gets you down?"

"Just." Sniff. "Keep." Sniff. "Swimming."

"Exactly."

The pair set off, in unison, "*Just keep swimming*," around the mezzanine, then descending to the shop floor, the lost little fish sniffing and wiping back tears, occasionally glancing up at Dory, who dutifully repeats, "*Just keep swimming*." Each gesture makes the little fish's giggles that bit louder. He slides the length of his orange, scaly forearm, his finned wrist and hand fully across his glistening, slimy nose and eyes, a cartoonishly big wipe that's reserved only for the under-fives. We lose this gesture as we grow up. In a few years he'll just use the knuckle of a bunched fist. Then a few years after that, just the tip of a finger, lightly dabbing an eye's corner. Then, after that, he'll be at the age when men don't cry. Judith's noticed that men only sob in specifically designated places: after a penalty shoot-out, at the death of a monarch, or at a Morrissey gig. That's what growing up is: reducing the surface area for the removal of tears.

And by the Tannoy desk, Judith can see a father — his inner turmoil scattered all around him as he paces on the faux-marble in circles, making the sensor automatically open, close, and reopen the sliding doors. He looks like King Lear on the heath, crazed in his chinos and sliders. He stops when he sees the pair approach and rushes towards them, sliders flapping. He scoops up his little fish, buries his face in the gills. "I'm so sorry, baby boy. I thought you'd walked out of the store." He turns to Judith, reaching out a hand to shake. "That was the worst four minutes of my life."

"Don't worry. That's what we're here for," replies Judith, removing her mask.

The father looks down at Judith's nametag. "Thanks... Judith? Is that your name?"

"No daddy, this is Dory," sniffs Nemo.

- - - - -

Today I am 'Judith', again. Judith, sister of the Bard — as Woolf designates her. Passing through the glass doors this morning, Judith registers the presence of the security guard at his lectern, with his rosary of sweetcorn for a grin. He nods, but she doesn't reciprocate. She's remembering something from a foggy, misted past. A guard like him, or maybe actually him, was calling out to a female colleague: "Oi, lov. You gonna let your hair down or wat." And so Judith walks on, along the aisles' central backbone, gliding between the separate ribs of aisle No.13, Baby/Sanitary, on her left, and aisle No.14, Toiletries, on her right, making a mental note to herself to take her price tag gun along both aisles and reduce the fuck out of the tampons, luxury bubble bath, and hot water bottles.

Up on the F&F mezzanine, she's humming along to the store's playlist. '*I woke up like this*.' She checks herself in one of the mirrors. It's impossible not to, they surround and reflect and refract and reproduce her. When her shift starts, she'll have to scrunch her hair up into a messy bun, but for now, she lets it flow down to her shoulders. She runs her fingers through the curls and flattens down her eyebrows.

Flawless. '*I woke up like this*.'

Smooth face. Clear skin. Throughout the nine days she's been working here on the F&F mezzanine, Judith's noticed a growing awareness of the environment she moves through and her own body in the space. She feels the cold coming from the many aisles' many fridges, and she tucks her hands into the warming folds of her work jumper. She feels the impulse to linger in aisle No.1, to flick through the back of magazines — *POUT*, or *Vogue,* or *Take a Break* — to scorn the horoscopes. She feels like chatting to her colleagues, getting to know them on an emotional level. So when a member of her F&F team approaches and greets Judith with a compliment about her luscious locks, Judith receives this warmly, replying in kind:

"Morning, Siobhan. Thanks. You've got to finish telling me about your cinema date."

"OMG, yeah. Like, loads to tell."

Siobhan's one of F&F's most sought-after workers, always being requested via Tannoy to pose for this or that photo op. Most recently, she featured alongside that Lib Dem MP in Angus Caarht's article about Tesco customers. Over their lunchbreak the other day, Siobhan told the F&F team that she was going out for dinner and a film with a mystery man. Frankie & Bennies followed by a trip to the Vue Cinema in Shepherd's Bush to see *Under the Skin*, which Judith's already seen, but she'd like to hear another POV.

"Looking forward to it," Judith calls after Siobhan before returning to her task of folding, hanging, and draping clothes on various racks. Judith fixes that future interaction in her mind's diary — as something to look forward to. She's noticed a vast unexplored chamber of her heart has rolled away its stone. She feels both a heightened sense of empathy but also the pressures that come with seeing other perspectives: to engage, to understand, and sometimes to forgive.

Judith looks down at her work boots, and past them, through the metal grates out of which the mezzanine floor is made. She can see down to the shop floor, and the balding heads of men and women's roots showing through as they all go about their shopping. She leans on the balcony and watches the queues building at the checkouts, notices how many of them are carrying only a few items in their hands. That's what self-service was brought in for. Her eyes linger on Marilyn and Shel, the two most experienced women who work the tills, both of them scanning items at a furiously efficient pace. Judith hopes they'll be okay — that they won't be culled like most of the other staff over sixty.

The rest of this morning's tasks involve setting out a new range of coats, removing the winter products, and replacing them with spring wear, draping the mannequins in a selection of outfits ready for warmer weather.

She's noticed in herself a recent impulse to check in, to register and absorb the feelings of customers as they pass by. She doesn't always want to smile, but she does feel an urge to find out how their day's going. It's like her sudden impulse with that pair of pretty mules she saw a customer buying the other day. She desperately wanted to try them on. It's like she wants to walk in other people's shoes.

During her lunchbreak, she opts for a chickpea and buckwheat salad from aisle No.3 (Ready Meals), and joins the table of F&Fers in the Staff Canteen.

"You're just in time for me to tell everyone about my date," Siobhan says, tucking in to a Ryvita smeared with goat's cheese. Classic Siobhan — always the same lunch.

"When we got to the restaurant..." and Siobhan is off, describing first her outfit, then her journey on the Tube, then the dinner — split bill — and then the cinema. Throughout the retelling, Siobhan's colleagues are really listening, giving her plenty of verbal feedback, gassing her up:

"...hmm..."

"Oh yeah?"

"Oh really?"

"Uhuh."

"OMG... no, really!"

"I get you."

All of this buttresses Siobhan's story until its final moments, where she concludes with an evaluation of how she felt about it all. "I just feel like... I dunno. Like it could've gone, like, better. But who knows. Maybe it'll be worth it if we meet up again."

A colleague asks, "Have you organised it?"

"I'm waiting for him to contact me," Siobhan replies.

"And what about the film?" Judith asks.

Siobhan crunches down on her Ryvita. Chews. She does that hand waving gesture in front of her mouth, signalling demure mastication that she's hurrying to complete so she can answer.

"*Under the Skin*. Scarlett Johansson. I liked it more than he did. It was all about how easily men can be lead, can find their heads turned. Like, in one scene, Johansson seduces a silk-shirted man in a night club. Then he drowns or gets submerged in like all this black tar stuff. And she does it again and again to all these different men. Her victims, I guess that's the word, the men, they should be pitied if nothing else. Most of them aren't menacing or overbearing, just very simple and susceptible to Johansson's eyes and lips."

When Judith returns through the store towards the mezzanine, she passes aisle No.14 (Toiletries), and notices an advert for sanitary pads. The shoehorn-shaped material in the photo is pure white, except for a dollop of minty blue liquid which drips meekly onto the woolly pad. There is no blood in sight, and Judith wonders if the general attitude of shock and disgust towards menstruation is due in part to the absence in adverts like this of the red colour which defines the natural process. The messaging is: let's create a euphemism for bodily functions, so we need not face the fact of blood. What would happen if men menstruated? Well, the film series *Jackass* would've had a different slant from the strictly scatological. There would've been prank after prank with Johnny Knoxville introducing himself, then introducing a gynecoLOLogist to oversee a period blood drinking game: Steve-O and Bam dressed in Roman military gear, each with a *vitis* held aloft, and their *pugios* flashing in their sheaths, as they downed shot after shot against the clock, all the while the rest of the cast hoot, cheer, and high-five with Centurion camaraderie, in all its bloody strength and honour.

As her shift comes to its end, she passes the Fish Counter, where Dan is descaling a hake. As with the security guard, out of the dry ice haze of memory Judith remembers that Dan, or someone very like him, admitted to suicidal impulses. She approaches and asks, "How are you, Dan?"

"Fine. Why?"

"But how are you in yourself?"

"Why d'you wanna know?"

"I sense a bit of hostility."

"Nah, mate. It's just I've got lots to do and it's already four o'clock."

Judith perseveres, using words like 'interested' and 'concerned' and 'wellbeing'.

Dan looks at her, frowning. "You've been up there with the gals on the mezzanine too long, mate."

"Maybe women see and understand more than men."

"Pah," Dan exclaims midway through splitting open an oyster. "I don't know a single woman who could imagine what it's like to be me. Women can't imagine what it's like to be a man."

"I'm not sure about that," replies Judith.

"Oh yeah?" Dan glances up with narrowed, challenging eyes. "Alright. You tell me what you think a woman would think it's like for a man working here."

"Okay. Which man?"

"Dunno, you choose."

Judith looks around, notices a young shop-floorer on his knees, shelving books on aisle No.1. She points. "Look at him. I'll tell you what a woman might think it's like for him working here. Imagine that he likes books. Let's say he's got into a habit of working hard for forty minutes to free up twenty minutes to do some reading in a toilet cubicle. He hides a book in his trousers' waistline and secures it in place by tightening the cord on his apron. As long as no one hugs him on his journey between the shop floor and toilet (*"Is that a book in your trousers, or are you just pleased to see me?"*) then he can sneak away for a good quarter of an hour of lavatory reading without being found out. If the cubicles are in-use, he stands at the urinal and feigns stage fright. Waiting, waiting for the cubicle to become free. He inspects the white tiles, their blemishes and the lightning bolt cracks in the porcelain. He inspects the urinal closely, which contains in its fragrant grill a cluster of semi-porous balls, the colour and shape of fish roe, through which the piss seeps. Sometimes a stressed colleague will have spat his white fudge of Nicorette gum into the grill, and it's wedged itself between the balls of roe. No cleaner has ever voluntarily ventured to remove these, nor should they feel obligated. He hears a flush, and a cubicle door opens, and he's duty-bound to avoid the gaze of whoever it is, wait for them to wash and dry their hands and leave, while the hot air yells from the shiny nozzle that looks like a tapir's snout. He enters the cubicle, locks the door, sits on the lid and reads... well... what would he read?"

"I dunno. Shakespeare?"

"I was going to suggest Jean Rhys, but why not. So he's there reading *Hamlet*, and he's getting really engrossed in the scene where Ophelia says, '*to the noble mind/Rich gifts wax poor when givers prove unkind,*' and he looks up to catch a warped reflection in the toilet paper dispenser's silver surface: a young man sitting on the toilet with the lid down, in a white apron, in a hairnet, with a white kitchen cap perched on top, reading a book. This is the first time he's ever caught himself in the act. He hears the clatter of a door, the jangle of a belt buckle, and the shuffle of trousers loosed to the floor as someone in the neighbouring cubicle sits and shits. He can hear his fellow colleague's relief: there is nothing like reading to the sound of a grown man defecating next to you."

"Doesn't sound like any bloke I know." Dan shrugs. "And also you've got anuva fing wrong. How many lads do you know who'd wash their hands after a piss? A shit, maybe, but not a piss."

"CAYG, Dan, always remember CAYG. And what do you think it's like for a woman working here?"

Dan sighs, picks up a handful of black mussels, begins to net them in blue mesh. "CAYG, mate. CAYG."

As she leaves the store, Judith passes into the lamplight of spring evening. She steps down to the crossroads, where car horns yelp at her. The trench opened up earlier today by the group of workmen is deep and dark, but the men in hi-viz have gone. Standing by the trench where they've been laying cable, Judith unpins her nametag. And she throws it in. The nametag flashes, glinting in the lamplight as it tumbles into the dark.

I side-foot loose soil from a reddish heap on top of it, burying Judith at the crossroads, wondering when the day might come for her to rise again.

- - - - -

Going for dinner with Billie Piper. That's on this evening's agenda. *Going for dinner with Billie Piper*, followed by some live jazz, performed by Lance. Alby had suggested that we come to Soho before the gig. *Going for dinner with Billie Piper*. There's strategy to this. A system, logic. GFDWBP. *Going, for, dinner, with, Billie, Piper*. That's Greek, Frith, Dean, Wardour, Berwick, Poland — the kind of mnemonic that helps keep Soho's streets well-patterned, and that helps lighten the mood a bit. I suspect Alby, like me, is aware that there's been some tension between us at Tesco. So, here we are, in Soho, on Dean Street, that's *dinner*, wondering what to eat.

"Could go to Burger and Lobster," I suggest, "for a bit of surf and turf."

"A bit dear, innit?" Alby objects.

"I don't think they do venison."

Alby shakes his head, "I don't even like you."

"Alright. What about The Montagu Pyke?"

"Lad. I've not come all the way to Soho for Wetherspoons. 'Ere, I know. Follow me."

We set off along Dean Street, passing beneath the blue Karl Marx plaque (*K.M. woz 'ere, 1851–6*). The streets are already rammo with the spillover of drinkers from The City, briefcases and laptop bags by the shins of men holding pints, talking stock.

We turn onto Greek Street — that's *going* — Alby leading us into a poky diner called Pollo, an Italian retreat from the extortionate coffee shops that enshrine Soho. Its delicious gourmet food does a lot of heavy lifting to make up for an appalling wine menu — £3.75 gets you an inky red glass from a nearby off-license, to which Pollo adds a few quid. The waiter brings our drinks and food, and the glasses tremble in subordination to a dish of great, and affordable, pasta. Décor: if these wooden panels could speak they would unburden decades of gossip about its low-income diners, of which Alby and I are just another in a series, looking up over our steaming plates of linguini gamberoni e cozze, to chew and gaze through the oven-fogged glass at the knot of streets beyond, where The Three Greyhounds meets Ed's milkshake bar, while theatre-goers spill out from the Prince Edward. Pollo's poor wine makes these woozy connections somehow more profound, though no self (dis) respecting MA student-cum-Tesco worker would bother sharing them, and so I keep them to myself. Alby, by contrast, is without the affliction of still being a student, and so shares his thoughts more easily.

He's holding up the *Evening Standard*. "Listen to this," he says, pushing his plate to one side and reading aloud: "With her new role as Brona Croft, an Irish lady of the night in foggy London, Billie Piper resurrects an old, familiar character. She has metamorphosed from dimpled girl-next-door, through the gel-pen pink of the life of a call-girl, and now reached her final imago, as the frayed lace-wearing and mascara-smudged Victorian wench." Alby looks up at me. "Can you believe it? We're literally going for dinner with Billie Piper and she's fuckin' showed up!"

I spool some spag onto my fork, nodding. It's a frail travelling coincidence that neighbourhoods in London bring about. The same kinds of characters crop up in the same postcodes throughout the decades. Soho, for instance, has always attracted the same bohemian types, from the orgy-obsessives of the reign of King Charles II all the way through to the burlesque shows of now.

I glance at my phone. "We need to eat up so we're not late for Lance's jazz performance."

Alby reads on, ignoring me: "*Penny Dreadful* is a gothic-horror for the small screen, a Frankenstein's monster in its own right, comprising the spliced limbs of every well-known ghoulish tale in popular imagination. There are references to Mary Shelley, Sweeney Todd, Dorian Gray, Sherlock Holmes. Yadder yadder blah blah. And then there's this. Listen. Billie Piper's Brona Croft is a victim of the progress that threatens us all, of technological advancement. Brona explains at one point early in the series that she worked in a looming factory in Shoreditch but was soon replaced by more efficient industrial machines."

Alby looks into the middle distance with an ominous face.

I sip my wine. I can already feel myself getting woozily raged up, a deadly combination of tired and drunk that makes the drinker indignant, sulky, and antagonistic.

"Ey, lad. This journalist is sayin' exactly what's happenin' to us at Tesco. I'm tellin' you we need to do summit about it." That expression crosses his face — of plans and schemes, of calculations and strategy. It was there when he told me about the map he'd procured. It was there when he spoke to Nick about the door sensors at the store front.

"Well, I don't know what you have in mind, but before anything else, I need somewhere to live. I'm fucking sick of sofa surfing. Maybe if this journalist was reporting on that, I'd be interested." I shift in my seat — Pollo's imitation marble tabletops and close-packed chairs flatter neither the décor nor the patron's spine. "And anyway, who is this journalist? I could've fucking written that article. I could do reviews."

I grab the paper, glance at the article, at the author's name.

ANGUS CAARHT, FREELANCE.

I feel myself deflate. The linguini suddenly feeling very stodgy in my stomach. I check my phone again. "Come on," I mutter, "let's pay and get along. Lance's going to be on soon."

We split the bill and leave, rounding the corner onto Frith Street — that's *for* — where a queue has already assembled itself along the pavement outside Ronnie Scott's. Fortunately, Lance's got us onto the guest list, and we sidle up next to the tutting queue and announce our names to the hi-vizzed bouncer. His head is the same shape and colour as a jicama, and with it he nods us through. We take our seats at a low-lit table, the walls behind us a mosaic of framed photographs of bloated faces blowing into trumpets, wearing shades and smoking.

To polite, turtle-necked applause, Lance and his band of moustached jazzheads shuffle on stage and pick up their instruments. None of them takes to a microphone to introduce themselves, instead allowing the watery sizzle of the cymbals and the stabbing piano chords to initiate what the audience largely recognises as Miles Davis's 'So What', and then the rest of *Kind of Blue* unfolds.

Not a brayed note in the place, just calmly and quietly revealed to the nodding audience. Lance and his troupe lead us through a drowsy, boozy soundscape that for me pulls up onto the mind's projector lantern images of taxi cab windows hashed with raindrops, and their tyres splashing through puddles. This is the opposite of frenzy, a tonic which cools the tired jealousy I felt when Alby was reading Caarht's article at Pollo. *Kind of Blue* is all kinds of blue, a sequence of watery repeats, repeats, repeats, each musicianer earning his rightful place on the prestigious wall of sound.

By the final ovation, I'm wobbly on my feet, with the large glasses of red I've continued to order. Alby and I wait by the club's entrance, while Lance gradually peels himself away from audience-members who pat him on the back and compliment his double bassing. After that, the three of us wind our way through Soho, briefly stopping at bars to top up, until they call last orders. We decide to buy a bottle of wine from an offy and share it as we walk and stumble.

Alby and Lance hadn't met before, and there's always a risk in trying to orientate your friends into one another's orbit, particularly those from different epochs: the childhood pal seldom syncs with the workplace buddy; the colleague-turned-comrade rarely gets along with the uni companion. But Alby and Lance hit it off well, with Alby waxing lyrical about our time spent at university together, and Lance talking proudly about becoming an uncle to his sister's baby, then enthusing about the poetry-jazz collaborations he and I occasionally record at his flat.

At this, Alby stands in the middle of the road on Wardour Street — that's *with* — his head upturned to the dark sky, swigs from the bottle of wine, then recites his memorised Borges story in Spanish, '*Del Rigor en la Ciencia*'.

Lance and I wait on the pavement, and our applause redoubles up the narrow, tall buildings.

"That would be great to record," Lance exclaims, taking the bottle from Alby. "It'd work best if we laid down a version of Miles Davis's 'Flamenco Sketches' behind it."

It's rowdily suggested that we just fucking do it, right now — get the bus back to Lance's flat and just fucking record it this very night. Lance's sister is away with the baby, so we'd not be disturbing anyone.

By this point, the night air is lacquered with spring heat, and we wind our way along Berwick Street – that's *Billie* – along Poland Street – that's *Piper* – and we're wandering past Oxford Street's illuminated shop fronts. It's so bright that if you squint, it could be daytime. If a bus arrived now, we'd likely get on it. The three of us trip and tumble along the pavement, taking it in turns trying to leapfrog postboxes. We're moving in the direction of TCR which, at this time, will have its mesh visor firmly down, and we can see the great glowing monument of Centre Point high above the station, its cross-hatched windows on so many floors like an enormous kleroterion, that purest of ancient democratic devices which selected Athenian citizens to the βουλαί. In my hazy state of wobbly knees and unsteady eyes, the proportions and shape of Centre Point shift, and its kleroterion aspect changes to that of a CAGE, with the lattice slots which comprise each window of the building now the dimensions of wire and mesh, and my drunken mind soars back to the warehouse, to the waste.

"But first I need a piss," Alby announces, interrupting my unwelcome imaginings.

"Second that," Lance agrees. I wait while they disappear down a flight of stairs into an alleyway off Ramillies Street. In this moment of stilled, fuzzily quiet drunkenness, the tinny hiss and thump of the jazz swills in my ears. It had a take-it-or-leave-it tone, an unurgent force which allowed the audience to absorb what we wanted: resolve, comfort, surprise, warmth, hate, love, anger. A truly democratic sound that laid out all the options to the listener and handed over the decision-making to us. I fumble in my pocket for a pen and pull out a ream of plasticky Tesco parchment, planning to scribble this down, but by then Alby and Lance are back, and they're giggling.

Alby: "There's a couple of blokes down there, really goin' for it."

"Bollocks," I reply suspiciously.

"I'm serious!" Alby squeals in protest.

The three of us walk down the steps and sure enough, silhouetted at the alleyway's far end is a pair of figures, one standing behind the other, gripping his shoulders. They're swaying, not quite in unison. I move closer, an ugly memory coalescing behind the booze: the leg-jiggling, the gripped shoulders.

"I've seen this before," I whisper.

"I bet you have," Alby sniggers. "There're websites for this kind of thing."

"No. I mean, they're not going at it, as you say. I saw this on a crime documentary. That one is mugging the other one."

As a trio we march towards the figures, and only when we're about a foot away do they separate. One releases the other and the other falls to the ground, groaning as he slumps face down. The one still standing stares at us, eyes wide and panicked. He's thin, very thin, with a wispy clump of dark hair on a smooth chin, and the smears of early sideburns painfully sculpted. Nervously he toggles the zip of his donkey jacket.

"Are you two friends?" Alby asks.

A panicked pause, then: "Yes, my friend. This is my friend. He is my good football brother."

"What kind of mad accent's tha'?" Alby mutters.

It's not one I recognise, with my drunken state and swilling ears.

Lance crouches and shakes the slumped figure's shoulders. "You alright, mate?"

Groans rise from the ground, then a slurred, "Jussstt whhhheresss mmmy wallllettt… annnd mmmy pphoone?"

Our attention turns back to the man in the donkey jacket. Alby grabs his chest, pushes him back against the filthy wall. "Give us his stuff, prick."

The pockets of dj's drainpiped jeans with those bleached tears in the thighs are turned out: wallet, phone, cigarettes. We take them all.

"Those mine," dj says, pointing at the packet of Benson and Hedges, the same brand that Tesco stocks behind the sliding metal panel by the Tannoy desk. This packet's image is a close-up of a porcelain toilet bowl, the water clouded a dull red. SMOKING INCREASES THE RISK OF BLADDER CANCER, reads the label.

"We're having them, too," I add, vindicated in my boozed state to inflict harm.

"Okay, okay. I sorry, my friend," says dj, panicked.

"Just an accidental theft, was it? Butterfingers?" Alby mutters, loosening his grip.

The guff of fans bolted to the wall above our heads is potent, and for a moment there's silence. Suddenly, without noticing the thought transfer to action, I pull back my shoulder, clench my fist, and hit dj as hard as I can in the face. Knuckles lodge into the shelf of his cheek. His head knocks back against the wall, and he yells out. I push him and try to knee him in the gut, but Alby and Lance are pulling at my shoulders, and I fall backwards. There's the tinkling of glass as one of us must've dropped our wine bottle. As I land on the ground, I can feel pain in my palm, sharp and delicious, as I lean my weight onto the shards of glass.

"What the fuck's wrong with yer?" Alby yells at me, then turns to dj. "You. Fuck. Off."

Dj moves – gallops – off along the alleyway, rubbing his head.

I sit up, next to the slumped body of the muggee. I inspect my hands, and can see glittering glassy diamonds imbedded in the bloody flesh.

"I say again, lad. What the fuck was that about?"

I can't quite answer, my jaw is locked. I just sit there picking glass from my hand while Lance and Alby discuss what to do.

Lance elicits from the muggee his address.

"It's in Lambeth, not far from my uncle's flat. I'll get this guy into a cab, drop him in Lambeth then I'll just walk back to mine."

"Alright, mace. And I'll take this fuckin' poor man's Paddy Monaghan back to my place and get him cleaned up."

"It's just my hand. Big deal," I slurrily shrug.

"You're sitting in our piss, as well," Lance points out. "Alby, I'll be in touch. I reckon we should collaborate on one of those poem-jazz tunes."

"I'm up for it," Alby agrees, then sighs as he hauls me upright, and the two of us return to Oxford Street and wait for a bus in silence.

This silence elongates until I ask, "So how come we're going back to yours?"

Alby, impatient, sighing as if to a pestering child: "You're too drunk, and you're bleeding, and you were sitting in piss."

"What about your twin?"

"What about him?"

"Still staying with you, isn't he...divorce?"

"Our Elis has gone back to his missus, so they can sort out the paperwork. His room's free tonight."

This isn't said with the kind of celebratory tone I would've hoped to be invited to crash at his. My hand hurts, but I don't say anything.

We're in silence, Alby pacing the perimeter of the bus stop, while I'm leaning my head against the smeared glass. "Cccoome on Albs," I protest, "You should've backed me up just then."

"Ey, lad. You need to chill the fuck out. Right now. The bus'll be here any minute and I can't be dealin' with tha' chat when we get on."

"All I'm saying is you should've backed me up with that mugger."

"Oi, look, I know you're all sensitive to theft and stealin' and stuff 'cause of yer brother, but you were way out of line hittin' that fella."

The bus arrives, we board, and shudder to Canonbury. Again, in silence.

There's no traffic, there's no one else onboard the bus. It's an empty, silent journey and I'm not sure what do with this. It's like darkness, apparently a lack or privation of light, but it feels very active, very realised. An object of noiselessness.

Having endured the injury of constant muzak, and metallic fuzzy announcements over the Tannoy, I might've felt in the past that silence is not only an actual thing but is a rare commodity, a treasure to be valued on the odd occasion it is stumbled upon. But this journey towards Canonbury with Alby is no treasure — it's leaden.

The next stop is CLEPHANE ROAD

We disembark into Alby's neighbourhood. There are many prefixes which could be added to this neck of the woods. To 'urbia' the obvious attachment is 'sub-', but it's not that. It's not established enough; it's not cosmetic enough. 'Ex-' is too definitive, too deathly. 'Pre-' is ahistorical. So 'post-urbia' will have to do. It's very quiet and chilled out, set back from a main road by the fortifications of a converted rice mill, and behind that there's a courtyard, and beyond that a system of corridors and alleyways that leads to a gate, and beyond that is Alby's flat. All of that muffles the sound of the city.

Without much small talk, Alby directs me to the bathroom, where I shower, wash my hands, plaster my palms with antiseptic cream and micropore, and when I leave the bathroom, there's a T-shirt and boxers laid out for me. And there's a freshly folded pair of Tesco trousers and dark blue Tesco fleece, which will be vital for work tomorrow morning. Straightforward fraternity, despite the rupture earlier in the evening, re-establishes itself in these gestures — the sharing of a bottle of wine, the borrowing of clothes. I collapse onto the bed and dizzily swirl into sleep.

I wake to the sound of Alby humming jazz tunes in the shower. It's early morning — that cruel trick which hangovers play by waking you before you'd usually get up. I'm still reeling from what he said last night about me being out of line for punching the mugger, but I'm grateful for the fresh work uniform he left for me — even if it doesn't quite fit.

Once I'm dressed, I go to the kitchen and make coffee, in an attempt to remedy the hangover. Although Alby's twin, Elis, has left for the foreseeable, there are still remnants: his clothes still hanging up in the room I slept in last night, legal letters addressed to him left on the countertop, the second bottle of blue-top milk in the fridge. Hopefully, he won't be back, and I might — possibly, maybe, just maybe — be able to move in here.

While the coffee percolates, I open kitchen drawers in search for more plasters and antiseptic cream to rewrap my cuts, but then I stop, suddenly noticing on the kitchen wall a corkboard on which is pinned the map of Tesco Kensington, with all its demarcated aisles. For some reason Alby has drawn in red felt-tip a series of arrows routed around the store, leading in and out of the warehouse. Where the sliding glass doors of the entrance are located, he's drawn a thick red circle, and next to this he's stuck a smaller, torn piece of paper on which is printed a photograph of a Dalek. It looks like it's been torn from one of Nick Dale's magazines. I inspect the rest of the corkboard more closely, on which Alby has pinned other curious stuff. There's a small drawing of a CAGE, with annotations showing its height, width, and depth. There's a £1 coin sellotaped to a card on which Alby's scribbled, '*For the lad with the trolley* '. There's a brochure for Barclays Boris bicycles. And there's a list of phrases, two of which are crossed out. I'm sure I recognise them, even if my hangover prevents me from placing them:

~~Ease out of pain through labour and endurance (Book II, Line 261–3)~~
~~Tedious havoc (Book IX, Line 30)~~
To obey is best (Book XII, Line 561)

Just as the shutter to the mind's memory bank is about to be raised, I notice another piece of paper, distinct from the rest, not in Alby's blocky scrawl but, I realise with confusion and shock, my own handwriting. It's an old draft of a letter to my brother, it's Draft No.4, the missing draft, the one which I thought I'd lost. I tug it from the corkboard and begin reading it through, forcing my eyes past the hangover's protest. The letter pleads, in the purest tone I could muster, for an explanation for why he stole what he did, to account for himself. The language is grey, the paper itself is grey. I feel grey.

But why the fuck has Alby got this?

Just then Alby enters. "Why the fuck've you got this?" His face is pinkish from the shower, but it looks like a blush of guilt.

"Eya, come on, lad. Just you settle down there and I'll..."

"No. This is fucked up. This is a private letter to my brother and you've got it."

"Look, I'll explain," Alby says, darting to turn down the hob under the bubbling coffee.

"Alby, I'm hungover as fuck, and you're a prick. You should've backed me up last night with that mugger, and now you've got my letter for my brother who you know is guilty of theft, and oh yeah, about what you said last night, yeah I have got a really fucking big problem, with thievery and stealing. So what are you doing then, stealing from me are you?"

"You're the one bein' a prick lad, listen to yourself mouthin' off right now."

"I've been looking for this for months. And what's all this on the corkboard?"

"Chill your fuckin' self, lad."

At this, I'm done. I turn away, retrieve my boots from the room I slept in, and trip towards the door, shouting as

I go, "I've got to get to work, and I'm taking my letter back. Wanker."

"Dick 'ed," Alby shouts as I slam the door.

The journey from Canonbury to Earl's Court is long and treacherous. I read and reread the missing Draft No.4 of my Letter to an Incarcerated Sibling, my head pounding with anger and booze as I pick out phrases where I ask why why why he stole what he did, where I concede that there are different kinds of theft but that what he did was unjustifiable, where I gesture towards a future relationship. But very soon, I can't seem to see the words on the page — for some reason, the ink begins to blur.

CHAPTER NINE

HOMEWARE

They say that the amount of time humans have existed, compared to the overall lifespan of the planet, is equivalent to the thickness of a layer of paint on the wall of a room. That single coat represents the entire history of humankind. Maybe that's why we feel so distraught when we witness a wrecking ball smashing into the side of a derelict house, as we pass a site cordoned off for gentrification. It marks the destruction of the room that contains the wall on which human history is scrawled. Maybe that's also why we feel so despondent about the hue of grey or beige paint which lacquers so many offices. It indicates how dull, forgettable, non-descript so much of a life is.

Distraught and despondent — that's the combo I feel right now, as I stand to attention in a small, grey-walled office. About ten minutes ago, as I was entering the store, I felt my elbow roughly seized.

Wart and Feral were on me, gripping my arms while Monojit stood in front of me: "Today you will bear the decision of your case. This way." I was escorted through the staff double doors, up the stairs, past the canteen, and along the network of managerial corridors. One particular part of this white-collar warren terminates in the doors marked UPPER MANAGEMENT in silver lettering. As always, on the floor is a cardboard box printed with the outline of a champagne flute. This time the box was open and empty. But just before reaching the doors, Wart and Feral, following Monojit, steered me into a side room. This room: a small, grey office in which I now stand. Metal cabinets upright like sentries surround me on all four sides. On the table is a computer and a pot of pens, each biro pointing upwards like black stakes.

By the window, Bisera leans, arms folded. Sitting at the table, his face paler than usual in the computer screen's glare, is Nick Dale. Next to him kneels Akin, writing on a pad of paper, taking notes like some kind of understudy. Monojit's behind me, barring the door. There are no chairs, except for Nick's, and I can hear he's doing leg-jiggles that make the plastic joints creak.

"Really difficult, this," begins Bisera, eyeing me stonily.

I look to Nick, but he's fixed on the computer screen.

"Difficult. Difficult." Bisera repeats. "You've been doing so well. A proper improvement. And now this."

Nick leans towards Akin, murmuring: "Always start with a compliment." Akin dutifully writes.

"And now this what?" I ask.

Bisera sighs. "Nick?"

From a cabinet by his side, Nick takes a small, tattered rectangular object. It's smeared with dried mud, or maybe coagulated blood, but the ice rink sheen of laminate still glints in the strip lighting over our heads. It's a JBT booklet, the very same kind which I received all those months ago when I started working here. Its metal ring binding is loose, like a car's valve spring bent and buckled by a traffic accident. Nick carefully puts on a pair of rubber gloves — the same kind which he and I used to clean up the smashed wine back in March — and delicately turns the pages. Bisera leans over his shoulder, looking down at the dog-eared pages.

Akin's pen hovers, waiting. Nick examines the JBT like he's beginning an autopsy: "Spine has been removed, leaving a two to three centimetre part of the binding still attached."

Akin writes.

"Pages 1 through 7 contain graffiti of what looks to me like a genital nature. Or perhaps root vegetables."

"Someone, and we don't know exactly who," Bisera explains, "has graffitied this precious booklet. With filth. Utter filth. Here" — she snatches up the booklet and holds it out — "just look."

On the page which describes Tesco's history, someone with a fairly decent understanding of male anatomy has amended the margins with a number of differently sized, variously proportioned erect penises, with bulging veins and swelling hairy testicles. One penis in particular has been drawn in such a way that the several dashes which comprise the blue line of the Tesco logo resemble ejaculated sperm.

"We cannot, will not, allow this kind of desecration of our brand."

I supress a smile. "Come on. That literally could've been anyone. Isn't there a school nearby? It could've been a teenager just doing what teenagers do."

"This is not the only piece of evidence we have that leads us to suspect that someone is seriously trying to jeopardise this store. Nick?"

From his cabinet, Nick takes a form. Without any intonation, without looking up at me, he recites: "I am now going to ask you a series of questions about recent suspicious activity around the store, and I want you to answer truthfully. Can you do that?" Then to Akin he murmurs, "always frame commands as questions."

"What choice does he have?" Monojit sneers behind me.

I am presented with a list of questions which, though I genuinely don't know the answers, prompt me to feel that I must pick my way to avoid dangerous pitfalls, trying not to be trapped in an outright lie, or to claim false cluelessness. I try to guard myself against any remark which could implicate me in whatever it is that Bisera is looking for, though I have a fairly decent idea that it's Alby who they're after.

I deny knowledge of why Tesco-branded trolleys have been dredged from the Serpentine.

I deny the accusation of participating in illicit gambling on the outcomes of staff tribunals.

I deny knowledge of why an empty CAGE had been discovered in Felon Place.

I deny knowledge of what an ex-employee named Heath has been doing since he was sacked.

I deny an accusation of deliberately sabotaging the Euphorium Bakery's range of Ploughwoman's sandwiches.

When I'm asked what I know about door sensor technology, I look meaningfully at Nick, who is still staring at the form in front of him, and answer with a shrug: "Only that it puts doormen out of work."

My replies to their questions are evasive but not untrue.

Bisera taps her fingertips together, ruminating up to the ceiling panels: "I can't tell if you're being very, very clever, or just really don't know what's going on."

"I can't help you there," I reply, "how would I know what I don't know?"

Monojit sniggers. Bisera gives him a sharp look. "Monojit, that's enough. He might be telling the truth."

Monojit steps forward. "Might be. Might not. But what about the CCTV footage? Get him to explain that."

Bisera nods reluctantly. "Okay. Nick?"

Nick obediently swivels the screen, to show me silent, grainy footage of an aisle on the F&F mezzanine, of a sepia figure crouching down low by a smaller, sepia figure.

"We can't get the audio," Nick explains neutrally.

"But it's clear that *that's* you there, and you're talking to that child in this clip," adds Akin.

Nick turns to him: "Remember you're here to learn. Leave the discussion to us." Akin nods and continues to write.

The footage skips to another clip, recorded on a different CCTV camera, as the pair of figures descend the mezzanine stairs — the taller in a Dory mask, the smaller laughing and wiping his eyes.

Bisera points to the screen. "That is not your role."

My role, if I remember that day, was as a Dory fish who returned a lost child to his father. Admittedly it isn't in my job description, but on that occasion I was willing to work *pro bono*. "I felt it was necessary in the circumstances, to ensure a customer's safety."

"But that is not your role. You should've contacted an appropriate member of staff. As a result of your actions the F&F was temporarily short-staffed, and the store lost revenue in your absence."

"And also," interjects Monojit, "if you're so concerned about the customer, how do you explain the thing with the homeless man? Nick, load the clip."

On the screen there appears flickering footage from another CCTV camera, this one overlooking the forecourt outside the store, and up its steps come two figures carrying between them a supermarket trolley. One of them is obviously me, and the other is evidently Trolley Fella.

"What's going on there, then?"

"He needed help carrying the trolley up the steps. One of the wheels was broken."

The footage continues to play. At the top of the steps, one of the figures — me — enters the store, while the other, Trolley Fella, in his big thick, worn coat, begins to tug the trolley along to the line of those already parked, using the key fob of one trolley to release the £1 coin from the trolley we've just returned.

Nick loads up two more clips from different days which show the same thing: me helping Trolley Fella to haul trolleys up the steps, then him using a parked trolley to release another £1 coin.

"He made a proper business out of this, as you can see. With all his 'savings' he came into the store and bought an entire wheel of our best brie."

"He's got good taste," I shrug.

"In the end we had to ask Haroon to take over and replace all the £1 coin trolleys with ones that don't need currency."

"Is that the best use of the store's resources?" I ask.

"Look, the fact is that you've contravened all sorts of policies and subclauses with this. Where in the JBT does it say that you can freely take what's on the aisles, as with the mask, or create an income for a homeless man?"

"What I did may've been thoughtless but only because I was following the Policies to their logical conclusions."

Monojit whistles: "Careful. Sounds suspiciously like you're having a go at the Policies."

I dig my teeth into my lip. Along with the sacred text of the JBT, the store's Policies are off-limit to voiced criticism.

Nick's fingers going full-on Elgar over the keyboard. There's the sound of chunky metallic scrapes and beeping, and out of a printer positioned on top of a cabinet, a piece of paper emerges. Bisera takes it, and begins to read aloud: "Team Member, ID number 6655321, the Commission of Inquiry having completed its work on this day in June 2014, has concluded with the consultation of a mix of shop floor and senior staff council that the accused worker is condemned to firing..."

The meaning of these words begins to take hold, just as through the window the sun breaks the clouds and blinds me.

"We're the firing squad," Akin murmurs so only I can hear, "and you've got to..."

He stops as we're all suddenly aware of a loud commotion in the corridor outside, whose stark walls and rubbery flooring makes the slightest noise bounce and amplify. There's a tumbling sound of shoes and squeaking of soles, and the door opens. In walks Connor McConcavity, followed by Cármen, whose expression is that hell-fury-scorn variety which men are warned to avoid provoking.

"Good morning, everyone. Right, I know what's going on in here, and I'm giving orders for it to stop. Yes, there is a lot of suspicion in the store at the moment, and yes, we know there is someone who is causing trouble, but I do not think it is this young man."

"Well hang on there–" remonstrates Akin.

McConcavity cuts across him: "There is another possible suspect, and we are looking into it. We'll have more to report soon as, but I'm sure you'll be concurrent with me that we've got a reputation to keep up, particularly after that article in *Our Tannoy*."

Behind McConcavity, I can see Cármen — she's nodding slowly. This must be her revenge on Alby. Maybe this means I'm in the clear.

"That's final," McConcavity says firmly. "But I will say to you" — looking at me directly — "take this as a warning. We are watching everyone. And if you hear of anything, you're to report it to Bisera or Monojit. Is that understood? Bisera, I leave it to you to decide what to do with him while the investigation is continuous."

McConcavity leaves, along with Cármen, closing the door behind them.

"Well. You're very lucky," Bisera says, "and you owe us, you owe the store. As such, I think what's best now is that you take on some hard labour in the warehouse. You've shown some real promise of late. Jasmeen told me you excelled in The Great Insertion brainstorm for the Danielle Steel book launch next month. But you need to prove your loyalty. Stay in the warehouse and keep out of the way for a bit."

"Don't forget the guided tour," adds Monojit.

"Oh yes, but before you're assigned to the warehouse, you will give a guided tour of the supermarket to a group of new recruits. Nick will walk you down and introduce you. Akin, you stay here. We've got some things to discuss."

I leave with Nick walking at my side, almost escorting me, down towards the shop floor. We're silent until he says abruptly: "It's clear that you were helping the child," he's still not looking at me.

"Why didn't you say anything just then?"

"I didn't want to go against what Bisera was saying. I had to show Akin what store loyalty looks like. And besides, she is our superior and this place relies on hierarchy."

"So what's changed in the last five minutes?"

Nick pauses. "While your punishment was being discussed, I watched the footage again, and I had a chance to think about it some more. Sometimes, when I watch things through a screen, it becomes clearer to me what's really going on."

A wave of adrenaline passes through me. Oddly, I do feel somewhat grateful for McConcavity's appearance. "Lucky that the boss showed up."

Nick explains: "That was all just for show. McConcavity sometimes does this — threatens to sack a colleague — and only after all the preparations have been made for the colleague to get the sack does he rush in to tell them that their job is safe. He says it makes them grateful to him and loyal to the store."

Ha. I'll fucking show them. Or maybe I should wait — until I've got some leverage in the form of my own accommodation. "Why are you telling me this?" I ask Nick as we push open the double doors.

He hesitates. “As I said, I don’t think that on this occasion they’re being fair. And also I think I owe you for not telling them I told Alby about door sensors. Anyway, I’m going to introduce you to the new Food2Go recruits now.”

“New Food2Go recruits?”

“Yes. Didn’t you know? Akin’s being promoted to join Bisera and the rest of the Leaders, and they all want more staff on Food2Go in case you...well...if a vacancy comes up. Here are the new guys. Be careful, Upper Management will be watching you closely.”

We walk to the end of aisle No.13, where a large group of fresh faced, wide-eyed new Team Members are gathered, clustered round one another. Nick introduces me as “your capable and *loyal* guide” and leaves me to it. But he’s right about Upper Management — Wart and Feral shadow me and the new recruits as I lead them from aisle to aisle, ad-libbing information which might be important, about price checks, REDUCED labels, and CAGEs. Feeling still slightly dazed from my mock-execution, I embark on a diatribe about wasting, but then back out:

“And of course, there’s the store’s attitude towards wasting, which... you’ll find out about in your own time. Ah, but here is an important place, if you’ll follow me.”

I can feel the store Stasi’s panopticon gaze passing over me every time I look around. I feel Wart and Feral watching, listening, taking note. I look up at all the bulbous CCTV cameras above, the same filmy black shape as a shark’s eye. Luckily, just when I feel I need to prove my loyalty to the store, we turn onto Homeware — and there is the ancient Mrs Mollie Friel, hobbling along, wielding her stick like a baton. I’m not going to miss this opportunity, and I announce to the herd of newbies:

“...and one of the most important responsibilities of working here at Tesco is taking care of our beloved regulars.

Here is Mrs Friel. Good morning, Mrs Friel. I think I know how I can enhance your supermarket experience."

From my pocket, I take my wallet, and from my wallet, I take the Freedom Pass. I'll be sorry to lose out on all the free travel, but I need a publicly witnessed win. Before Mrs Friel has time to reply with a thank you or a snarl about "fucking darkies" and "sending them back," I'm calling out loudly over everyone's head, so that any Upper Management in the vicinity can hear, "Don't mention it. Don't worry, Mrs Friel," before shepherding the new recruits past the mad old idiot and along the aisle, all the time emphasising to them again the importance of customer care.

We approach the Deli Counter, where Alby is hunched over the spinning, gleaming blade, pushing the pinkish leg of some bovine through the whir and buzz. I've not seen him or spoken with him since that AM at his flat, but now's not the time to go into it. There's loyalty I need to prove.

"Heya, Alby," I raise my voice with all the singsong I can muster, over the sound of splitting flesh and bone. *Heya*... I've never used that word before. I can see Wart and Feral making notes on their tablets.

Alby turns, notices me and the herd gathered round, and turns off the blade. He faces us, palms on the granite butcher's slab.

"Could you tell us what you do?"

He squints at me, or maybe he sniffs, with folds suddenly appearing over his brow and across his nose. He goes to speak, checks himself, maybe notices Wart and Feral close by, and says more slowly, with the affected grin, wide eyes, and faux-jolly tone of a children's TV presenter: "Hello, everybody. Welcome to Fresh Meats. This 'ere" — he holds up a wad of dripping flesh in his gloved hand — "is Angus beef, and this" — he holds up half a chicken, blemished and dangling — "is poultry. But you wouldn't know it, would you? I bet none of you have ever been to an abattoir, or throttled a hen. You just think of meat as what's wrapped in cellophane." He slaps the flesh down on the slab. "And I tell you, your tour guide was like you once, but now look at him here, leading you around, tellin' you what's what, askin' me to perform. He's goin places — maybe right to the top of this 'ere store. Maybe one day he'll even take my job!"

The blade has finally slowed to a stop, the final pneumatic hiss from the machinery is a sigh, a gasp. I recover myself, aware that behind me the new recruits are waiting for a response. I laugh, not heartily, not even throatily, but nasally, trying to carry it off as a bit of banter.

"Ha, ha. This is the sort of banter you can expect from everyone here," I offer to the herd. "We're mad here."

Banter…Mad. This has never been my language before.

We move on, towards the F&F mezzanine, and I turn to give Alby a look which I hope communicates the incommunicable sentiment *you owe me for not selling you out upstairs*. His back is to me, and the blade begins to whir again as a flabby piece of pig is sliced.

- - - - -

In what feels like the makings of a habit, I've missed yet another seminar for the MA. Nevertheless, when I finish my shift, which yet again prevented me from attending, I Tube it into central to meet my coursemates. I should be frustrated, given that each seminar, attended or not, costs around £280 (that's £2.33 per minute) in tuition fees, but with my shifts at the store as they are, I couldn't afford to attend. And for some reason, of late my enthusiasm for the whole MA has dwindled. Maybe I'm just tired. Maybe my loyalties really have shifted. I arrive at the Fitzroy Tavern just in time to be included in the round. One of the professors has recently been promoted, and so we've been joined by a lot of senior staff who are celebrating.

I'm wedged in the corner by the wall, so that my upright rucksack beneath the table is out of the thoroughfare. These days I'm trying to be more conscious of the baggage I carry around with me. By happy luckenstance, the newly promoted professor is next to me. Mair Llewellyn — elegant, reserved, polite, thoughtful — she's generous with essay feedback and delicately critical in her responses during seminars, so I've heard. Her research is cutting edge, in vogue, the kind that fills column inches in the *Times Literary Supplement*. We talk about books — she getting more tipsy and candid, owning up to concerns about the way the humanities is going:

"It's like, I read *Sweet Tooth* so that I could teach all of you lot for this course, and it got my back up and bristly because of how the humanities was being funded by the government, and I worry that I might be, that all of us here might be, stooges and rubes for a new Cold War."

"I agree," I agree. "At my workplace, it's starting to feel like I'm being used by them or whatever. Like they're controlling me."

She shrugs. "That's just the way it is. It's the same in every job, I think."

I rearrange my legs beneath the table and knock my rucksack, which topples and falls onto her feet. She looks down, slides her varnished toes back into her glittering flats. "What's with the bag?"

I'm panicked, not wanting to share the embarrassment of my continuous status *sans maison*. Instead I mumble, "Oh yeah, it's crammed with books. Done a big haul at the library. Just lugging these around until I get them home."

She looks fully at me, for a few seconds, her tipsiness momentarily clear, until I turn away to fiddle with a soggy beermat.

"Yeah," she says carefully and quietly, "I remember when *I* didn't have anywhere to live, too, when I was studying at Columbia. It's hard. I can relate."

I'm taken aback at how easy it was to see through my yarn — the clarity of her drunken vision — but before I can arrange a retort, she continues, almost wistfully, "Listen, this isn't really the way of things, but I can see you're in need. When do you next need somewhere?"

"Tomorrow, actually. I've just removed myself from some accommodation." After Freddy's housemate returned, I had to stay at the bedsit in Bethnal Green again, above the chicken shop. It didn't work out. The guy who lent me the sofa always wears a kimono, makes Bloody Marys at all hours, and there's only a beaded curtain between the kitchenet and my sleeping quarters. To top it off, his ancient golden retriever pisses on everything.

"That bad is it? Fine. Here's my address. Here's my mobile number, too. We have a spare room, my housemate and I, which we usually use as a study, but you can use it for the time being. You come by after 5PM tomorrow, and I'll give you a key."

The rest of the evening is a golden shimmer of reassurance as I consider the prospect of staying at an academic's place — maybe I can borrow her books; maybe I'll become her apprentice, her understudy. Aristotle surely crashed at Plato's from time to time.

So buoyant is my mood at this new possibility that I don't even mind bedding down in the library for the night. So vibrant is the idea of the new, scholarly accommodation that I skip into Tesco the following morning, not even caring that I'll be in the warehouse, proving my loyalty. There's a lightness in my step at the relief of having somewhere sorted for the foreseeable. And the symbolism of a spare key. It's an instrument of significance, which, once inserted in the key-hole, turns and fuses the ridged wards of the lock with the key's corresponding incisions, and suddenly every fixed bolt and solid bar of iron and wood easily unfastens. You may now enter. You have suffered long enough.

"Oi," Monojit appears before I can pass through the plasticky tendrils into warehouse. There's a grin on his face that, while I don't trust, I refuse to let ruin my vibe. "You may've convinced Bisera, but I've still got my eye on you."

"I know, I know. Prove my loyalty and all that."

"Oh good. So you *do* understand. In that case, you won't mind participating in an Ice Bucket Challenge then."

"What?"

"An Ice Bucket Challenge. For charity."

"I can't. I..."

"...need to prove your loyalty."

I shake my head. "I've not got a pair of shorts or a spare T-shirt or even a..."

From behind his back Monojit produces a towel, a T-shirt, and a pair of shorts. The F&F labels have almost been completely covered by REDUCED stickers.

"It'll take place at midday" — Monojit smiles toothily — "in the front of the store. Make sure you bring these with you."

At noon, the Tannoy summons me from the warehouse to the foyer, where a child's swimming pool has been inflated and a plastic chair placed inside it. Angus Caarht is there with his camera, as are Monojit, Bisera, Akin, and a few giggling colleagues. And lots of curious customers. No Alby, though. Either in solidarity or disinterest. I step into the empty pool and sit in my T-shirt and shorts. There's a countdown, which customers are encouraged to chorus, and then my scalp goes numb, shoulders numb, thighs. Lungs. Demand. Air. I gasp, chest heaving like the cusp of a panic attack as ice water cascades around. There's a cheer, photos are taken, and then I'm discharged, squelching through the store with those shivers and shudders you get at the swimming pool. In the ♂ Changing Room, I towel off and put on my dry, familiar Tesco clothes. I'm suddenly at ease, in a wholly forming uniform, an outfit to fit in.

My pocket vibrates.

Hey there, this is Mair. i'm really sorry to have to do this but we're going to have to cancel the plan for you to stay at ours. I'd had a few too many last night and recognised another in need, but because I'm teaching you and most likely marking your essays etc. it's not appropriate. This is a professional thing, I'm sorry to say. Anyway, I've referred your situation to the student liaison committee, and they've already responded to me that they've set up a meeting for you to discuss with them the troubles you've been having. Check your emails and they should get in touch soon. Again, really sorry but I hope this helps.

I'm shivering again.

I check my phone's credit. Remaining credit is £00.15.

I'll need to use this wisely, to quickly ask someone else if I can stay at theirs tonight, so a reply to Mair will have to wait. But I need to makes sure that my silence conveys coolness, but the right kind of coolness. It must be a 'hey-yo-no-worries-no-biggy' sort of coolness, not an iciness that says without saying that the best place to find revenge is in the refrigerated aisle.

I retreat to a toilet cubicle, and begin composing an SOS message to Lance.

I wait for a reply, my head bowed over my knees as I sit on the lowered toilet lid, the floor tiles beneath my boots sticky with the grain left by a swabbing mop. Colleagues come in and out, I can hear them hocking up phlegm as they enter, sniffing as they leave, and while they're in here, near-total silence, other than a bladder's or a cistern's trickle. The smell of ammonia is tangy in the citroned air.

Ammonia = amoneya.

Money and urine are interchangeable. We spend a penny when we wee, and we piss it all away when we're broke.

A delay of ten or fifteen seconds, then comes Lance's reply.

Yeah sure

This is followed immediately by O2's automated text: **Remaining credit is £00.00.**

- - - - -

Lance's skipping rope is spinning so fast it gives him an oval outline, like he's inside an egg. Already there's a shadow of sweat blotting out the letters of the Under Armour logo on his T-shirt.

"He... llo," he gasps, mid-skip. "Sorry... about... your accommo... dation." His eyes flash beneath a veined, beaded brow as I enter the apartment.

"That's just how it always is. Thanks for helping me out, though. Can I use your radiator?" I hold out the T-shirt and shorts, still wet from today's humiliating Ice Bucket Challenge. No one at Tesco has asked for them back, so I'm going to put them into regular circulation.

Lance pauses his workout. "You don't need a radiator. It's about 22°C outside. Look." He slides open the glass door of the balcony and a rush of hot air hits us, like walking past the exhaust pipe of a bus. I hang the dripping T-shirt and shorts on a plastic line stretched from the outer wall to the balcony railings, finding a space between baby grows, baby vests, and muslins.

"Here, wear these." Lance hands me a running top and running shorts, made of that arse-gripping Lycra that young mums like to go shopping in at Tesco. For some reason, Montgomery and the other old fogies never object to that kind of lower-income customer.

"Not bad. Almost a complete jogger" — his sinewy forearm points at my work boots — "but those will not do. What are you, size nine? Yeah, I've got another pair of running shoes. They're upstairs by the treadmill."

I ascend the spiral staircase to the apartment's even brighter, glassier, top-floor, humid as a greenhouse, where there's an array of weights, pulleys, and a treadmill. It's all part of Lance's recent commitment to bulking up, getting hench. It's about time jazzheads became beefcakes. As I approach the treadmill, I discover how Lance is getting on with his new title of 'uncle'. The treadmill is humming away, and on its smooth conveyor belt a pram has been positioned. Its handle is tied to the bar of the treadmill, and another skipping rope has been knotted to the pram's opposite axle, pulled taught by a stack of weights piled up on the floor like iron bagels. The to-and-fro tug keeps the pram stationary while the treadmill's motion keeps the pram trundling. I peep inside, and there is the pinkish bundle of Lance's niece, tiny eyes and tiny mouth sealed in total calm. I take the trainers and tip-toe back down the stairs.

Lance's grinning. "Do you like my set up?"

"It's a novel method of parenting."

"Uncleing, dude. A totally different skill set," he replies, midway through a stretch which would baffle even Shiva.

"Is it safe?"

"Yeah, I reckon. I've done it before, and it's been fine."

I must look uncertain.

"What?" he asks.

"How old is she?"

"Four months. Don't worry. My sister's been leaving her with me whenever she goes to yoga."

I don't know when the maternal grip loosens enough to let a newborn out of sight, or when a newborn ceases to be a newborn and becomes instead a straightforward, open and shut, bona fide little baby. This niece arrived in February, so maybe after four months it's okay.

"We should only be gone for fifteen minutes or so, if you can keep up."

Lance's really taken to this fitness regime. He's much more lively and springy on his feet than when we first met. He holds himself taller, still sinewy and slim but with what's evidently an improving core strength.

I change into jogger's garb, and we ping ourselves down in the lift to the ground floor, exit the foyer with a nod to the concierge, spin through the flattened hamster wheel of the revolving door, and out from Astrocity Tower's air-conditioned slickness into the dense heat of June's afternoon heatwave. The river rushes and sparkles, as Thames Clippers cruise from Chelsea to Greenwich, laden with tourists who want to see where Mean Time begins.

While Lance programmes a stopwatch around his neck, I inspect my appearance in the window of a parked car — a Lamborghini Huracán, no less — the colour of blood orange. It's not uncommon on this bend in the Thames, though you tend only to see these at night, doing growling laps around Sloane Square, or parked up on double reds with wasp-patterned tickets slapped on its windscreen. As if a £280 fine will dissuade the offspring of oligarchs or oil barons, for whom a Lambo is what they use to pop into town.

Through the car's narrow window, I can see a passenger seat of surprisingly un-Huracánian disorder: a child's car seat, dried peelings of ancient fruit, crumbs, crumbs, crumbs, an adolescent's trainer in the footwell, with its dirty laces splayed and scurrying like a triffid. These are the remnants of a household transported into the confined space of a luxury car. I wonder which of Astrocity Tower's apartments belongs to someone whose whip is the site of such mess. It's odd that these objects have accumulated in such an unembarrassed way in a car so ostentatious as this. Maybe that's what huge wealth permits. If this mess were spread throughout the house and there was a visitor, there'd be a rush to tidy or organise or apologise. But here, there's something unapologetically dignified in the chaos of it all.

Like a camera refocusing, I retract my gaze from the car's interior to the window's surface, to inspect my reflection. The Lambo obliges, my features at once discernible and disappointing. Yes, I have my face, my eyes, my mouth — and yes, that's an improvement on having none — but the face and the eyes and the mouth are, in sequence, gaunt, blood-shot, and thin. I wish I had a hoodie to put up to shade myself from myself.

"Right then. Our route is the following. Over Vauxhall Bridge, the MI6 building will be on our left when we turn right along the riverside, onto Nine Elms Lane, around Battersea Power Station, up onto Chelsea Bridge, back onto Grosvenor Road, all the way to Astrocity Tower."

"Are you sure that'll only take fifteen minutes?"

"I can do it in that time, and you're not *that* unfit, surely. I tell you what. Do as much as you can, and if you have to slow down, I'll run on ahead to check on my niece."

We set off in sync, strides landing neatly on each paving slab like a multiplayer platform video game. A pair of Mario Bros. on the London level. We pass the MI6 building, that Lego castle of concrete and glass. There's something eerie and hieratic about it. Like many glass totems on the Thames — most recently the Shard — the MI6 building wears its hallmarks prominently, its barcode of shadowy deals with government officials, lobbyists, and private money. But it does all this blatantly: transparent dishonesty. It wasn't until it was built and operational that the government actually acknowledged its existence as the place out of which agents operated. It's a fiction that everyone agreed about but never recognised, a nameless entity.

We get as far as Chelsea Bridge before Lance puts on the burners, or I put on the coolers, and just as I feel sharp gravel filling my lungs, I watch as Lance shrinks along the bridge then disappears. He's had a head start of months and months of exercise, regularly running away from and back to the comfort of Astrocity Tower. Give me a place like that, a route like this along the Thames, and I reckon I'd get fit and healthy pretty quickly.

Cities shouldn't be moved through at that pace anyway, I conclude as I limp off the bridge, passing plywood that walls off a construction site, where more glass and concrete will soon assemble themselves. Building and construction sites agitate the walker, probably because of the association with demolished stories. Though surely they should cultivate an optimistic feeling for the flâneur, since they are a place of renewal, of reconstruction.

I get as far as Grosvenor Road before I stop entirely, remove a trainer and sock, and pop a blister. It's yolky and painful. I'm desperate for water and something to eat, so I hobble off onto the high street. A car passes slowly, its windows down, its scudding music making a group of school yoot in front of me bob their heads and roll their shoulders, their school ties flapping.

'*Dreams is lucid, loosely based on music, swallow my mucus,*
Hope your pussy get herpes…'

The yoot throw up their arms, recognising the song, chorusing the lyrics, and finishing off the rhyme:

'*Swallow my mucus,*
Hope your pussy get herpes and yo' ass get lupus.'

One of them points at a street sign framed by a thick, orangey hedge.

"Lupus Street, fam."

They all shriek and clap fists into palms at this frail

sonic coincidence. One of them throws his school bag up in the air. The others laugh. They exude that loose-limbed jubilation of teens approaching the end of a school term.

"What are the chances," one of them whoops.

"Nah, that is mad, fam."

"Bruv, that's God's work."

"Swear down."

It certainly does appear determined, like something prearranged. If it's God who organised things just like this, so that a song about lupus played as a car trundled down Lupus Street, then it was God who also invented the disease and dished it out all over the planet. Flannery O'Connor might concede that it's a punishment with a plan which humans can't comprehend. God moves in mannered and mysterious ways. Like the shape of the store, all laid out and foretold. I slow on the pavement, knees aching, blister squelching, and lean against the glass of a greasy spoon café. I try to catch and secure my breath.

Through the window, there's the familiar figure who is present in every greasy spoon on every street in every town and city throughout the country. The W.I.R. Usually this stands for Writer in Residence (think Alain de Botton's tenancy in Heathrow airport, or Fay Weldon at The Savoy), but here in the high street's greasy spoon is the irregular regular, the Weirdo in Residence. Born into this role, you can't imagine their life being anything other than what it is in front of you now, amongst the cheap cutlery and spills on the tablecloth, the bottles of red and brown sauce. The W.I.R. might even predate the institution in which they sit, the café's fatty walls may've been built around them as they sat there murmuring to themselves, slobbering on their shoes. And this W.I.R. is not just tolerated but honoured, loved, and cherished by the people who work there, treated like a dear family member instead of a scabrous drain on footfall business. But you, the non-regular — the

W.*not*.I.R. — you're just passing through. You're the one who is tolerated, and you envy that irregular regular who will one day have their own framed photo on the wall and a commemorative plaque:

'*In memory of Genine (dates unknown)*, who used to sit by the window with her bin bags and empty buggy, the café's self-appointed maître d' beckoning customers in.'

Or:

'*In memory of Old Nath (dates unknown)*, who used to volunteer himself as a lollipop man on the street outside this café.'

This disproves the widely reported opinion that the city's misfits are workshy or lazy. These people *are* in fact looking for work, constantly wanting purpose, seeking the social validation that labour seems to bring. If only the world would adjust its dials to accommodate them. Maybe step one is to stop referring to them as scabrous drains or W.I.R.s.

My back's against the glass, and I feel a vibrating knock. I turn, and through the window is the angry face of an aproned worker. Although the street is busy and the glass muffles the sound, I can make out what he is mouthing and gesturing: FUCK OFF. YOU'RE MAKING THE WINDOW DIRTY. Over the worker's shoulder, I can see the W.I.R. turn towards me, shake a large, greasy head, then turn back to the TV mounted high up on the wall, on which the weatherman is forecasting a Britain the colour of uncooked Angus beef.

I hobble along and into the next shop, Oxfam. Here you find another of the high street's brood: the student on work experience — the good-willed possessor of the short straw. In this particular establishment, the musk of old lady perfumes and WD40 sticks to my sweaty clothes. It's busy, with a broad demographic: not just pensioners but teens, thirty-somethings, and the middle-aged. Charity shops promote the paradoxical sentiment that only once an item has arrived at Oxfam or Scope does it regain its value. Macklemore's 'Thrift Shop' song has demonstrated there's a lot of money to be made from such a sentiment. A volunteer is fighting with a mannequin to get a garment over its bare head and motionless limbs. It's a London 2012 Olympics hoodie, dark blue, with a series of jagged red shapes huddled in the middle of the chest. If you squint, the red shapes merge into an almost-legible Olympic logo, but at first glance, they resemble the kind of fragments of slate and rubble from a construction site. We likely have Stella McCartney to thank for the 2012 Olympics uniforms, all of them different shades of blue, all of them a broad tribal allegiance to state-of-the-art art of the state: Kapoor's twisted red steel thing, Keith Wilson's big upright colourful crayons, and Monica Bonvicini's installation which simply and accurately commanded: RUN. The Olympics was all about a particular kind of tribalism, the worship of a particularly gifted athletic body. These were welcome within London, but no others.

It's worth asking who really wanted the Games. Presumably it wasn't those East Londoners whose playing fields were sold off so that the stadium could be built. It probably wasn't those who'd been promised opportunities for local people, for whom shit service industry jobs did not count as aspirational. In the year and a half since it finished, the whole Olympic apparatus of open armed welcome to the world has disappeared. It's been replaced with something coarser, more inward-looking, but no less obsessed with tribal allegiance. The sentiments circulating about immigrants confirms an attempt to make the whole island into an Olympic Village, where only certain types of bodies are welcome within its borders.

"'Scuse me, sir," squarks a spotty volunteer whose voice hasn't yet broken, "could you move along please if you're not buying anything."

The customers glance at me with suspicion.

Back to the street, hobbling to the next shop, I find my place. It's a Tesco Express. In the taxonomic ranking — Kingdom, Phylum, Genus, etc. — this small establishment is the Class variety, with fewer choices but more expensive produce. They tend to grow on high streets, springing up alongside betting shops and Savers, where impulse purchases form the bulk of their revenue. It feels like a home away from home for me, the layout of aisles different, the workers' faces different, but the same outfits, the same Tannoy announcements, the same playlist. Since I'm in civilian attire, unrecognisable to staff and to myself, I move freely, without any anchoring. No CAYG for me to enforce. No CAGE for me to waste. No duty to enhance anyone's supermarket experience.

By the time I've lugged myself back to the apartment, stopping only to pop another blister and scold my bare foot on hot tarmac, Lance's cradling the baby, who is happily awake, her big blue eyes scanning the world, her moon head swivelling owl-like. Lance's warm-down music seems to double as a calming agent for his niece: Alice Coltrane's 'Journey In Satchidananda'. Swaying to the sound of tinkly piano keys, pebble-shingle shushes of cymbals, and undulating harp-pluckings, Lance murmurs: "You alright, dude? Have to say, I thought you might've fallen in the Thames."

"I'm good. How's the baby?"

"She's fine. Alice Coltrane helps her sleep. She's almost ready to drop off now." Indeed, her wide eyes look brightly tired, and her limbs jerk like a wind-up toy whose cog is wearing down. "Would you mind playing with her while I have a quick shower?"

My throat yo-yos dryly. I've not spent any time with a baby since I was one, so any notion of 'playing' would be ad-libbed. Lance lays her down in her cot, and I approach. Her tiny arms and feet wave softly, inviting a stroke, a tickle. A fuzzed, frayed memory of a nursey rhyme floats, grudgingly, into view... Something to do with cattle and feet, is it?

Trotters?

No.

...It involves counting, I think.

...Cattle and counting. *This little piggy...*

But this half-formed memory is quickly butted and lassoed by literature, by a whole library in my mind, and I can't get the learning out of my head — I can't just be in the moment — so when I reach out to lightly pinch her big toe, what comes out of my mouth is:

This little piggy's called Napoleon, and he's based on Stalin.

This little piggy's called Snowball, and he's based on Trotsky.

This little piggy's called Squealer, and he's Napoleon's propagandist.

With each piggy named, I wiggle the pinched toe, the size and shape of a single green pea.

This little piggy's called Minimus, and he's the farm's poet. He pens the song to replace 'Beasts of England'.

And this little piggy is called Pinkeye, and he tastes Napoleon's food to check if it's poisoned.

By the time I've got to the littlest, pinkiest of the five, her face has turned from Sudocrem white to the red of the Sudocrem logo, and a wailing sound drowns out Coltrane's stuttering, hypnotic jam. I scoop her up, holding her arms like she's a glass trophy, bring her towards me, and begin to march, limping, blistering, up and down in front of the windows, trying to point out various places beyond the glass.

"Look over there, little baby. That's Battersea Power station. That's the Oval cricket ground. And if you look over there, you'll see Westminster and the Houses of P—"

But before the first syllable is out, there's a squirting sound. A dirty protest. Something like a percolator bubbling while a drill penetrates damp wood, while a washing machine drains, while rubble tumbles after a controlled demolition. And, at the same time, there's a sweetish, sour smell, like aisle No.4 after a spillage of a thousand Müller Corner yoghurts. And then I can feel, across my palm, my forearm, my chest, a warm ooze.

"Wheyy," Lance applauds, towelling his head. "She's made her mark." He nods at a stain on the T-shirt he's leant me as he takes hold of the baby. "Yeah, she's leaked through."

I'm looking down at the continent of browning yellow spread across my front.

"Sorry, yeah. My nappy skills are still amateur. I probably did it too loosely." He weighs her in one arm. "You could dead lift that nappy, it's so full. Grab the Milton, would you? I'll get your T-shirt from outside. It'll be dry by now."

My heart leaps. "Milton?"

"Look in the pram," he calls out, beginning to assemble on the kitchen island a conveyor of vest, baby grow, Pampers, and cotton wool.

Up onto the top floor I go again, into the pram on the treadmill, my literary snout rootling for the Milton. But we're very far from *Areopagitica*. I stand with hobbling difficulty, holding a pack of antibacterial wipes in my sweaty palms. Milton. *Baby expert since 1916*. I begin the CAYG of the T-shirt, the motion of the white material a wave of surrender.

- - - - -

The day is clear. My diary is empty of any Tescobligations, so I'm going to claw back some time for the MA. Oh yeah. The MA that I moved to London to do. I've turned my phone to silent. I've got a day of research and reading planned in the British Library. Dom and I approach the entrance, and the security guards instruct us to empty our bags.

"How was the rest of the weekend at Flo's?" I ask as my rucksack vomits up books, dirty clothes, toiletries. I don't really care about who sees what anymore. Embarrassment and shame are too time-consuming.

"Florence's, you mean?"

"Now that we're out of the Shire, I think I'll stick to 'Flo'."

"It was good," Dom goes on, slotting his laptop back into its bag. "Sorry again for not driving you to the station. I was way too drunk."

"Nah, it's all good. Flo's cleaner gave me a lift."

"Yeah, she was there when we all had breakfast, cooking us a full English and cleaning up all the mess at the same time. It was very impressive plate spinning."

We mount the marble steps towards the Library's Reading Room. It's quiet today, most people preferring to be outside enjoying this utterly unbearable weather. The store's aisles' newspapers have been warning that it's going to get worse.

"What else did you do?"

"Everyone was very hungover, so lots of lounging by the pool. The girls just swam, some completely naked. Tara in particular."

"Oh yeah?" The image of her ribbed, bare chassis in the darkness comes to me. Her diesel-breath: *Take me like a cockney would.*

"Yeah. Actually it was very funny, that night with her. She slept with like three or four of Flo's friends, one after the other."

"You're joking?"

"I think it was a mechanic and three waitresses, or maybe three mechanics and a waitress. I forget the order. And some of their costumes were not too okay. Yeah, she's hilarious. Flo says she's a, how do you say, a 'cereal fucker'."

"Shit."

"I don't know this expression. Is it like a fucker of cereal?"

"No." Shit shit shit. "She means, 'serial fucker'. S-E-R-I-A-L. It's a homophone. It's 'serial' like 'one after another.'"

"Oh right. A fucker of many in a sequence. Yes that makes more sense."

"Please tell me you're joking."

"Not at all. Even Flo said to me when we were driving back to London that Tara's known for spreading herself around. It's like a joke in their friendship group. Tara the Terrible, they call her. Tara uses the name herself." Dom gives me a look. "Why's your face like that?"

"What? No. I'm just umm stunned that Flo would talk about a friend like that. A bit sexist isn't it?"

"I guess. Maybe. She's what Chinua Achebe might call 'an iron horse.'"

I think back to Flo's introduction, to the semi-circle of toffs all guffawing, the way they all fell back into the crowd, giggling, as if they all knew. Then I think back to the mousetraps, the hairnet, and realise that there was a key object missing from my time with Tara.

Durex (aisle No.14).

Immediately, I'm wondering just how terrible Tara the Terrible really is. Suddenly, I want to commission a survey on STI prevalence in the upper classes in South East England. I need Nick and Akin to draw up pie charts on birth rate in the Berkshire area. Surely the British Library has an archive. I didn't think about it when Debra drove me to the station — clouded as I was by a Calvin and cognac hangover, by the need to get back to London, by the need to sort accommodation — but of course, of course for sure Tara and I have done a terrible trade: I've got her pregnant and she's given me an infection. Inevitable, one hundred percent guaranteed. It's as predictable as the layout of a Tesco.

At the Reading Room's entrance, my hands are shaking so much I can't find my library card. Dom goes on ahead, flashing his ID, while I'm still fumbling. Eventually, I thrust my card in the guard's direction. He gestures me through, though I'm expecting him to sniff out some lethal disease that I'm riddled with. By the time I'm through, Dom's already found himself a table, and there's no way I'm going to stage-whisper to him my current head spin. So, I set up at a nearby table and silently kick myself, as tracer bullets fire off into the interminable theatre of conflict in my mind — different names for babies. Bruce? Harry? Omar? Zoe? Siobhan? Mitch? Sharon? Daryl? Jonno? Tara'd insist on something double-barrelled: Tarquin-Avery or Clementine-Ottilie. I'm also sitting here fret-sweating about the certainty of some sort of STI I've been carrying around. My task force training makes Tescomodified slogans out of each condition:

Putting the 'E.R.' in 'herpes'.

Putting the 'tit' in 'hepatitis'.

Putting the 'art' in 'genital warts'.

Putting the 'hoe' in 'gonorrhoea'.

Putting the 'rich' in 'trichomoniasis'.

Putting the 'lad' in 'chlamydia'. This one wouldn't make it onto Jasmeen's shortlist; the sequence 'lad' doesn't appear consecutively.

I want to go home. I want to have a home, where I can throw a duvet over my head and die.

Putting the 'STI' in 'domestic'.

Instead I stack books into towers around me, sitting in their tombstone shadow, trying to find solace and answers in the library. I turn on the uni-loaned laptop, get online, swiftly search 'NHS clinics near me', and start filling in the form at a rapid rate. It asks for an address, and I smear my fingers over the keyboard, entering the only one which

I know by heart: Lottie's in Angel. I've not seen her since the *onan interruptus* in February, but it'll have to do.

Have you *engaged in unprotected sex*? I tick the box. Always I, I, I. Why can't it be someone else ticking the box?

Putting the 'I' in 'HIV'.

Putting the 'ID' in 'AIDS'.

Maybe Lance's sister will donate the pram and baby clothes, though Tara'd surely insist on brand new gear — state-of-the-art apparatus for our little nipper.

I scroll down the form to the section asking what conditions I want to be tested for, and I type into the box SEXUALLY TRANSMITTED INFECTION.

Maybe Tesco offers generous paternity leave. Doubt it. By then I could be working at Regal Tuition. How might that work, turning to Tara in bed next to me to ask my boss for time off and to ask the mother of my child to help me with the nappy?

"Hi," a light voice at my side.

I turn.

Standing by the table is a pretty woman with a bob, blushing, with lips quivering, eyes sparkling like a clear mountain stream. "I'm Millie." She smiles, mouse-ish. "I saw you across the library like a month ago, and I wish I'd come over to like say hi, and I didn't, and I was like, oh no, but I just saw you come in, and I was like, yay, and so I was wondering if you wanted to..." Her eyes flick to the screen — she takes in the NHS logo and the three words on the screen, which seem to have grown in font size:

SEXUALLY TRANSMITTED INFECTION

Her mouth is still small and round from the end of pronouncing 'to', but now it tightens as if spitting out something unpalatable.

"Wanted to?" I ask, voice trembling in all the wrong ways.

"...to... um... actually, sorry, I think I've got you mixed up with someone else. Sorry, my bad." She's already halfway across the carpet in the direction of the exit before I mumble, "No worries." I return to the screen and type in the rest of the info, stabbing each key so that it echoes out into the silence.

- - - - -

Today I am 'Bertie', and Bertie's been in the warehouse obeying a new company directive to secure the dustbin lids with zip ties. This is to prevent the homeless from retrieving the perfectly edible bags of waste.

He's extracted from the warehouse and instructed by Akin to provide a personal shopper experience for one of the regulars, the bejewelled, sherry-infused, mink-wearing elderly daughter of Lady Harding.

"Ittt'ssss Pimm's o'cloccckk," she slurs, which Bertie takes as a signal to accompany her around the store collecting the ingredients for the cocktail.

"Oh yes, Ms Harding, an integral part of the drink," Bertie remarks as she grabs a bottle of cloudy lemonade. "It rather reminds me of my youth. Yes, I'd leave my thatched cottage and cycle out to the River Orwell, waving to the vicar or the village bobby." Since Akin's arrival Bertie's been leaning into this poshness stuff loads more, in an effort to reclaim something that was never Bertie's to begin with. "The church's bells used to ring out, sending nested birds tumbling, with my jars and net tied to my bicycle's frame. I'd arrive at a sunny clearing by the flowing Orwell, rest my bike on the grass, its wheels still spinning, rush down the green bank to sit by the river, and sip lovely, English lemonade."

Bertie leads the way to aisle No.8. "Oh wonderful, Ms Harding. Apple, orange, lemon, strawberry — all inspired choices. You know, when I was a boy, I would sit on the crown of a hill under an apple tree, where I could pluck lovely red fruit just like these. Oh yes, I would sit there and survey the field through which I'd come, this rural champaign so glittering and gold and..."

And suddenly Bertie is struck by a memory that infiltrates the idyllic fiction he's providing. No longer a young boy with his bike, but a twenty-something sitting on a hill overlooking a field, in the late summer of 2013. Across this pastoral setting, he'd watched his father appear. Families adhere to the principle of equilibrium, whereby if one member is delighted or calm or successful in some endeavour, then another must be miserable, or down on their luck. Thus, Bertie's father had approached with the newspaper in one hand — its headline about the brother's incarceration — and in the other hand, Bertie's university acceptance letter.

"Get to London. Get a good job. Get a good degree. You're the best thing we've got," is what he recalls his father saying. This had precipitated everything that's happened since.

From aisle No.8, Bertie directs Ms Harding up to aisle No.17 for a chopping board and knife so she or her housemaid can slice the fruit. But Bertie's fawning manner has been hollowed out by the memory, by the feeling that this whole endeavour in the capital has not succeeded if this, here, now, is where it's lead him. He holds Ms Harding's mink-draped shoulders firm and escorts her from aisle to aisle to get the rest of what she needs. It's only 10AM — way too early for Pimm's — but the customer's always right. He sends her on her way to the checkout and turns back towards the warehouse.

He passes the end of the aisle, where the newspapers are shelved. It was a burglary that his brother had taken part in — the kind of burglary which could only ever occur in the countryside, the kind that creates a provincial scandal, which shunts other headlines to the back pages for months and months. You don't have to be Angus Caarht to know that BURGLARY trumps TOWN HALL REPAVED; that BURGLAR ARRESTED trumps CHILD DISCOVERS DENTIST'S LOST WATCH; that BURGLAR NAMED trumps DUVET SHOP TO CLOSE; that BURGLAR COURT DATE SET trumps CAFÉ LAUNCHES VEGAN OPTIONS. Provincial life is dangerously dull, where there's nothing to distract from a family rift.

Bertie is vibrated out of this reverie by a text in his pocket. He jolts each time he checks his phone, worrying it'll be Tara (Im preggers) or the NHS (U R a disease bag), but to his relief, it's from Freddy:

> Yo turns out that one of my housemates, the one whose room u were staying in, isn't coming back. Moving on. So there's gonna be a room in our house that needs a tenant. Later tonight, everyones attending a House Meeting, and will put it to a vote. Obvs I want you in this house and I know a lot of the other housemates want you here, but not everyone. Nothing personal, it's just that there's another guy who is also a friend of the house who also needs a room. He's a DJ. He's vying for a space here, too. So tonight there'll be a vote

Bertie thumbs a quick reply, explaining that this is positive news, that he intends to cook a meal for the house this evening while they debate and vote.

can't hurt your chances! is Freddy's reply.

So for the remainder of his shift, Bertie mulls over what he should cook. Money is tight and his cooking isn't great. Pasta and pesto is too bland; oven pizzas are too basic.

The only other recipe he knows how to do is the one Dom described in the car on the way to Flo's estate: Nick Griffin's BNP Beef Stew. Admittedly, Dom added a 'Hungarian twist': a unique, traditional blend of herbs and spices which Bertie can't get hold of without a swift flight to the Békés vármegye county on the border. Everything else in the recipe, however, he can purchase here.

At the end of his shift, Bertie goes along the shelves with his REDUCED pistol unholstered, and unloads on a bunch of ingredients: potatoes, onions, parsnips, carrots, chopped tomatoes, Tabasco sauce, mixed herbs, stock cubes, Lea & Perrins, and a bottle of ale, and British beef (obvs.). Under his breath, he murmurs the phrase, "Can't hurt your chances. Can't hurt your chances."

With Bertie's nametag unpinned and returned to the veg box, I collect my bags of shopping and my rucksack, then head for Streatham to prepare for what I hope will be the First Supper of many.

The vote won't take place until later, which gives me a couple of hours to prepare it all and get it simmering. In the kitchen, I begin peeling and chopping. First, the onions, which I dice until my eyes are streaming. I whack these in the pan. I cut and brown the beef as it joins the softening onions. Then it's the carrots, the parsnips, and the spuds.

I'm feeling good. I'm feeling energetic. I'm feeling hopeful. The house keeps an old CD player on the kitchen side, so I choose from their stack of albums Spacemen 3's *The Perfect Prescription*. It's a curious house, with lots of high-tech DJ equipment but also these throwback devices. In the living room, for instance, they keep a Victorian tripod camera, which they hook up to a laptop when they webcast their DJ performances. I sling in the chopped tomatoes and stir, stir, stir — letting the flavours mix, intermingle, get to know each other.

Once the album has finished, I open up the case to replace the CD, and four or five of the little teeth that grip the disc fall onto the kitchen surface. Shit. It's not my fault that the plastic has become brittle and finally broken into shards, but it's the kind of thing that could count against me.

Yeah I like him 'n' all, but he can't look after other people's belongings. I vote no.

Best hide the evidence. I scoop the pieces into my palm and bin them, each tiny translucent tooth twinkling in the light, like diamonds on a bed of parsnip skin and onion peel.

I hear movement in the hallway as the housemates rise from their DJ slumber to congregate, ready for the vote. There's muffled laughter through the wall. This bodes well. If everyone's in a good mood... "Can't hurt your chances. Can't hurt your chances."

I select another CD (Spiritualized's *Ladies and Gentlemen We Are Floating in Space*), dial up the volume and turn back to the hob, where the stew is bubbling well.

I peer around the corner to see them all troop into the living room and close the door. I add a decent glug of Lea & Perrins, with a dash or two of Tabasco, and stir, stir, stir — still letting the flavours mix, intermingle, get to know each other.

By the midpoint of the album ('Home of the Brave') the stew is almost ready. I pour in the bottle of ale, swigging the dregs.

"Yo, man." I turn, and one of the housemates is there. "Good choice of tunes."

"Yeah, I love this album." I've never listened to it, but I figured it would only improve my chances to pretend.

"You know this was the last band to play at The Hacienda? How about that for a claim?"

I don't know the album, nor The Hacienda, so I go with the non-committal: "Yeah, that's incredible."

"I know. Imagine being the last artist of a great institution before it closed?"

I stir the stew and ask casually, "So, have you finished the vote yet?"

"Nah, man. I'm just getting a glass of water."

I move aside from the sink, watch the water slowly fill up his pint glass, desperately trying to act like it's no big thing about the possibility of the vote going my way. Yeahnobigdeal, yeahnoworries, yeahnobiggy — all phrases I don't have in my lexicon.

"I'll have to lend you another one of their albums," the housemate says as he leaves the kitchen. "Smells good, by the way."

That must be a positive sign, I think, it means that he hopes I'll move in and we can share music. Maybe we'll start a band. I'll recruit Lance for some double bass/jazz-electronic fusion. The Waddle Cantos Remix. We could webcast our performances with the tripod, and between band practices I could go jogging around Tooting Common to get healthy. The smell of burning jolts me. I've left the stew too long in the pan without stirring. It's salvageable, but the base is charred.

Yeah I like him 'n' all, but he can't cook for shit. I vote no.

I continue to stir, paying closer attention. Nick Griffin's recipe clearly requires meticulous scrutiny, not to be overlooked or disregarded, even for a second. I wonder what'd be worse: if everyone gets food poisoning, or if everyone really enjoys it.

Freddy enters the kitchen, removing his goggles like a 1920s aviator weary after a test flight: "We've had the meeting. We've done the vote."

"And yes, what?" I grind pepper into the pan, hands shaking.

"Right. I can tell you that the vote came down fifty-fifty. Right down the middle."

"But there's nine people that live here," I point out.

"Yeah, we had one abstention."

"On what grounds?"

"Well, he'd snorted so much ketamine, he couldn't actually speak — physically couldn't unclench his jaw to talk. So we put him down as present but not voting."

"So what does all that mean?"

"What's been decided is that you and Perc should have a game of Scrabble."

"Perc?" I ask.

"Georgie Perc. He's the other guy in the running for the room. You and he will play Scrabble against each other. I know — you can thank me later. I know that words are your forte, so I've stacked the odds in your favour." Freddy's tapping a butterknife against his vambrace. "But you won't be playing Scrabble until tomorrow evening. So rest up, get yourself ready. Read whatever words you need. It's on."

I serve up the beef stew to the house, then retreat to the cupboard to revise.

- - - - -

I wake with words on my mind. On the Tube into work, I'm scribbling all the different combinations I can think of, reordering words into interesting and distorted configurations. I'm finding words within words. During my lunchbreak, I linger in aisle No.1, skimming the pages of our bestsellers (J.K. Rowling's *The Casual Vacancy*, Stephen King's *Doctor Sleep*, Donna Tartt's *The Goldfinch*) to pick out random words.

I take a ream of notes from my pocket and scribble 'vacancy' and scribble words I find living inside it: 'cava', 'navy', and 'cyan'.

Inside 'doctor' I find 'cord', 'root', and 'door'.

Inside 'Tartt' I find 'tart' (aisle No.11).

This is my wheelhouse.

As I leave the warehouse on my lunchbreak, four young women with Jedwood haircuts approach. One of them asks me where the DIY aisle is. In her basket is a four-pack of white tank tops and a two-pack of white underwear. She explains what they're looking for:

"Sledgehammers... like in the Miley Cyrus video."

"Yes, I'll show you. Just give me a sec." I scribble 'sledgehammer', then 'degrease', 'emerald', and 'hearse'.

As we walk, they're all chitter-chattering, using their smartphones as palms, behind which their giggles ripple out. They're referring to a recent, potent, fragrant guff from the zeitgeist: a music video in which Miley Cyrus uses a Thor-ish hammer to smash her way sideways — no, not upwards through any glass ceiling, but yes, sideways — through plaster and mortar walls. And the hook is that she's not wearing very much. This is the 'Wrecking Ball' song, which plays all the fucking time here, and which brings to mind a piece of graffiti I saw when I left Alby's Canonbury flat in a rage. Despite my high emotional state, I noticed that someone had stuck to a wall a huge poster of the November 2006 High Court order banning the destruction of the nearby Dalston theatre. And then, next to the poster, was a photo of cranes dangling wrecking balls poised to flatten the protected area to make way for the Olympic Village.

Having metastasised from her *Hannah Montana* origins (a late 2000s TV show about a teenage girl with a pop star alter ego), M.C. appears nowadays in a boyish pixie guise, playing the part of a woman with a heavy metal fetish. No, not the music genre of heavy metal, but literally licking the flat, leaden head of a sledgehammer. I point the four gigglers towards our assortment of tools on aisle No.17 and leave them to assess their costumes.

I scribble 'costumes', then 'outc mes'.

No one likes to deny an artist their agency, but it's worth turning away from who is in front of the camera to who is holding it. This is Freddy's influence. The 'Wrecking Ball' music video was directed by Terry Richardson, whose other recent work includes the video for Beyoncé's 'XO', in which a casually clad Beyoncé — a low-key Queen B. — walks through the glittery lusciousness of a fairground. It's a place of harmless clarity, in which things are as they really are. So we see Beyoncé's 1,000-watt grin as she strolls amongst the candy-flossed crowd, wearing a pair of pink flashing cat ears and the same white tank top that Miley wears in her vid, too. Beyoncé wanders on, as fruit machines spin and big dippers dip and rise. She coyly peeps out from behind a bleached fringe, rides a dodgem, a rollercoaster. There is a sense that all senses are being served by the fairground. Everything is as it really is. Beyoncé strides on, clutching a huge dollar-bill patterned cone. Very torch-like. Combined with her flashing feline crown, the torch gives her the status of a statue. Liberty fragranced with the brine blowing in from the Atlantic to Coney Island. Beyoncé's fairground is a far cry from Great Yarmouth's Golden Mile, with its rickety and rusted rides. Some of us still bear the scars from Norfolk's rollercoasters and its wobbly Ferris wheel. You get the sense from her trip to the seaside, her walk through the crowd, that the air is perfumed with the sweetness of belonging, and not that stubborn coppery trace on your fingertips from the lonely Yarmouth 2p slot machines, where you get lost with every penny you lose. That's the problem with Beyoncé's gorgeous smile in the midst of the dancing crowd. She wants to be Found in the Funhouse.

On my ream of paper, I scribble 'fairground', within which I find: 'adoring', 'rigor', and 'unfair'.

After my shift, it's back to Streatham in the evening, and I'm feeling confident.

I enter the living room, which is already arranged ready for the game, with the low sofas pushed back, the Victorian tripod packed away, and a round table placed in the middle of the room.

Freddy makes the introductions.

"This is Perc."

I shake a cold, thin, and exploratory hand. Perc is pale, freckled, with O–O eyes that focus laser-like on me. His hair is the frizzy backend of a peacock, and he's got an untamed goatee protruding like a tuft of seagrass from the cliff-edge of his chin.

He leans over the table, fiddles with some tiles. "I heard you made a stew last night," he smirks, eyes wide. "A bit watery, I heard. Like it'd been left too long."

I flinch as I sit opposite, remembering the burning onions. "The idea with cooking," I parry, "is to let the flavours get to know each other."

"Well, it would seem that your flavours got to know each other, became neighbours, began an affair, moved in, had a fight, and got divorced."

Shit. He knows how to extend metaphors. No matter. This can't psych me out.

"Oh by the way, Freddy," Perc says casually, "I've got that DVD of Alain Corneau's *Série noire*. Don't let me forget to give it to you."

"Oh great," enthuses Freddy, his goggles steaming up with delight. He rubs his fingerless riding gloves together, and my stomach tumbleturns.

Perc leans forward and murmurs to me, "I hate 'mainstream' cinema, don't you?"

This can't psych me out.

On the table is the OED. And next to it is the Scrabble board, which resembles the messy square of a QR code.

We begin.

After a few plays I've laid $B_3A_1R_1R_1E_1L_1$ on the board, and Perc's responded with $A_1L_1L_1E_1Y_4$, the A_1 of which is the neighbour to my L_1.

$$
\begin{array}{l}
B_3A_1R_1R_1E_1L_1 \\
A_1L_1L_1E_1Y_4
\end{array}
$$

My rack is $A_1D_2L_1I_1O_1S_1$.

Out of the velvet bag I take a tile.

G_2.

I swap my tiles around on my rack, creating total disorder, looking for a pattern.

And then I see it.

If I lay my tiles over the L_1 of $B_3A_1R_1R_1E_1L_1$ and the A_1 of $A_1L_1L_1E_1Y_4$ I can make $G_2L_1A_1D_2I_1O_1L_1A_1S_1$. A nine-letter word that would scoop up all sorts of bonuses and double points. I put down my tiles, one after another.

Perc looks at the tiles, nods in approval, scratches his cliff-tuft, then leans forward and points out: "There are two LAs in GLADIOLAS. You could've repositioned the whole word and got a triple word score."

I feel myself begin to flail, the wheel of the cart in my mind shaking all to pieces. Then Perc lays

$$
\begin{array}{c}
I_1 \\ N_1 \\ F_4 \\ E_1 \\ C_3 \\ T_1 \\ I_1 \\ O_1 \\ N_1
\end{array}
$$

— and my head goes. Flashing in front of me is the memory of the British Library, with STI glowing from my laptop screen, and Millie's face contorted in repulsion and panic... then I'm in the clinic, leaning over the counter to whisper that I'm here for an urgent sexual health check-up, and the matronly nurse is asking me to speak up a bit... then I'm in the bleachy room with the doctor; he's swilling my pot of piss, and he's asking me to drop my trousers, to lie back on the papery roll on the bed, ready for the swab, and he's gloved his hand, and he's holding what looks like a long glass ear bud, and he's got rheum in his right eye, and he's inserting the glass thing into the | of my penis, where nothing should ever go back *that* way, and he's practically whisking and...

My head's gone, and soon the game finishes. I lean over to shake the hand of the new tenant.

Words failed me, or I failed words.

All the work that I did, all the money spent on ingredients for a nationalist meal, all the time and resources wasted. As I settle down in the cupboard, I check my emails:

> **Dear student, your case has recently been referred to us by a member of your department's faculty. We have scheduled an appointment to discuss your current situation. You should arrive at the Student Liaison Support office for 2PM on 18th July.**

Well, that's something. A silver sliver of a lifeline instigated by Mair Llewellyn to sort my accommodation. As I fall asleep, I can hear the muffled thud rising up through the floorboards, gathering in volume, making the cupboard shake. The house welcomes its new tenant. They're playing a dubstep remix of 'Our House' by Madness.

CHAPTER TEN

CHECKOUT

There's nothing more triumphant than a completed shopping list. Each item found and ticked off. I've come across many scattered on the shop floor or scrunched at the bottom of baskets. If you've ever scribbled a shopping list, and taken it with you to the aisles, you can call yourself an author. It means that You stood in your kitchen checking the fridge and the cupboard for what you needed. It means that You wrote a cuneiform, a modern-day Kish tablet, and hoped that the You of the future would decipher that code in the supermarket. With a few strokes of a pen, You were in dialogue with your future self. You made a future friend. Some lists, of course, remain incomplete. These I often find abandoned in a trolley, some items ticked off but others still unfound, telling a terrible story of insufficient funds, of a loss of nerve, of a last-minute change of heart:

~~Whisky~~
~~Oven-ready pizza~~
~~Ice cream~~
~~Paracetamol~~
Baby shoes

All those products centrifugally spread around the store are collected together into the contained, ordered space of a shopping basket — with all the opal skies of every day ever spent, and all the sapphire seas bottled up, and all of time and space crunched together into the narrow, mesh vessel. This pendent of a universe, so precious as it swings at a shopper's side.

Once the items have been gathered, the customer must join the truly British phenomenon of the supermarket queue. The dead line. Ordered, quietly polite, simmering with internalised rage and impatience, tutting, always tutting. Everyone surreptitiously judging everyone else's choice of items (Rustler microwave burger, Lambrini, *The Daily Mail*).

At the front of the queue is the checkout lady. Whereas God declared Man banished from Paradise to till the ground, at Tesco it's Woman who works the till. She's the *Última Mujer*. At the conveyor belt's end sits Pat, or Marilyn, or Shel, and she scans each item, totals up the cost, then reads it back to you. She scans, totals, reads, repeats. Scans, totals, reads, repeats. Everyone shuffles. The Tesco two-step towards her, in flats, boots, heels — their heads lowered at half-mast, all with the bland, bleary-eyed anxiety of a hospital waiting room. The £ sign affixes itself to the numbers she reads out — an insignia, a designation, like a mangled musical note that tolls for the funeral.

The trolley is shaken all to pieces, and the conveyor belt is very near its end. Stacks of mesh baskets at shin height; the continuously unravelling grey rubber tongue of the conveyor; the heartbeat beep of each scanned item; the retail reaper who tells you the price; the packing area beyond her, where you stand to receive your barcoded lot. Each moment brings you to your finale — brings this most modern of interactions to its death. You pay your toll, and you check out.

Today I am 'Adam', and Adam stands on aisle No.1 and looks on with astonishment as customers queue to buy a book. He's never seen excitement like it. This AM he was in the warehouse, tasked with unpaletting a huge delivery of a newly published release. And now, in the faces of the excited queue, he sees the fruits of his labours. Out of curiosity, he'd opened a box, sliding the Stanley knife along the brown shiny tape. The box burst open like Pandora's, and into the darkness of the warehouse spilled hardback after hardback, the front cover brightly coloured, printed with a Getty-ish image of a mother and child sitting on a tree branch, heads together.

The novel's tagline: *What if perfect isn't possible?*

The novel's title: *A Perfect Life*.

The author: Danielle Steel.

Adam had flicked to a page, glanced at the words '*Work always came first*', and taken Steel's instruction and got on with his graft.

And now he watches the queues grow and snake around the aisles, thick with crazed customers, all desperately trying to get *A Perfect Life*.

Ex-gentry Montgomery appears, points his stick at the shelves of books on aisle No.1. "So what's all this hoo-ha, young man?" He asks this gruffly, tapping the end of his stick against the book's cover on the shelf.

"It's a new novel," Adam replies, "by Danielle Steel."

"A woman? Steel? *Yupyup* there's only ever been one female who was worthy of metal: The Iron Lady — God rest her soul."

He launches into a Thatcher lament: "Ah, my dear boy, you will be too young to remember when we the people were graced by the presence of *Spitting Image* on our television screens. I was but entering the latter half of my fifth decade when I first guffawed at that sketch. I must tell you. Picture if you will, Margaret Thatcher's cabinet at table in a restaurant. The waitress asks dearest Maggie how she likes her steak. 'Raw please,' Maggie answers. Then the waitress asks, 'And what about the vegetables?' Maggie looks around at her cabinet and answers, 'They'll have the same.' *Yupyupuhuhyup*, such incredible writing, such wonderful wit that couldn't possibly be repeated today."

There's not a moment for Adam to interject — to tell Montgomery that yes, in fact, he *has* seen this clip, and that more or less everyone has seen it, because it's the clip from *Spitting Image* that's always trundled out to indicate the series' quality, its longevity, to prove that it's not dated.

Montgomery goes on: "And what was incredible for the time was that it was really a great badge of pride for those public figures who were caricatured on *Spitting Image*."

Yes it was, Adam thinks, and that tells you everything wrong with it. Satire of this kind, which appeals so much to those whom it satirises, has a very brief sell-by date. Not because the public figures move on or die and drift away from the zeitgeist, but because if it's an accolade to be cartoonishly pilloried, then it's not successful satire. *Spitting Image* was too close to what it purported to despise.

Montgomery, wistful now, puts his hand on Adam's shoulder to support himself. "You know, her origins were not dissimilar to the hallowed hall in which we find ourselves conversing now. Oh yes, oh yes — Thatcher was the child of a grocer. It was while helping out in her father's fruit and vegetable shop that she developed her politics. In fact, her critics, and even some of her admirers, get it wrong — she never rejected the wartime foundations of the welfare state. And actually, it's often overlooked that it was the Tories who introduced the finest food rationing system during the war. Like our foodbanks here, of which I, for one, think we should be immensely proud."

Adam remembers a woman he saw the other week, leaning forward on her tiptoes to rummage in the foodbank box by the checkouts. As she hoisted herself back up, she had an assortment of items collected in her arms — tins, toothpaste, a box of cereal. She put them on the faux-marble floor to lean back over the box. Again on tiptoes, her pastel-coloured Crocs slipping from her feet.

"Excuse me," she'd asked another, taller customer as he passed by, "My lanyard's fallen in and I can't reach the bottom. Would you mind?"

He'd obliged, reached in and retrieved her lanyard, the NHS logo emblazoned on the plastic card and, as if to labour the point, printed on the fabric cord: STAFF STAFF STAFF STAFF. She'd thanked him, picked up her items and went on her way. She must've come here from Charing Cross Hospital during her break.

"*Yupyuhyup*," continues Montgomery, "taking care of our most downtrodden, out of the goodness of our hearts. That's the British way. Help me, would you dear boy? With this list of mine."

He thrusts a piece of paper into Adam's hand. On it, Montgomery has written his usual daily order of a bottle of champagne, but today there's also pork loin, plain flour, chicken stock cubes, cranberry sauce, and honey.

"And for Thatcher, her focus was not really the welfare system at all, but rather she was more concerned about tackling the abuse of that system, which for her meant ending the militancy of unions."

"Onions?"

"No, my boy. *U*nions."

"I understand, sir. I'm just asking if you need red onions added to your list."

"Oh yes. Quite right."

"And would you prefer gammon?" Adam cajoles. "It's on sale."

"Jolly good, my fine fellow."

They move slowly towards aisle No.2 (Fresh Meats): "Most of all, what she defeated comprehensively was 'dependency culture'. Do you know what I mean by that? The laziness of youth. No, no — not you, of course. The laziness of the *un*employed. The laziness of the lower classes. She disliked the habits of the surplus population, what Winston Churchill disparaged as 'Queuetopia'. Her experience as the daughter of a wartime shopkeeper convinced her of the powers of national emergency organisation and the necessity of free markets."

Montgomery and Adam saunter through the store, occasionally finding their path blocked by another excited coil of the Steel queue. Surely neither Thatcher nor Churchill could object to this kind of congregation. Perhaps there are particular kinds of queues that provoke scorn — queues at passport control, queues at the dole office — while others deserve praise: the supermarket queue is a sign of good business, of busy business.

"This is quite a big list today," Adam remarks. "Is it a special occasion?"

"Oh *yupyuh*, young man. It's for my tenant. Well, my ex-tenant. A sad day on which I will bid farewell to her. She's lived in one of my properties for a decade. Yes it'll be very sad with the house all empty now."

"Where is it?"

"Oh, a few minutes away, on Yeoman's Row, off Brompton Road. It's a lovely spot, but I can't get up the stairs anymore" — he taps his stick against his leg — "so for years she's resided on the first floor, had the whole place to herself, and just kept it all clean. That's how Mayari paid for her lodging, by being a live-in cleaner, but now she's moving back to Manila."

Just as Adam is about to go full-on sycophantic Jeeves, and suggest himself as the replacement for the house on Yeoman's Row, a senior colleague passes him and murmurs the word 'cage' in his ear.

Does this mean CAGE, or CAYG?

Adam leaves Montgomery and catches up with the colleague. "Where do you need me to CAYG?" Adam asks.

"No. It's Cage I need you to help with. We need you to remove all those Nicolas Cage DVDs from the shelves to make space for another delivery of this Danielle Steel book. I've never seen so many people excited about a bloody novel like this before."

As if conditioned, Adam notices himself compelled to leave Montgomery and fall to his knees to remove the ludicrous number of films starring Hollywood's most famous Cage. *Leaving Las Vegas*, *The Rock*, *Face/Off*, *Gone in 60 Seconds*, *Captain Corelli's Mandolin*, *National Treasure*, *World Trade Center*, *The Wicker Man* (the remake) and *The Croods*. For some reason *Captain Corelli's Mandolin* and *The Croods* are the most popular, and thus those which are most regularly restocked. *The Croods* is more understandable, it being a recent child-friendly retelling of Plato's Cave Allegory.

By the time Adam's finished removing all the DVDs and filled the spaces with rows of Danielle Steel's novel, Montgomery has long since departed from the store. No matter. Next week, Adam has his meeting with the university to discuss accommodation. Hopefully, they will offer him a place and he won't have to fawn over or cosy up to Montgomery.

He passes a few members of Upper Management, tapping away on their tablets and watching the large queues of customers clutching Steel's book, shaking their heads: "We might need to empty some of the other aisles to make room for all this demand."

At the end of his shift, Adam unpins the nametag and returns it to the veg box.

I emerge into the ♂ Changing Room and begin pulling on my civvies. Naked, except for these two-day old boxers, there's a metallic throbbing sound as my phone begins to vibrate on the bench. I examine the screen. It's a 0151 number, Liverpool's area code. My first thought is of

Alby, who I've not seen for some time. Perhaps it's just coincidence that our shifts aren't aligning, or maybe Upper Management are monitoring us and keeping us apart.

"Yes?"

"Hi there, this is Becci from the University of Liverpool's Student Alumni Development Team."

"Yes?"

"And I'm calling you today because I have a few questions for you as one of our esteemed alumni on our database."

"Yes?"

"Did you know it's already been exactly twelve months since you graduated with us in July 2013?"

"Yes."

"And we'd love to check out what you're up to now, a year on. So, could I please ask you some questions?"

"Yes."

"Have you, in the last year, gone into full-time work?"

Unintentionally. "Yes."

"Have you utilised the skills obtained throughout your degree?"

Sometimes. "Sometimes."

"Can you give an example of how your degree has helped you in your employment?"

I can do a Tannoy announcement in the style of John Keats. "My language skills helped to design a marketing campaign for a Danielle Steel book."

"Oh fab! I'll put 'advertising'. And have you gone on to further education?"

Tried. "Yes."

"What are your living arrangements?"

"I'm between places."

"Where in the country are you based?"

"London."

"Would you consider yourself single?"

Very. “Yes.”

“What have you gained in the last year?”

Quite possibly an STI and/or a child. “Experience.”

“On a 1–10 scale, how satisfied are you with where you are right now?”

I look around the locker room, catch myself in the mirror — in my dirty boxers. My long hair is greasy, my beard is gutterfluff, and my bare chest an oven-ready Margherita of acne.

“It’s off the scale.”

“And finally, can I ask if I can call you in another twelve months to check out where you’ve got to?”

“Hello?

“Hello?”

“Are you still there?”

- - - - -

As long as I sit here and look at the pretty girl from this distance, there’s a possibility that she’ll fall in love with me. If I stand up, go over, and introduce myself, or invite her to have a drink, that’s when there’s a risk that the universe will end. So I’ll stay sitting here, brooding over today’s events, looking at the pretty girl.

I’m on terra unfamiliar — south of the river, far from Bloomsbury, far from Earl’s Court. I’m in Southwark, and I’ve been sitting in The George Inn for nearly seven hours, since I left the meeting room at the university and got this far before collapsing. Everything’s gone south. I feel like I’ve been stood up, let down, mugged off, led on.

The pretty girl is still there, rocking on her bar stool, picking at honey roasted nuts that the barman brought her.

Today was the day of my university appointment to help secure some accommodation. Or at least, that's what I'd been led to believe was going to happen.

While the pretty girl readjusts herself on her stool, like a gorgeous garden gnome, I unpocket my phone and reread yet again the text which Mair sent me last month:

> **Hey there, this is Mair. i'm really sorry to have to do this but we're going to have to cancel the plan for you to stay at ours. I'd had a few too many last night and recognised another in need, but because I'm teaching you and most likely marking your essays etc. it's not appropriate. This is a professional thing, I'm sorry to say. Anyway, I've referred your situation to the student liaison committee, and they've already responded to me that they've set up a meeting for you to discuss with them the troubles you've been having. Check your emails and they should get in touch soon. Again, really sorry but I hope this helps.**

No mention of anything like a mental health intervention. I repocket my phone and pull out my laptop, flip the lid, adjust my bloodshot eyes to the ignited screen, open my inbox, reread yet again the email which the university sent to me:

> **Dear student, your case has recently been referred to us by a member of your department's faculty. We have scheduled an appointment to discuss your current situation. You should arrive at the Student Liaison Support office for 2PM on 18th July.**

Again, no mention of anything like a mental health intervention. By 'your situation', as Mair's text put it, and 'current situation', as the email puts it, I'd assumed they meant a crisis of housing, not a crisis of sanity. So imagine my shock, surprise, wrong footedness, when I'd entered the scheduled meeting earlier today, ready to point to a big fuck-off map of London and say *THERE, THAT'S where I want to live*, only to discover...

The pretty girl flicks her hair. It's dark as coal.

...only to discover that I was the subject of an assessment for whether I was fit enough to study or *compost mentis*. Give me a million Tannoy announcements for the rest of time. I'll gladly waste whatever you want. Take me back to Tesco. Just get me out of here. All of that went through my head as I faced the three faces sitting in a row.

Far right: "You've got to accept this as a defeat; there's no shame in that."

Far left: "You're clearly very good at hiding what you're really going through, but you need to be honest with us."

The face in the middle said nothing and busily filled in a form, based on my responses. I felt myself fold like an IKEA table, ready for the tip.

Their conclusion, recited aloud to me, then written on the form that's in my pocket now: "We advise a suspension of studies and we refer the student to mental health support."

The pretty girl is reapplying her make up. Maybe this means she's moving off soon.

So I'd stepped out of the meeting and got off campus ASAFP. I just started walking, fucking off out of there, in any direction. I didn't look up from the reassuring order of paving slabs until I noticed first Southwark Cathedral and then The George Inn. I went straight in, ordered a whisky, and slumped in a nook facing the bar. I've been in here for nearly seven hours. There is a wide wound in my chest that I'm trying to heal with whisky — and by watching this pretty girl from a safe distance.

On the wall in a glass case there's a flinty looking badge: a relic dredged from a mudlark on the Thames, depicting the martyrdom of Thomas Becket. Inscribed on the knobbly metal are the letters: THOMAS MA. Even the turbulent priest is closer to getting a Master's degree than I am.

She's so pretty. Flat pumps. Bare ankles with those knobbly bits that invite a nibble. Her skirt, lavender and nettley, is all swishing, and her blouse is cream. Her hair is perfect. She's absolute and complete, so fully possessed of self-knowledge, grace in her gestures, what she wills or says seems wisest and best. She's talking amicably to the barman: "...and so I said to him, you're a cunt, mate. Do one."

Ah the sweet lyricism of a perfect being. Her voice is familiar. A timeless lilt. She's not flirting with him, their body language tells me, just engaged, focused. I pick up snippets of what she's saying:

"....after that night I moved my stuff out of his place and never saw him again. Which is better coz my poetry's been properly improving since."

Barman's nodding, while he clinks freshly steamed glasses onto the shelves.

I gulp the last of whisky No.9. I'm trying to drink for each aisle in the store. I was averaging about one and a half an hour but slowed down when this pretty girl arrived. Didn't want to look uncouth in this near-empty pub.

Time for whisky No.10, in honour of the World Foods aisle. I close the laptop's lid. I'll probably have to return it to the university's library under some subclause of the loaning policy that makes the mentally ill unsafe around electronics.

Standing, now, gradually, I find that the floorboards shift and seesaw beneath me. I'll order mine, and ask her if she wants one. But first I need to get across the room.

It feels like I'm in an old rerun of *Star Trek*. Whenever they need a plot point, an asteroid'll strike the USS Enterprise. All the crew and aliens onboard will lunge for the nearest bit of furniture to steady themselves. It is with that momentum and in that manner than I tumble to the bar, hoisting myself to the vertical.

"Same again, please. Ta. And er..." I turn towards her, seeing her in profile like the poise of a postage stamp. Again, familiar. Beauty is timeless, too.

She turns.

"...the fuck do you want?"

"I heard you say you're into poetry?"

She nods. "And you?"

I nod. "Who do you like?"

"John Milton."

I feel lifted by these three syllables — I'm on safe ground. My chest practically bursts as I recite:

"'*Into this wild Abyss — The womb of Nature, and perhaps her grave...*'"

The pretty girl interjects, "...dadidaditumtitum '*the wary Fiend Stood on the brink of hell and looked awhile, Pondering his voyage...*' Yeah, everyone knows that one... from the beginning of the Philip Pullman books."

I'm floored, I'm flawed, as I remember myself reading those books as a child. Put away childish things.

She laughs. "It's a good bit, don't get me wrong, but it's just that's the only bit of that poem anyone ever seems to know."

Before I can tell her that I know more of Milton than just this, I notice that she's looking at my T-shirt. "Why's your T-shirt say 'BE MY LEVANTINE'? Is it a Syrian solidarity thing?"

It feels wrong to use a humanitarian crisis as a chat-up line, but she might well be the love of my life.

"Yes," I answer. "Can I get you a drink?"

"Well, I commend you then, but I'm not interested. Thanks, though," she says, then turns back to her postage-stamp poise.

I turn to the barman and order for myself. The same order as the previous nine, but it feels weird to say, "The usual, please." From my pocket, I take my wallet, withdraw my card, and hold it near to the glowing reader held out by the barman, minding the gap, between the pretty girl and me, between the reader and my bank card. Its beep is the flatline of my attempt to woo her.

While the barman fetches the whisky bottle, I go around the bar and through the 🚹 door. The trickle of the drains behind the chipped tiles, the basin's bouquet of bleach and ammonia. It brings me to my senses. I piss, hosing down a skidmark in the toilet bowl, and while I wash my hands, I wonder what else I've got in the *Now That's What I Call Poetry* of my mind. If not Milton, then Christina Rossetti, or maybe Coleridge, or Chaucer.

Back at the bar, she's got her head bowed over a piece of paper. Crumpled. Familiar looking.

"This yours?" she asks.

Fuck. "Yeah it must've fallen from my pocket." It's the form that was smooth this afternoon, slid across the table to me by the Student Liaison Support team. Crumpled now.

She looks more closely at me, down at the letter, and back to me. "*This* is the good stuff. 'Sleeping rough', 'anxiety', 'prone to hallucinations'. Why didn't you try and chat me up with this? I'll have a red vodka with lemonade. And a packet of salt and vinegar crisps."

The barman gets her order. The beep of my bank card above the reader signals the starter pistol on my quick sprint to woo the pretty girl. It's almost last orders.

"So, c'mon then," she says, opening the packet down the side and spreading it out into a very small shiny picnic blanket, "tell me something that'll dazzle."

I take a crisp and crunch, but wonder, what can I say? That I'm one official form away from exiting my MA? That I'm homeless? That I've almost certainly got an STI and/or baby?

"Oh, I dunno. Not that interesting, really."

"Pfft, you know it's very few blokes who can get away with the vague, mysterious thing, and self-deprecation is not very in vogue these days."

"Okay. I work at Tesco. Better?"

"That *is* better. It's not particularly attractive, but at least it's honest."

"And the Milton stuff is just generic?"

"All that literature and culture is just a stand in for the fact that you lack a personality. Believe me, I've known loads of men like that and to be honest I'm just sick of being the one who has to hold someone else's head together. But this Tesco thing, that's a proper USP."

"It's really all I've got now," I confess.

"That's the good shit. The true desperation of the poets. What, do you think Blake was fucking around at a Freshers' Fair or a book club? No, he was grafting, living, trying to get by. So what's it like there, at Tesco?"

"Oh, y'know, same old really."

"No, I don't know. That's why I'm asking."

"That's time," the barman interrupts, "and also, your cab's outside."

"Cab?"

"Yes," she says, hopping down from her stool. "To the station. I live in Canterbury, so I'm cabbing it to the station for the last train. Shame. I feel like there was more stuff you could've told me that might've made it into a poem."

"That's time, mate," the barman repeats.

I go to the nook to retrieve my rucksack and return to the bar.

She downs the last of her drink. "Nice to meet you." She extends out a hand and as I go to shake she swerves it and reaches for the bowl of nuts on the bar. She scoops up a few, throws them into a wide, chuckling mouth, nods knowingly, and is out of the door.

I stand here, the barman collecting glasses, reorganising chairs. I sip the last of my whisky.

So, she's gone. Back to Kent, and the pub's clock is flicking the Vs at me. 23.05.

"You'll see her again, bruv," says the barman, tolerantly consoling, "she does the poetry night regularly."

"She *performs* poetry?" The pilot light of memory clicking on.

"Yeah. Not just here but all over London's open mic circuit. But, as she said, she lives in Canterbury so she always stops off here on her way back down."

"Where else does she perform?" I ask eagerly, the memory now a hob's blue flame. "Like in North London?"

The barman whistles, thinking. "There's The Woodman in Highgate." He starts to laugh. "You know what's fucking hilarious about that pub? It's got a backroom that's named after—"

"Rod Stewart. I know. I've been there." An asteroid slams into the USS Enterprise of my heart, and I grip the bar to steady myself. I've been there. I've met her. I've whispered poetry to her.

"Anyway," the barman announces pointedly. He's done with his professional duties and wants me and the other loiterers to drink up and get out. "It's time, mate. Fuck off, in other words."

In other words. Words, words — the kinds of other words I couldn't muster during Scrabble, couldn't conjure to a pretty girl to convey the world I inhabit at Tesco. There's really no point in learning all these words if I can't use them when it really matters.

I pick up my crumpled form from the bar, yank my rucksack onto my shoulders and barge the pub's door. As I walk across The George's old Tudor-beamed courtyard, I try to focus with whisky-hazed eyes on the words on the page. I turn onto Tabard Street and have to keep looking up from the paper to avoid lampposts. By a hefty, leafy roundabout that takes me onto New Kent Road, I'm almost knocked down by a delivery van. A Tesco delivery van, obviously. Throughout this assault course, the same phrases leap out at me, doing a few laps on the skidmarked racetrack of my skull: *This student has been sleeping rough and should suspend his studies. He needs mental health support at an appropriate accommodation suitable for such an intervention to prevent any further instances of his imagining himself to be other people.*

Beneath this, at the bottom of the page, a different hand, a more looping handwriting. A telephone number, and the name *Harri x*, and the words *call me when you've got a story to tell. Words, words. I have many to use.*

I should call her, and tell her a tale. I bring my phone from my pocket, thumb the screen, type in her phone number and press the call key. Over the traffic, the *burbburb, burbburb* of the phone goes on and on.

New Kent Road ages abruptly and I'm walking along Old Kent Road, the only discernible difference being that here are fewer Betfreds and more healthy trees. I stop at a corner shop and buy a 35cl Famous Grouse. I can feel the enamel stripped from my teeth and my throat's cartilage peel with each swig.

At a crossroads, there's inevitably a fuck-off massive Tesco Superstore. Tomorrow, I'm due back in work, but what's the point what's the point what's the point. Instead, I will go to Kent, right fucking now. I don't have Mollie Friel's Freedom Pass anymore, but fuck it, I'll walk to Kent to see Harri. I will walk to Canterbury, to where there are apples and cherries (aisle No.6), where there are hops (aisle No.20), and where there's a woman (the ultimate aisle). Maybe I'll get as far as Dover, and Harri and I will ship out to Europe together. Start again on the high seas, sharing stories.

I lean against the metal of a Shard-shaped obelisk outside the Tesco, which still retains the heat it's absorbed throughout the daytime. Above, its constellation of arrows spin and turn as part of the monument. A plaque tells me its credentials: Peter Logan, 1995. Despite the nearly imperceptible breeze, the arrows are pointing in unwieldy directions, as if blown in a gale. There must be some kind of internal momentum. This way, that way, pointing down Humphrey Street, then up to Burgess Park.

Then the arrow turns back to the Tesco.

Even by the lamplight that shades the nearest trees, I can make out a face reflected in the obelisk's metal. It's the face of a storyteller.

"Hi, you've reached Harri. I can't take the call at the moment, but please leave a message and I'll get back to you."

I press the red button to cancel the call.

I keep walking, a big green street sign with the dimensions of a tennis court directs me towards Dover (A2) and the Channel Tnl (A20), where my white dove of a Kentish maid has surely fluttered.

I call again.

"Hi, you've reached Harri. I can't take the call at the moment, but please leave a message and I'll get back to you."

I press the red button to cancel the call.

Outside Old Kent Road Fire Station, there's a fragrant lavender bush. I snap off a sprig and rub it between my fingertips. Through the big glass windows, I can see red trucks at rest. I rub a bit of the scent into my neck — a herb cologne to impress my Kentish maid when I reach her. I snap off a few more sprigs and tuck them into my rucksack.

I cross over at a traffic island, passing by a mural which is momentarily ignited by the glare of oncoming headlights. I can make out the figures in stony profile: a dagger-bearing yeomen, a knight beneath a tower, and a nun on horseback with her eyes closed and her palm raised, as if placating her fellow travellers.

"Hi, you've reached Harri. I can't take the call at the moment but please leave a message and I'll get back to you."

I press the red button.

I pass The Windsor, on whose swinging pub sign is perched the statue of a proud golden cockerel. I keep walking, and realise that at some point Old Kent Road merged into New Cross Road. It veers left, and the buildings are now more squat, the barbershops larger and more regular, the wig and weave outlets more wiggy and weavier.

A plaque on a graffitied wall by Iceland explains that, on 25/11/1944, a V2 rocket landed here, killing 168 people. I keep walking, to the lower end of Deptford High Street, where I rest a boot on the sharp hook of the anchor statue to retie my shoelace, pressing the Nokia between my collarbone and my cheek to call again. The sooty sky is smearing its shadow wherever the lamplights' amber doesn't reach. On the horizon, the neon pyramid of Canary Wharf has snagged a cloud on its glass point, and the cloud trails limply off to the west, like sheep's wool on a bramble.

"Hi, you've reached Harri. I can't..."

I press the red button.

Along the broadest, widest part of New Cross Road, I notice a plaque on the wall of a tall house on the opposite side of the road. The roaring traffic prevents me crossing and I feel angry that the city has denied me knowledge of itself.

"Hello?"

I press the red button. But no — shit, wait — I think that might've been her actual voice. I redial, but I'm walking beneath the railway arches of Deptford DLR, where my phone signal cuts out.

I redial and hear only the metallic beep of disconnection. The water under the bridge is very low, showing up its muddy cargo of glistening tyre rims or the funnel of welly boots lost to the mire.

I re-emerge and dial again.

"Hi, you've reached Harri. I can't take the call at the moment, but please leave a message and I'll get back to you."

I press the red button.

I can make out the grubby emerald façade of the Greenwich Magistrates Court on the other side of the road.

"Hi, you've..."

I press the red button.

I keep walking, along the gently curving, ascending slabs of Blackheath Road. There's a synthetic rubber smell wafting across from a retail park, then the road's gradient suddenly inclines, and the smell is replaced by the thick, syrupy musk of pine needles, more usually associated with Christmas than fierce July heat, where summer night's scent sparks the weary into wariness.

"Hi, you've..."

I press the red button.

I keep walking, the combo of rucksack+Grouse+hill making me heave. The road narrows into the dimensions of a shooting range. The traffic slows, and the houses on both sides become grander — elderly, somehow — as if cowering in all their finery for a quiet life. Their porch carvings like old grey moustaches, and through their wide bay windows, thinly opened, dim chandeliers dangle.

"Hi, you've..."

I press the red button.

Then, up onto the flat, dark plane of Blackheath, oddly silent despite the thread of traffic. The sounds of axles, horns, and exhaust-pipes spreads and dilutes into a whisper across the grassy park and its porous trees.

"Hi, you've..."

I press the red button.

I keep walking, over crispy, crackling grass, past a pond

walled on all sides by grungy mop-headed willow trees. They sway, very slightly in the coming wind, as if something's in the way. I keep walking, between a pair of posts holding up a much bigger green sign — the dimensions of a football pitch — announcing Dover (A2) and Woolwich (A207). Along the edge of the road fissuring Blackheath, there are gorse bushes, in whose thorny stems bits of rubbish are tangled. A pair of tights trail ominously, tugged and torn from a body, left laddered and billowing.

My phone cuts out again. Not because of signal but because, as I look down at the screen, of the familiar problem: **Remaining credit is £00.00.**

I keep walking, along Shooters Hill Road — long, long, endlessly long, with terraced houses on either side whose roofs share a tall, thin chimney sticking up in silhouette like a mohawk.

Remaining credit is £00.00.

A petrol station appears out of the dark, glowing anemone orange. Time to top up phone credit and alcohol levels.

Trillaling goes the door as I push it open. This is an automated jingle, not a windchime or bell dangling above the doorframe. I peruse the shelves of alcohol, pick out another 35cl — Bells, this time — and join the queue. Ahead of me is a young woman carrying a tote that sags with bottles of spirits. On the tote's canvas is printed a faded image of a school's crest and the words LEAVERS 2014. Ahead of her is an elderly man ordering scratch cards and lotto tickets. While he uses a coin to rub at the silvery film of each, discarding one after another at the rate the cashier can present them, I glance out of the window, where a Tesco delivery van has pulled up. Out jumps a middle-aged man who doesn't pause to fill up his van but walks straight across the forecourt and enters.

Trillaling

The cashier looks up, over the flat-capped head of the old man. "Evening, Arthur."

"Alright there, Omar," calls back the Tesco delivery man, already scanning the shelves. "You got any Red Bull in?"

"Over there."

The old man has scratched his final card. "Just my luck," he mutters as he waddles past us in the queue and out of the petrol station.

Trillaling

Omar and Arthur continue chit-chatting while the young woman gets served. Arthur's complaining about traffic and exhaustion: "How am I meant to get these deliveries in if the roads are this chocka?"

"Where is it tonight?" Omar asks.

"Canvey Island."

Omar winces. "Bit out of your way, isn't it?"

"You're telling me. There's some big demand all of a sudden, so I'm doing plenty of extra drives. Pain in the arse if you ask me."

"I know," Omar sympathises. "Too many cars out there. That'll be £35.90 please, love. You don't need a bag, I see."

"And where are those vegan sausage rolls, mate?" Arthur calls from across the aisles.

"All sold out, I'm afraid. Next please."

Trillaling and the young woman leaves. I step forward to the till as Arthur joins behind me. He's holding up a newspaper. "You sin this, Omar? ITV2 announces it will commission a six-part series called...Get this...*Dapper Laughs on the Pull*. It's going to be executively produced by Holly Willoughby's hubby, it says here. Ha ha. He says Dapper Laughs is the new Cilla Black. Can you believe it? Honestly."

I pay for my bottle and ask for phone credit.

"You need to get a contract, mate," Arthur says behind me. "Much cheaper for using internet data. When I'm driving, I just clip my iPhone to the dashboard and talk to my mates as I drive."

"He looks like he's talking to ghosts," Omar murmurs loudly as he hands me the top-up card. "I see him through the window of his van just sitting on the forecourt mouthing away."

"Oi. Watch it," laughs Arthur.

"I don't have a smartphone," holding up my Nokia, "just this."

"No smartphone? Where d'you work?"

"Tesco."

"Bollocks."

I flash my ID from my wallet.

"As if! What branch?"

"Tesco Kensington."

"SW. Very nice. Bit far from home out here, aren't ya?"

"Very."

"Lemme ask ya. Has your branch bin getting all saughtsa books in? Steel or summit?"

"Danielle Steel. *A Perfect Life*. Yes. Crazy isn't it."

"You're tellin me. I bin all over tryna keep up wiv demand. I tell you though, whatever she's written ain't got nuffink on the Blackheath Bowmen."

"The?"

Over my shoulder Arthur calls out: "Oi Omar. He don't know about the Blackheath Bowmen."

"Well he should do," Omar calls back.

"Shall we tell him, Omar?"

Omar nods. "Alright!" — darting out from behind the glass — "Wait for me."

Arthur: "Come outside."

Bells and top-up card in hand, I follow Arthur and Omar onto the forecourt. Arthur holds his finger to his lips. "Listen," he whispers. "Just listen."

Omar, too, is silent, his eyes closed.

All I can hear is the machine whir of traffic, the rush of exhausts, the hum of the cables and lights of the petrol station.

"This was told by one of our best storytellers. During the Great War, 300,000 Germans had a small English company of troops on the ropes. Our Tommies in their trench were under fire day and night, and they knew they were about to die. Those who hadn't already been blown to bits prayed and shook hands with one another. Others improvised songs from the music halls or made jokes. Some even gave stupid names to the shell that they reckoned would kill them. An officer told his men to keep firing at the 300,000 Germans, to enjoy what time there was left of shooting practice. One Englishman followed these orders and aimed his rifle at the grey mass. And, as he did, he remembered a vegetarian restaurant he used to visit back in London that made dishes of lentils and nuts posing as steak. This soldier suddenly saw the plates these dishes were served on, which were printed with the red flag of St George on the white porcelain, and the motto printed in blue: *Adsit Anglis Sanctus Geogius*. Now, do you know what that means, mate?"

"May St George be a present help to the English," Omar interrupts excitedly.

"Omar's right. *Adsit Anglis Sanctus Geogius*. And when the soldier muttered these words to himself he saw, suddenly in front of him, amongst the shell cavities and fallen bodies and shrapnel of no-man's land, a whole line of men facing the advancing Germans. These men had bows and aimed them upwards. They let fly, and a thousand arrows sailed into the grey horde. Again the bowmen let fly, and the Germans were stopped in their approach towards the English trenches. More and more arrows were fired; more and more found their mark, and more and more enemy soldiers fell. Eventually, the vegetarian soldier realised that there were no more Germans left standing. His incantation had helped them win the battle. He looked around for a sign of the bowmen, but there was none. Even when the English inspected the bodies of the fallen enemy, they found no entry wounds, and not a single arrowhead was discovered anywhere on the battlefield. The English soldier began to doubt himself, but he knew that those spirits he'd summoned were real. They were St George's bowmen of Agincourt, come to protect the English whenever they were most in need. And do you know why Blackheath is so special in this story? In 1415, that's 599 years ago, after the victory at Agincourt, those valiant soldiers first entered London through this very heath."

A shiver from the booze, or a fizzing of electricity from the garage, makes me pause. So quiet is it all around that I think I can make out an echo, not a machine whir but a metallic scrape, not the rush of exhaust but the wheezing of horses, not the hum of cables but the distant thump of a drum beating and boots in unison.

"And if you're quiet now," Arthur drops his voice to a whisper, "you might hear the Agincourt parade that came this way to celebrate its victory, their bows clattering skyward, the victory songs peaking to the treetops, the locals throwing garlands."

Omar nudges me back to whatever this is. "Great story, isn't it?"

"It is." To Arthur: "Who told you that?"

"I told you. One of our best storytellers."

"Who?"

"The boss of my branch of Tesco. At our regional meeting, he said there are plans to make it into a Christmas advert for this year. Yeah, the word is that Sainsbury's are planning a World War I advert about the trenches and football, so we're hoping to get ahead of them."

I keep walking, wriggling through shadowy streets, demarcated only by traffic lights. Along the edge of gated communities and through gulag underpasses. As I walk, I try to thumb the keys of my phone, looking from the screen to the top-up card, desperate to call Harri, to recount to her what I've just heard. But my hands tremble — more than those of the old man with his scratch cards. Along Charlton Park Lane, I pass copper green cemetery gates, carelessly left open, the rusted padlock like a hand giving a thumbs up to enter. I have to keep looking up from the top-up card to see where I'm going. High above, the great hubcap in the sky leads me, and as I keep walking, the smell of dung and the snort of some hidden mare comes from my right, where I can see the outline of a paddock. To my left are the blazing lights of the Woolwich barracks, lit up and brooding.

Finally, I enter the top-up card digits in the correct order and hold my phone out in front of me as I walk, waiting for a credit confirmation text to come through.

London is nestling close, like a lover seeking comfort. On the far horizon is a hill, with crane cabins above building sites, flashing their red-jewelled warnings to incoming aircraft, and the aerials and the wheezing smoke from factory funnels — the city adorned like Leviathan's ballooned head. And likewise, the promise that all of this is benign and benevolent — while always the threat of sanctioned violence and legislated cruelty. Parked cars with engines on, lining the curb, headlights giving me evils; or casting shadows of dark tree trunks splayed upwards, like giant arrowheads jammed in the soil. I look up above the leaf line. The further from the city's amber glow I am, the brighter and more viscous become the constellations and the infinite dark which illuminates them. These blasted stars stricken by astral influence, suffering in their isolation as I suffer and—

Automated text from O2: **You have successfully topped up. Your remaining credit is: £10.00.**

I immediately scroll through my phone to Harri's number and press call. It rings, it rings.

"Hello?"

"Harri? Hi, it's me from the pub. I have such a good story for you..."

I step onto a dark path between the glare of the barracks and a line of trees, but step through the path, find myself falling forward, pulled by the weight of my rucksack, tumbling down a steep slope, rolling and then stopping, my head knocking against a brick wall.

Somewhere vaguely above there's the sound of a car slowing, and a window rolling down: "Y'alright, mate?"

Another steady squeal of brakes as a second car slows down, another voice calling from another open window: "Ey, he's fallen in the Ha Ha."

"Wheyy. Wanker." And the sound of laughter and two cars accelerating.

Lying there, back fucked by how I landed across my rucksack, looking up at the narrow strip of sky framed by the mossy lips of this steep slope, I'm struck by a memory: I'd just turned eighteen, the first time I went out boozing, led into this adult world by my older brother, long before his incarceration. The plan was to have a pint in every pub along the stretch of dark country roads in the Fens. My brother, steadily, patiently, leading me from pub to pub, holding a torch to light our way along the lane. But suddenly, I was jolted by a boozy impulse and, foolishly, snatched the torch from his hand. In my head, I'd planned to run off into the darkness, to hide behind a hedge and then jump out at him. But as I reached a field's edge, turned off the torch, and stepped onto the patch of dark grass to hide, my foot passed through what I thought was grass. It was empty air, where a gully sent me down, down, down to lie there, like I am now, tangled in brambles. A person of the abyss. Unable to move, hoping for a brotherly hand to hoist me up from the dark.

▬ ▬ ▬ ▬ ▬

Today I am moss. I am dent. I am can, leaf, mud, stone. The *compost mentis* of ages and nations here in the ditch — detritus scattered from passersby who've used this Ha Ha as a wasteland: the crinkled bow-tie of a dozen Tyskies thrown from a nearby bench; a child's toy, coated like chainmail with snail shells; a few Bags for Life. If I rummaged in amongst it all, I might find the severed heads prophesised by the occult seer Cagliostro. I retrieve my phone from the leaves. There's a new message.

Harri: dont call me again

What a waste.

I claw my way up the Ha Ha's steep side, hauling my rucksack behind me. This is where the joke stops. The early morning dew has already been melted by searing heat. Marzipan sunlight ignites the countless spiderwebs spread out like trip wires from one blade of grass to the next. I'm sweating as I emerge from the dugout, needled, pined, soiled, and so, so hungover. And I'm late, stuck on Woolwich's periphery. The terraced houses which make up the moored tanker of a council estate along the meadow's side seem to stretch on forever.

It's not just my proximity to the Royal Arsenal that makes me think about war. It's not just Arthur's tale, which already belongs to the spirits. It's that the city itself, even the weather, seems to be preparing for conflict. Parakeets perform flight manoeuvres. The colour of tennis balls, they pelt en masse from tree to tree, while bees' backends froth with collected pollen. Badgers are the clay-kickers in their burrows; stinging nettles glisten like green shields ready for revolt. Tufts of wheat could be a piece of helmet battledress. Foxes think up strategy. Conkers have appeared unseasonably soon, fully grown on their branches, like that bit on the end of a medieval *Morgenstern*, or a spiked Ferrero Rocher (aisle No.19). Spread all over the place are propellers from those helicoptering seedpods that spin off from sycamores, and there are grenade-shaped blackberries ready to detonate and smear their stains.

I limp along Grand Depot Road, a parade ground to my left, where military men already stomp and bark their morning drills. To my right are the ruins of a church, a roofless neo-Byzantine crumble, with ornate, blossoming columns that prop up morning's blue sky. Through its gates, patterned with the wheels of Saxony demi-cannons, I can see a raised altar with its gold-leaf mural of a soldier rearing up on his horse to crush a green dragon beneath its hooves.

I keep limping, turning away from the start of Nightingale Road, where Alexander Blok might pen a poem ('*the hand will not return to its labour*'), with cars fizzing much faster than the 20mph printed on the beetle-coloured tarmac. I'm going downhill, into Woolwich, passing the great cave of a store's backend. A sign announces that it's a Tesco Delivery Yard. A truck reverses into the cave, and workers scurry around unloading palettes. As I pass, the driver says to a hard-hatted foreman, "It's another delivery of that metal woman's book."

Then I'm limping by a porridge-coloured house that calls itself St Peter's Presbytery, outside which an old woman clad in red frock and a hat heaped with fake flowers slows on her mobility scooter to cross herself. I have to dodge her, so as to avoid God's wrath, as I limp on swiftly towards the station. I'm going to be late for work.

Prompted by the delivery truck's red, white, and blue logo, I start running, now that I can see the station at the bottom of the hill, shaped like Hypno-Disc from *Robot Wars*, but I have to squint suddenly against the flashes from the Tesco Extra's huge glass front. It blinds and scolds my eyes. I stop for a second, in the midst of a déjà vu: I've seen this Tesco before. Yes! That's it! Last month, in the *Our Tannoy* magazine, this Tesco was nominated for the Carbuncle Prize — its yellow comb-shaped panels like a cubist beehive, and, inexplicably, along its brow-shaped terrace above the store's entrance, a series of bicycles.

I'm really rushing now, along the edge of General Gordon Square, ducking as two men cross my path carrying between them a set of metal poles to assemble the stalls, like festival tents, to sell discount fruit and veg, knock-off watches and branded clothes. These are the exhausted stall owners who glare angrily at the big, gleaming Tesco on the public square's far side, which has sucked away their daily trade. These street grocers who get up earlier, work later, sell less, seethe more, are now relegated to the status of prospectless moons orbiting planet Tesco. Here are the satellites Miranda, Ariel, Umbriel, Titania, and Oberon, all spinning around the retail Uranus.

I leg it into Woolwich station and I beep my Oyster card. Then I'm away — on the train towards West London.

I have to change into my work clothes right there in the Tube carriage. My rucksack vomits up my uniform, which I peel on awkwardly like I'm on a beach removing swimming shorts behind a sandy towel. I receive disapproving looks, but without a nametag of my own, there's no one for these commuters to complain about. Tesco employs like 300,000 staff. I've seen people do much worse on the Underground.

The sweaty grossness of my morning efforts, combined with last night's long, slow assault on my liver and dermis, necessitates talcum powder as the train sets off. But I have to be careful. Talc leaves white prints on every surface, including this carriage's floor. It looks like Freud's study.

At Earl's Court I rise with the heat up the escalators. There's no whiteboard at its entrance. I have to invent my own inspirational quote: '*The plague will rouse its rats and send them to die in a joyful city*.' Maybe Camus is a bit harsh for mid-July, though when I reach Warwick Road, the pavements are a filthy plane of bitumen boiling up from underground.

The wide black stretch of Cromwell Road dry heaves traffic along its gullet. I dodge cars to get into Tesco. The cool curtain of air that greets me when I enter is a relief. But instantly things are not as they should be. Usually, at the store's front there is the pleasant sight of colourful flowers in buckets. Celestial roses, immortal amaranth, orchids, hyacinths, lilies, crocuses, and pots of myrtle, their white tentacles tipped with fairy lights.

But not today.

The flowers and their buckets have been thrown aside and lie on the faux-marble floor, wilted. In their place, stacks and stacks of books have been piled up. Rows and rows of Danielle Steel's new novel. Crowds are trying to get at them, only just held at bay by the frantic warnings from the security guard, who shouts, "Get back! Get back!" as the crowd surges forward, to grab, to snatch.

"I need *A Perfect Life*!" yells a crazed man, pulling at his hair.

"We'll get it to you soon as, once the queues have gone down at the checkouts, sir," calls a terrified shop floorer hiding behind the security guard.

All along the other aisles, people are clambering to get at copies of the book. Entire shelves which would've usually stocked tinned beans, or toilet roll, or apple cider, have been replaced. And still the crowds come, like locusts, wrenching the books from the shelves and racing towards the checkouts.

"Just please, I beg you, give me *A Perfect Life*," howls a woman carrying a toddler under one arm, while with the other she gouges fingernails down her cheek. Everywhere I look, there are wild eyed customers.

At various times this supermarket has taken on aliases of its own: a cathedral, with its vaulted ceilings of wire and pipe, its architraves of scaffolding; or a Parthenon, its steel girders like patternless Doric pillars, and freezers in place of friezes. It's been a farm, a panopticon, an airport. But today it is a lazar house in a heat wave. I rush up to the F&F mezzanine to survey the scene, from the privileged position of Google Map's dangling yellow man.

From Fresh Meats by the front of the store, all the way up to Wine & Spirits by the warehouse's entrance, a monstrous crew appears; in a miserable failure of abstinence, their malady is the avarice for *A Perfect Life*. In ghastly spasms, the crowds shriek and scratch at one another to get at the books, and there erupts to the vaulted ceilings the sounds of torture, of fever, of agony born of insatiable longing. In a demonic frenzy, cures and medicines from the Pharmacy are thrown to the floor as the crowd searches for Steel. Dire is the waste of these balms.

Through the plasticky tendrils that hang down at the warehouse's entrance, a palette of Steel's books is wheeled out. Immediately, a mob descends on it, the warehouse workers scattering in terror. The rabble grabs armfuls of books and runs the gauntlet to the checkouts where, as fast as colleagues can scan the books, there are mechanics trying to wheel in brand new self-service machines to deal with the demand. The machines beeps like obsolete life-support machines. Their intermittent toots and honks are the glitches of ineffective heart monitors.

"Just use real people," roars a furious man stuck in a rapidly disintegrating queue.

The crowd bays in agreement, and shop floorers are grabbed by their blue collars, dragged through the crowds to the checkouts to speed up the yearning for *A Perfect Life*.

"Beautiful, isn't it, lad?"

I turn, and Alby is at my side. His uniform is open, unbuttoned, loose. "I'm glad you're finally here. Was worried you were gonna miss it."

"What's going on?"

"The marketing campaign for Danielle's Steel's book. It's been pretty fuckin' successful, I'd say, and now everyone's gone insane trying to get hold of it. All the customers have fucked off the rules. You should see aisle No.12. There's a gang tryin' to gut the freezers in case there are copies of the book hidden in the sides. It's exactly what I've been hoping for."

"What d'you mean?"

"Because of how well the marketin' has gone, no one wants to buy anythin' else. Look, you can see how everyone's throwin' aside all the other stuff just to try and get hold of a book. You know what this means?" He turns to me, his eyes bright, excited, manic. "It means that all that other produce will be wasted. Unless we do summit about it."

"And where's Upper Management?"

"They've all been barricaded inside their offices," he says, grinning.

"What?"

"Yeah, my handywork. Well, with Nick's help, though he didn't realise."

"What are you on about?"

"Okay, come with me."

We descend the stairs, fight our way through the crowd, dodging a tussle between a granny and a yoot, both of whom are gripping an opposite end of *A Perfect Life*. The yoot gets the better of the granny and dashes off with his booty. "But I'm a librarian," she protests after him.

We cross the aisles and duck the carnage to the FIRE EXIT, out into our old haunt, Felon Place. Very overgrown since our previous visit back in January. Triffids have made advances, the whole alleyway colonised by lichen. It's very humid, and apart from the rush of traffic along the main road, it's quiet.

Alby turns to me. "For months now I've been waitin' for just this sort of thing, where we can finally push back against all the stupidity and bureaucracy of this place. How many times have we complained about all the wealth and the waste? Well today, my mace, we can do summit about it."

He hands me a pair of workman's gloves.

"Put these on. I've already locked Upper Management upstairs, scrambled their offices' door codes. They'll work it out at some point, so we don't have long to do everything else."

"What d'you mean, everything else? Is this all part of that stuff you had up on your corkboard? The drawing of the CAGE, the quotes about disobeying? What is all this you're dragging me into?"

"There's not much time, but trust me. Just follow my lead. We're going to get the CAGEs that are filled with everything that's gonna be wasted, all the food that no one's allowed to have. It's all just sittin' there, and we're gonna give it away."

"Who to?"

"To the people — to everyone outside on the street. It's all already ready, lad. Look, I know we've had a rough time with each other, but I've just been waitin' for yous to get here so that we can get it done properly and then make our escape."

"I dunno. We'll get bollocked."

"We'll get more than bollocked, lad, but you know what?" He takes hold of his nametag, plucks it from his shirt, tearing the white material, and drops it to the ground, the silvery pinhead glistens like a comet. "I don't give a fuck. This place isn't for us."

"This is all mad." I'm racing through the implications. It's... What?... A theft? ... A crime? If I leave this place, I'll have lost my USP. No degree, no home, probs an STI, maybe a baby, no job.

"Lad, I know you're sensitive to stealing and thieving. I understand where you're comin' from. I'm sorry I didn't tell yous that I had your brother's letter. But I read it, and I *know* that you also want all this to stop. Like that bit in the letter when you say to him that his was the wrong kind of stealin'. Well, now we can do it right."

Rage flares. Or maybe it's the heat and the last swells of alcohol poisoning my system. "How did you get that? It wasn't yours to read."

"Remember when you leant me *The Diary of a Nobody* by the Grossmith brothers? Back in January at The Troubadour? Well, I found it inside — it just fell out. And I get it, like, I understand you're not comfortable with anythin' like burglary. But, mate, listen, this isn't burglary. It's not theft. It's salvage."

"We'll lose our jobs."

"Fuck it." Alby shrugs. "No wage is good enough for what we're bein' asked to do. To look the other way while all this wasting goes on. There's other work in this city. Lad, I refuse to accept a future where there's no consequences for all this waste, all these adverts, and box-ticking and spectacle — where success is decided by bullies; where greed runs riot. I'm tryin' to get you to see that we need to be proactive, and we can do that. Startin' now. We need to focus on redistributin' resources. Equally, fairly. Today can be a gift. But you need to come with, so come with."

I look down at my work boots and see his nametag flashing brightly in amongst the weeds.

I bend to retrieve it.

"Alby?" I call out, but looking up, he's already disappeared through the FIRE EXIT doors.

- - - - -

In this chiarotescuro Alby and I pull CAGEs to block the stairwell leading to the staff area. We wedge then kick down their brakes so that each fortifies the next, like a wiry Roman testudo. Then, as one, we rush the double doors, both of us hauling weighty CAGEs full of produce — we're at full speed down the aisles.

Customers see us coming. "They've got more books here!" they shout in pursuit, but when they see that it's only gourmet food, wine, luxury chocolates, they fall back, losing interest, on the hunt elsewhere for *A Perfect Life*.

We run along aisle No.20, and I join Alby in his rhythmic chanting, "To disobey is best," while around us bottles smash on the floor as customers clamber for a copy of the book. Immediately, all colleagues who are not holding back the churning fiery wall of crazed customers dash over to fulfil their CAYG duties.

"To the Tannoy!" Alby calls to me, and we rush to the Customer Service Desk, Alby bringing from his pocket a Dictaphone.

"I need to stick down the button," he says quickly. From the drawer behind the desk, I take tape and scissors. Alby presses the red button, tapes it down, and clicks on the Dictaphone.

Over the store's speakers I can hear the tinkling, chiming sound of cymbals and piano. John Coltrane. 'My Favourite Things'.

"What d'you think? Music by Lance." Alby's grinning.

"But how did…"

Alby holds up a hand for quiet, and we hear accompanying the jazz instrumental a strange crackling, droning, booming voice. A Scouse voice.

"*To disobey is best.*"

“And that’s my voice. Lance and I collaborated. Not bad, eh? Come on, lad. We’ve got more to do.”

We pull the CAGEs in the direction of the glass doors of the entrance, where there stands blocking our way the formidable shape of the guard, his reflection in the sliding door’s glass doubling his stature. His vest and numerous sewn badges make a scaly fold of authoritarian fabric. His mouth is open, and he breathes heavily.

“Lead him down one of the aisles while I deal with the door sensor,” is Alby’s instruction. “Nick showed me how to make the doors only open from the outside.”

I goad the guard, picking up a fillet of mackerel from the ice bed on the Fish Counter and lobbing it at him. This sets him off — the minotaur in pursuit. I dart and skid, first along Dairy, then Canned Goods, zigzagging to avoid the Steel mob, but he’s close behind — so close that he manages to grab my hairnet, loosening my hair, in direct contravention of Tesco policies. I dodge, see his reflection in the glass panels of the aisles, tripling like a Cerberean sentinel.

“This way,” shouts Alby. The glass doors slide open briefly, and Alby is through, then I’m tumbling after him just as they close behind me. There’s a thud as the guard’s mass collides with the glass. On the other side, his face is red and furious, his heavy breath misting the window. And we’re out onto the forecourt, where there are all these CAGEs in a line across the pavement. Dozens of them. Maybe fifty or more.

“What are these doing here?” I ask.

“This is what I’ve been plannin’, lad. I told you. It’s the unwastin’.”

He beckons to a figure standing by the CAGEs. It’s Trolley Fella, scrawling words in block capitals on a whiteboard, the same one from Earl’s Court station:

TO DISOBEY IS BEST, Milton, PL, book xii, line 561

Through the closed glass doors, the furious face of the security guard has been joined by other colleagues, some angry, some confused.

Alby is shouting out to passersby, "Roll up, roll up! Get your free produce!" while he goes along the line of CAGEs, unlocking them so their doors swing open with an inviting creak. "Everything you see here was goin' to be wasted in the dustbins behind the store, so we'd rather that you had it. Please, take freely."

At first the passing pedestrians turn heads but keep walking. But then some stop, then others come forward. Alby encourages them: "Come on. We've got Borettane onions, pitted colossal olives in piri piri marinade, mixed pitted Kalamata olives with basil and garlic, olives stuffed with garlic and pepper, cava, sanitary pads, Phish Food ice-cream, bread, bread, bread, cereal, chocolate. Come on! There's plenty to go around."

Within minutes a huge queue has formed, winding across the forecourt as people gather and whoop and clap at the great giveaway. Everyone takes part, passing boxes, packages, and parcels out to those behind them. Salad, pasta, pizza, pasties, fruit, veg, tins, toiletries. All the while, behind the glass, the colleagues continue to assemble to witness this outpouring of generosity — this repurposing of resources. Upper Management have amassed in a dark cluster like cypress trees, while their Team Leader and Counter Manager minions are reduced to inept flunkies.

The queue for this unwasting is so long it begins to stretch into the road, halting traffic. The cars' tyres begin to sink into the viscous tarmac. They've become stuck in the tarry mire, and although there is an orchestra of car horns, against the queue's noble temper, all that futile aggression fails. The queue does not rage; there are no brazen shouts.

Instead, everyone smilingly proceeds, waiting for their turn, helping others. In this moment, nothing is wasted, nor a word misspoken — every gesture aimed benevolently, all brimming with meaning.

The roads are so much like a cauldron that the city's entrails — pipes, wires, cables — boil up to the surface like the veined roots of some great black tree.

My pocket vibrates. It's Lottie:

> **just got a letter through the door and opened it before I realised it had your name on the front. It's from the NHS, with test results, and it says that...**

But the message stops abruptly, because my inbox on this shitty phone is full, and before I can delete messages to make space, the glass doors slide open, and the enraged Upper Management and the rest spill out on to the forecourt.

"Ey, lad, take this!" Alby shouts to me as he appears with a pair of Boris bikes, and he's already swinging a leg over the saddle, pedalling furiously. I do the same, wobbly and swerving in his wake. As I cycle, my ankle is straining in pain from the fall into the Ha Ha. Pedalling forth through viscous black ink, briefly looking back to the warped visage of the store — the growing queue stretching and weaving through the stilled traffic, the joy on the faces of those receiving the waste — before I return my gaze forward to the world ahead, where Alby, his arms outstretched, seems to rise in sunlight, as he takes his solitary, labouring way. The wheels of my bike begin to sink into the bitumen, and I'm pedalling faster and the wheels are spinning, but the more I pedal, the further I sink downward, as Alby somehow glides away.

But I feel buoyed by Alby, by Huw, by Samuel, by Kevin, and Michael, and Eric, and Judith, and Bertie, and Adam, and all those others whose names I've taken. We are legion. We are Tescomrades.

Of course, none of that happens. I don't go along with Alby or his scheme. Instead of following him back through the FIRE EXIT doors from Felon Place, I go upstairs to the Upper Management floor, unlock their office, tell them of the plan. They quickly alert the security guard via the tablets which Nick introduced. Alby is accosted before he begins smashing up any aisles, before he can commandeer the Tannoy, before the CAGEs can be seized. He loses his job, and for my efforts I am promoted to the Deli Counter, given fresh white overalls and a white mesh hat. Until my own arrives, I'll wear Alby's nametag. The blade spins. I cut with it.

ACKNOWLEDGMENTS

Isi and Anouk.

Ollie Hancock, Marta Zanucco, and Wendy Liu.

David Hering and Daniel O'Connor.

Sadie and Rachelle, for the sofa and sweet water.

News from Nowhere, West Kirby Bookshop, and Sefton Park Library.

Alex Niven for his generosity, Tariq Goddard for the commission, Carl Neville for his support, and Christopher DeVeau for his guidance.

The University of Liverpool's Centre for New and International Writing, and its monthly meetings at The Belvedere.

The Leslie Clan, for that first fountain pen.

REPEATER BOOKS

is dedicated to the creation of a new reality. The landscape of twenty-first-century arts and letters is faded and inert, riven by fashionable cynicism, egotistical self-reference and a nostalgia for the recent past. Repeater intends to add its voice to those movements that wish to enter history and assert control over its currents, gathering together scattered and isolated voices with those who have already called for an escape from Capitalist Realism. Our desire is to publish in every sphere and genre, combining vigorous dissent and a pragmatic willingness to succeed where messianic abstraction and quiescent co-option have stalled: abstention is not an option: we are alive and we don't agree.